COFFIN MOON

COFFIN
MOON

A Novel

KEITH
ROSSON

Random House • New York

Random House
An imprint and division of Penguin Random House LLC
1745 Broadway, New York, NY 10019
randomhousebooks.com
penguinrandomhouse.com

Published in the United Kingdom by Black Crow Books.

Library of Congress Cataloging-in-Publication Data
Names: Rosson, Keith (Novelist), author.
Title: Coffin moon: a novel / Keith Rosson.
Description: First edition. | New York, NY: Random House, 2025.
Identifiers: LCCN 2025017147 (print) | LCCN 2025017148 (ebook) |
ISBN 9780593733400 (hardcover; acid-free paper) |
ISBN 9780593733417 (ebook)
Subjects: LCGFT: Horror fiction. | Paranormal fiction. |
Thrillers (Fiction) | Novels.
Classification: LCC PS3618.O853544 C64 2025 (print) | LCC PS3618.
O853544 (ebook) | DDC 813/.6—dc23/eng/20250411
LC record available at https://lccn.loc.gov/2025017147
LC ebook record available at https://lccn.loc.gov/2025017148

Printed in the United States of America on acid-free paper

2 4 6 8 9 7 5 3 1

First US Edition

BOOK TEAM: Production editor: Cindy Berman •
Managing editor: Rebecca Berlant • Production manager: Nathalie Mairena •
Copy editor: Lawrence Krauser

Book design by Fritz Metsch

The authorized representative in the EU for product safety and compliance is
Penguin Random House Ireland, Morrison Chambers, 32 Nassau Street,
Dublin D02 YH68, Ireland. https://eu-contact.penguin.ie.

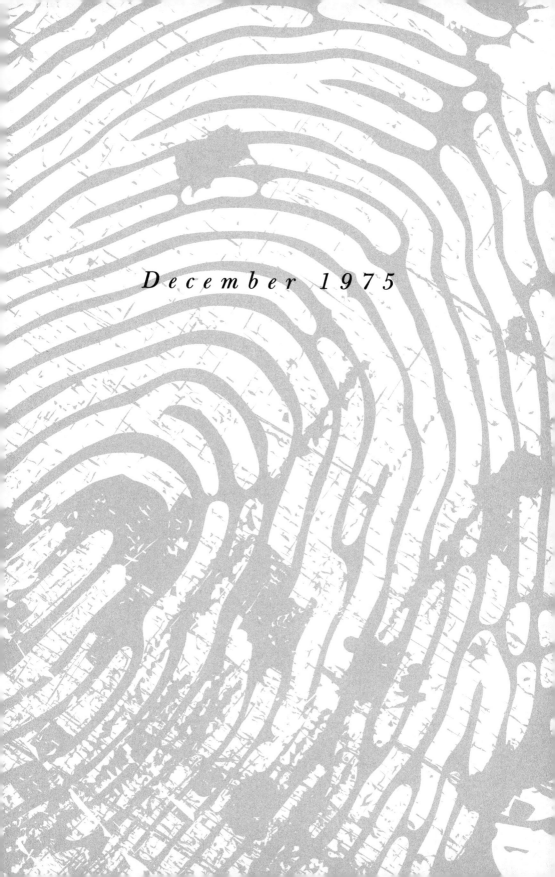

December 1975

1

HELL'S LEITMOTIF

*trouble at school • couple of uninvited guests • reluctantly, minor
gets involved • secrets upon secrets • a palaver is interrupted •
minor and john varley make their introductions • that terrible,
familiar stink of blood • a head made of smoke*

1

Early afternoon, with bruised, ugly clouds hanging above the notched teeth of the buildings across the street, the sleet all coming down sideways, holiday lights blinking red and green in the windows of the bar. The waist-high Christmas tree in the corner done up in silver tinsel. Cold winter light on the floor. Duane Minor, alone in the Last Call twenty minutes before opening, puts ashtrays on the tables. Makes sure he's got his lemon slices and his cherries, that the racks are stocked with clean glasses, there's enough ice to get him through to early evening at least. A night of shit sleep gives the world a blighted, gritty cast, and he's got Blue Oyster Cult on the jukebox in the back, turned up high enough to rattle window glass; it's only the break in the song that lets him hear the phone ringing.

"Last Call Tavern," he says. "We open in twenty."

"Hello, Mr. Minor. It's Patty Garent over at Joseph Middle School."

Minor's heart sinks. "Hey, Mrs. Garent. Just a sec, please." He sets the phone down and trots over to the stereo console at the far end of the bar, lowers the volume on the jukebox. Walks back and closes his eyes for a moment before picking up the handset.

"I'm here, ma'am." He fishes a cigarette out of the pack on the counter, lights up.

"Well, Mr. Minor, I'm the bearer of unfortunate news."

"Ah, damn. Another fight?"

"Yes, I'm sorry to say, and the girl was hurt this time. We need you to come pick Julia up and discuss the issue with Principal Reed. You and your wife both, if that's a possibility."

Minor looks at the clock. There are odd, mismatched stitches of sorrow and shame and anger all sort of roiling inside him, the most prevalent one being the certainty that he's failing miserably at this. That guardianship—parenthood, whatever the hell the state of Oregon wants to call it—is a thing simply beyond his means. This child has brought him out of his depth. He runs a hand down his face, and notes the day's first desire for a drink. "Okay," he says. "My wife's in class right now, but I can make it. Give me twenty minutes?"

"Thank you, Mr. Minor. She'll be in the office when you get here."

Minor hangs up, calls Joanne, his mother-in-law. Ed picks up on the second ring, spends a moment coughing before he says hello.

"Ed, it's Duane."

"Oh, boy," Ed says, not unkindly. "Let me guess. It's either something with Julia or someone burned the bar down."

"Former. Gotta go talk to the principal."

"Oof. Fighting?"

"Again, yeah."

"Shitfire," he says. "I'll let Joanne know."

"I appreciate it."

The *thunk* of the handset, and then he hears Ed and Joanne talking. Ed comes back on. "She'll be there in fifteen. She says to just lock the front, she'll take care of the rest."

"I appreciate it. How you feeling today?"

"Oh, upright and taking solids, you know. Tell that girl not to be such a hard-ass, would you? She's got every right to, but still."

"I hear you."

Minor hangs up, gets his coat, his keys. Spends maybe a little too long looking at the gleaming tiers of bottles behind the bar. Just a nip wouldn't be noticeable, he thinks, and it'd maybe sand off the barbs of this anger he's feeling. But one drink's a road that twists, he knows it full well, twists and then turns down a darker trail, and it's been eighteen months since he's had a drop, a lot of that time spent white-knuckled. It'd be some real sad-sack shit to throw away all that time, so a minute later he's outside, shoulders hunched against the sleet, still sober. Locking the Last Call's front door behind him, running toward his truck parked around the corner.

Joseph Middle School hasn't changed a bit since Minor was a kid. A one-story, L-shaped building with bike racks out front, chipped cement steps. An American flag rattles on its chain, and through the school's long banks of windows, the bent heads of children can be seen. Minor walks inside, makes his way to the front office, where Mrs. Garent peers at him over her bifocals. She'd worked here when he was a kid, and had seemed old to him then. Since Julia's moved in with Minor and his wife, Heidi, he's become intimately familiar with the place again, the staff. Mrs. Garent promptly directs him to Principal Reed's office, and he sees Julia slouched in a chair next to the man's open door; she won't look at him, so Minor steps inside. Reed, bald and mustached, wearing a mustard-colored shirt and brown tie, looks up from his desk with hound dog eyes. The air of the perpetual administrator about him.

"Hey, Duane," he says unhappily. "Why don't you shut the door."

Minor does, then settles himself into a chair that faces Reed's desk.

"So," Reed says, sighing heavily, "sounds like it was a fight in the lunch line."

"Alright. Damn."

"Far as I understand it, someone took cuts in front of someone else, and Julia objected. Something was said in response, probably an unkind thing, and she hit the other student in the mouth. Twice."

"What unkind thing was that?"

"I don't know," Reed admits. "We're going off stories from multiple kids here. But hopefully you'll agree with me, Duane, when I say it doesn't really matter that much. Even if someone said something, it doesn't justify what happened."

Minor doesn't know if that's necessarily true, but also knows Julia's on thin ice here. "No, yeah, I hear you."

"Can't have people getting punched over a disagreement, you know?"

"Absolutely."

"The other student's currently at the hospital waiting to see if stitches are necessary."

Another moment of drowning, wishing like hell Heidi was here. "Yeah, you're right. She crossed the line."

Tony Reed's not a bad guy. Not really. They've filled him in on Julia's story: Mom doing a life sentence in upstate New York, stepfather dead, Julia separated from her stepbrother. The whole heartbreaking thing. At first, it was all harrowing enough to afford her some disciplinary leeway, but looking at the principal right now, it's clear that ship has sailed. *Stitches?*

"So, the other student's parents are requesting expulsion," Reed says, and Minor looks at him in alarm.

"Tony, I—"

Reed holds up a hand. "I'm not going to do it, Duane, but I want you to know that that's the point we're getting to."

"I understand. It won't happen again."

Tight-lipped, Minor nods. His gratitude from moments before has evaporated like smoke, and he feels that familiar fury in him, that sliver of heat that makes his hands flex against his thighs. This little speech feels practiced, and it sets off in Minor the same bells as any rear-echelon motherfucker that ever gave his platoon an ass-chewing over something beyond their control. People just feel the need to jaw at you sometimes, feel big. Reed's likely behind the pocket himself a hundred times a day, getting his own ass-chewings from parents and superintendents and all the rest; sometimes you just need to pass the misery around. And really, he's not far off on his assessment of Julia— this isn't the first time Minor's sat in this chair, after all.

"I understand," he says again, the anger gone as quickly as it arrived. Just tired now. "I want to thank you for giving her another chance, Tony. She's had a hard road."

"I know it," Reed says. "And I'm sorry for it. We all want her to succeed."

He and Julia are getting in the truck across the street from school when the bell rings and kids begin spilling out the doors. Laughing, running, jumping off benches. The sleet's stopped and kids unlock their bikes and begin gleefully slaloming through puddles, trying to splash each other. Julia sits in the passenger seat with her arms crossed, chin dipped to her chest, watching it all from the corners of her eyes. Newly thirteen, wire-thin, ink-black hair that falls to her shoulders and a scowl like a minotaur. Minor cracks a window, lights a cigarette. He's trying to stay calm, trying to feel like a *parent*, like an adult. Julia's been with them for a little over a year now and he can count those instances of feeling like he's got his shit together on one hand, maybe. He threads the truck out into the street, waits for kids to pass in the crosswalk.

"So you're not going to say anything?"

A mumble.

"What's that?"

She turns and looks at him; she has a scratch laddering one cheek and her mouth is a small bow of resentment. "I didn't do anything wrong."

He laughs. "Tell that to the kid with stitches."

"It's not like I punched her for no reason. That's not what happened."

"Okay. Well, why don't you tell me what happened, then."

More silence. Rain ticks on the windshield. The inside of the truck is quiet save for the clack of the wipers, and Minor sighs and rolls his window up. Puts his cigarette out in the ashtray and turns the radio on. He hears the words *local authorities are asking anyone with knowledge of the girl's disappearance* and moves the dial, but there's nothing else besides disco and evangelism, so he turns it off.

•

They have an early dinner, he and Heidi and Julia, the sound of the Last Call below rising up through the floorboards. Julia's still quiet—kid's rarely a font of chatter on the best of days—and beyond the bass-throb of the bar downstairs, there's little noise in the apartment save for J. J. Cale's *Okie* on the turntable, snaking low and sinuous from the speakers. Heidi's occasional attempts at conversation die horrible deaths. Minor eats quickly, and notices, not for the first time, how he and Julia handle their food the same way: hunched down, their free arms curled around their plates. It was something he picked up in chow halls throughout his tour; Julia earned it by living with Ray Ray Sikes, her stepfather.

She pushes away from the table, asks if she can be excused. There's still a mess of spaghetti on her plate, a half-eaten piece of garlic bread. Minor's distracted, feels bad that Joanne's down at the bar by herself now, tackling his shift for him. He and Heidi have had the requisite talk with Julia, about her anger and where it should go. How she has every right to be furious, given what's happened, but that there's a right way to express it and a wrong way. She'd responded with mute impassivity; they might have gotten a single "Alright, fine" out of her. It's a conversation the three of them have had many times before. As ever, Julia takes it in and gives nothing back.

Heidi points at Julia's plate with her fork. "You got to finish your dinner, babe."

"I'm not hungry."

Heidi sets her fork down, just looks at her. Julia is her niece, her sister's child, blood of her blood. In the past year, quiet or not, Julia's become attached to Heidi in a way that she hasn't to Minor. It's understandable: he's a man, and Heidi had relayed enough info from her sister's trial to know what kind of a man Ray Ray Sikes had been, what he'd done to earn that bullet through his mouth. Julia hangs on to Heidi like something born of necessity.

Heidi shrugs. "Yeah, well. You still got to finish it."

Julia rolls her eyes, sits back down. Picks up her garlic bread and takes a bite like it's been doused in arsenic.

"I gotta go help downstairs," Minor says, wiping his mouth with a napkin and running his plate to the sink.

"See ya," Heidi says, then lifts her face up to his for a kiss.

"I'm gonna close tonight, send Joanne home," he says. "Your dad didn't sound great on the phone."

"Got it," she says, then looks at Julia, who's giving her plate the death-stare. Heidi winks at the girl, unbothered by all of it, patient as ever. "Us girls will hold down the fort."

It's four A.M. when he makes it back upstairs, showers off the smell of the bar.

He's stepped to the kitchen for a drink of water, standing quiet amid the dark press of the room. The world outside the kitchen window is a chiaroscuro of power lines, black sky, the apartment buildings across the street. Glass in his hand, he listens to the ticking radiator, a sudden spat of rain against the window.

Buried under the other noises, he hears Julia crying softly in her bed down the hall.

That night, the dreams come at him, teeth bared.

It's been like this since he stopped drinking. Like the drinking smashed all the fear down. Sober, everything bubbles up bloody and foaming. He'll fall asleep and then, most nights, *boom*—a riff on the same brutal melody, dream-logic that merges horror and history.

They almost always start, the dreams, with Minor walking the wet darkness of the jungle. Almost always a squad of three: Lyle in the rear, then Minor, then Ferris, another grunt that Minor hadn't even hardly known in life, a guy who'd drawn READYMADE MEAT in painfully careful marker strokes on the fabric of his helmet cover. The dream-logic is malleable as taffy, but Minor, without even turning, knows the three of them are spread out too far, knows that something's behind them, that it's about to start picking them off one by one. Lyle gets got first, dumbass hillbilly Lyle who in actuality had been on his third tour when Minor shipped in in '72. Lyle, a crazy motherfucker who was feverishly strung out on heroin by then, shooting dope between his toes even while in the bush, and thinking he was invincible. In real life, Lyle had gotten his jaw pulped by a sniper's round at the fence line of their fire base one night, high as shit, but in *this* dream, he's right behind Minor, and the *thing* is there too, this monster, and then it gets Ferris, his helmet suddenly rolling on the ground, and Minor's got two choices—run back or run ahead, with the understanding it'll be death either way. Like so much of Vietnam, there is no good answer. There is no right thing to do, there is only the world happening to you, the world encroaching upon your body and your heart and your will, and then he looks up from Ferris's helmet at his feet, its bowl filled to the brim with blood, and then the two men, the ones from last year, chunks of glass gleaming in the face of one of them, their twitching, animated bodies, the dirt on their faces turning to mud beneath the rain, in their hair, both striding toward him like something out of a stop-motion film, and then fingertips graze his face—

He wakes, gasping, Heidi shouting in panic and then pressing a hand down on his chest, trying to calm him. He dreams this dream, or something like it, three, four, five nights a week. Zero fucking desire to rest his head on the pillow afterward. You'd think that he'd grow more acclimated to it, but no. Not at all. Every night feels like the first night. If anything, the dream's grown sharper with time, more cutting.

2

Middle of the week and the Last Call's, weirdly, about as busy as it gets. Smoke clouds the ceiling, the room throbs with R&B, disco, pop songs, and he and Joanne and Andy, the college kid Joanne's hired to do barback, are hustling their asses off. Minor's in the zone, slinging drinks, keeping an eye on stock, cracking jokes, knifing beer foam from glass tops with a magician's flourish, all the while bopping like a jackass to whatever the jukebox's kicking out. Working at the Last Call has come to feel like home in a way that nothing else really has, a fact that consistently surprises him, especially given his sobriety, as tenuous as it can feel sometimes. He loves it all: the black-and-white framed photos of Prohibition-era speakeasies on the walls, the half dozen circular tables moored in the middle of the room. The black hockey pucks of plastic ashtrays that populate every flat surface. It's early in the evening but someone's already fallen over in the corner, taking the Christmas tree down with him; Joanne hadn't even booted the old guy, just sat him down amid the noise and gave him a cup of coffee. "You're gonna put my picture on the wall, aren't you, Jo," he'd slurred, snarls of silver tinsel from the tree still wreathing his shoulders, referring to the wall of Polaroids behind the bar that Joanne and Ed have taken over the years—pinned snapshots of folks who have fallen asleep at the rail or passed out in their booths. "You're good, Vince," she'd told him. "Just have some coffee and get your head on straight, for Christ's sake."

She's got a soft spot for drunks, Joanne. She'd inherited the bar and the apartment above from her father some thirty years before; she and Ed had handed the apartment over to Heidi when she and Minor had gotten married, and Heidi had lived there alone during his tour in Vietnam. Now he and Heidi and Julia all live upstairs, and while Minor appreciates his in-laws, he also understands that Heidi feels trapped here sometimes. She's grown up in the shadow of the Last Call, after all, been here her entire life. Minor's own parents retired to Taos immediately after he graduated high school and moved out, and while he calls them once a month or so, they all seem fine with the distance, and the calls have long had a perfunctory air to them. Meanwhile, he likes his in-laws very much, and they seem to like him back: Ed and Joanne are no-nonsense people, tough as hell, and they've risen up to help out with Julia in a way that Minor's profoundly grateful for.

"Duane, gimme another one," croons Bobby Liprinksi over the din of the bar, putting his elbows on the wood and leaning over, face flushed. "Another pint, my good man."

Minor pulls a beer, gives him a face. "Wait your turn, Bob."

Flipping him the finger, eyes at half mast, Bobby puts a cigarette in his mouth backward, almost lighting the filter before he catches the mistake. *Gotta watch him tonight,* Minor thinks. Bobby's his closest friend, but he spins into wildness sometimes. Missing the last two fingers of his right hand from a piece of shrapnel he caught in Dai Do three years back, Bobby's unpredictable, wound wire-tight. Can veer from fun-loving drunk to vicious in an eyeblink. They didn't serve together, but they know some of the same guys, and Bobby plants his ass on a stool at the Last Call most nights of the week.

Minor's humming, serving drinks, giving change, tossing little barbs to the ballbusters at the rack. Busy, but he and Joanne and the kid are holding their own. Everything feels as right as it gets, and the nightmares of the previous evening seem ludicrous under the electric light. *I live in* this *moment,* he thinks, slamming the cash register shut with a metallic clang. *I'm safe. I got no problems at all.*

They don't have a bouncer at the bar. It's a relaxed, long-standing dive, a regulars' spot. A Southeast tavern populated by folks from the neighborhood, by Korean War–vet buddies of Ed's, by blue-collar guys making the short trek from the industrial warehouses along the riverfront to drink Budweiser and grouse about gas prices and play stick in the back room. They don't do hippies here, don't allow drugs. Prostitutes are kindly but firmly given the boot if there's even a hint of them plying their trade, and if you want to bet on college basketball or the horses, you better do it where Joanne can't hear you or you'll be getting promptly 86'ed.

So when a pair of guys in biker vests and ponytails come in, it gets noticed.

There's nothing like a record scratch or anything, nothing so Wild West-y, but people pay attention. A ripple of awareness kind of moves through the place. Bobby, Minor sees, gets his hackles up right away: he leans on his elbows again and dips his head down, squinting one eye at them. A couple of the old guys on their stools swivel their heads and give the bikers a brazen, unapologetic stink-eye as they pass. They're wearing denim and leather, these boys, swaggering along in their shit-kicker motorcycle boots. Blurred green tattoos on their arms that, to Minor, never really signified more than that you'd spent time in lockup. That you got caught. He puts it at fifty-fifty that they're carrying, and would bet a paycheck they've at least got knives on them. He feels his legs go a little watery, adrenaline's precursor.

Bobby turns and looks at him with something close to a leer. A loop of hair falls in one eye and he swipes it away. Guy looks happy, is what it is, which doesn't do shit to calm Minor's nerves. Does the opposite, even. Bobby says, "What in the blue fuck we got *here*, Duane?"

"People can drink. No law against it." Minor saying this while pushing his own nervousness down. He's aiming for casual and getting close—the Last Call really is so far removed from a biker bar that these guys might as well be visiting the moon. He passes over a pitcher and three glasses to a waiting customer, hands the lady her change, then starts putting together a G&T for one of the white-hairs at the rack.

Except the bikers don't sidle up to the bar or go to one of the booths lining the wall. They don't have a seat at one of the tables. They stride through the room, taking up space, and walk down the tavern's rear hall. But they don't head to the back where there's more booths and a pair of pool tables. They stop and open up Joanne's office door there in the hallway. The one with the sign on the door that says NO ADMITTANCE.

They walk in without knocking. Walk in like they don't need to think twice about it.

Bobby catches it too, gives him another look. "The fuck is that all about?"

"Yeah, hold on," Minor says, and holds up a finger for the next customer. "I'll just be a sec."

He makes his way through the bar, heat prickling his scalp. That feeling you get where violence becomes a possibility, maybe even a likelihood.

There's a part of him, it's true, that's missed it.

Missed it a lot.

He raps on the door, opens it. Joanne's sitting behind her desk in the cramped room, the two guys standing on the other side of it. Joanne looks like he's just walked in on her using the bathroom—shocked, maybe embarrassed. One of the bikers has a long red ponytail shot through with gray, a beard the same. The other's clean-shaven. Both men stare at him with little smiles, like Minor's about to do a particularly cute parlor trick.

"What's up?" Joanne says to him, her voice clipped.

Minor's eyes rove among the three of them. He catches the patch on the back of the men's vests—a skull with a snake writhing out of the open mouth. *Crooked Wheel* done in blackletter script above the death's head. The rocker patch on the bottom just a white *MC* on a black field. *Motorcycle Club.*

"Hey," he says, "we're running low on tallboys, you want me to call the distributor?"

Joanne gives him a look that's faceted, complex—one that says she knows that his excuse for coming in is bullshit, and that she's still embarrassed too. That she's been caught in something. "We'll make it through," she says, folding her hands on the desk. She's a big woman who has spent her life in this place. She knows how to take up space in a room. But before these two men, she looks small, and there's some imbalance here that he can't pin down: subservience or fealty or something.

"Alright," he says. He eyeballs the man with the red ponytail and says, "Just let me know if you need anything. Me and Bobby are right outside."

The guy grins, looks at the other biker, then back at Minor. "You think this is a shakedown or something, brother?"

"Leave it," Joanne says sharply. To Minor: "I'll be out in five minutes."

Bobby stays while he closes the place down. Sam Cooke low on the jukebox while Minor mops and dumps ashtrays and rinses the beer mats, stacks the drying pint glasses in their racks, the two of them smoking cigarettes, occasionally talking. Joanne seems to have made it a point to avoid him the entire evening, and she's still holed up in her office. The bikers had left shortly after Minor had made his way back to the bar, the ponytailed one offering him a wink as they stepped out. And that'd been that. It all meant something—it all felt so *off*—but he can't say exactly how.

Bobby's about to fall asleep at the bar, eyes half lidded and dreamy, when his boyfriend comes in. Ian works the swing shift down at the bottling plant, and him picking Bobby up after work is not an uncommon thing. Bobby turns his head at the sound of the bell above the door and slurs, "Oh, there he is. Mister Fantastic."

Ian smiles. "Another good night, huh, Bob?"

"Ah, he wasn't too bad," Minor says.

Ian sits down and the three of them have a last drink. Soda for him, beer for the other two. Couple years older than Bobby, Ian got a deferment, something with his knees; first time Minor had seen the two of them drink in the bar together, it being obvious what was going on, that they were together, there was a stink about it among the clientele. Some of them. You could see it happen; folks had a vision of what was right and what wasn't. Minor felt like if Bobby had lost most of his hand in service to his country, guy should be able to do what the fuck he wants. Nobody's business, and now if anyone makes any comments under their breath, gets too lit and mutters that Bobby ought to find a bar that serves his own kind, him or Joanne are usually right there to cool things down, hopefully before Bobby winds up putting a fist through the guy's teeth. He and Ian live in the neighborhood, can hoof it back to their apartment easy enough, and Minor likes these last drinks, the quiet way the three of them put a mark on the end of the night.

When they're done, Bobby jabs his half-smoked cigarette toward Minor in some kind of blitzed acknowledgment, then slowly clambers off his stool. He begins the arduous task of putting his jacket on until Ian helps him. Minor's good feelings from earlier in the night have soured. The air feels charged with this thing between him and Joanne. He doesn't want to overstep his bounds—she's his mother-in-law and his boss and beyond that, he's become indebted to her for a multitude of reasons, reasons that are hard to consider—but those men have brought the feeling of trouble with them, and he can't slough it off.

He and Bobby slap hands and Ian salutes him with a finger to the brow and the two of them step out into the night. Now it's just Minor and Joanne and Sam Cooke doing "Twistin' the Night Away." He finishes up, turns off the juke, shuts the bank of lights down so that the room's only illuminated by the streetlights outside, the gleaming strings of Christmas bulbs blinking around the front windows.

He puts his coat on and walks down the hall. Stands at Joanne's door for a second before knocking.

"Yeah."

Minor opens it, leans his head in. "We're all set for tomorrow."

Joanne's still behind her desk, a sheaf of papers and manila folders spread out across its top. A calculator with its loop of accounting tape and the ever-present ashtray. Her glasses are perched on the top of her head and she's got Billie Holiday turned low as a whisper on a little transistor radio by her elbow. She nods. " 'Night, Duane."

"Listen, Joanne—"

"Yeah?"

"Those guys have anything to do with, uh, with what happened?"

"What do you mean?"

He's almost afraid to say it. Saying it will give it life, will exhume it. Bring the blood and dirt and horror up to the forefront. "With what happened last year, I mean. That thing you helped me with."

She blinks, her lips pursing for a second. "No, hon. This is my deal."

Relief, then, like a tide through him. "Alright. Listen, I'm sorry if I walked in on something tonight. Your business is your business."

Joanne scratches her chin with a thumbnail, opens her mouth and stops. Like she wants to say something to him, but all she manages is, "We're good, Duane. I know you're just looking out. Heidi still up?"

He smiles. "Not a chance. She's asleep by ten most nights, unless she's got a paper due."

"Gotcha. Kid alright?"

He considers telling her about Principal Reed, Julia's in-school suspension, but he's tired, and it's a whole other thing he'd have to unpack with her. "She's fine," he manages. Both of them deciding to skirt the trueness of things, apparently.

"Good" is all she says. "Thanks for everything."

Upstairs, all is silent. In the bedroom, he takes his clothes off as the first flakes of snow begin whirling like ash outside the window. He gets beneath the comforter and presses himself to his wife, his nose in her hair. *Me and you,* he thinks, *me and you for good,* trying his best to push away that small blooming flower of dread inside him.

3

The next afternoon, he relieves Ed behind the bar. A rare thing, his father-in-law doing a shift at the Last Call, even the morning shift, and it heartens Minor: the man's been sick for a while, a cough that just won't let loose of him, migraines and dizziness. He's been reluctant to get it checked out, changing the subject whenever Joanne insists he visit a doctor. He's in his fifties and hung up on that old man logic: *If I ignore it, it can't hurt me.* Today, he sips coffee from a brown ceramic mug and greets Minor with a lift of the hand while a couple of regulars sit hunched like crows on their stools, each at opposite ends of the bar.

Julia's upstairs doing homework while Heidi's getting ready to jump on the bus and go to class downtown. All this family, this life, in close proximity—a year-plus back from Nam and he's still getting used to it. This clutch of people that know him, that expect things of him. Insist, even, on loving him, in spite of all he's done. In spite of all that's happened. He'd awoken last night with the sheets in a mad tangle around his legs, the same throat-stuffing panic, Heidi there with a stilling hand on his chest. The dreams are terrible in the way they button-mash the same dumb touchstones of grief and horror: the dripping jungle, Minor raking his rifle across the darkness, he and Ferris and Lyle, chosen for some goddamn reason to be the stand-in avatars of his fears. Abstractions, details, war shit, dream-junk, all of it nonsensical but white-hot with clarity. The roar of the mounted guns, blood jetting, men screaming. Trunks of trees shivering and bending against the gunfire. A hooch burning, its roof sheathed in Day-Glo orange flames. Then, on cue, the closing act: the boys from the bar, the two of them made a pair of monsters in this dream, their wet and seeping faces, jaws distended, those two boys, the secret he shares with Joanne, what happened last year—

Ed coughs, pulls him from this jagged, glassy daydream he's in. "How we doing today, bud?" he asks, the old man's standard greeting. He rinses his coffee cup in the sink beneath the rail, walks over and gets his coat from the hook on the wall.

"Hanging in," Minor says, "how're you?"

Ed zips up his coat and makes a seesawing gesture with his hand. "Been slow so far." He starts coughing again, this time bending a little at the waist, the engine of his chest struggling to turn over. He stands up straight, takes a slow breath, offers a self-conscious smile. "Well, taking a nap is in the cards, looks like. Damn."

"I hear you," Minor says, that small worm of dread moving through him again. The old man looks bad.

"Anyway," Ed says, making his way around the bar and patting one of the regulars on the shoulder as he heads toward the door, "you have a good one, Duane."

"You too."

"Call us if you got any problems. Joanne can head over."

"No problem. Take care."

It starts to pick up a little around four, folks clocking off early from work, and the bar's hopping for sure by six. He and Andy the barback are working alone but cruising along well enough. At seven, with Bobby having just taken up his perch near the rail, Minor clocks the same two bikers sauntering in, though instead of going to Joanne's office this time, they head straight for the back room, with the pool tables. Maybe a minute later the big one with the red ponytail walks up and plants himself at the bar with that same smirk. Minor makes him wait, takes other orders from folks down the other end, and by the time he walks up to the rail where the biker's leaning on his elbows, he and Bobby are already getting into it.

"The fuck out of here," he hears Bobby say.

The biker's got these big hands laddered in silver rings. Minor's worried about guns, or a sticking knife in the guy's boot, but even a punch from rings like that will mess up a man's face something serious. But the biker's unfazed. Just grins and says, "Why, *you* got a mouth on you, don't you? Want to be careful with that, brother, someone might decide to shut it the fuck closed for you one day."

"What can I get you?" Minor says, his voice tight.

The biker keeps his eyes locked on Bobby a few more seconds, Bobby's lips pulled back in a sneer, both of them big-dogging each other, but at this point Bobby's still sober enough to show some measure of self-restraint. Later in the evening, it'll be a different story.

The biker turns to him. "Pitcher of Bud, two glasses."

Minor pulls the beer, cuts the head of foam with a knife, passes it and a pair of pint glasses over. A couple bills get pushed his way and Minor bangs in the register keys, passes over the change.

"This is a stand-up place," Minor says.

"Oh, is it now? Okay."

"It is, and I don't want any trouble tonight."

"Don't plan on making any," the biker says back to him. "Might want to talk to Three Fingers over here, though," he says, hooking a thumb at Bobby.

"Fuck you, man." Bobby spits as the guy walks away.

Bobby's seething, and that bad feeling inside Minor is starting to blossom into something like panic now. He's no stranger to violence—Christ, far from it—but the unsurety of what's going on with these guys makes it seem like everything's built on quicksand. At the same time, Joanne's obviously cool with them, so it's not like Minor's got much room to be concerned, right? *Everything's fine,* he tells himself. *You're just tired.*

"Man's patched," an old-timer a few chairs down rasps. He's got massive gray sideburns, and a thread of cigarette smoke climbs in an ashtray by his hand.

"What's that supposed to mean?" says Bobby, standing on his tiptoes to watch the biker go.

"Means those boys are in a chopper club, and they're patched. They been sworn in."

"Big fucking whoop," Bobby says.

The old man shrugs. "Well, I'm just saying he's no one *I'd* mess with. Never heard of no Crooked Wheel before, but they got that air about them."

"Yeah? What air's that?"

The old man scratches a sideburn and shrugs again. "Type not to give a fella too many chances to shut his mouth, I guess."

"Oh, I got you jumping on my balls now too?"

Minor thinks of Joanne, that look she'd given him in the office, how she'd seemed small and scared, two things very unlike her. He tells Bobby to leave it alone.

The night keeps on. As the hours pass, a weird, raw cast falls across the evening, and Minor can't help but notice a lot of new faces, folks who stop in for a beer at best and then jet. One biker—not the red-headed one, the other guy—stays on the pay phone in the hall almost the entire time, and it feels to Minor like a fight's continually about to take place. This strange undercurrent. Meanwhile, the redhead orders pitcher after pitcher. At one point, someone drops a glass. Andy's swamped, so Minor's got to clean the mess up and can't pour while he does it, and then there's a backlog of people wanting drinks. All these new faces, these drop-ins, but there's still this odd, slow-motion feeling to everything.

The hell is going on?

It's pushing eleven o'clock when that same regular who'd talked about patches comes shuffling from the bathroom and gingerly sets himself on his stool and goes, "Son, you know they're dealing drugs back there, don't you?"

It clicks, then, the underwater slowness of the evening. So fucking stupid on Minor's part. Like he hasn't seen a million guys strung out on dope before—here and in Nam. Christ, Lyle alone. Jawless, sniper-shot, dope-fiend Lyle. Minor should've been able to recognize the stilted, molasses-like quality of folks in the bar tonight.

Son of a bitch, he thinks, *they're dealing dope out of the back room,* and he picks up a fish bat they have tucked beneath the rail. There's also Ed's service pistol, a .45 ACP in a lockbox underneath the bar, but even as furious as he is, there's no way he's brandishing a gun at those two. Recipe for a gunfight.

Still, he feels puffed up with a kind of holy righteousness—it's rare that moments in his life are simple like this anymore. This clear. He strides past the tables—Jesus Christ, there's a woman *nodding off* in one of the corner booths, right there with her boyfriend next to her, he must have been blind not to have noticed it. He feels a flaring trill of embarrassment, imagining Ed or Joanne seeing the bar in a state like this.

Down the hall and then the back room opens up; people see the look on his face and step back. He hears a single kiss of a pool ball at one of the tables and people scatter when he brings the fish bat down on the bikers' table. Pint glasses jump, the ashtray jackrabbits up in a cloud of ash. The sound of wood on wood like a pistol shot. An empty glass rolls off the edge of the table and someone screams when it explodes on the floor like a bomb.

"Get the fuck out," he says, pointing the fish bat at the red-headed biker. "You're done."

Both of them sit there cool as shit, their hands raised a few inches off the table. Someone—Bobby, maybe Andy—has gone behind the bar and turned off the jukebox. It's quiet as a fucking grave back here. Everyone standing around, waiting to see what happens next.

"Relax," says the other biker.

Minor pivots, points the bat at him. "Another word to me and you'll need bridgework, motherfucker. Tell me to relax. Dealing dope in this bar? You fucking brain-dead or what?"

Bobby, behind him, says, "Get the fuck out, boys. Now."

Minor steps back as the two bikers lumber out of the booth. The one with the ponytail locks eyes with him. He grins, softly shakes his head. "You're making a mistake here."

"That's what your mother told herself," goes Bobby, and a few people titter.

They walk out of the room, down the hallway, Minor pacing them a few steps behind, ready to swing. Past the bathrooms, past Joanne's office with its NO ADMITTANCE sign. Those scuffed Crooked Wheel vests, the skulls with the snakes rippling between the jaws. They thread their way past the tables and out the front door, the bell jingling overhead, and Minor yells out, "Don't come back." Ponytail turns and smiles at him, and if there are things that Minor might discern in that look, fear isn't one of them. Fear isn't even close.

4

He's asleep, his hand resting on his wife's hip, when the downstairs buzzer starts ringing, metallic and insistent and *loud*. Minor's slept the sleep of the dead, dreamless and unbroken—like the little showdown with the Crooked Wheel had scratched some itch that his brain's been demanding, which is a scary thought—and he wakes to the sound of the buzzer bleary-eyed but strangely rested. Heidi groans and puts a hand over her eyes. "Do me a favor," she says. "Lean out the window and pour boiling oil on whoever that is, would you?"

Another harsh buzz, this one lasting ten, fifteen seconds.

"The heck?" calls Julia from her room.

"I got it," Minor says, pushing himself out of bed, pulling his jeans on. Grabs his coat flung over the back of the chair in the corner and trots out of the apartment and down the stairwell. Shoeless, the cold snakes up the hall and against the soles of his feet. It's only when he gets to the bottom landing that he considers how he'd left things the night before with the bikers, and fear almost keeps him from turning the doorknob; last night's bravado, that eagerness he'd felt, is gone.

But peering through the peephole, he sees Joanne, red-cheeked and puffy-eyed, a black knit cap on her head, bundled up against the cold. A thin scrim of new snow on the hoods of cars across the street. It's dawn, pretty much, maybe a little later. He's only been asleep a few hours.

He opens the door. "Hey," he says. "What's the—"

She pulls a hank of hair from her mouth, looks him up and down. No shirt beneath his jacket, hair corkscrewed with sleep. "Get your shoes on, Duane."

"What? Is everything okay? I—"

"Get your goddamn shoes on, now," Joanne barks, like he's a child, and Minor realizes that she's furious at him.

"Okay. You want to come in?"

She blinks at him, her face a mask. "I'll wait out here."

He trots upstairs, gently shuts the front door behind him.

Back in the bedroom, that dread's expanded: whatever he's been waiting for has arrived. In some way he doesn't understand yet, Minor has stepped off into the dark.

"Who was it?" Heidi asks, a pillow covering the top half of her face.

"Your mom."

"Funny."

"No, seriously."

Heidi lifts the edge of the pillow, peers at him. "Really? What's she want?"

"I don't know," Minor says, sitting on the bed and putting on his socks. "She wants to talk to me."

"To you?"

"I guess so."

Heidi puts the pillow back on her face. "Bar stuff."

"Probably." Trying to sound even, calm. Thoughts pinwheel wildly through his mind: *she found a rig in the bathroom, someone overdosed, those Crooked Wheel dipshits sold to a UC cop and the bar's getting shut down.* Who knows. He finds his boots, and zips up his jacket after making sure his smokes are in the pocket.

"Not even putting a shirt on, huh? Mister Casual."

"See you in a bit," he says, then is out of the apartment, clomping down the stairs again.

Out on the street, Joanne's already got a cigarette of her own, her hair beneath the cap a wild tangle in the wind. The cold is fierce.

"Walk with me," she says.

Minor lights up, keeps pace. They round the corner away from the bar, a mishmash of turn-of-the-century apartment buildings and two-story homes. The wind makes little eddies with the snow on the ground.

"I'm going to tell you something," Joanne says, crossing the street after a delivery truck slowly trundles past. "And you're going to keep it to yourself. You're not going to tell Julia, and you're sure as hell not going to tell my daughter. Do we understand each other?"

"Yes, ma'am."

She puts her hands in the pockets of her coat, leaves her cigarette in her mouth. "You know Ed's sick." The cigarette wags as she speaks.

"Yeah," he says cautiously. "His cough seemed pretty bad yesterday."

"I finally talked him into going to the doctor. They ran their tests, took their blood samples, all that. Got him in this machine, this CAT scan, it's called."

Minor knowing what's coming then.

"It's cancer," Joanne says. "Started in his lungs, apparently. It's in his brain now."

He swallows, his throat clicking, suddenly dry. "Jesus Christ."

They pass a woman walking a small dog that leans hard against its leash to sniff Minor's leg, the woman smiling with her head dipped down.

He waits until there's some distance between them and says, "How much time does he have?"

"Not much. Months. But there's chemo, which, I don't know." She looks up at the sky and blinks, pulls another hank of hair from her mouth. "Ed doesn't want to do it."

"The chemo?"

Joanne nods, takes a greedy drag on the cigarette. He watches as a single silvery tear falls from her eyelash, runs down her cheek and lands on the scarf wrapped around her throat. They cross another street, the sun rising now, sunlight beginning to wink off the chrome of parked cars. A crow caws on the power line above their heads.

"Says he's too tired. I tell him, I say, 'This'll help you not be tired, you old bastard,' but he's right. Chemo, radiation, it's just hell on you. On the body."

They're passing an apartment building and Joanne runs her cigarette along the brickwork and then tosses it in a garbage can as they pass. She immediately lights up another one.

"But, Duane," she says, not looking at him, looking out at the street before them, at the trees and buildings, the cold blue throat of the sky, "there's someone who can help him."

"Help him how?"

She just shakes her head, her mouth a grim line. "You wouldn't believe me."

"Okay," he says, annoyed at this sudden shift—Joanne's never been one to act cagey—"and I suppose those two guys in their skull vests and their state-time ink have something to do with it."

"They work for someone. He's the one that can help Ed."

"*How,* though, is what I'm asking you."

She turns and looks at him. She seems impossibly old in the morning light, pale and drawn and exhausted, freighted with all of this. "Duane, just listen to me—"

"They're dealing heroin out of the back of your bar, Joanne. *Heroin.* Did you know that? The bar you inherited from your old man, the bar you and Ed have run for years. Jesus, you could *do time,* Joanne, so could he. Hell, so could I."

"They're being careful."

"They're *not* being careful, I promise you. They don't give a shit. And it's gonna bring heat down on me for the thing last year, I guarantee it, and once the cops start looking around—"

Joanne's eyes widen in surprise, a kind of terrible mirth. "Oh," she says. "Oh, I get it. That's what this is all about, isn't it? Your *thing* last year. You're just worried about yourself."

"That's not true at all."

"You son of a bitch, you owe me."

Minor tenses, shocked into silence.

She nods, knuckling a tear away, her eyes burning into his. "That's right. You owe me, Duane."

"I know I do." She's never spoken to him like this before.

"Then step aside."

"So you can let these guys sell dope in your bar?" He scrubs at his chin with the back of his hand, still stunned that she's willing to use his past as a cudgel. It has been an unspoken thing between them until now. His ghosts, the skeletons that rattle the cage of his heart at night. What the dreams, at their core, are all about. He throws out his arms. "So, what, I can get arrested for trafficking and have Julia taken away from us? The fuck is Heidi going to do if you and me and Ed are in prison? What are they promising you, man?"

She tucks a hand beneath her elbow, looks away from him, holding the cigarette close to her face. After a moment, she says, "Like I said, you wouldn't believe me if I told you."

"Try me."

But it's the wrong thing to say. Joanne jabs the smoke at him again. "No. You listen to me, Duane. The Last Call is *my* place. *My* bar. Those men are going to be back tonight, and you're going to let them do what they do, and if they ask for anything, you're going to give it to them. You understand me? Or else."

Softly, afraid of the answer, he says, "Or else what, Joanne?"

Wiping another tear away, blinking madly, her face seems cut from stone. Fierce and resolute. "Or I'll tell Heidi what happened last year. What you did. I'll tell Heidi and the cops."

There it is.

Before he can speak, Joanne says, in a fierce whisper, "*Ed's* my family, you understand me? My husband's my family. If I can help him, goddamnit, I'm going to."

She fixes him with a baleful stare, her lips pursed, daring him, and then she turns and walks away, not waiting to see if he follows.

5

An hour later, he and Julia are in his truck, heading to school. He's numb, the back of his mind feathery with panic, trying to work out the knot of Joanne's ultimatum, trying to push back at the blur of old memories—boots scraping the floor, the wet red gleam of shattered glass—all while giving Julia the calm and impassive face of an unbothered parent. Julia's been thrown back into gen pop, as it were, her three-day suspension over. She doesn't say much to him, her dark eyes forever watching the street, carefully gauging the world. She talks to Heidi all the time, he can hear them chatting away when he's in another room, but when he's around Julia closes up like a fist. Ray Ray, he imagines, coloring the way she looks at men. Though maybe, who knows, maybe she sees inside him just fine, sees that fury Minor's tried so hard to push down since he got sober. Some vital shortage in him, some necessary human component he's just missing.

Morning news is on the radio. Sports scores, weather, and then the tickertape of misery—local and national—begins unspooling. Gridlock in city council over a proposed gas tax. A dismal update on the oil tanker that's spilled 180,000 barrels of the stuff off the coast of Nantucket. The body of fourteen-year-old Karen Malone, missing for days now, has been discovered, savaged and limbless in the weeds some hundred yards behind her home. She'd been going to a friend's house to do homework. This is the first confirmed death, the reporter says, after a marked rise in recent missing persons reports—

"Jesus Christ," Minor says, turning the radio off. Thinks of the two men. The truck ride after, the tarp.

Julia's wearing this oversized sweater, a knit one that she's borrowed from Heidi, cream-colored with black at the waist and the cuffs. It swallows her up, and she picks at a thread on the hem and says quietly, "Some kids from school knew her."

Minor looks at her. "Who?"

"Karen Malone. The girl they're talking about."

"She went to your school?"

"No. But some kids were friends with her. Casey and them. Everyone's all, 'She ran away, she was on drugs,' and Casey's like, 'Not a chance.' Casey thought she ran away to her dad's. She's gonna be fucked up by this."

Minor doesn't call her out on the language. Mom's doing life in Bayonne? Dickhead stepfather murdered in front of you? You get a free f-word every once in a while.

"I'm sorry to hear that," he manages. All these deaths, the idea of it, pinballing around him. *I'll tell Heidi and the cops.*

They drive on, the weather turning to rain now, little ridges of ugly brown snow on this side of the street or that. More hard weather coming, though, according to the radio. Minor can't stop thinking about what Joanne's said to him about Ed. The plaintive quality in her voice, like she's come up against the edge of something, something that Minor, in spite of his history, isn't even close to understanding. Cancer in the lungs? Spread to the brain? The fuck could a bunch of deadbeat heroin dealers possibly offer her? Must be money. Maybe Ed's insurance won't cover the treatment.

"How long can I live with you guys?" Julia says softly, looking out the window.

Minor's thrown back into the moment. "What?"

"Are you gonna send me away?"

He looks at her, shocked. "Man, what're you talking about?"

"Like if I get in trouble again. Would you send me away?"

"What? Hell no. Absolutely not. What's going on, Julia? What's the matter?"

"I don't know," she says, staring down at her lap. Her small pale hands twined there beneath the giant cuffs of that sweater. "Me and

Little Kev already got taken away from each other, after Ray, and now I just get worried that I'm gonna get sent away from you guys too. And then I won't know anyone wherever I go."

There's this urge to make a bold proclamation, stop the truck, put his hand over hers. Something grand like that. But in truth, Minor's not that type of person, and Julia would be mortified by the gesture. So all he says is, "Not a chance. You're stuck with me and Heidi until you're eighteen, and after that we can figure out your next move together. All three of us."

"Grandma and Grandpa too, though?"

"Grandma and Grandpa too." Minor says it without hesitation.

She's frowning furiously down at her lap, which in Julia's lexicon can sometimes mean anger or sadness, but can also mean a happiness she doesn't really know what to do with.

"It'd help," he says after a moment, "if you could hold off on the ass-kickings, though."

Julia gives a small nod. He gets the tiniest smile from her. "Yeah."

Minor smiles back. "Yeah?"

"Okay."

He lets her out at the corner, down from the school—he remembers being thirteen, the embarrassment he felt whenever he was in forced proximity to his parents—and watches as she walks through the doors. A small, thin girl with her head bowed, a black ponytail, rain *papping* against the shoulders of her coat. He feels a fierceness inside himself, this desire to protect her that's so physical it's almost a pain; this, coupled with a nattering, serpentine belief that no matter what he does, it's never going to be quite enough. There's no magic answer, no elixir that might protect her from her own past, from whatever future might be rocketing toward her. He should be thrilled—she's never opened up to him like that before, such things usually reserved for her talks with Heidi—but everything still feels off-kilter after Joanne.

He makes it home and finds Heidi in one of his oversized shirts, eggs and bacon sizzling in a pan. He leans in and kisses her neck, presses himself against her, then goes and pours a cup of coffee. Sits down at their small kitchen table, lights a smoke. Watches her cook, listens to her talk about her book, school, all the endless damn *reading* she has to do. He's continuously impressed by her—she works part-time as a typist for a construction company and is a few months away from getting her BFA at Portland State. It's nearly all men in her classes, *writers,* and Minor's done his level best at fielding his insecurities about them. Smashed down, as well as he can, all those fears of her falling for some asshole in a turtleneck who's going to write her love poems. The feeling that one day their differences may become too insurmountable—she's an artist, he's whatever he is, a bartender, a man besieged by bad dreams of the things he did and saw in some other life. In this life.

She's written a novel, Heidi has. *The Hollow,* it's called, and beyond the barest synopsis he knows almost nothing about it. *You're the person I want to read it the most, Duane, but not until it's all the way done,* she's told him, and he's finally learned to stop asking when that's going to be. She started the first draft when he was in Vietnam and has been revising it ever since. Only thing he's sure about is that it involves a young woman in a 1930s Oregon mill town who slowly goes mad from mercury poisoning amid a number of scandalous affairs. She'll be presenting it to her graduating committee in the summer—the "most striking" fifty pages. So right now, she's embroiled in a decision to either section it out into a handful of short stories, or simply hand it to the committee as a whole *piece.* "I mean, I'll graduate either way, but why half-ass it? Right?" This is how Heidi moves through the world, this patient, evenhanded consideration. The manuscript—the current incarnation of it—lies on the kitchen table next to the fruit bowl, the title page of this draft already emblazoned with a coffee ring in the corner. It's her paperweight, her beating heart, the loving anvil she's chained herself to.

They eat breakfast, the radio on low. Jazz, quiet and soft. At some point, Heidi asks him what Joanne wanted to talk to him about. "It was early," she says.

Minor keeps his eyes on his plate, pushes his eggs around. "Yeah, just bar stuff."

"Everything alright?"

"Yeah, everything's fine," he says, and that's a line crossed right there. You make these little decisions in a marriage, a hundred of them a day. Some of them mean nothing, so inconsequential that you don't even notice them, and some of them have the potential to echo through time, through the rooms of your life. Minor swallows, sips coffee, looks out the window, knows this will be the latter. Knows that he's made a mistake.

He picks Julia up from school that afternoon before his shift at the bar. Given her talk earlier that morning, he wants to try to connect. Try to reassure her. But he's himself, always and resolutely mired in his own skin, and can't come up with anything beyond the most inane ideas. Baking cookies. Bowling. He thinks too of getting his pistol from the bedroom closet and maybe taking her shooting somewhere outside of town. Then immediately winces at his own thoughtlessness, given how she'd come to be with him and Heidi in the first place. *Fucking idiot,* he thinks. *Jesus.*

He decides to keep it simple, and it's only when they pull into a parking lot instead of home that she looks up. "What're we doing here?"

"I mean, there's the sign right there."

"Donuts?"

Minor shrugs. "Yeah, why not?"

Inside, there's that first hint of a smile. She walks over to the cases, and he notes again how small she is. She looks back at him. "Can I get two?"

Minor shoves his fists in his pockets. "Long as you eat dinner tonight, you can get ten if you want."

A real grin then, and she orders two, and asks if she can get one for Heidi as well and Minor's face almost crumples with tears. He's like this sometimes, all of his emotions rippling right under the veneer.

But the idea of this kid, after all she's been through, thinking of Heidi, wanting to please her. Just about makes him cry.

He gets a maple bar and a cup of coffee and she gets hers, Heidi's bear claw in a grease-spotted paper bag, and they sit in the corner at the window while old guys at another table gripe at each other and smoke cigarettes and a little boy comes in with his mom and the world keeps moving along. If he's hoping for her to suddenly open up to him, it's a hope unmet. But she chews and smiles and wipes her fingers with a napkin and it's the two of them for a little while in a companionable enough silence. If he's not her father—and he's not, and never will be—he is an adult tasked with her safekeeping. He and Heidi both.

Traffic outside, and in the shop it smells of the old boys' cigarettes and the coffee and the jubilant, cloying scent of sugar and vanilla.

"I know what you're doing," Julia says, licking her fingers.

Minor makes a face. "What am I doing?"

"You feel bad about me asking if I'd get sent away."

He shakes his head, fishes out a cigarette from his pack and puts it in his mouth. "I don't feel bad about it. I just want you to know that you're with us. Me and Heidi and Grandma and Grandpa."

She raises an eyebrow. "So you bribe me with donuts?"

"I mean, I figured it was better than bribing you with coffee?"

Her first open smile of the day. She leans forward, arms on the table. "I can have *coffee*?"

So ten minutes later they're heading home, Julia holding a steaming Styrofoam cup of coffee carefully with both hands, taking little sips from it, Minor already trying to figure out what he'll tell Heidi when she busts his ass about giving the kid this much caffeine.

He starts his shift after dropping Julia at the apartment, Heidi giving him a *What the hell* look when she waltzes in with her coffee cup and heads to her room.

"Was that a giant cup of coffee I saw?"

"We were bonding," Minor says.

"Jesus Christ," Heidi says, rolling her eyes, and Minor laughs out loud.

He heads downstairs for his shift then, his good humor vanishing like smoke, but despite what Joanne had told him, the men from the Crooked Wheel do not come back that night. It's a normal enough evening, all told. He squashes a couple fights before they start, most notably Bobby mouthing off to another one of the regulars, the two of them almost squaring off in the middle of the floor before Minor's able to get around the bar. He gives the regular a pitcher of Hamm's and sits Bobby on his stool, putting a cup of burnt coffee in his hands and hissing at him to calm the fuck down, suddenly exhausted with the whole thing, these repetitions they get into every damn night. He's on edge his whole shift, waiting for the Crooked Wheel to roll in, maybe a whole crew of them this time. Nervous especially with Bobby sloppy as he is, like he's the spark that might set everything off. But Minor knows himself well enough to understand that if they do come in, it's his own pride that's going to be the spark. That pit of rage in him he's tried so hard to push down. Ed's sickness be damned, and to hell with Joanne's fears. None of it matters when he gets to a certain point. Minor thinks he's *right,* is the thing, and if you think you're right, lot of times it gives you breathing room to do whatever the fuck you want in the name of some supposed justice.

Then it's last call, and then night's end. He cleans and preps, closes up, heads upstairs. Everything's quiet. It's one of those nights where he knows sleep won't come. Now's the time for what Joanne said this morning to flex its wings and decimate any notion of rest inside him. He sits on the couch in the dark and smokes and honestly, there's a part of him that's entirely unsurprised to hear, sometime later, the blat of chopper engines on the street, and then the sound of someone walking around downstairs. A part of him has been expecting it. Sound of doors closing, pipes gurgling.

Someone's in the bar.

He imagines the men in their vests emptying Joanne's safe in the office. The slop of gasoline flung across the back room, soaking the felt of the pool tables. The tang of smoke, flames lighting up the bar and licking their way up the stairwell, crawling the walls. The doorknobs of their apartment grown too hot to touch. The charred, curled corpses of his wife and niece.

He thinks, too, of last year, of what he owes Joanne and can't bear to speak of out loud, and it's this, finally, that gets him moving.

He creeps down the hall and into his bedroom. Heidi, always a deep sleeper, is a hunched shape beneath the blankets. He goes to their closet and reaches up onto the shelf until he feels the steel lockbox and takes it down, pausing when the hinge of its handle creaks, waiting for Heidi to stir. She doesn't, and he makes his way gingerly out into the living room, where he uses the key on his key ring to open the box. An M1911 .45, the same model he'd carried in-country. He checks that it's loaded, the safety's off.

In the stillness, he hears someone laugh downstairs.

Minor creeps down the stairwell and steps outside; the night is flensed with cold rain. Streetlights haloed in mist. Snow melting. It's been an hour, maybe an hour and a half since he closed up. He walks to the corner of the building, the pistol low at his leg. That pregnant moment before violence begins. The simplicity of the world, everything viewed through the narrowest of apertures.

There's a pair of choppers parked at the curb.

He strides around the corner, peers into the big picture windows of the bar. Lights are on in the back room, and then he catches a man's silhouette going into Joanne's office, illumination suddenly spilling into the hallway when he turns the office light on.

The front door's unlocked. He opens it, the .45 held out in front of him. Creeps slow. The front of the bar is dark, just the Christmas lights and the thinned wash of streetlights outside. He smells beer and smoke, the industrial cleaner he used on the floor. Men's voices drift low from the back. He makes his way to the hallway.

When the man comes out of Joanne's office—the red-headed biker from the other night—Minor steps up and jams the barrel of the .45 hard behind his ear.

"Hands up," he says softly.

"Oh, you dipshit," the man says, but he puts his hands up. Minor takes a step back, makes space.

"How many of you?"

"Fuck you."

"Bradley," a man's voice calls from the back room. "You alright?"

A momentary pause and then Bradley calls out, "Boss, I got a pistol in my ear," and Minor almost shoots him right then.

Whoever it is in the back room laughs. "Well," he says, "why don't you and your friend come on back so we can figure this out."

"Go," Minor says softly.

He follows Bradley down the hallway and into the back room. The pool tables, the dartboard, the two booths.

Seated at the rear booth is the other biker, and opposite him is a man Minor doesn't recognize. Huge guy in a dark denim jacket. An open-throated shirt the color of ash, blond hair that brushes his collar. Week's worth of beard. Just radiating this kind of easy, jolly menace, like everything's a big joke. There's a couple pints on the tabletop, still with heads of foam on them.

And there's Joanne, seated across the table from the big man. She turns and looks at Minor. A napkin's balled in her fist. She's been crying.

"Oh, Duane," she says, her voice thick with resentment. "Damn it. Why didn't you listen to me?"

6

"So this is Duane," says the blond man to Joanne. And then, to Minor: "You're the man currently rat-fucking my business endeavors, from what I hear. Well, nice to meet you, Duane." He smiles, stretches those massive arms out across the back of the booth. If Minor was expecting some Crooked Wheel lieutenant, some grizzled outlaw done up in jailhouse ink, he's not getting it. He puts this guy at about his own age, mid-twenties, that big bear paw hanging off the edge of the seat back. He's massive, fearsome, but a biker he's not.

Minor looks over at Joanne. "You alright?" To the other man blocking her in: "Let her out."

The blond man raises those big hands up, then returns them to the booth's back. "You're misreading things."

He's still got the .45 on Bradley, who starts to turn, and Minor tells him to stop. He does. "You move one more time," Minor says, "and your riding days are over. You'll be shitting in a bag while they wheel you around to the titty bars, son."

"I get that gun off you, it's going up your ass," Bradley says over his shoulder.

The blond man grins again. Might be a television show for all he's concerned. He says, "We were in the middle of a business meeting, Duane."

"Duane," Joanne says, her voice wavering, "put that damn gun down, now."

"What the hell's going on," he says. And to the blond man: "What's your name?"

He puts a hand to his chest. Knuckles all done up in scar tissue. "Me?" he says with mock surprise.

"You, yes."

"My name's John Varley, Duane. Surprised you haven't learned that yet, given the degree that you've been concerning yourself with my activities."

"The deal's off," Minor says. "Whatever shit you got going on with Joanne, it's not happening."

"Fuck you." Joanne spits. "That's not your call."

His eyes still pinballing between Varley and Bradley, the third one still seated next to Joanne, he says to her, "Think about it. You let these dipshits move dope through here, what happens? If they sell to some undercover cop, or someone dies in the bar? You get busted for distribution, the bank seizes the place, Julia goes right back to the state. After everything that's happened to her."

"Why, who's Julia?" Varley says. "*She* sounds important."

Shoot him, Minor thinks. *Right now.*

"Shut up," Joanne says to Varley, and something happens to the man's face. A blankness, all that good humor evaporating like smoke. Minor tries to get a feel for him and can't do it. Guy's mannerisms feel off, prim or dated in some way that Minor can't pin down. But it's real clear that Joanne's just crossed a line with him. Varley's not one who takes well to being talked down to.

"Eugene," he says, still looking right at Minor, and with that odd, cavalier smile returning to his face, "go ahead and stand up against that pool table there. Bradley, you too."

Eugene scoots out, and he and Bradley sidle over to the table.

"What exactly is it you can do for us?" Minor says, the gun on Varley now. "That Joanne's willing to torch her whole fucking life for?"

Varley makes a face. "I'm thinking that's a bit melodramatic, Duane."

"I look like I care what you think?"

Varley squints and picks at the corner of one eye with a fingertip. "What you look like, to me, is a big fucking stop sign, and it's pissing me off. I'm trying to work out business logistics with this lady here, and then you come in pointing a gun at people. I think you're stepping out of bounds."

"Joanne," Minor says, "go get the Polaroid behind the bar."

To his surprise, Joanne does just that. Gets out of the booth, moves past him, goes down the hall to the dark bar. The three of them stand there, Bradley letting out a long sigh, until Joanne comes back with it.

"Take their pictures," Minor says. "All three of these assholes. John Varley, and Bradley, and—what was your name again, bud?"

The other biker mumbles something.

"Say what?"

Joanne takes their photos, the camera spitting a pair of gray squares into her hand.

"Eugene," the man says.

"Eugene, John Varley, and Bradley," Minor repeats. "All of you hooked in deep with the Crooked Wheel Club, looks like, and I'm sure the Portland police are familiar with *that* outfit, am I right? Give me those photos." She hands them over to him, openly weeping now, a fist pressed to her lips, and he puts the photos in his shirt pocket, the images just starting to rise from the murk to reveal themselves. "Stand behind me," he says, and she does.

"You're making a mistake," Varley says softly, putting his hands flat on the table.

"What mistake is that?"

"Crossing me," he says.

"That so?" He pivots on his heel and pistol-whips Bradley, gets some muscle into it, gets him right under the eye. That good feeling, that rightness, big inside him. Bradley cries out, falls back onto the table; Eugene reaches out for him and Minor jabs the barrel of the .45, quick, into the hard knob of his throat. Eugene sputters, gags, drops to his knees. Minor stands there, his legs feathery with adrenaline.

"Get the fuck out," he says, turning and raising the pistol at Varley. "Or you can be one of those guys that catch a bullet with their teeth."

Varley stands, slowly—Minor taking a step back, making sure Joanne's behind him. The man's even bigger than he first thought. Six-five, maybe? Christ. Varley gives Joanne a reproachful, dead-eyed look. Any previous humor scoured clean. "I offered you the world," he says.

"I know," Joanne says in a wooden voice, a voice Minor has never heard in all the years he's known her. "He doesn't want it."

"Five seconds," Minor says.

Varley nods. Black jeans and that black denim jacket and a gray shirt, all of it with a certain weathered quality, like the man's stepped out of time. He hums with a weird, dark vitality, and he walks over and claps Bradley on the back, and Bradley hoists Eugene up by his arm. "I'll see you around, Duane."

Minor motions for them to go down the hall to the front of the bar. "You won't see shit. You come near anyone I know, you ever come close to this bar again, come down this fucking *street,* and your photos are going straight to the first cop I see. Now *go.*"

He watches the three men walk through the empty bar, following at a distance. Bradley even takes care to gently shut the front door behind them. They stand outside for a moment and then Varley says something and Minor sees through the window the two bikers get on their rides. The sound of their choppers fills the street, impossibly loud after the taut-bowstring quietness of the past few minutes. Varley walks the opposite way. Just walks on down the street, hands in his pockets, like he hadn't had a gun pointed in his face moments before. Minor wonders if he's circling back.

"We should get out of here," he says, turning to Joanne.

She stares at him, incredulous, until her face slowly crumples.

"Joanne."

She covers her face with her hands. "You idiot. Christ, Duane. What have you done?"

"Joanne, you'd have lost everything. I promise you. Guys like that, they don't give a shit—"

"I wish she'd never met you." She looks up at him and her face is one of resignation, a kind of stunned, bomb-blasted wonderment, like she can't believe where she is at that exact moment. "Your goddamn pride. Your anger."

Minor looks at her, his jaw working, unable to say anything.

"I'd trade ten of you for Ed," she says. "*Ten*. You understand me? And the fact that my daughter has to raise that girl with you? My God. You and Ray Sikes are more the same than you are different. Same type of man. Small and vicious and weakhearted. Thinking your way's the only way there is. Ed had a *chance* until you fucking stormed in."

He stands there, a kind of abject horror moving through him slow. That this is what she thinks of him. What she's always thought of him, apparently. "A chance at what?" he says, and she holds up a hand to stop him.

"You're even worse than Ray," she says. "You're a killer, Duane. I should've never helped you. Never picked up the phone that night." And then Joanne turns. With her face in her hands, she walks out into the night. A small shape out in the dark where Varley was only moments before.

He wants to call out to her—it's not safe out there—but something, some weakness, stops him. She's already said what she means, hasn't she? What good will he do, going out there?

Maybe he is a coward after all.

So he does nothing. He stands in the silent, ticking bar with a pistol hanging limp from his hand. His head is a dark and empty star, just his heart and lungs working. A head full of nothing, and this notion that he has done the right thing suddenly twisting away like smoke, like a trick of the light, his own hollowness his only companion.

7

"Hon, it's gonna be fine," Heidi says to the kid, grinding her cigarette butt out in the ashtray on the kitchen counter. "Just call me if anything comes up. I'll take the truck and get you right away."

The three of them in the apartment, rain spattering the windows outside, the past week's snow mostly gone but the day already turning dark. Julia in her puffy winter coat with her backpack slung over one shoulder. Beneath it, she's dressed in her favorite outfit—blue jeans and a black T-shirt, heavy black boots of Minor's that she's stuffed with newspaper and claimed as her own. No tie-dyes for her, no bell-bottoms or flares or any of that. It's her first sleepover since moving in with them, and Heidi has already talked to Casey's mom on the phone, double-checked everything. As sick as he feels over all of this shit with Joanne, Varley, as numb as he is, and with this secret about Ed he's apparently chosen to keep from his wife, there's a small kernel of happiness inside him. She deserves it, Julia. She's been to hell and back, and a part of him seizes on this notion that she might have a chance to be a child in spite of all that's happened to her. "Everything'll be fine," Heidi says again.

"I know," Julia says, then looks at Minor, a look that's just there and back, real fast. And then, incredibly, she's walking over to Heidi with her head down, blushing furiously, the line in her scalp where her hair's parted, and she's wrapping her arms around Heidi, burying herself in the crook of his wife's neck. Heidi gives him a surprised smile over the top of Julia's head, a look like *What the hell*. Then Julia pulls free and shrugs her shoulders to adjust her backpack and says, "Okay, I'm ready."

Minor casts his wife one more wide-eyed glance as he and Julia head for the door, Heidi grinning like she's just won the lottery.

Julia's stepped out into the hallway when Heidi calls out, "Love you, kid. Have fun tonight."

"Love you too," Julia says—another first, *huge,* and it sounds so normal, another dizzying thing—and then Minor's following her down the stairs.

They thread their way along I-5, heading toward Casey's house. Julia's fidgety, nervous, and, to his surprise, actually talking to him. Minor's head is still dismantling the night before, what he did, what he could have done, but he's trying to be in the moment. She's riffing, this kid.

"I'm just saying, what if I get scared? Casey's mom said we could watch scary movies after her little brother goes to bed, but, like, what if I get *too* freaked out?" This from a girl who saw what she saw in New York. What her mother did to Ray. The boundless lives inside a person.

"Like Heidi said, just call."

"You guys won't be mad? Even if it's the middle of the night?"

"I keep pretty late hours, Jules. Not sure if you noticed."

"Yeah, but what about Heidi?"

"Heidi'll be fine. But honestly, I think you will be too. Just, you know, be a kid for a night. Have fun."

It sits there between them, what he's said. All her past history—why it's so damnably hard for Julia to *be* a kid—suddenly feels like a tangible thing, a third person inside the truck's cab.

"I haven't really told you guys thank you," Julia says quietly. Her backpack's in her lap. She twirls one of the straps around her finger. The high-rises of downtown throw a mess of glittering light across the shimmering face of the Willamette River.

"Yeah, you don't have to," Minor says, thinking of what Joanne said the night before.

"I do, though. Thanks."

"Sure," Minor says, his voice suddenly thick. "No problem." He has another one of those moments, those feelings like he's drowning. But it's a strangely *good* feeling this time, in spite of everything, and he thinks, *Protect her, man. You gotta work this out with Joanne. Ed, the Crooked Wheel. You gotta clear it up with her somehow. That, and the thing last year. Who knows how, but it's gotta be done.*

"There was a part of me that was glad she did it," Julia says, bringing him back, the words so soft he's not even sure he heard her right. She's still looking out the window. "My mom. There's a part of me that's still glad, actually. Even though it made everything different."

"Yeah, well, Ray Ray was a real piece of shit," Minor says, thinking of Joanne's crumpled, sorrowful face as she said, *You and Ray Sikes are more the same than you are different.*

"I hated him," she says.

"I know," Minor says quietly. "You got every right to."

"I just want to let you know. You guys didn't have to take me in. I know that."

"Oh, come on."

She looks down at her backpack, gives that strap another twist. "For real. I could be in some home that HHS put me in. I miss my mom, but this place with you guys, it's—it's better in some ways."

And then, before he can say anything, before he can navigate the confusing, heartbreaking mix of love and pain and sorrow that means being a guardian of this child, Julia rescues him and turns the radio on. Rod Stewart, oh God, but it saves him from trying to speak through this sudden lump in his throat, and then, wonder of wonders, she actually starts singing along, her voice high and plaintive and not exactly great, but lovely just the same, singing beside him and working hard at the business of being a child, a kid going to her friend's house to spend the night.

There's the quick "Hi, nice to meet you, I'll come get her in the morning" talk with Casey's mother in their living room, Casey's old man giving him a brief wave of the hand while he lies splayed out in a recliner in his socks, a tallboy in one fist, Casey's little brothers running around raising hell, the two girls slipping like smoke down the hall to Casey's bedroom. After that, he threads through traffic on the highway and tries to figure out what to do about Joanne. Tonight's her shift downstairs, and he considers popping in on her, telling Andy to sling drinks while they talk in the office. But what is there to say? Minor still thinks he's *right,* is the thing. Still believes he's done what he did with family in mind—and that's not really an apology, is it? That's an excuse. Then he thinks of just manning the door, keeping an eye out. Even with the threat of the Polaroids, retribution seems not just possible but likely with those three. They don't seem like the type to let things fester. What was it Varley had said to Joanne? *I offered you the world.* And what was it she'd said back to him? That Ed hadn't wanted it, after all?

It reminds him—he's got to put those Polaroids somewhere safe. He hasn't even looked at them yet, and spends a panicked moment patting his jacket before feeling the square rigidity of them in his pocket. At some point soon, this thing with Ed and Joanne—and the Crooked Wheel too, and the thing last year—all of it will collide like a meteor against the rest of his life. He knows he has to tell Heidi. All of it. She's bound up in it. They all are.

He parks the truck on the street and clomps back up the stairwell, shaking rainwater from his coat. Smells weed before he makes it through the front door. He finds Heidi sitting cross-legged in a tank top on the couch, listening to a blues record and taking little sips off a nail-thin joint, her hair done up in pigtails. She's got her manuscript on the couch's armrest, and has a spiral-bound notebook open on her lap, making notes. Minor sits down next to her, feels the press of her leg against his.

"How'd it go with drop-off?"

"Great," he says. "She thanked us."

Heidi turns to him, makes a face. "Shut up."

"I'm serious."

"And she told us she *loved* us when she left? Kid must be getting into our stash or something."

He laughs. "She also told me she was glad your sister killed Ray. It wasn't all sunshine."

Heidi nods solemnly, takes another hit. "Being thirteen and having to live with that shit."

They sit there for a bit, listening to the man on the stereo lament his lot in life. *Baby*, he wails, his voice like broken glass, parked somewhere right on the edge of a howl, *I done wrong, bad wrong, and I mean it when I say I'll do wronger still.*

"Listen," Minor says, "I got to tell you something," and then—and he will think on this later, will wonder how much destiny or bad luck or God's impeccable timing played a part—the phone starts ringing.

Heidi arches her eyebrows at him. He's on the precipice of it, of confession, some lizard-brain part of him insisting he let it ring, that he just *tell her.* Tell her all of it. Ed and Joanne and the Wheel, Varley, those two men—

"It might be Julia," Heidi says, and Minor says, "Right, right," and jumps up, walks into the kitchen, picks up the phone.

"Duane," Joanne says on the other end.

"Hey, Joanne." Minor blinking at the floor, surprised.

"Look," she says, "Ed's not doing well. I need to be at home with him." She clears her throat. He can hear the din of the bar behind her. "And Andy's not ready for a shift by himself yet." She speaks almost formally, last night like an open wound between them.

"You want me to head down there?"

"Please. It's— He's having a rough night."

Minor scratches an eyebrow. "Alright. Be right down."

She says, "Thank you, Duane," and he figures that's as close to an apology as either of them can manage right now. He sets the phone in its cradle.

The record's stopped. "Is it Mom?" Heidi calls out.

"Yeah, she needs me to cover for her."

"Damn. I wanted us to party tonight. No school, the house to our-selves? Why's she need you to cover?"

"I don't know," he says. "Something with your dad."

A pause. "He's not doing great, is he?"

"Yeah, I don't know," he says. *Fucking* tell *her,* he thinks, and then Heidi asks if he wants her to bring him down dinner later.

"Yeah, maybe," he says, cursing himself once again for his coward-ice. This whole story's become too big to thread his way through. He walks over and kisses Heidi, her hand slipping around his neck, her tongue snaking briefly in his mouth. She tastes like grass, her fingers trailing gently on his thigh as he walks to the coatrack by the door and puts on his jacket. Heidi stands up to put a new record on.

"Love you," he calls out.

Heidi, leaning over the stereo, the black circle of the record held in her tented fingers, smiles at him and says, "Love you too, babe."

He and Andy are busy, but Joanne's done a good job of prepping for the night and things run smooth. Bobby's already there by the time Minor comes down, and Minor asks him if he can keep a lid on his drinking tonight and watch the door for him. Bobby agrees, stations himself on a stool with a Pepsi. Minor cruises in that spot where time passes without him hardly being aware of it, and come midnight or so, between the jukebox going and his line of customers at the rack, Minor hardly hears the phone ringing.

He picks up the handset, sticks his finger in his ear and says, "Last Call."

"Hi, Duane?" Even through the noise, Minor recognizes Julia's voice as plaintive, embarrassed. He looks at the clock on the wall. Eleven minutes past midnight.

His voice softens. "Hey, kid, what's up? You alright?"

"I'm sorry, man, I just can't do it. I thought I could, and Casey and her mom are being really cool, but I just— I'm freaking out." Her voice catches. "I keep thinking about Ray, for some reason. I just want to sleep in my own bed tonight, you know?"

"Okay," he says, holding up a finger for a regular hoisting his cocktail glass Minor's way in annoyance. "It's cool. Just give Heidi a call upstairs, she'll come get you."

"That's the thing," Julia says. "I called up there and no one answered. I thought maybe she was down there with you."

"Alright," Minor says, sticking the phone into the crook between his shoulder and ear, taking the guy's glass and dumping its ice in the sink beneath the rail. "I'll run up there. She must've fallen asleep. One of us'll be there in a bit, just hang tight."

"Thanks, Duane. I'm sorry."

"Don't be sorry." He hangs up, looks at the regular. "You can't wait till I'm done with my phone call, Barry? You need a drink that bad?"

The old man's at least got the presence of mind to look sheepish. "Just hoping to get a G&T, Duane. Sorry."

"Andy, hey," Minor calls out. Andy, a dish tub in his hands, turns and looks at him like Minor's about to punch him in the mouth. "I got to run upstairs, make this fine gentleman a gin and tonic, please."

"Duane, dude—"

"Just do it, brother. I'll be back down in a second."

He walks around the bar, heads toward the front door. Bobby gives him a look when he steps past him. "You alright?"

"Yeah, just gotta run upstairs for a sec."

Bobby nods, hoists his glass. "Godspeed, young traveler."

Minor runs outside, around the corner, fishing his keys out of his pocket. Just in that short distance, the shoulders of his jacket get soaked. Rain in his hair, down his collar. He keys open the door, takes the stairs up to the apartment two at a time. Bummed that he's gonna have to wake Heidi up, preparing in advance for the sleep-blasted, gummy look in her eyes. A heavy sleeper to begin with, and grass always knocks her for a loop. Ever since they were kids, since high school, she's always been like that—

The smell hits him at the top of the stairs. Before he even opens the door.

It's a scent, metallic and warm, that's ingrained in the very fiber of Minor's past, and his reaction is an animal one—a flood of adrenaline, that thunderous fight-or-flight response that turns the world grainy and hyper-bright, makes his heartbeat *poom poom poom* in his throat. Time gone all slow and taffy-like.

He keys the front door. Pushing it open, he calls out Heidi's name. There's no answer. Place is *cold,* too, cold in spite of the clang of the radiator beneath the windows in the living room. He takes a step inside. Takes another step, and as he does, the bedroom door at the end of the hall slams shut. Minor jumps. Just a draft, he tells himself. But where's the draft coming from? The open front door and what?

The bedroom.

The bedroom *window.*

That's why it's so cold up here.

Because the bedroom window's open.

"Heidi?" His voice is small in his ears. Timid as a child's.

He turns and takes a step toward the closed bedroom door and sees, ah God, Jesus, right there, a smear of blood along the hallway now, chest-high, and there's a framed photo—the three of them standing in a bowling alley, taken within a week of Julia first getting here— that's fallen to the floor, a slivered crack running through the glass. The sound of his breathing through his own pinched throat like a bellows in his ears.

He walks down the hall and touches the bedroom doorknob. Smells the blood. The radiator, working hard, pings and rattles behind him, this insistent knocking like someone seeking entrance. His hands are weighted, useless clubs at the ends of his arms. He sees the wedge of light under the bedroom door.

He opens it.

Inside, the curtain flutters at the other side of the room, snared against the shards of window glass still intact on the frame.

The room's freezing and heavy with the close, pressing reek of blood.

And there's *so* much of it.

His eyes drift from the bed to the walls and the floor, the ceiling—*it's on the ceiling*—unsure at first of what he's even looking at, the parts of her, her wet red hair, a strange, almost Cubist block of pale, blood-slathered flesh on the floor, another on the bed, the room done up in great red splashes and gouts, and then he releases a single choked cry, steeped in realization and disgust and horror at what he's discovered, this kind of halving of himself, who he was before he stepped in this room and who he is now, and then Duane Minor steps backward into the hallway, sagging against the wall, his hands held out at nothing, pushing at the air as if he might stuff the vision of what he's just seen back into the past.

8

Three hours after he discovers the savaged, dismembered remains of his wife in the bedroom of their apartment above the Last Call Tavern, Minor finds himself seated across from a pair of Portland Police Bureau detectives deep inside the downtown precinct. It's a small room and they're sitting at a wooden table, its edges chipped and splintered, all kinds of dumb shit written and carved onto its surface. The detectives across from him each have their own yellow legal pad in front of them. All three men are smoking cigarettes; they've bought him a pack of Winstons from a vending machine in the hallway, and a cup of coffee that tastes resoundingly of scorched plastic. The two cops have made a good show of talking softly to him, calling him by his first name, keeping it respectful, low-key and mournful. They're so sorry. He's not in handcuffs. His legs, he can't stop it, they'll randomly start spasming beneath the table. Everything else inside him is numb, scoured out. The detectives have done a good job of ignoring his legs.

They look like quintessential cops, these two. Beefy, mustached, big sideburns. One's balding and one isn't, and that's about the only difference Minor can discern. Both of them white. They're wearing dress shirts and ties, their sidearms and badges on their belts. They might be thirty or fifty. Minor just keeps touching the coffee cup in front of him, pushing little half-moons into the Styrofoam with his fingernails until its surface is pebbled with them. He can't cry, nothing like that, can't imagine ever crying again. Just these leg spasms and this numbness. The detectives have informed him that they have Julia in another room, that she's okay, but Minor can't imagine such a thing is possible. The fuck does *okay* mean? Who will ever be okay again?

The detectives have told him their names. There's Scoggins, the balding one, and Davis. Or David? It doesn't matter. Most of Minor—the necessary, integral, working parts of him—is hollowed out with shock. It's just his body sitting here. Heart, lungs, twitching legs.

They've exchanged all the necessary niceties. Informed him that they've both spent their whole lives here, Scoggins over in the Piedmont neighborhood, Davis—it's Davis, he decides—out in the wastelands of Gresham, where he played tight end in high school, got a scholarship to OSU and promptly got himself a greenstick fracture in his right fibula six minutes into his first game. He knows that Scoggins's son ran a .50 cal on a swift boat near Hoi An, that he did two tours and came back in '72 and now works selling cars at a lot right there on Eighty-second Avenue. Minor's listed his own tour by rote, and they've both politely thanked him for his service and subtly professed gratitude that he hasn't turned hippie or burned his draft card or any silly bullshit like that.

Scoggins, minutes ago, has also informed him that Ed and Joanne Shaw have been found murdered in their house in North Portland, ripped apart and disemboweled in the same manner that Heidi was. Minor takes this in, and he is hollow, hollow, he is a sounding board for these words, that's all. He inhales smoke and blows it out. He sips cold, scorched coffee.

"So, Duane," says Scoggins, who has clearly been eyeballing him for his response after news of Ed and Joanne's murders, "I was just hoping we could go over the timeline again. Want to make sure we got it all right."

"I've told you everything," Minor says. He drags on his cigarette and his left foot does another one of those little tap-dance flurries under the table. The two detectives share a look. "Told you like ten times now."

"I know it. And I'm sorry for it, Duane. Just one more time. Tell us about the men you fought in the bar."

"I didn't fight them, man. I kicked them out."

"Right," Scoggins says, flipping a page on his pad. "Right, sorry. Three guys. Two in biker vests, and another in, what was it?"

"Like a jacket. Denim jacket. Gray, or like a faded black."

"That's right. And this was the ringleader, correct? This John Varley?"

Minor nods. "Yeah."

Scoggins flips the pages and smooths down the pad with the flat of his hand. "How'd you know he was the ringleader, Duane?"

"I mean, it was obvious. They listened to him. Did what he said."

"Alright. And you described this John Varley as six-two to six-four, two hundred and thirty pounds. Twenty-five to thirty-five years old. Blond, shoulder-length hair. That about right?"

"Yeah."

"See, here's the thing I don't get, Duane," Scoggins said, leaning forward, squinting one eye shut. "Why are they listening to him if he's wearing a denim jacket?"

"I don't know what you mean."

Davis rolls the edge of his cigarette around the rim of the ashtray. Doesn't look at him. "You know anything about biker gangs, Duane?"

"No."

"Well, let me tell you, they're real precise with their structure. A hierarchy, right? First you're what's called a hang-around, then you're a prospect—where you're being initiated into the gang and they just run you into the damn ground, haze the hell out of you—and then, if you stick with it, you finally get your colors. You get patched in. They give you a vest with the club's rocker on it, the patches and all that. And then?" He shrugs, goes wide-eyed. "Then there's a whole other hierarchy after you've been patched, with lieutenants and men-at-arms, all that stuff."

Minor waits for him to keep talking but that's it. He can't figure what Davis is getting at. "Point being," Scoggins says after a bit, turning his hands palms up. "It just doesn't make sense, Duane."

"What doesn't?"

"That this John Varley, big as he is, scary as he is, he's telling these Crooked Wheel guys what to do? They're not the biggest outfit in town, but they're no one to mess with, you know? But this Varley, he's not patched, he's not wearing their colors, nothing. The, uh, the *accoutrements* are so important to these guys, Duane. The protocol involved, it's almost military in a way. So it's just weird to us. This story about these guys following him around, a guy who's not in the life, it doesn't make much sense to us."

Minor, for the first time since being brought in, bristles. The lightest feather of rage arcing up his spine. "So this guy's not wearing a fucking jacket with skulls on it and you think I'm lying?"

"I'm not saying that. Not saying that at all. I just don't see them hitching their cart to a guy who isn't patched, much less even affiliated."

"So, what? I'm making it up? That what you're saying?"

The words hang there, everyone quiet after that. Scoggins and Davis waiting him out.

Dully, he says, "I should probably get a lawyer then, right? At this point?"

The detectives share another look. Scoggins leans back, the overhead light curving across his bald spot, and he squares his legal pad up against the edge of the table, sets his pen down on top of it. "I mean, you can. You're not being charged, Duane, but you can lawyer up if you want. Mostly what I'm hoping you'll do is tell me the truth."

"I am telling you the truth."

Davis crushes out his cigarette and crunches his face up like he's got indigestion. "Okay. So some guys from this one-percenter club are strong-arming your mother-in-law into using her bar to run heroin through. That right?"

"Yeah."

"But you, in your wisdom, put a stop to it."

That sense of hollowness inside him finally gives way. Terror seeps in like groundwater, and fury, and a sense of loss so big he can't even discern the edges of it yet. All of that pales, though, to the sense of guilt that marches through him. Blooms huge and ruinous. The understanding that none of this would have happened had he done what Joanne had asked of him. How he owns the corpse of every

loved one. Of his wife. The detectives see this shift in Minor's posture, how he hunches forward, how his face tightens into a mask of
pain. Davis seems to take it as some facade giving way. He leans in,
eager.

"See, maybe, hear me out, maybe you were working *with* these
guys, Duane, and things got away from you. Maybe they wanted a cut
that was too big and you told them no. Or you mouthed off a bit, and
things went south. Not your fault. You didn't think they'd respond
like this. You were just trying to make a little money. No shame in it."
His eyes search Minor's face, and he holds out his hands and shrugs,
like *What can you do?*

"I want a lawyer."

"You have any violent tendencies, Duane?" says Davis. "Lot of
you guys come back from Nam with pretty short fuses, I hear."

Minor looks at Scoggins for help, father of Mr. Two Tours, Mr.
Swift Boat, and gets back a flat, unblinking gaze. No love there. Bad
cop and bad cop.

"Lawyer," Minor says.

"Look," Scoggins says, seeing that he's hit a wall and trying to
backtrack. "It just reads funny to us. The bar owner who needs cash
for her husband's cancer treatments? She gets in deep with a biker
gang to move dope? Run, apparently, by a guy that's never been on a
bike in his life? No colors, no affiliation. I'm sorry for your loss,
brother, but there's something you're not telling us."

Minor reaches for the Winstons, puts another one in his mouth. "I
told you everything there is," he says.

"What about Julia?" Davis thumbs through the notes in his pad.
"Her mother's doing a life bid, right? Where is it again?"

"Bayonne Correctional," Minor says, shaking out his match and
dropping it in the ashtray. "Upstate New York."

"Bayonne, that's right. For killing her, what was it, her husband?
Shot him in the face, didn't she?"

Minor nods.

"And Julia saw it?"

"Yeah."

"You know, you mentioned she's got a temper. Trouble in school. Fighting. Any chance she's involved in this?"

"What? She's thirteen years old."

"You don't think she could've had something to do with it?"

"She's thirteen," Minor says again.

Davis looks up from his notepad. "That supposed to mean something to me?"

Scoggins, almost imperceptibly, touches the other detective with his elbow, and then scoots forward in his chair. *Here it comes,* Minor thinks. "Duane, I want you to listen to me. Alright? I can't—*we* can't imagine what you're going through. But those bodies, Duane— I know you don't want to hear this, and I'm sorry—but the damage done to Heidi, to your in-laws, it's like something an animal could do. Sick people are behind this, and I know by looking at you, brother, that there's more you're not telling us. And that breaks my heart. You want to know why?"

"Why?"

Scoggins leans in, so close that Minor can see the pores on his face, the bristles of his mustache. "Karen Malone is why," he says softly.

Some dim remembrance in his head—where has he heard that name?—but before he can figure it out, Scoggins says, "Karen Malone, couple days back, we found her in a bunch of junk weeds by the train tracks behind her house. She didn't have any fucking *arms,* brother." He nods, chews at his cheek for a moment. "You hear me? No arms. Had a head like a balloon someone had popped. Fourteen years old. We always have missing persons reports, kids run away, all that shit. But we got an *uptick,* Duane, and in wintertime? Makes no sense. And now we got three *new* bodies here. Your wife and your in-laws." He waits, blinks. Taps a finger on his yellow pad. "And their bodies look a *lot* like Karen Malone's. So, no, I personally don't think you did it, Duane, but I don't think you're being straight with us, either. So if you know something, why not be a stand-up guy and help us out?"

"I just came upstairs and saw her," he says. "That's all."

He remembers the way Varley had told Joanne, regretfully, *I offered you the world,* and even now there is some small, dark part of him turning vengeance over in his heart like a jeweler with a loupe examining a stone.

Davis has had enough. He leans back. "So that's all you got for us?"

"What else do you want?"

He points at Minor. "I want whatever that thing is in your eyes. That thing you're not telling us."

"I've told you everything there is." How the lie gets easier each time you say it. "My whole fucking life just ended."

Davis looks over at Scoggins, nods. Some message passing between them.

Scoggins says, "Remember when we frisked you, brother? When you first came into the station? We took everything out of your pockets for safety purposes, took your coat?"

"Yeah," Minor says.

Scoggins lifts up the middle of his notepad, pushes something across the table.

Two things, actually.

The Polaroids Joanne took that night in the Last Call.

She'd done a good job. The flash had washed everything into a morgue-like brightness, and in the first photograph, the two bikers looked pale as cadavers, their leathers blown out to a pale gray. The pupils red. Bradley, the closer of the two, has his lips pulled back in a sneer.

But it's the other photo that catches Minor's breath in his throat.

He recognizes Bradley, in the forefront again, can make out the blackletter OOKED of the patch on the back of his vest. And behind Bradley, he sees Varley's dark jeans, sees that gray shirt he'd worn, its open throat. That dark denim jacket. Recognizes the inherent *shape* of a man standing up from a booth, sees in stark clarity the pint glass sitting on the table, nearly full of piss-yellow beer.

But where Varley's hand should be in the photograph, there is something like a burst of gray-white smoke. Minor can see the edge of the table through it. *Nothing,* he thinks wildly, *a fuckup, a warp in the chemicals on the photo paper.*

But no.

Where Varley's head should be, his face, there's that same rippled quality. The barest suggestion of his features, warped and furling and gray-white, *foglike,* with two piercing white holes in place of the eyes. A head made of smoke.

Varley, looking like some errant ghost, like something unwilling— *unable*—to be captured on film.

Scoggins stares at him, eyebrows raised. He's almost smiling as he taps the Polaroid with a blunt fingernail. "What the hell is *this,* Duane? That's what I'm asking you. What exactly is happening here? We're supposed to believe *this* is John Varley?"

December 1975 –

January 1976

2

FOREVER OR
THE NEXT SUNRISE

1

During his admittedly brief and tumultuous partnership with the Crooked Wheel (the beginning of which was the brutal disemboweling of the Portland chapter's lieutenant in front of the rest of his crew), John Varley had taken refuge in the club's headquarters, a large, low-squat building of cement and brick and milky opaque windows, there on MLK Jr. Boulevard, a place dark and cavernous and smelling strongly of marijuana, motor oil and body odor. A three-bay garage took up the bulk of the space, but there was an inner office that Varley had refurbished in such a way—via two-by-fours and plywood sheeting—to block out the light and afford him some sleep. After the dispatching of the lieutenant, a three-hundred-pound mustached biker they called Zips, due to his penchant for methamphetamines, Varley had assumed responsibility of the club, though his knowledge of the ins and outs of biker culture was nominal at best. He was a hardcase of a different sort. Still, you run your hand up under a man's rib cage and pull out his entrails, shattering the ribs like yellow shards of kindling, the people watching will either follow you to the brink of hell or run away screaming. While the majority of the club had run away—after several woefully misguided attempts at killing him there in the garage—Bradley and Eugene and a few other boys had chosen to stick around with Varley at the helm, under the premise of making some real money. It had been a nice couple of weeks before everything imploded.

Like so many events in his past, it was Varley's temper that torched it all. The garage is once again filled with the corpses of the remaining crew, this same ragtag group of men who had sworn fealty to him, all of them wearing their cute little vests with the skull on the back. He'd meant it when he said they'd be able to make some cash, but after he'd slaughtered the bar hag and her man and her daughter, the remaining members of the Wheel had rebelled against him. *You're bringing more fucking heat on us,* Bradley had said, before Varley drove his fist through the man's mouth. Varley's rage ever his north star.

The garage is an abattoir now, a half dozen dead men flung about; it's an unsafe place to sleep in and will soon be full to the brim with either pigs or Crooked Wheel boys from other chapters seeking revenge. So Varley's beat feet and found an outbuilding in the industrial section of town, its roof furred in a thin carpet of snow, its interior a kind of storing house for train yard trash, the stink of the nearby river all run through it. He cannot bear someone telling him no, telling him he's wrong, it's like mercury in his blood. Better this than another night with Bradley and his kind.

It's night now, leaning toward morning, and snow is falling. Apart from the distant clatter of trains, all's quiet. Inside the shed, Varley pushes a fifty-five-gallon drum full of creosote-soaked lumber scraps against the door and then covers himself with a crackling blue tarp he's found, weighing it down on three sides with refuse—rebar, an old oil drum that leaves his hands red with rust, a stretch of rotting plywood lashed in ice. The shed's windows are broken out; daylight will get inside, and he can only hope for the best.

His hand reaches blindly outside the tarp's edge, and puts a heavy railroad spike, fat and nearly shapeless with rust, on its fourth side. Feels the weight of the plastic over him, tries to take comfort in its fragile protection, this rattling skin he hides beneath.

Portland, after what he's done—made nine or ten corpses in a single night—is lost to him, at least for a while. He'll leave when he wakes.

But for now, sleep, or what passes for it.

John Varley's dreams are stilted, jump-scare affairs, populated with the endless number of faces of those he has killed. Faces in repose, faces with their lips pulled back in terror, faces in the sweet and damning moments when death has finally gripped them. A collage of faces, and Varley in his dreams supping at their necks, drinking. He dreams, and his body takes note, rust-dirty fingers twitching on the hard ground as his eyes rove beneath his blue-veined lids. The clouds clear and the moon hangs there in the dark above the windows.

The sun makes its inevitable arc across the sky and dips down again and Varley awakens with a thin skein of gritty snow weighing down the tarp, the howl of the wind creeping inside. Another night he's alive, and he feels that—that life—stride through the scaffolding of his blood.

He sits up, pushes the tarp aside. Removes the drum from the shed door and steps out.

The streets are lined with cars and he tries doors, then looks for keys behind visors until he finds one, a Chevy Impala, so blue it's almost black, a boat of a thing with a fingernail's worth of gasoline in the tank. Some distance away he hears a police siren and imagines that some of his bodies have been found. The old woman from the bar, maybe. Her blood-sick husband. The woman's daughter, there above the tavern. He'd been hoping for the woman's son-in-law, *Duane*, Mr. .45 himself, but no luck. Now, sirens, and that familiar song in his heart, the one he's sung to himself a hundred times over the years: *Time to go, time to go* . . .

He gets in the Impala, leaves Portland. After days of sleet, the snow is falling true now. Grays stacked on grays stacked on white, and the dark sky above. How many times has Varley done this— made inroads toward some vestige of life, the seizure of some sort of lasting power—only to have his own boundless rage break that life like a stick of kindling across his knee?

He turns on the radio, hoping for a song, but finds instead a man clamoring about end-times. Still, Varley finds himself entranced, and listens as Portland's lights fade behind him, replaced with industry and farmland and then just that flat featureless expanse of highway, the whirling snowflakes lit up in the glow of his headlights. He drives, vows to head somewhere with more opportunity, another place where they don't know him, or no longer remember his name.

A place, really, where they'll treat him right.

The familiar refrain.

Minor's released from the station without being charged, and he and Julia step out into a slate-gray morning. There's a certain blankness to the kid, a robotic quality, as they trod down the steps of the downtown precinct, the city slowly coming alive around them. Shock, he thinks, and figures he looks the same. Minor usually likes cold mornings like this, so different from the endless humidity of Vietnam, but right now, it's like he could run his face through the wall of any of these buildings and feel nothing at all.

Moments after showing him the photograph of John Varley, Scoggins had been called out of the room, Minor and Davis spending the next few minutes staring at the table. Scoggins had eventually come back in and handed Minor his two photographs. Handed him everything, actually: his wallet, his own cigarettes and lighter, his keys, all in a paper sack. An illegal search, Minor figures, given that he wasn't being charged. He and Julia stand on the corner now, and he thinks about smoking a cigarette. His mind slowly catalogs the gestures necessary: cigarette in mouth, put lighter to cigarette, inhale.

"Can we get some food?" Julia says quietly.

"Yeah, you bet," Minor says with false brightness. For a moment, he pats his pockets for his car keys, and then remembers he'd been taken to the station in a police cruiser.

They walk, shoulders hiked against the cold, and find a diner a few blocks away.

The waitress, with a bouffant of jet-black hair and a face that's seen no shortage of rough times, softens when she sees them, puts the pair of them at a table by the window. The coffee revives Minor a bit and he looks out the window and smokes. Julia orders pancakes and bacon and toast, eats with her head tucked down.

He's about to speak, to say something, when the waitress comes back and fills his cup. He waits until she's gone and then says, "Did they tell you about Grandma and Grandpa?" He can't look at her when he says it.

"Yeah." She pushes a wedge of pancake around with her fork. Blinks.

"And Heidi."

A pause. "Yeah."

Minor doesn't know what else to say. He holds his cup, feels the warmth against his hands. Lights another smoke. Looks out at the snow that is just now beginning to whiten the streets. There is nothing inside him that indicates the world will continue on a minute after this. There's only this second, sitting here, the smell of bacon and cigarettes in the air, the scrape of forks against plates. Julia still has her clothes on from last night. So does he. He thinks of the pair of photos in his coat, the rippled, smoky quality of John Varley's face. Thinking of Heidi is like staring at the sun, impossible to do for more than the briefest second.

Julia looks out the window too. A single tear starts to trek down her face and she deftly wipes it away with a knuckle. Her hair needs to be brushed.

She's still looking out the window when she says, "Would that have happened to me too, do you think? If I wasn't staying at Casey's?"

"I don't know," Minor says; it's a lie that comes easily. He reaches into his pocket and feels the sharp edges of the photographs and the business card that Detective Scoggins had given him after hitting Minor with what he imagines is the standard refrain: *We'll be in touch. Don't go anywhere out of state. Your apartment is considered a crime scene, so please notify us when you know where you're staying. You're a witness in a triple homicide, Mr. Minor; failure to contact us with your whereabouts will land you a warrant with your name on it.*

"You should have some food," Julia says, and Minor nods like what she's said is perfectly reasonable. He lights a cigarette even though one is burning in the ashtray.

They have to wait until the coroner is done with the autopsies before he can call the funeral home to make arrangements. They take a taxi home and quickly get in the truck, pointedly ignoring the police tape done up over the entrance to the bar, the side entrance to the apartment. He gets them a room in a motor court deep north, on Interstate; the Palm Sands, it's called, like they're somewhere tropical, and there's a sign in the parking lot with the name done up in neon. Theirs is a corner unit, bottom floor, with the dumpsters and the parking lot butting up against their wall. He goes out to smoke and then, after his cigarette, opens the door of the room and peers in; Julia is sitting on one of the twin beds, the television light bluing her face. The rear curtains, which had offered a dismal view of a chain-link fence and the back of an auto detailing shop, are drawn tight.

"I'm gonna get us some groceries," he says. Julia nods, not looking at him. "Lock the door behind me."

She nods again.

"Julia."

She turns to him, slowly. Face blank as a ventriloquist's doll.

"Lock the door behind me," he says.

"Alright."

He drives back to the apartment. The front of the Last Call and the side door that leads up to their place, everything slashed in those criss-crosses of yellow tape. Knowing it's wrong, knowing it's the worst move, and yet he's drawn here like someone's put a fishhook in him, pulling him along. Besides, there's shit here he and Julia need.

Up the stairs, his breath loud in his ears. His key still works, and he dips under the tape across the doorway, a doorway he's stepped through hundreds of times, if not thousands. Walking into the narrow hall is like stepping off the edge of a cliff. Like living in that split second of time before you start tumbling earthward.

He hears the tick of the radiator—it's been left on—sees the black smudges of fingerprint powder on the walls, the floor.

He thinks, distantly, distractedly, of going into the bedroom and seeing if they've taken the pistol from his lockbox, but such an idea feels like leaping headfirst into his own grave. He can't go in there. His heart thunders in the narrow confines of his rib cage. Breath still whistling, his throat threatening to close with panic.

Walking away from the bedroom to the archway that leads to the kitchen, he sees more signs of the police's presence. Yellow markers scattered around that denote evidence of some kind. More spills and scatters of fingerprint powder.

He comes to their kitchen table, that scuffed thing that'd already been beat to hell when Heidi had bought it at a garage sale, the two of them lugging it up the steep staircase one blistering summer day, bumping their fingers against the walls and laughing their asses off.

He sees it then, his heart like a fist in his throat: *The Hollow.* Heidi's manuscript.

He picks up the stack of pages, straightens their edges. Lifts it, tests its heft.

Taking it feels like kissing her and exhuming her body all at once.

Get Julia some clothes from her room at least.

But he can't.

I have to leave.

He walks out of the apartment, ducking beneath the police tape again. Shuts the door, locks it.

There is a part of him that wants to rend and tear and fall into that redness inside him. Wants to exact on Varley what he'd exacted on Heidi. Eye for an eye. Death for a death. And another part of him thinks back to what had happened last year—Joanne saying *You owe me*—and knows that he might not return from it if he does. Like you've only got so many chances to put your hand in the flame before you get burned.

But this feeling inside him, he doesn't know if he can stand it. His culpability. How his goddamn pride had turned everything upside down. How his family—Ed, Joanne, his *wife*—had reaped the whirlwind because of it. He doesn't know if he can survive it.

Minor puts the manuscript beneath his jacket. Holds it like the most precious jewel.

Practically runs down the stairs, mad to escape.

The manuscript goes in the glove box and he finds another bar three blocks away. Inside, there is noise and electric light, basketball on TV, smoke crowding the air. He doesn't realize he's looking for Varley until he feels a fluttering moment of disappointment that he's not there. Imagines he will scan every room like this, some part of him eternally hoping for it. A loud man leans on the bar a few stools down, yelling his endless story at the bartender as she pours drinks and pointedly ignores him. The familiarity of it all. One, two, three shots of whiskey inside him and the growing panic is pushed down a bit. His first drinks in a year and a half. He smokes, sipping his fourth shot, this one with a beer-back, as the minutes tick down. He tries to picture Heidi, all their years together, and can't do it. He can see her but there's no *feeling* to it, it's just this empty space. Their entire life together is subsumed right now by the red horror he'd seen in the bedroom. He closes his eyes and groans audibly, enough so that the loud man, still talking, peers over at him.

He visits a grocery store, a liquor store. Fills the truck bed with sacks. Bread, canned meats, soup, fruit, toilet paper, three half-gallons of Jameson's, a carton of Winstons. Pays cash, which leaves him little in his wallet. In the parking lot, the snow is finally starting to come down in earnest. It reminds him of the time he and Heidi went up to Mt. Hood to go skiing. The winter before he got drafted, the two of them just kids, Minor so bad at it, busting his ass over and over again. Heidi laughing at him so hard she couldn't breathe, snow like minute crystals in her hair. He feels then the first savage red coil of grief and knows that if he gives into it, he'll never stop. He'll keep falling. He's drunk, and for a moment he wishes for the pistol in his lockbox. The feel of the barrel in the meat under his chin. *Get me out of here.*

Back at the motel, he knocks on the door of the room. The manuscript's tucked beneath his arm, a sack of groceries held to his chest. There's no answer. He peers up and down the walkway to make sure he's gotten the right room number. He knocks again.

"What?" says Julia on the other side.

"It's Duane." He tries hard not to sound drunk.

The locks rattle and he steps inside, Julia walking back to her bed and sitting down. She's watching cartoons, the cat and mouse and their unending violence committed upon each other. Explosions and violin strings twanging.

"You went drinking," she says without looking at him.

"I did. I stopped at the bar."

He busies himself making trips to the truck, putting groceries away. Carefully sets the whiskey and cigarettes in the single cabinet above the sink, and next to it Heidi's novel. If Julia sees it, she doesn't say anything.

When he's done, she says, "I was thinking about something," and he realizes that they've both taken on the same numbed intonation. Her speech is as slurred as his, robbed of any animative qualities. Couple of wax dummies, listlessly moving through the world.

"What's that?"

She says, "It was either me or you, right?"

His back's turned to her and he shuts his eyes for a moment. "What do you mean?"

"Like with Grandma and Grandpa and Aunt Heidi. They either got killed because of me or because of you. Right? Because if it was just one of them that was killed, it could have been a robber or something. Just an accident. But it was at two places. It was at our house and Grandma and Grandpa's—"

"No. Julia, it's not— I don't know why it happened," he says. He looks down at the chipped porcelain sink in their little kitchenette.

His legs feel like they want to give out beneath him. On the television, a bomb explodes. "The police are trying to figure it out."

"Heidi didn't do anything bad. Neither did Grandma or Grandpa. Right?"

Minor swallows. "Right."

"Then it had to be one of us." A moment later: "Do you think it was because of something I did?"

He turns, horrified. She is cross-legged on her bed watching TV. He sees the weight of it in her frame, the way her spine curls. "Jesus Christ, *no*, Julia. No. Why would you say that?"

"I don't know. First it was the thing with Ray Ray, and now this. Maybe, I don't know, maybe it was the man who killed Karen Malone. Maybe he saw me or something. Maybe I did it somehow."

"Jesus, Julia," he says, louder than he wants to, trying not to let his fear turn to anger. "You didn't have anything to do with this."

"Are you sure?"

"I promise you."

Julia nods and looks away. She picks at a pill of fabric on her blanket. "Then it must be because of you, Uncle Duane." She cuts her eyes to him for the first time but can't keep them there for long. "What did you do?"

Two days before Christmas, couple days spent in the motel, and he and Julia are driving to breakfast when he sees Bobby Liprinski on the sidewalk, Bobby's eyes going big in recognition before Minor stops the truck in the middle of the street. Bobby trots up to the driver's side window.

When he rolls down the window, Bobby stands there, hooking his fingers over the window well. "Jesus Christ, Duane" is all Bobby can manage. "Christ in heaven, man."

Minor offers a smile like a rictus on his face. "How you doing, bud?"

"I don't even— Where you guys staying? I saw the tape over the door of the apartment."

"We got a room over on Interstate. The Palm Sands."

"Jesus. Yeah, they taped it all up, Duane. Cops all over it. They been interviewing everybody." He bends a little, looks over at Julia in the passenger seat. "Hey, kid," he says.

"Hi."

A car pulls up behind the truck, and Bobby gestures madly for them to go past. He looks back at Duane and says, "We gotta talk, brother."

They go to Valentine's Lounge and get a booth. Minor gives Julia the quarters in his pocket and she hits the bank of pinball machines in the back. It's morning, and Minor tries to buy a beer from the waitress. She tells him that he'll have to go into the other room, on the bar side. He and Bobby order coffee instead.

"Cops fucking sweated every one of us, man," Bobby starts off.

"Yeah?"

"Yeah, these two detectives. I didn't say shit, Duane, but they caught the gist of it from the old guys. Barry and them. Couple of the guys had bench warrants and the cops said they'd misfile them somewhere permanently if they talked."

"It doesn't matter."

"Point being, they know about those two guys that night, about you booting them. Crooked Wheel or whatever the fuck it was." He holds up his hand with the missing fingers and takes a drag off his cigarette, blows the smoke off to the side. "It was them, right?"

Minor tries to imagine his future. Can't. Heidi had not wanted too much from him. She had wanted him to calm his heart after he came home from overseas, to not let that ever-present rage of his rise like acid to the top, and for the past year and a half, even before Julia, he'd done that. Tried his best anyway. Sober, no fighting, going to work. But now? Now he feels the urge to fall back into it, the comforting hand of fury. "I came downstairs couple nights after that shit you saw," he says. "Heard people down there. Those guys, they'd come back. They'd made a deal with Joanne, I guess. Ed's sick—*was* sick. Cancer."

"Shit."

"So I guess Joanne gave them the green light to move dope through the bar."

Bobby screws up his face. "For real?"

"Yeah."

"That don't sound like her, man. Fucking *why*?"

"She said they had some way to help Ed."

"Who, the biker gang? How the hell could they help?"

Minor shrugs, looks out the window. "Maybe they were giving her money for his surgery or something, I don't know. For chemo."

Bobby scratches his neck, makes a face. "What'd you do?"

"When they were down there? I ran 'em out. Last Call gets raided? Gets shut down in a fed bust? Joanne would lose the place and Julia'd be put in a foster home."

"Yeah. Was she pissed? Joanne?"

"Yeah," he says, guilt making the words thick in his mouth. "She was pissed. And then, you know, this *guy* . . ." He sort of groans, wipes at his mouth and reaches into his coat. Takes out the Polaroids. "I had Joanne take these, right? So I'd have something to hang over these guys if they came back." He hands Bobby the Polaroid of Bradley and Eugene, and Bobby peers down at it.

"Yep. I remember this one. Yep."

And then Minor pushes the other photo across the table. "And that's the guy that ran the show. John Varley, his name was. I watched Joanne take that fucking picture with my own eyes, Bobby, I swear to God."

Bobby picks up the photo, scratches at an eyebrow with the hand holding the cigarette, those bubblegum scars crawling down to his wrist. Smoke haloes around him. "What is this?"

Minor hoists an arm over the back of the booth and turns to look at Julia's slim form at the pinball machines. He turns back to Bobby. "That's him. That's the guy that killed Heidi."

•

They drive Bobby back to his apartment, Julia sitting between them. Bobby tells them to wait; he runs upstairs and comes back out a minute later. He hands Minor a rubber-banded roll of money through the window. "We took up a collection for Ed and Joanne. For Heidi. The funerals and all that." He winces, looks sheepish. "Everyone's doing their drinking over at the Roundhouse now, the fucking traitors." He dips his head, looks in at Julia. "Sorry, kid."

"I haven't— I can't do anything with the bodies yet, Bobby. The cops have to finish their autopsies."

"No, I hear you, Duane. It's just—it's for you guys. Keep it." He reaches out and touches Minor's arm, and something in Minor almost breaks at the notion that he's deserving of such a thing.

Christmas Day they spend in the motel watching television. It snows in earnest. Minor buys Julia comic books, a stuffed animal, a pack of pencils and a notebook, gives it to her in a paper bag with the name of a department store across the front. She tells him thanks, and that's Christmas. They go to a Chinese restaurant down the street for dinner; it's packed, loud. No one wants to be alone. A fistfight breaks out in the parking lot as they're leaving. One man gets punched in the mouth and he staggers and falls down, his shirt and coat rucking up, his belly a bright pink against the fresh snow. Julia watches as blood spills from the man's mouth and dots the snow around him, almost entranced, until Minor gently leads her away.

The next day, he calls Scoggins from the Palm Sands pay phone, and the detective tells him he's been given permission to pick up the bodies, to go ahead with the funerals.

Then Scoggins says, "Duane, I need a number, brother. An address. I know you and that child aren't sleeping in your truck. I need a way to get in touch with you."

After a moment's pause, he says, "I'm at the Palm Sands."

"There on Interstate?"

"Yeah."

"Alright." He gives Minor instructions on how to retrieve the bodies from the coroner's office. Minor listens, and as he does he wonders what madness feels like, wonders if this is it.

One hundred and seventy-eight dollars. What the folks of the Last Call put together for them. Minor and Julia get into the truck and drive to First Pacific Credit, where he and Heidi had banked since before he'd gone to Nam. He empties out the account, and with the funeral money and their savings there's over eight hundred dollars. The cash sits in an envelope in Minor's coat, next to the two photos.

Something is beginning to happen. He is moving toward an idea like a man navigating a dark room.

That night, he goes into the bathroom and turns off the light and takes off his clothes. He sits in the tub with his knees pressed to his chin, the water scalding. The knowledge of Heidi's death, of all of their deaths, is so profound it feels as if it's altering the shape of his bones. Calcifying his heart. Something in him has begun to lean toward violence. What else is there to do? He had been quelling this rage inside himself for her and her alone, and now she's gone.

After a while he stands, drains the tub, gets dressed. He steps out into the room and watches Julia's eyes open in the dark. She's lying on her bed.

"What did you do?"

He puts on his coat, opens his mouth to speak.

"You did something to someone," she says. "That's why it happened. Right?"

"I'm going out," Minor says, his voice quaking. "I'll be back in a bit. Get some sleep. We'll do the funeral stuff tomorrow."

At his back, quiet but lethal as an arrow finding its mark: "What did you do, Uncle Duane?"

He cabs out to Southeast, manages a decent drunk at Valentine's before he starts a fight with a guy and gets his lip split open, then gets tossed by the bouncer. He staggers back to the Palm Sands, walks it the whole way, miles and miles across town, scooping up palmfuls of fresh snow off the hoods of parked cars to press against his face.

Hours later he keys the door, if not sober at least closer to it, and walks into the room to find Julia sitting on her bed, the television once again throwing wild shadows about the room. He walks over and turns the lamp on that sits on the end table between them. Julia blinks, looks at him. Takes in his face, says woodenly, "What happened?"

Minor tosses the Polaroids on the bed next to her.

"You're right."

"What do you mean?"

"It's not about you," he says. "It's not because of you. Don't ever think that."

She picks up the photos.

"Those are the men that did it," he says. His lip's ballooned up and he sounds funny. "That guy there, Julia? With a fucking—with a *cloud* where his face should be? John Varley's his name. He's the one that killed them. He's the one that killed Heidi."

3

The next morning, Julia is showering and Minor is staring at the Polaroids when there's a knock on the motel door. He freezes, his heart snared in his throat, and then carefully puts the photos in his jacket. The blinds are drawn and the television's turned to some cop show, guy in a mask brandishing a gun, holding a woman by the arm. Minor looks at the empty glasses on the counter of the kitchenette, the bottoms ringed in whiskey, and feels a starburst of shame strong enough to surprise himself.

Minor puts his eye to the peephole and isn't surprised to see Detective Scoggins standing there, wearing a heavy coat with a fur-lined hood. Minor opens the door and the detective spends a moment sizing him up.

"Okay if I come in, Duane?"

Minor steps back, welcomes him inside.

He watches Scoggins take everything in. The two beds—one made, the other a mess of curled sheets, a blanket twisted on the floor. The closed blinds, the mounded ashtray. The water glasses, the bottles of Jameson's. Food wrappers and takeout boxes with their skins of congealed grease shoved in the garbage can. Scoggins's face is blank and impassive.

"How you holding up?"

Minor shrugs. "You're looking at it."

Scoggins nods, smooths down his mustache. "I came by to see if you wanted a ride to the coroner's office."

"Not quite ready for that yet."

"No?"

"No."

He sees the question Scoggins *wants* to ask—*When* will *you be ready, Duane?*—but instead he gestures at his own face and says, "What happened here?"

Minor remembers the bar fight, gingerly touches the scab at his lip. "I fell."

The detective laughs. "Fell into some guy's fist?"

"Something like that."

Scoggins nods and looks back at the bathroom door, the line of light at the bottom. "Julia in there?"

"Yeah."

"She alright?"

"Hell no," Minor says right away. "Would you be?"

"Fair point." The detective walks over to the TV console, where a cop's chasing the robber down an alley. He turns back to Minor and says, "Duane, I got something I need to ask you."

"Alright."

"John Varley," Scoggins says, his arms folded at his chest.

"What about him?"

"Well, I looked into him, Duane, and things aren't coming up in any way that I can understand."

"What do you mean?"

Scoggins looks over and sees a whiskey bottle on the counter of the kitchenette. "Any chance I can get a nip of that?"

"They let you drink on the job?"

He walks over, rinses a glass at the sink. "It's my day off, actually."

The sound of water in the bathroom stops. The woman on television screams, and the policeman squares up and fires his gun down the alley. Scoggins turns to him, the glass held at his chest.

"Turns out John Varley's been arrested before, Duane. Here in town."

"Okay," Minor says. "So now you know I'm not bullshitting you."

Scoggins's face tightens then, like he's eaten something that doesn't agree with him. He rubs at his chin with the back of his hand.

"Well, the funny thing is, he was arrested, and on the way to jail, he apparently escaped."

"So you never got his fingerprints. His photo."

"Uh, no," Scoggins says, smiling down into his drink. "Cops didn't get the chance."

"I don't get you," Minor says, but some part of him already understands.

"A man named John Varley, according to police reports, was arrested on assault charges and disorderly conduct, and was being transported to jail when he escaped his cuffs, put both the arresting officers in the hospital with multiple injuries, and *ffft*, vanished into the night. One of the cops died in the hospital. Guy's physical description matches the one you claim was trying to run dope through the Last Call."

"But there's some catch," Minor says.

Scoggins laughs. Not an ounce of joy in it. "Oh, there's a fucking catch, Duane." He drains the glass and grimaces. "John Varley caught these particular charges on a lovely March evening in the year of our Lord 1931."

Neither of them says anything for a moment, and then Minor fishes out his cigarettes, lights one. His whole body feels cold. "Alright. So it's a different guy."

"Could be," Scoggins says. "Could be a relative, or even your John Varley's old man."

"But you don't think it is."

"Me? I don't know *what* to think, brother. I wish I did. But I'll tell you what, the spring of 1931? In Portland? That was a bloody one. Five unsolved homicides in three months. And guess what, Duane? Here's the kicker."

"What?"

"Those murders, they match what's happening now," Scoggins says. "Five bodies ripped to hell. The last one taking place three days before Varley got arrested in '31, and then nothing like it for decades. Until now."

"Like he skipped town."

"Like I said, we got plenty of missing persons, same as any city, but something like this? We got these killings in 1931 and we got 'em right now and that's about it."

"Okay."

Scoggins smiles, reaches into his jacket and takes out a notepad. "Mind telling me what bar you were at last night?"

Minor's thrown. "What?"

"Just being thorough."

"I thought you were off the clock."

"Oh, we never sleep, Duane. So where'd you do your drinking?"

"Valentine's."

Scoggins points at the wall with his pen. "Valentine's Lounge? Over in Southeast?"

"That's the one."

"That's not far from the Last Call. What were you doing so close?"

"Getting drunk."

"Fair. Any witnesses?"

"Lot of people probably saw the bouncer throw me out."

Scoggins smiles, writes something down. "How long were you there for?"

"Couple hours."

"You left your niece alone?"

"I mean, she's old enough."

A suck of his teeth, like Scoggins doesn't agree but doesn't want to say so. "When did you leave Valentine's?"

"Probably ten."

"Probably ten or exactly ten?"

"Probably ten," Minor says.

"Then what?"

"Then I walked back here."

"You walked the whole way?"

"Yeah," he says. "Tried to sober up. What's this all about?"

Scoggins sighs and clicks his pen. Puts the notebook away. "Well, last night we were able to get a warrant on the Crooked Wheel's little clubhouse they got over on MLK? We found a half dozen bodies, every last one of them done in the same fashion as your wife, your in-laws, that girl Karen Malone, and all those folks back in '31. But these were big dudes, Duane, and most of them were armed. One guy was pushing three hundred pounds, and it looked like he'd been put through a wood chipper."

Still with that coldness through him. This sense that even in this room, with a door that locks, he's too close to what's happening, to what's already happened. He's made Julia too vulnerable. He thinks, *Take the kid and run. Heidi, she wouldn't want you up against this, whatever it is. You really care about keeping Julia safe like you claim to? Fucking run. Whatever this is, it's too much for you.*

"Why you telling me this, Scoggins? I can't tell if you think I'm a suspect or a victim."

Scoggins laughs, rubs at an eye with his knuckle. "Yeah, me neither, man. My boss'd shit a brick if he knew I was here. I guess I'm trying to get you to consider that girl's welfare." As if mirroring Minor's own thoughts, he says, "Whatever this is, you're neck-deep in it, and I'm asking you to consider getting police protection."

"Is that on the record or off?"

Scoggins cuts his eyes away. "I'd need to see. Check with some people."

"Yeah, I don't think so."

"Look, if you'd seen what I saw in that garage, you'd be asking if you could sleep under my fucking desk, I promise you."

"We're good," Minor says.

"Yeah, see, you're far from good. Light-years from it." He looks at Minor with those hound dog eyes and then pushes off from the kitchen counter. Minor's disappointed him. Whatever good grace he might have had with Scoggins—a grace born of empathy, of an attempt at understanding his sorrow—it's coming to an end.

"That's all you got to say on the matter, then?"

Minor holds out his hands. "I'm not trying to jam you up, Detective. I don't know who Varley is. I don't know what the picture means. I just, I want to grieve. I want to figure out how to do that."

"Alright." Scoggins raises his hands, mirroring him. He walks over and hands Minor a business card.

"You already gave me one of those."

"Did I?"

"At the police station."

"Well. Doesn't hurt to have two around," he says, holding it out until Minor takes it. "Call me if you think of anything else, Duane. That's my office number and my home number on the back. Call anytime. Call me in the middle of the night if you want."

"Alright."

"And please, reach out to the coroner. Put your old lady to rest. Her folks."

Scoggins walks out and Minor locks the door behind him, deadbolts it. A moment later, Julia steps out of the bathroom, dressed, her hair in wet strings. Steam clouds the bathroom mirror.

"So it's true," she says.

"What?" Minor says.

"What you told me. That John Varley killed Aunt Heidi and Grandma and Grandpa. And that girl too. Karen Malone. That he's, I don't know, a ghost or something."

"I don't know what he is," he says, though that's not exactly true anymore, is it? He has an idea. Something so ludicrous and nonsensical and terrible he can't bring himself to say it. Because such a thing shouldn't be possible. And *yet*.

And yet there are the Polaroids, and Scoggins telling him about the murders in 1931, and the more recent murders, and, well, if you took it as fact—John Varley being something like a vampire, something that might live forever, that doesn't age—it sure would explain why poor, terrified Joanne was courting his favor, wouldn't it? Would have likely done wonders, or at least done *something,* for Ed's terminal condition.

"I don't know what he is," he says again, no longer believing it, and that small pearl of rage continues to grind itself against his heart. Even as he tells himself to run, run, that dark part of him wants the other thing. Wants to move forward, to stride forth. Wants to head *toward* John Varley, whoever or whatever he might be.

He spends time on the pay phone out front. Calls the coroner's office and makes arrangements for the funeral home to pick the bodies up in the morning; it will be a closed casket affair for all three of them, and Minor has an appointment with the funeral director at ten A.M. tomorrow to go over plots and details. Picking out a gravestone and casket for his wife will, he knows, murder some substantial part of him, and by six o'clock that evening, with the press of everything on his shoulders, he's going stir-crazy. "Let's grab something to eat," he says, just to get out.

"Can you bring me something?" Julia says. She's lying in bed with the covers over her. Just the top of her head visible. "I'm not feeling good."

"Yeah," he says, and a part of him is secretly grateful that he'll be alone.

Just a drink or two, he thinks. *Two drinks, tops.*

He eats Chinese food and gets Julia an order of fried rice to go, puts it on the seat next to him in the truck. Snow is coming down again, lying on top of the ice that's already there. He makes his way past the Last Call, his heart thunderous in his chest at the sight of the yellow tape still over the doors. Heads to Valentine's.

It's the same bartender from the night before, and he takes one look at Minor and points at the door. "Nope. Out."

Minor holds up his hands, leaves. Hits up a liquor store for another matching set of half-gallon jugs of Jameson's.

He brings everything into the room at the Palm Sands.

Where he finds the lights on and the television off. Bathroom door open.

The room telegraphing its profound emptiness.

Julia, she's gone.

4

She leaves the motel, almost daring her uncle to come back. To find her in the parking lot, to try and stop her. She'd thought for a while that they might be united in their horror of what had been done to their family, be moved to some sort of action. But Uncle Duane doesn't feel the same way, or doesn't care, or has been broken by the murders in some way she can't understand. He started drinking immediately after coming back from the police station and drinks every day now, all the time, sitting in the dark cage of himself. The man who cared for her, who said those things in the truck on the way to Casey's, about all of them sticking together? That man seems to be gone. She's alone, as alone as she was the day of her mom's sentencing, alone as the night the sheriff shepherded her out of the kitchen in Transom after her mom shot Ray Ray in the face.

At the doorway, she takes one more look at the room with its cast-off sheets and green shag carpet, the oil painting above the beds of a ship on a frothing sea. She leaves her backpack here and says, "Good night, Uncle Duane," as if he were asleep, as if he hadn't left her alone. She steps out into a night that smells of cold, crystalline and bright.

She walks with her back arrow-straight and thinks of the photograph he showed her. How the things he said, the things she heard the detective say, cannot be right and also *feel* right, somehow. Of *course* he's a man with no face, a burst of gray cloud where his face should be. Of *course* he would be the one to kill her grandma and grandpa, who'd doted on her like they'd known her their whole lives, even though she'd only met them once or twice before, back when she was just a little kid, hardly able to remember.

"He's the one that killed Heidi," her uncle had said, his voice raw as he tapped a nail against John Varley's warped face on the plastic sheen of the Polaroid.

"What does he look like?" Julia had asked him, seeing in her uncle a rare willingness to talk to her since the murders had closed his heart the way someone would shut a door.

Duane had picked up the photo from the bed, ran a hand across his mouth. "Varley? Big fucker, Julia. Big, pale, blond hair. Taller than me. About my age, maybe. Hard-looking. Dressed all in black. Gray."

And then, after the policeman had left, what had he done? Nothing. He'd gone out to get food. To drink more. The same quicksand he's put himself in since they left the police station days ago.

So if she wants to do things right by her aunt and her grandparents, she's got to do it herself.

No one's going to rescue her.

No one's going to save her.

Her mom taught her that.

She walks north down Interstate, cars and noise and cold all heaving around her, Christmas lights here and there, and it starts snowing again, the flakes granular as sugar. She wonders what Little Kev is doing right now. What her mom's doing right now in her cell in Bayonne. It's the middle of the night in New York. Is she asleep? Is she lying in bed, staring at the curlicued springs of the bed frame above her, the pocked cement wall? Is she dreaming of Julia? Is it a good dream, a dream where they're happy together?

She passes a man smoking a cigarette, tapping out a rhythm with his free hand on the thigh of his jeans. He's leaning against a brick wall scrawled with graffiti and his eyes shine like hard little jewels in the dark.

"You know John Varley?" she says. Best to just be out with it. Ask everyone she sees. Ask a thousand times.

The man looks around like he's in a crowded room, then turns back to her and touches a finger to his chest. "You talking to me?"

"Yeah," Julia says. "You know John Varley?"

He pushes himself from the wall, looking up one side of the street and then the other. Wind blows a breath down Julia's collar, and she shivers.

The man puts his cigarette to his mouth and takes it away. He says, "Darby put you up to this?"

"I don't know Darby. I'm looking for a man named John Varley."

He gives her a hard, assessing look, his eyes traveling up and down her body, and it occurs to her, finally, to be afraid.

"How old are you?"

"Thirteen."

"Jesus Christ," the man says, and walks away, pitching his cigarette into the gutter. A little chorus of sparks against the street. "Jesus Christ," he says again. His back to her, big loping steps as he walks down the sidewalk, smoothing his hair down.

Julia waits until he turns a corner and then she continues on her way. Walks and walks until she comes to a large intersection. Squinting, she reads the street signs: LOMBARD and INTERSTATE. A big grocery store there, a parking lot, the windows gleaming, everything closed at this hour. A gas station across the way.

She turns, walks the length of Lombard now, with its dive bars and auto repair shops and long stretches of undeveloped lots behind chain-link fences. Weeds and slabs of cracked pavement, drifts of garbage with a thin dusting of white snow over the tops. Her breath in tatters behind her. She goes to a bus stop where three, four people stand bundled against the cold, each of them a careful distance from the others, no one talking, and she drifts among them saying Varley's name like something totemic. Walking up to each of them and saying his name in the hope that the saying will rob her of her fear. She's ignored by everyone until an old lady in a blue hat, the small brown oval of her face showing above the collar of her coat, asks where Julia's mother is. If she knows she's out at such an hour, and oh, that sends Julia walking away from the bus stop with an aching, wounded heart. Her mother? Her mother would shit a brick, to quote that detective, if she knew Julia was out here. She would be angry because being out here was risky, and if her mother had taught her anything, it was to make yourself small in the face of a risk. That was how they survived in the house in Transom until they couldn't survive it anymore.

Julia has begun wondering if her mother did what she did to Ray Ray for *them,* in some way she can't yet fathom. For her and Little Kev. Maybe so. Maybe there was no more room to run away, in her mother's mind. That what she'd done was the only way to end things. There's so much she doesn't know.

She walks on. Dark mouths of doorways, the crooked fingers of alleyways. Wind shirring the weeds, trash fluttering down the four-lane street, cars passing by, wheels hissing against the snow. She sees a group of people walking her way, and through the knifing wind she hears their laughter and it is the laughter of children. Teenagers. The cold wind sends her the smell of cigarette smoke.

They pass her, some half dozen young people parked in that age between hers and Duane's. In high school. Scowls and flared jeans. One boy with an Afro, one boy with a dusting of a mustache on his lip, a black leather jacket. Children out late, children with parents who do not care where they are. She sees a girl's face among them, her mouth a red bow and mascara applied like she's done it in her sleep, and the group of them drift around Julia like water around a stone until she reaches out and touches the boy's arm, the one with the leather jacket. He looks down at her with curiosity, like a zoo animal has reached through the bars and touched him. How do you find a person? You just ask.

He stops, and the group of them mill around her. He smiles at her and has a black tooth in his mouth. The smile's a mean-hearted thing, and once again she becomes afraid.

"I'm looking for John Varley."

"What?" His eyes jump from hers to the girl with the red mouth and back, and Julia understands that he wants to impress her above all.

"I'm looking for John Varley."

One of the boys mimics her voice, high-pitched, and the rest of them laugh. But the boy in the jacket doesn't, and neither does the girl with the mascara.

"I don't know who that is," the boy says, but his eyes cut away.

"He's got a face like a cloud when you take his picture," Julia says, seeing a flash of understanding—of fear or recognition or *something*—in the girl's eyes. "He kills people."

More titters behind her, one of the boys in back of her saying, "Kid's high as the fucking moon, man."

"Gotta be," says another.

But the boy in the jacket—he's maybe seventeen, she decides—his Adam's apple jumps like it's on a lure; he digs into his pocket and comes out with a cigarette and tries to light it but the wind's too strong. "What do you mean, he kills people?" He has small green tattoos on each finger, fuzzy and indistinct.

"He killed my aunt. My grandpa and grandma." The people in front of her suddenly go wavery, her tears threatening to spill out. She hasn't cried in front of Uncle Duane, not one time, but out here in the cold, where no one knows her, it's different.

The boy looks like he's about to speak, and then he laughs, one of the other boys nudging him with his shoulder, the moment breaking apart. "I can't help you," he says. "I don't know who that is." He puts his cigarette back in his pocket. "You should go home," he says. "It's dark out." And then he walks away.

The group follows him, and Julia watches them go. Just as they're about to cross Lombard, the girl says something to them and turns back. She hunches against the cold and walks quickly back to Julia. She crouches before her, a hand gripping shut the collar of her jacket. Her eyes are beautiful and green, ringed in that black.

"Did he bite them?" she says, and it's like a secret between them.

"What?"

"The man you're looking for. Did he bite them?"

Julia blinks. "He ripped them apart, is what my uncle said. He—"

"He killed your parents? For real?"

"My grandparents. My aunt." She swallows, puts the heel of her hand to one eye. "The people taking care of me."

"You should stay away from him."

"I can't, though."

"He's dangerous."

"*I'm* dangerous," Julia says, and the girl laughs; her front teeth are a little crooked and Julia maybe falls in love with her a tiny bit.

"You need to talk to Adeline," the girl says, and pulls a strand of hair from her mouth.

"Adeline," Julia repeats.

"There's a park back there," she says, gesturing behind Julia. "Kenton Park. You can see her there most nights."

"When?"

One of the boys yells something, and the girl stands up. "I don't know," she says. "She's there a lot. She lives around there. If anyone knows where to find him, she will."

"Okay."

"But be careful. She has a man there with her and, just—don't go by yourself. You have someone you can go with? A grown-up?"

"Yes."

"Good. Talk to Adeline, then. Ask her about the Children's Museum. But bring a grown-up and be ready to run."

5

John Varley stops at a service station some thirty miles outside of the city. Two pumps with a convenience store attached. When the attendant trots up to his window, Varley feels a small starburst of desire. What happened in the garage of the Crooked Wheel Club will keep him sated for a while, but blood is blood. The scent of it at the nexus of the man's jawbone and neck, the sullen way the man takes Varley's money and hands him his change; there's an allure there that borders on the sexual. There is something almost intimate in the imbalance of power between them. But no, gaining distance is more important, getting away, escaping, and after he fills the tank, he is about to continue on when he sees a man, a boy, really, leaning against the wall of the station, hunched against the cold.

Young, Varley notes, with blond hair like his own, hair that brushes his shoulders. A ridiculous leopard-print coat that falls to the boy's knees, its hem choked in bulbs of ice, as if he's been walking through the snow. Blood is blood, certainly, but here is another one of Varley's guiding lights—the simple embrace of *want*. Varley has insisted on getting what he *wants* in this life of his, seizing it, and when he wants something—a throat gripped between his teeth, say, or money, or a new thrall with an air of desperation about him—then he takes it. His desires and ferocities have wounded him in the past, and will again, but oh, they've also afforded him some great measure of joy and power, haven't they? He sidles the Impala up next to the boy and rolls the passenger window down.

He smiles. "How you doing?"

"Colder than a witch's asshole out here," the boy says, and Varley laughs. He's got some trace of an accent—European, but one Varley can't quite pin down. Regardless, he's charmed immediately. Lust and blood-want all entwined. He thinks of Bradley, with his coarse red beard, the yellow, picket-fence teeth in his mouth, the joyless, resentful ways he'd allowed Varley his advances in their brief time together. And, later, in the garage, the way he'd spun Bradley's head backward until his shocked, purpled face was staring at him over the logo of his vest. "You got the crooked part right," Varley had joked, but there had been no one left alive to hear it.

For the hundredth time in his life, the thousandth, Varley looks at this boy and tells himself he needs no one. That he can walk this world alone just fine. That a thrall is as much an entrapment as an aide, and that his own hand is as serviceable as any man or woman's ministrations.

But oh, you do get lonely every once in a while.

The boy crouches down in the window. Varley hears the roar of his blood, feels the stirrings of an erection. The boy's eyes rove the interior of the Impala, then fall lastly on Varley's face. He tucks a hank of blond hair behind his ear.

"What brings you out here?" Varley says.

"Car broke down," the boy says, though there is no car in the parking lot besides this one. He laces his fingers over the sill of the passenger door. "Where you heading tonight?"

"West" is all Varley says. "You want a ride?"

A smile, and the boy turns and trots back, staggering once on the ice, almost doing a clownish pratfall, his laughter bright as he rights himself. He goes around the corner of the building and retrieves his backpack, then comes back to the Impala and cracks open the passenger door. He sits down, the interior suddenly full of the boy's thrumming heat, the scent of his blood and body odor trilling Varley's nose.

Yes, the men of the Crooked Wheel had turned on him, but what the Wheel couldn't understand—what none of them ever fucking understood—was how damnably *replaceable* they all were. Fodder and food and bodies for Varley's will to be enacted upon, and that was all.

The boy smiles at him, once more tucks a hank of golden hair behind his ear, drums out something on his thighs. "I'm ready," he says.

"So am I," Varley says, and puts the Impala on the highway.

6

Four, five times he makes it out to the parking lot, keys in his hand, ready to go look for her. Furious and fearful and sick in his heart. *My God, Heidi, I've lost her. I've lost her.* Only to turn back and head inside, telling himself he should be here if, *when,* she comes back. Finally, the panic gets too great and he leaves her a note on the kitchen counter—*Out looking for you, STAY HERE*—and gets in his truck.

Gray streets, snow, people here and there, but none her age, her size. Occasionally he rolls down his window and describes Julia, asks this person or that if they've seen her. All the while the memory of Heidi's drawn face when she'd gotten the call from the New York DHS office about her sister, Linda, murdering her husband. That there was a daughter, Julia, twelve years old—Heidi only barely remembering her as a toddler, before Linda had met Ray and they'd headed cross-country to the East Coast. The child would need a place to live, guardians. How Minor had at first been stunned— a child? They wanted them to take care of a kid?—and then a kind of numbed, quiet joy at the idea, and then the fear. The sense, like Vietnam, that he had entered into an agreement that was beyond his capabilities. And yet, she had needed a safe place, hadn't she? Needed people to guard her—that term, *guardian,* sticking with him in a way that little else did—and what would happen to her if they said no? Ed and Joanne were too old. The girl would wind up in foster care, moved from home to home. He pushes the truck through the dark night with fear threading its way through his heart, the words in his head as close to any religious incantation that he might muster: *Heidi*

I'm sorry I'll watch her I'll be careful I'll save her I'm sorry I love you damn it Julia be alright—

And then he sees her.

She is walking with her arms wrapped around herself, head dipped, but even with that dark fan of black hair hidden beneath a hat, he knows it's her, knows it by her walk. The set of her shoulders. He lets out a blubbering cry of relief, ugly as hell, and turns down the street, screeches to a halt. Gets out.

Julia stands there, poised to run, eyes wide, until she recognizes him. Sees the look on his face, the panic there, and she begins weeping, too, and runs to him and they collide, and he bends to his knees on the freezing concrete and holds her, her face buried in his neck. How small she is, Jesus. They weep together, and Minor's tears feel transformative, feel different than they were the other night in the motel, the bathtub. This is Minor leaning into grief instead, moving toward the boundaries of that territory.

"I'm sorry," he says, his hand cupping her head. He just keeps saying it. Tears burn hot down his cheeks. He wants to say it a million times. "I'm sorry, I'm sorry."

"Me too," she says, her face muffled.

"You don't have anything to be sorry for," he says, and he tells Heidi—her ghost, her memory, the thing buoying him to the world— that he'll do whatever he has to do to protect this child.

"But I snuck out."

He laughs, runs a hand down his face, lets her go. "Well, yeah, there's that." They look at each other and smile, both still crying. Minor reaches out and touches her hand, holds it in his own.

Me and this kid, Heidi. We'll keep each other safe.

For you.

"Uncle Duane," Julia says, her dark eyes roving his face, the sorrow suddenly gone, replaced with something else. "I know how to find him. We have to go see someone named Adeline."

7

"You're different," the boy says from the passenger seat, and Varley smiles in the dark.

"Like no one you'll ever meet."

"So what's your story, then?" the boy asks. They're driving west on 26, the highway here salted and paved, the radio playing disco, something the boy had found. Sounds like idiots yammering on xylophones and keyboards to Varley, but he's never been much swayed by music.

"My story?"

"I can tell you mine, if it helps," says the boy, pushing in the car's lighter and then holding its reddened coil up to his cigarette.

"Alright." Hours to go until sunrise, this boy beside him with his tang of blood and sweat, *life* all loud and brassy in him. Varley is, for the moment, content, and that's a fine thing to be.

"Let's see. My name's Johan Claasen."

"Alright."

"Born in Utrecht, studying in Seattle on scholarship until I dropped out."

"Lofty. Studying what?"

"Art. Painting."

"You're a painter?"

"I'm all sorts of things," Johan says, but there's nothing suggestive about it. He says it darkly, moodily, looking out the window, the clear delineation of snow and sky.

"You dropped out of school?"

Johan nods, cracks his window, a scream of wind inside. Varley doesn't mind. Varley minds nothing right now. "I lost my scholarship, my visa expired. I left Seattle, messed around in Portland for a while, thought about Boise."

"Boise? Good lord, name a good thing that's ever happened in Boise. Snow and hillbillies. At least in Alaska, there's polar night."

"What's that?"

"Two months where the sun doesn't rise. You go far north enough, it's unbroken night."

"That's appealing to you?"

"It is," Varley says. "A dream of mine for a long time now."

"Well, I *like* the snow," Johan says, laughing. His hand touches Varley's arm for a moment and then withdraws. "But I don't know about two months of no sunlight."

"Alright. What else?"

Johan ashes through the narrow wedge of window. "Let's see. Two sisters, both younger than me. My father's an academic at university, my mother's a scientist."

"Again, lofty."

"Suffocating," Johan says, rolling his eyes. "I miss painting sometimes, but I also think it's fine to take a break, to live life, see what there is to see." He looks over at Varley, his eyes glittering in the dark. "I think it's important to *experience* things, don't you?"

The Impala's wheels churn the dark, devour the miles. Fling Varley down the dark passageway of his own bloody history.

Summer of 1903, horse-drawn carriages on the cobblestones, the clatter of hooves, steaming piles of horseshit all around. Trolleys trundling their way through the muck, their metallic tracks lacing the streets, the brick buildings of Seattle seemingly brushing up against the sky.

John Varley stands splay-legged in a saloon, dumb and towering and fearless, ready—always and constantly ready— to hurt someone.

Twenty-three years old. Shoulders wide as a fucking beam. Heart infused with a cruelty that even by then had become second nature and was perfectly suited for his new line of work, which was breaking fingers for a tavern owner by the name of Jim Templeton. In Seattle's Pioneer Square neighborhood, this was, and Templeton old enough to be his father, with a penchant for ferocity and violence that matched, if not surpassed, Varley's own. The two of them getting on famously, with young Varley a kind of catch-all employee when it came to the business of menace. Most of his work involved standing next to doorways looking severe or, occasionally, laying a sap across the back of some drunkard's neck. Snapping the thumb of a fellow reticent to repay a debt. All of which Varley found enjoyable enough, though he sometimes grew bored if made to stand still for long periods of time. He'd been on his own for seven years at that point, cast from his hometown of Duluth out into the vastness of the world by a father whose love affair with a bottle had finally reached terminal pitch, the man wanting nothing to do with Varley after his mother had fallen ill with the cough. "Old enough to wander on your own now" were his father's parting words, eyes rheumy, silver stubble on his cheeks. "Time to hit the road, boy, stop knocking your giant empty skull against the rafters of my house." Varley in those interceding years had wandered Arizona, Nevada, Utah, found the seasons too severe. Too hot, too cold. Had tried at being a farmhand, at cowboying, working a derrick, all of that coming to a crescendo when he'd killed a lover after he'd found the man going through his bedroll one night, looking for Varley's wallet to rob him. In Redding, California, this had been at Oregon's border, and thinking about it still made him angry.

So, Seattle now. Hard-luck part of town. Templeton's saloon was called the Bloody Bucket, low-ceilinged, with windows that overlooked the main drag. Varley had stumbled in with a thirst that first night when Templeton, uncharacteristically in the tavern himself, laid eyes on him. It had really been that simple, Varley's whole life done or undone in that moment, depending on how you looked at it, simply by Templeton sizing him up and thinking: *Here's a man might do some harm for me.* "You are just a *massive* sonofabitch, aren't you?" Templeton had said, wandering over, a snifter of brandy in his hand. Old, silver-haired man in a velvet waistcoat, that mustache arced into points at the ends, a murderous, happy gleam in the eyes. Varley had nodded the affirmative, strangely bashful.

Templeton had brought him to his back office that very evening, given him a free shot of decent whiskey, and asked him point-blank if he was a hardcase or not. Varley, the shot glass tiny in his hand, empty now, whiskey burning deliciously through him, asked Templeton what he meant.

"I mean," Templeton said, "can you, without flinching, righteously fuck a man up when I tell you to for thirty dollars a week?"

Varley had gently put the glass down on the edge of Templeton's desk while the old man sat staring at him, fingers tented, eyes glittering in the oily light.

"You for real?"

"I mean, hell, son. I don't know you, but you got a formidable look about you. Scars on your eyebrows, your nose, the knuckles of those hands. Looks like you're no stranger to dust-ups. Am I off on that?"

"No, sir."

"Well, then, if you want loyalty, you pay for it. Most people don't understand that but I do. Thirty a week ought to do it. You show up late, you're out. Show up drunk, you're out. Hesitate when I tell you to knock a man down, you're out. You ever talk to the cops about the goings-on here, you're out, and you'll be put in the ground as a bonus."

Thinking of the dead man in Redding, lethally perforated by the very knife resting now in a bag at his hip, Varley said, "I won't talk to no cops."

"Good," said Templeton. "Don't do none of that other shit, neither. You stand there in my bar and look fearsome, that's all you got to do most of the time. Every once in a while, throw a rummy out the door, put your fist into the teeth of a man I tell you to. Think you can handle that?"

"I can, yes, sir."

"Good." Templeton reached into his pocket and extracted a billfold, made a show of counting out some money, pushing it across the desk. A twenty and a ten. A month's worth of wages for the best-paying job he'd ever had, and all he'd done so far was drink a shot of the man's whiskey.

"We'll try it on a probationary basis, like. You understand what that means?"

"Yes, sir."

"Good. This bit here ain't even a loan, just to get yourself a room. I want you at the front door there at two in the afternoon tomorrow. And in a getup that doesn't smell like shit, you don't mind me saying. You show up one minute after the hour, I'm out thirty bucks, because you'll be told to hit the road. But show up on time, we both might continue to benefit."

"Yes, sir."

"What's your name, boy?"

"John Charles," Varley said, a name he'd been using after Redding.

"John Charles. Alright then. I will see you tomorrow at two P.M."

"You mind if I get another drink out at the bar, sir?"

"I would advise against it."

"Yes, sir."

Nine months passed in this manner. The pay more than suited him. Got himself some nice pants and shirts, a jacket, a room in a clean boardinghouse down the street. He found his temperament calmed greatly with the arrival of money. Who'd have thought? He managed to save, even. At thirty a week, it was not hard. He caught a few furtive glances from other men like himself, men with his inclinations, but what had happened in Redding seemed to have revealed some intrinsically broken thing inside him and he made certain nothing happened. With women too, just steering clear of the whole affair. Still, passions aside, he approached something like contentedness in those months. The police didn't worry him because Templeton paid off the police, a skinny, bucktoothed patrolman coming in once a week to collect his envelope to share with the rest of the precinct.

In truth, Templeton asked little of him. He stood, he escorted drunkards outside, he broke a man's fingers in a cupboard in Templeton's office one night. Punched a few kidneys, threw another man through the window of the bar after he'd been foolish enough to threaten Varley with a blade. Templeton, at that, had come out of his office with a cigar clamped in his jaws and surveyed the damage. He'd simply said, "It's coming out of your payroll, John. Now board that shit up and call the glass man first thing in the morning."

Nine months, and then, with the street outside churned to filth via a seemingly endless May rain, Templeton had stormed through the saloon doors one night holding a rag to his forehead, cursing like the seven winds, eyes glassy with fear and rage. His coterie of personal bruisers had followed—Pete, Big Steve, Tippy, Sticking Francis—all part of Templeton's brutal entourage, and each of them nursing their own menagerie of hurts. Worst of them was Francis, who took rabbit-sips of air and held his hands to his bloody stomach, and Big Steve, ashen-faced with shock and appearing to be feeling the effects of having the lower half of his arm turned entirely backward, the knuckles of his hand slapping against his own thigh.

"The God-blasted sonofabitch isn't of this world," Templeton had muttered, storming past Varley, quieting the entire bar with his entrance. Templeton making a point of rolling into the Bucket was not an uncommon thing, but it was usually a brash, showman-like affair. Never, in all the time Varley had been running the door, had the old man come in on the losing end of a scrap, and a profound unease shot through the room like an electric current. Templeton and his boys staggered to the back office and card games and conversations gathered steam once more, but slowly, as if the whole establishment was on notice. The doctor arrived soon after, headed back there with his black bag.

An hour later, Templeton called Varley into his office. The doctor was gone, and the old man was seated behind his desk once more, a large oak affair covered in green felt and, besides the large Browning pistol resting near his hand, bare of accoutrement. Looking at him,

Varley was reminded once again that Templeton was roughly the same age as his old man, something that he'd taken a quiet comfort in during those months of employment. He was also smart enough to recognize that he wanted to please Templeton like a child wants to please their father, and what a dangerous thing that could be.

Templeton's face was shrouded in shadow, his bandaged head gleaming a shocking white from the thrown illumination of the oil lamps. The fabric was already stippled red, leaking through. The least injured of Templeton's leg-breakers, Pete and Tippy, sat like chastised children on a velvet loveseat, both of them cowed with their hands in their laps.

Templeton leaned back in his chair and cast Varley an assessing eye. "How old are you, John?"

"Twenty-four now, Mr. Templeton."

Templeton nodded. "You ever kill anyone?"

Cold flooded through him. Varley cast his eyes to the floor. "No, sir."

"You're a bad liar, you know that? How many folks you killed?"

"None, sir."

"Lie to me again and you're out on your ass."

Varley cleared his throat, kept his eyes to the scuffed floor. "One man, Mr. Templeton. That I know of."

Templeton laughed, the sound sharp like pistol fire, and Pete and Tippy jumped in their seats. "*That he knows of.* I love it. Did he deserve it, John?"

"I figured so when I was doing it."

Another sharp cough of laughter from Templeton. He murmured Varley's response, as if filing it away somewhere. A tidbit to keep. He leaned forward then, his chair creaking.

"John, have you given any consideration as to where my man Wendell might be? Has that crossed your mind at all, watching us drag our sorry asses inside here an hour ago? Did you happen to think, 'Why, Wendell follows Mr. Templeton everywhere he goes, I wonder where he might be?'"

It was true, he realized. Wendell, the largest of Templeton's men, larger even than Varley, hadn't come back with the rest of the boys earlier that evening. But it hadn't crossed his mind at all. Why would it? His job was a simple and straightforward one. Menace was the bedrock of his occupation. And while well-paid, he wasn't like Tippy or Sticking Francis; he was not a part of Templeton's inner sanctum. It wasn't his job to consider Wendell or anyone else.

Still, he also recognized a prompt when he heard one. "Where's Wendell, Mr. Templeton? I didn't see him come in with you all."

To his left, Pete sighed like a dog who'd been kicked to the curb.

"Wendell," Templeton said, "has been moved on to the next life, John. Forcibly so. We'd gone over to Starling's supposed *meeting*"— and this was said acidly, rich with contempt—"and done so on good faith and with the purest of intentions. *Unarmed,* I might add. And were met with someone who, at Starling's direction, plowed through every last fucking one of these fellows." He cast a baleful eye toward the two men on the loveseat. "Ones with any backbone, at least. The fellow Starling hired cut open Sticking Francis's belly wide as a roadway, and turned Big Steve's arm all the way around on him. But Wendell, he got the worst of it."

"Chewed him up like a steak on payday," Pete said, his voice thick, almost weeping, and Templeton told him to hush.

Varley said, "So he's dead?"

Templeton nodded. "Oh, he's deader than hell, John. Dead as any dead thing might ever care to be. And it weren't with a knife, either. Man was *eaten.*"

Davis Starling was a name bandied around a lot in the months Varley had worked the door of the Bucket. Starling was from Wichita, supposedly, though maybe Memphis or New Orleans. Mystery, Varley had come to understand, was its own currency in a business such as this. Starling had lately begun buying property all throughout town, with particular interest in the Square. Jim Templeton was the head of no syndicate—he had his saloon, the barbershop across the street, a few seamstress shops that he ran ladies out of, and the rooming houses above most of those. He himself would insist he was no crime lord. But he was also unappreciative of extortion, and when a pair of Starling's men had swaggered into the Bucket and informed Jim Templeton that they'd be opening up another saloon three doors down, but could be convinced to set up shop elsewhere for a sizeable cash payment right then and there, Varley had held the door while Tippy and Big Steve had tossed them out, with the threat of worse to come should they ever darken the Bucket's door again.

But it hadn't stopped Starling. Renovations were begun on the place down the street, once an upholsterer's shop. Workmen coming and going all day, making it a point to scatter their materials along the walk, particularly in front of the Bucket, until Varley and Tippy had been sent to ask the gentlemen to clean it up, which the workmen reluctantly did under threat of violence. Still, this sort of thing happened more than once. A constant nagging embattlement, with Starling himself supposedly setting up shop, just like Templeton, in the back office of his still-nameless saloon. The whole thing took on a linear, easily understood arc: eventually someone was going to get hurt, or worse.

Windows were smashed after-hours at both locales. Varley began tossing patrons of the Bucket who Templeton suspected were Starling's plants. Honestly, he was surprised that it was only Wendell who'd been killed in this most recent exchange; the whole thing had taken on the inevitable momentum of a trainwreck. That said, Wendell being gutted was new, a clear line that had been definitively crossed. Someone was dead. They were on the far side of the moon now, all of them.

"What do you mean, Mr. Templeton, that he was eaten?"

Tippy, on the couch, lifted his chin and said, "He was chewed up, John Charles, is what Mr. Templeton means. He *looked* like a man, least from the neck down, but he chewed Wendell up like a fucking sawblade." Tippy held up a beefy forearm, blocked his own face with it. "Giant motherfucker too, 'bout chomped Wendell's goddamn hand off when he put his arm up like this."

"You're full of it."

"Hell I am. Mr. Templeton seen it with his own eyeballs."

"You're saying this fellow almost bit Wendell's hand off? Almost *bit it off*?"

"He's saying that and more!" Templeton barked. "Fucking blood-bath, is what it was. And during a supposed *truce,* that's the part that gets me. You understand? We'd gone there with no weapons, Sticking Francis not even with a toothpick on him. Gone there to talk business, finally see to some arrangement, and how were we met? With Davis Starling laughing in our faces, and then siccing this *thing* on us like some damn attack dog. And killing a man of mine!"

"It weren't human," Pete said.

Templeton whirled, pointed a finger his way. "You shut your mouth, Pete." He looked at Varley then, and there was a shrewdness in the eyes, the set of the mouth, that Varley had seen in the man's business dealings, but until now had never been leveled his way. He didn't care for it a bit.

"John Charles, a question for you."

"Yes, sir?"

"You ever been to California, by chance?"

Varley felt his blood go cold. "Been there once or twice, sir," he managed.

Templeton nodded. "I was wondering so. Wondering if you ever spent any time up north, near Redding, maybe?"

He made his face as blank as he could manage. "No sir, mostly down south."

"I see. Ever met a fellow by the name of John Varley? Looks quite a bit like you?"

"No, sir. Not that I remember."

"See, that's interesting to me. Was talking to an acquaintance from there a bit back and they was telling me there was a queer down there with that name, John Varley, who got in a fight with a fellow over a billfold. Fella he was shacking up with. This was maybe a year back. Big, blond-haired, Viking-looking motherfucker was what my acquaintance said. Claimed this Varley stuck him in the lung and the fellow died."

"Well, that's a rough one, sir. I don't truck with queers, though."

"I see. Because I hear the sheriff out there would love to be made privy to any clues regarding this fellow's whereabouts. Any clues at all."

Chilled sweat had broken out on Varley's back. The way the other men were looking at him now. "Wish I could help you, Mr. Templeton." Thinking *Run.* Thinking *Get Templeton first, get that gun of his, then get Tippy, do Steve last. Hell, get your knife out and do them all that way if you have to. You got enough money to run awhile.*

Varley's hand crept to his bag, and Templeton noticed, grinned.

And then Jim Templeton had stood up, wincing a little as he did so, and walked slowly around his desk. He was smaller than Varley, shorter—hell, most people were—but the hand he laid on Varley's shoulder was firm. Even after all this, Jim Templeton still hummed with life and dark cheer. He reached back and took the Browning pistol from his desktop. Matte black and heavy as all hell. He put it butt-first in Varley's hand.

"Here's how much I trust you, John. Giving you my own damn gun. Brand-new too."

Varley held it, blinking.

"Go on over there, John, in the dark of night. Tomorrow. And lay waste to them all. Whoever you see."

"Mr. Templeton, if Wendell really was ate—"

Templeton put up a stopping hand, patted Varley's chest with it. "You killed a man, John, by your own tongue you admitted it. You think I give a screaming shit about some dead queer in Redding, California? Hell no. You think I care if your name's John Charles or John Varley or Johnny Two-Dicks? I do not. I appreciate your temerity, truth be told."

"I don't know what that means."

"It means you are an audacious motherfucker, boy, with some brass balls, and this won't be any harder for you than putting down a dog. A dirty dog at that. This one that Starling hired, he's a man with some sort of teeth on him, sure, but a man nonetheless. I want him and Starling both laid down, you understand?" Templeton leaned forward, and Varley smelled pipe smoke and whatever ointment the doctor had plied his wound with. Softly, he said, "And I'll tell you this, boy, I will make it worth your while. This is the sort of thing makes a man a *business partner.* Makes a man a friend for life, doing something like this."

Pete muttered something under his breath. Varley couldn't make it all out, but *faggot* was in there somewhere.

Eyes still locked on Varley, Templeton said, "Another word from you, Pete, and I'll kick your useless skinny ass down the street myself. The men are talking, you understand me?"

After a moment, Varley nodded, flashed the old man a grin. He decided it the way he did most things—quickly, going off the jumping and mercurial swayings of his own heart.

"Sir," he said, "you point me in the right direction, and I'll make sure those fellows don't ever rise from their beds again."

Templeton nodded back at him. "Good man, John. Proud of you, and glad to hear it."

8

"She's at a park," Julia says.

"Who is?"

"Adeline. This lady who knows him. Knows Varley."

"A park."

"Kenton Park," she says. When he doesn't say anything, she asks him if he knows where it is.

"I mean, yeah, I know it," he answers. "But, Julia, this is nuts. Some kid told you that a woman hangs out in a park at night, and we're supposed to go talk to her? To get to Varley? Makes no sense."

"It makes as much sense as a guy with a cloud for a face," she says back to him. "A guy that looked the same as he did forty years ago."

They're in Minor's truck and he's far enough away from his panic at losing her that he actually laughs a little. "Good point."

He drives her to Kenton Park. What else is there to do? He'll humor Julia tonight, let her have this kernel of hope, keep her safe, and tomorrow, finally, he will begin the process of righting the ship. Meet with the coroner and funeral director, take ownership of the bodies. Notify Principal Reed of all that's happened. Start getting the line on something for work, maybe hit up Bobby about it. Find a new, more permanent place to live.

At the same time, Christ, something in him twists on a wire. He wants Varley to answer for what he's done, to pay for it. He knows Julia wants it too. Why else would she be out here, in the cold, looking for Heidi's killer?

They come to the park. It's large, quiet, the edges of its acreage lined in trees, a central field that dips down. A backstop and a baseball diamond. The park itself is ringed in sleeping houses. Minor scans the darkness around them from the idling truck.

"Yeah, I don't see anyone, kid."

"We should walk around."

"Julia—"

Staring at him, she unbuckles her seatbelt. Climbs out.

Minor curses under his breath, follows her as she steps onto the path. Pure *will* etched into her posture.

"This is pointless, kid." He throws out his arms, taking in all of it. There's the implied shape of a children's playground at the far end of the park, structures jutting up like the skeletons of things long gone to the ground. "There's no one here. It's too cold."

"Just *help* me," Julia says, and keeps walking down the path.

So he follows her, a memory coming to him as he walks—he and Heidi had picnicked at Kenton Park a few times, both before and after his tour. Summertime, blankets on the grass, sharing a bottle of wine while a jazz band played on a grandstand. The music bright as arrowed sunlight, dogs running around, children laughing. People trying to dance to it. Heidi with her hair pinned up, her hand on his thigh. Someone had lit a joint, he remembered, and the smell of it drifted among the crowd. The memory is as sudden and insistent as a hand in his face, and in that moment, Heidi feels close enough to touch. The mole on her shoulder. The green flecks in her brown eyes. The way she'd shake her head and say his name in mock disappointment whenever he made a joke that didn't land. Now that he's beginning to navigate the boundaries of grief, he's not sure he can stand it. This is what he thinks as Julia winds along the trail, the wind making lonely sounds through the fingers of branches overhead. The park's maybe ten acres, twelve, and they've walked almost its entire length when he says to Julia's back, "There's nothing here, hon." Then he hears the creak of a swing set. They've gotten closer to the playground, and Minor's mouth goes dry when, in the darkness, he sees a little girl on one of the swings, and a man sitting on a bench nearby, just his shoulders and his knit cap visible.

Middle of the fucking night. Twenty-five degrees out. *Snowing*.

The girl is turned away from them, and she wears a blue coat. He sees black penny loafers and white socks and, as she swings, the pale stalks of her bare legs.

Julia stops. He almost runs into her. Ice floods his blood. She takes his hand in hers.

Turn back, he thinks. *Whatever this is, turn back. No good will come from this.*

"Adeline," Julia croaks. She squeezes his hand.

The girl and her father—Minor assumes that's who he is—turn simultaneously. He's an old man, white beard and a ponytail, and he stands up to face them. Wearing a green peacoat and jeans, heavy gloves. A turtleneck a dozen years out of fashion. He looks dismayed to see them.

The girl pushes herself off the swing and the wind flattens her pink dress against her, pushes the hood of her blue raincoat down. That threatening dread Minor has felt for so long has finally arrived, been made whole: this is something they won't be able to turn from.

The girl walks toward them, her hair in a dark bob, and she takes a cigarette from her pocket and puts it in her mouth.

The old man walks over to her, bends at the waist and lights it. The flick of the lighter, the man chasing the wind with his cupped hand, trying to protect the flame.

He gets it lit and, still with that sullen look on his face, goes and sits down on the bench again. The girl walks over to them, her small black shoes scraping the gritty cement.

She looks younger than Julia. Nine years old maybe, ten. She is small and fine-boned and the cuffs of her blue jacket are filthy. The collar of her pink dress is ringed in black down to her stomach. Dirt or something worse. There's a disarming sort of *awareness* in the set of her shoulders, the way she walks unflinchingly toward them. The way she *smokes,* clearly. But mostly it's in the way her eyes quickly give Minor a dismissive once-over and then turn back to Julia. His scalp tightens.

"Are you Adeline?" Julia asks.

"Who wants to know?" she says, smiling.

From his spot on the bench, the old man asks Minor if he has any weapons on him.

"What?"

The man coughs. "You have any weapons on you, son?"

"No."

"Does she?" he says, lifting his chin at Julia.

"No."

The old man says, "You want me to frisk them?"

The girl blows smoke at the sky. "I'm not worried."

Insane. The whole thing.

Run.

Minor says, "Look—"

"Yes, I'm Adeline. What do you want?" The girl's eyes are large and liquid and in them Minor sees a complete and utter lack of fear. Curiosity, maybe. Amusement.

Julia lets go of his hand, takes a step forward and says, in a small voice, "I want to find John Varley, and I'm supposed to ask you about the Children's Museum."

"Ah," she says. "Well, that's two things, sweetness."

"I want to know about both, I guess."

Adeline smiles again and he realizes—and in that realization a horror unfolds, horror upon horror—that she's *old,* that's the thing that's making him want to run, even more than the dirty pink dress and the pale legs exposed to the cold. It's that she's *old,* this little girl. Her mannerisms, the way she speaks. An adult, somehow, frozen in this body, playacting at childhood. "The Museum's right across the street." She gestures vaguely toward the houses across the park; Julia follows her hand, but Minor can't see anything through the trees. "Old place, all boarded up to siphon out the light. You can't miss it. But you'll never get in, not without permission."

"Someone said you could help me."

"Frank," Adeline says without taking her eyes away from Julia, "do we help people?"

"Not for free," the old man says from his spot on the bench.

"Not for free," Adeline repeats.

"Listen, what the fuck is this?" Minor says, and Julia takes another step toward the little girl and says, "I want John Varley."

Adeline tilts her head like a dog, her eyes widening. She lets out a breathless little chuckle. "*You* want John Varley. That's all? Why not just throw yourself into a buzz saw? Why not try to catch the wind in your hand? You'd have as much chance of doing that as getting one over on him."

"Someone told me you could help me."

"Child," Adeline says, "I do admire your fierceness, as stupid and misguided as it is, but I'm not the helping kind."

"Please."

"You should take your broken-down man here and stay as far away from John Varley as you can manage. He's not the sort you go after."

"Julia," Minor says, "let's go."

Adeline smiles at him for the first time. "You're the one from the bar, aren't you? The Last Call, Last Chance? Something like that?"

Minor nods.

She grins then, that smile widening, and he swears that a blackness falls over her eyes. Just for a second. He puts a hand on Julia's shoulder, pulls her back a step. "Oh," Adeline goes on, almost breathlessly, "he *ruined* you, didn't he? Broke your heart. Left pieces of those people on the *ceiling,* is what I heard."

Julia stiffens beneath his hand.

"What is he?" Minor says, hardly aware he's said it.

Adeline waves a hand at him coquettishly. "Oh, you know what he is."

"I don't."

"Yes, you do. You're just afraid to say it."

"How do we find him?" Julia asks.

"You don't," Frank says from his spot on the bench. "You stay the hell away from him and count yourself lucky."

Adeline walks over to Frank, and Minor sees her lay a small hand on his throat. Not pushing, no violence to it, but Frank's eyes go wide with fear. A warning, Minor guesses, for talking out of turn. She takes her hand away and says, "John Varley's not like the rest of us, dear. Some of us—those of us in the Museum, for example—eke out our lives in unremarkable increments. Sleep, dream. Stay quiet, stay small. We eat when we have to, but we're not *gluttonous.* You understand?"

"Alright," Minor says.

"Varley, though? He's a dervish. He likes the bloody parts."

Run, Minor thinks again. *Get Julia, get away from here. Bury your wife and her family and protect this girl. It's not too late.*

And then Julia says, "I don't care. I want revenge," and some part of Minor's heart cracks in half at the pain in those words, and he realizes, in spite of everything, he does too.

He does too.

Adeline playfully runs her hand through Frank's hair, sees the man's face tighten once more. She says, "Revenge is an eyeblink, sweetness. There and done. Once you're finished with it, there's a certain hollowness."

"I don't care."

"You're too young to know about not caring."

"Why are you protecting him?" Minor says.

Adeline steps away from the old man and screws up her face, disgusted. "I'm protecting *you,* you ass. Protecting this girl here, who might still have some sort of life ahead of her."

"This is a dead end," Minor says to Julia, and he starts to steer her back down the path they came from. She lets him.

But then: "Varley isn't even here, last I heard," Adeline calls out behind them. "Word is, he slaughtered his thralls—"

"Thralls?" asks Julia, turning back to her.

Adeline points a finger at Frank. "Attendants. Familiars. You're my helper, aren't you, Frank?"

"Yes, ma'am."

"And you do it out of the goodness of your own heart, don't you? No coercion involved, right? In spite of the term?"

Frank nods.

"See?" she says. "So yes, Varley killed them all—probably because they were less than thrilled about the lawful repercussions of killing your people—and now he's on the run."

"Where is he?"

"That doesn't matter," Adeline says, enunciating each word and motioning with the hand holding her cigarette, "because you can't stop him." Her gaze is languid, unworried. "You two don't have the string for what's necessary. You don't have the heart for it."

What happens next happens so fast, he can hardly track it. Julia runs, leaps at the girl's throat and before Minor can move, before he can hardly blink, Adeline pivots, throws her to the ground, falls over her, her mouth inches from Julia's neck. Dozens of needlelike, nearly translucent teeth rise from the girl's gums over her existing teeth, nestling there at the hollow of Julia's throat. A black film slides over her eyes. He steps toward the two of them and feels cold steel pressed to the back of his neck. Frank says, "I got hollow-points in here. Not another inch."

The moment hangs there, Minor with his hands up, until Adeline stands and those needlelike teeth fall back into her gums and the black ink slides from her eyes. She breathes heavily once, twice, and steps away. Julia sits up, blinking. Minor feels the pressure leave the back of his neck.

"Heart or stupidity, I don't know," Adeline says, her voice bright as she brushes snow from her knees. "But I like it. I'll take you to the Museum, child."

"You will?"

"I will. And that's the first step for readying yourself against Varley. Except there's always an admission price."

"Julia," Minor says, "let's go."

Julia ignores him, stands up. "What is it?"

"Well, a life," Adeline says, as if she's a fool. "A life in trade." She hooks a thumb at Minor. "This one will work."

"He's not available," Julia says primly, and he has a sudden mad desire to laugh until he can't laugh anymore. Until he's screaming.

"Why's that?"

"He's my uncle."

Adeline makes a face. "Everyone's someone's uncle, child. Someone's father or wife or daughter. He's practically dead already, you can't smell it on him? The whiskey and the heartsick? The man has given up."

"I need him. I can't do this without him."

Adeline shrugs. "Well, we're at an impasse, then."

"Take me," Julia says. "Let me do this, and I'll come back to you. I promise."

Minor walks over to her, puts his hand on her shoulder. "Let's go."

Adeline ignores him too. To Julia, she says, "It doesn't work that way, dear. You go to the Museum, you're changed. That's the way of it."

Minor bends, speaks low. "Julia, please. Come on."

"He took everything from me," Julia says, her chin dimpling as she tries not to weep. "Don't you understand?"

"Well, of course he did," Adeline says, so softly Minor can hardly hear her above the rusty creak of the swing in the wind. "It's what we do. Varley's just joyous from it, is all. Happy with the hurt of it. The *mess.*" She takes the pack of cigarettes out of her pocket and finds it empty. Motions for another one and Frank walks over, offers her his, the pistol held in his other hand. "You should reconsider, child. He's getting farther away by the minute."

Minor asks how she knows that, and Adeline flicks two fingers at Frank, who hands her his lighter. She waits until she's lit her cigarette to answer him. "Because he's famous for it. His fury gets the better of him and he kills everyone and then he has to run." Minor thinks of the detective, the bodies ripped apart in 1931. "Not the first time, not the last."

"You seem to know a lot about him."

A laconic smile. "It would be a stretch to say we're a community. But he's a known quantity."

"Where is he?" Julia says.

Adeline sighs. "Honestly, I'm getting tired of this conversation. Come to the Museum or don't."

"If I put you in front of a mirror right now," Minor says to her, "what would I see?"

"Beauty incarnate," Adeline croons, waggling her eyebrows. Laughing drily, she holds her cigarette to her lips for a long time and then says, "You'd see a warp and a mystery. A writhe and buckle where there should be a face. But you already know that, don't you?"

"What happens in the Museum? What do you do in there that costs a life?"

"Why do you keep asking questions you already know the answer to?"

"Tell me."

"*Tell me*," she says mockingly. "In the Museum, you're made into something that might actually give you a chance against him."

Minor palms his sweating hands on the thighs of his jeans. Thinks of Lyle. Of Ferris and his helmet with READYMADE MEAT in marker on the front. Thinks of Heidi turned into something you'd find on the floor of a slaughterhouse. The *work* it took to do it. To reduce her to something like that.

He's caught between that brokenhearted howl for vengeance, buried under the false mask of something as lofty as *justice,* and what he knows Heidi would want him to do, for himself, for Julia.

"To be made," he says, "into something like you? Like him?"

She nods. "You still wouldn't stand a chance against him, but it would up the odds a bit."

"But it's forever, isn't it? What happens in the Museum?"

She looks at Frank, still holding the pistol at his leg, and laughs that bitter, childlike laugh. "Forever or the next sunrise, sure."

Julia turns to him. He is stunned to his core to see that hope hasn't died in her eyes. That it's *bloomed.* "Duane, please, we can do this."

"Christ, no, Julia. No."

Adeline turns to her. "See? He's weak. Your uncle, he's like an animal with its leg caught in a trap. Cut him loose, girl. Come see me. Whenever you want. We'll have a good time, you and I."

"*Please,* Duane."

"We're going," he says, and he takes her by the arm, and leads her back along the path through the trees. She goes with him, her shoulders slumped in defeat. Somewhere along the way she starts crying.

9

West, escape, snow in a mad whirl against the headlights. The green glow of the dashboard draws Johan's face in a beautiful monster-light. The boy going on and on about his life. His childhood friends, growing up in Utrecht, the litany of small, petty crimes he's committed through the years, earning him pocket money and, a more important currency, excitement. Varley is happy to listen to him filling the car with noise, the occasional strobe of red as they pass another car. There is the freedom of moving just to move. Of getting away.

"I'm talking too much," Johan says.

"I don't mind it."

"No?"

"You've led a life, that's for sure."

"What about you?"

"What about me?"

Johan's smile is freighted with so many things, and Varley thinks of the touch on his arm earlier. "Well, I've told you *my* crimes. What about yours? Are you a dangerous man?"

Varley considers it. Considers, too, reaching over, steering wheel be damned, and pressing his teeth against the boy's throat. Be done with it. Blood splashing the windows, the Impala jouncing against the guardrail, windshield starring. How the boy's screams would fill his ears like music. But there's something about him, and Varley pauses.

"Is it arrogant to say yes?" he asks instead. "Call me arrogant, then." He lifts his chin, peers at the sinuous, curling smoke of his face in the rearview mirror, a sight Johan has yet to witness. "I'm a dangerous man."

Johan turns to him, tucks his hair behind his ear. "Who's more dangerous, me or you?"

They drive for perhaps half a mile and Johan goes to speak again but Varley raises a finger, bidding him quiet. He takes an off-ramp and follows the winding curve of the road to a rest stop. A single cement outbuilding, a visitor's area with a small expanse of grass and a pair of picnic tables. The lot is empty at this hour, barren, snow-covered, everything surrounded by a thin stand of firs. A quiet little pocket of the world. He turns and looks at the boy.

"Let's find out."

Johan's gaze is one he's seen many times before. Breathlessness and a nattering of fear and a kind of exultant rush. The sudden understanding that Varley is one who will take you up on your dare. Will honor your willingness to test the edges of things. "What?" the boy says, coyly.

"What do you want in this life of yours, Johan?"

"I don't know," Johan breathes, smiling and knitting his eyebrows together, trying to lighten things, to steer Varley away from his sudden seriousness. He can see it at work in the boy's face: that understanding that he's here, in a desolate rest stop with no one around. Just this stranger staring back at him.

"I want you to consider it," Varley says. Behind them, a car approaches. A pair of headlights slowly wend their way from the highway and down that curving road to the parking lot of the rest stop. Not a big rig, either. A car. Varley turns, hoists an arm over his seatback. "What do you *want,* boy? Money? Women? Men? Power? Vengeance?" He shrugs. Feels the stirrings of desire. Not a need, but a want. There is even, look at this, the desire to *impress* this boy. "I can give you life eternal. See, you laugh at me, fine, but I can give you the gift of life. A life a mile wide and possible as anything. Believe it."

The headlights pull into the lot, parking three, four spots away from their car. An old man gets out, gives them a cursory glance, then begins walking toward the bathrooms, his steps careful in the snow.

"But first," Varley says, "you need to do something for me. Consider it a show of fealty."

They watch the old man push through the door of the restroom, and then Johan licks his lips and says, "What's 'fealty' mean?"

"Loyalty, Johan. Devotion."

"Alright."

"Alright," Varley says. "We're going in there, and I'm going to show you what I mean." He laughs a little, taps out a drumbeat on the steering wheel before opening his door. Johan will either go with him into that restroom or he'll run. If he chooses well, he'll walk with Varley into that cement room and bear witness to what Varley is, and then he'll face *another* choice: he'll either stand in wonderment and live, or turn from Varley and die.

Either way, John Varley gets to eat.

He steps out into a cutting wind that blows his hair from his shoulders. "Follow me, then. Let's find out who's the more dangerous man."

They walk into the restroom. Tiled floors, tiled walls, their footsteps echoing as the door whispers closed. A bank of three urinals and a pair of stalls. The old man's got his back turned to them, pissing at a urinal, and his shoulders slump at their entrance. Varley feels something inside himself at that—lust, the ache for blood, the joy that comes before hurting someone. Maybe all of it.

The old man's wearing a checkered houndstooth coat and pleated slacks, a little newsie cap on top of his thinning hair. Even from here his blood thuds weakly in Varley's ears. But feeding isn't even necessarily the point, is it? Fealty is what's at play here. Allegiance.

The old fellow clears his throat, zips himself up. He still has his back to them when he says, "You mind if I wash my hands before we do this?"

They are blocking the door, the two of them, and Johan gives Varley a grin, confused but game. Varley's impressed: the old man has spine.

"Before we do what?"

He turns then, fixing them both with a baleful eye. Mouth hardly moving beneath the broom-bristle mustache. "Whatever this idiotic slap and tickle is you two are about to do. Rob me? Take my car?"

There is a moment there where no one speaks, a delicate moment where the three of them are poised in this room, each of them unmoving, still as a frieze. And then, that second before Varley's teeth rise from his gums, that second before he strides to the old man and bends to his throat, that moment before he sees if Johan, too, will live or die in this mausoleum that smells of piss and disinfectant, Johan says to the old man, conversationally, "Actually, I'm going to take your life."

And then the boy steps forth, sound of his boots scraping across the floor, and he hooks a hand around the old man's neck, his cap falling off, and Johan's other arm is pumping, pumping, the bright and merry tang of blood in the air, the boy stabbing the old man in the guts with some kind of blade Varley hadn't even known was on him, stabbing again and again, and the old man's eyes widening enough to show the whites. The great surprise of death, how it strides through the door, takes a seat at your table. He tries to push Johan away, the blade pinning the old man's hand to his chest at one point, the knife snagged in the metacarpals, the boy grunting with effort to pull it free.

Varley watches, arms folded.

Both of them wet with blood. Then, with a gentleness that seems nearly intimate, Johan drops the knife, lays the old man down to the ground. The old man blinks up at the bathroom light, his mouth working as if deciphering some riddle. Which he is, Varley thinks. The oldest damn riddle of them all.

Johan finds the blade, folds it closed, puts it back in his pants pocket. Unconcerned with the blood. He stands up, watching. The old man's hands swim along the floor, seeking purchase, seeking an answer, seeking *more time* as he gazes up at the sputtering, buzzing fluorescent.

Johan looks at Varley then, the air electric between them, charged with this moment, and Johan says, "Watch this," and then brings a boot down on the old man's face. Once more, then again, the man's hand snaking up briefly, then falling back to the tiles.

The man is still for a long time before Johan stops.

And then Johan looks at him again, chest heaving, shoulders rising. Blood stippling a cheek. Smell of blood hot and cloying in the room.

Varley hears the smile in Johan's voice when he says, "That the kind of fealty you were talking about?"

10

Julia weeps in the passenger seat while Minor drives them back to the motel. "There's no other way," she says.

"I can't let you do it," Minor says. "I— I have to take care of you, Julia."

"Like you took care of Aunt Heidi," she says, and he winces like he's been punched.

"I'm sorry," she says a moment later.

"It's alright."

"We have to *get* him," she says, her voice so thick with tears it's nearly inaudible.

"No," he says. "This all— It's too much. It's nuts. Whatever that was back there, whoever those people were, we can't. *I* can't."

"He killed them," she screams, her voice cracking on the second word, the sound of it close in the cab of the truck. "He killed them and he meant to. He *liked* it."

"I know, I know," Minor says as they pull into the parking lot of the Palm Sands, reaching for her, trying to soothe her, but Julia slaps his hand away and steps out and for a moment, there at the truck's door, it looks like she's going to run. She starts toward the street, tensed, ready. But then she turns, walks to the door of their room, arms crossed. She waits for Minor to open it, and then goes into the bathroom, closes the door behind her.

She spends the night in there—it's the only space that offers any privacy in this little hell of theirs—and Minor sets about getting gloriously, wretchedly drunk. Does it to stuff the panic down. Does it with the abandon of a man who, he tells himself, will never drink again after this. Tomorrow will be the day that he fixes all the broken things. But tonight, Jesus Christ, after *Adeline*? Whatever *that* was? Oh yeah, he's getting shitfaced.

There's no fanfare, no staggering around the room, no grand proclamations made to the walls. He turns on the television and methodically hoists glasses of Jameson's to his mouth. At some point in the night, he lurches to the sink in the little kitchenette and vomits. Stomping back to his bed, his knees butt against the bed frame and he falls face-first onto the mattress. The room spins wildly.

He awakens to a sickening throb in his skull, a familiar feeling like molten steel's been poured into the space behind his eyeballs. Pushing himself from the bed, Minor looks around the room, but all's black. Staggering upright, the world seems built on quicksand, and he stumbles to the light switch. The room's empty, smelling of whiskey and that buried note of vomit. Minor's stomach tightens like a fist, bile rising in his throat.

Walking to the bathroom—weaving to the left, his shoulder bouncing off the wall—he knocks softly on the door. No answer. No wedge of light underneath.

"Julia?"

He tests the knob. It's unlocked. Opening the door and turning on the light, he sees the toilet, the water-spotted mirror, the open shower curtain. Nothing else. The *plink plink plink* of a dripping faucet.

She's gone. Again.

His mind in a slow, knocking circuit. So goddamn stupid of him. He cups his hands beneath the bathroom sink and drinks until his belly heaves with it. Doesn't help a thing.

He grabs his keys and walks out to his truck. The world is quiet and lunar and white. Two, three in the morning, something like that, he hasn't been asleep—passed out—for long, and he thinks, *If I actu-*

ally manage to drive out of this parking lot, first fucking thing I'll do is wrap the truck around a goddamn telephone pole.

So he walks instead, starts running. Makes it a block before he bends at the waist and heaves. Then he's running again, still drunk, stupid, slipping more than once on the ice coating the sidewalk. He rips his knee up at one point, and still he runs down Interstate.

She might as well have sent him a letter with the address on it. It couldn't have been more obvious where she's going.

But she'd also known he'd get shitfaced, hadn't she?

So damn predictable.

She just had to wait for Uncle Duane to do the thing he does.

11

She retraces her route. She's afraid of what comes next, yes, absolutely terrified, but also glad to be free of the confines of the Palm Sands. No matter what happens in the next hour, she's at least free of those four walls, the pressing closeness of the bathroom. How her uncle's sadness has frozen him in place.

She walks a long straight line, down this one street. Interstate? The blurred headlights of passing cars, the biting cold. Her history—her aunt and her mother and Little Kev and Casey and her grandparents—all clamoring around her, pushing her along. Her mother had not allowed Ray Ray to continue doing what he'd always done, she'd finally reached some point where she'd had enough of the man he was. Where the life she was living had become intolerable. And she'd put a stop to it.

And this, too, was intolerable. This half-life of Julia's. The same day spent in that hotel room, over and over again, her uncle perpetually afraid to do what needed to be done. But he was strong, John Varley, that was the thing. *That* she could understand. Stronger than Ray Ray. More cunning, more willing to hurt. Possibly not even a man at all, but something else. Uncle Duane won't say the word, but it's there behind his eyes.

She walks to the intersection and crosses Interstate, heads down Lombard, streetlights haloing the hillocks of icy muck mounded at the curbs. Her footsteps rasp on the fresh snow. From Lombard to Denver, and then she turns again and finds the park and walks among the trees, her heart now strangely calm in spite of her fear. There is a sense of inevitability to it all—at least that's what she tells herself. She walks the paved path where the snow is thinner and squints in the gloom and sees the empty playground. Adeline and her man are gone, the swings still.

The Museum's right across the street, Adeline had told her. This strange girl who smoked cigarettes and had an adult—a man, even—bend to her will. This girl with skin pale as a new shirt, who talked like someone older than she was, full of dark knowledge, unknown grievances.

She's a vampire, isn't she, Uncle Duane? Her and Varley.

Say the word to take its power away.

Not that he would answer. Since Aunt Heidi's murder, Grandma and Grandpa, his words are like a river that's dried up. His heart hard as the pit of some rotten fruit.

She heads off the path, crosses the park in a straight line, in the direction that Adeline had motioned toward. She finds the house, the Children's Museum, easily enough, the tops of her shoes choked with fresh snow now, her socks wet, feet like blocks of ice. And still there's no fear, just the sense that she is an arrow in flight, arcing and soon to arrive at some inevitable destination.

There are four houses on the block, each of them a crumbling Victorian, each one the color of slate in the gloom, almost featureless for it. No streetlights here. The street gently slopes down; there are no cars in any of the driveways. Plywood over all of the windows. Trash in the yards, clumps of yellow grass pushing up through the skin of snow. And then she sees, between the upper floors of two of the houses, a kind of *tunnel*. Made up of scaffolding and more sheets of plywood, scrap metal, sections of iron fencing, and the thought that scurries through her mind at last gives her a moment's fear: *All of the houses are connected. The Children's Museum is all those houses. It's like a* nest.

How do the police not come? Why don't people knock the buildings down and build other houses there? This close to a park, where children play? The driveways and side yards are cloaked in shadows, unbroken sheets of snow, even the sidewalk in front of them is mostly unblemished, like people don't walk here, either by intention or some unspoken distaste. She picks one of the houses—in the middle, where the tunnels connect—and walks up the path to the porch. The door is a massive oaken thing, the window in it leaded and rippled with age. The wood of the porch splintered, chewed at by animals. Julia's heart is loud in her ears.

She knocks, timidly at first and then louder.

A great rustling clamor above her head, the spring of metal, the shuffle of feet in the tunnels above. Someone on the second floor— how she can hear it she doesn't know—screams breathlessly and then laughs and Julia almost pisses herself in fear.

Aunt Heidi, like a flare in her mind, like a flashlight beam that leads her way. Aunt Heidi and the calm, resolute way she had loved. That and Varley, ending him, those are the guides that keep her rooted to the ground.

A shape appears behind the gnarled glass panes of the door, there and gone, and then the door opens as if of its own accord.

She steps inside, smells rot immediately. Old blood, something like that. And the jungly, pungent smell of mildew and wood gone spongy; the floor gives a bit beneath her. The sound of hurried footfalls above, lots of them, and then one of those breathless screams again. To the left is a large stairwell, and as her eyes adjust to the gloom, she sees the room to her right is empty, the floor paint-spattered, all the light fixtures gone. Tendrils of wires hanging from the holes like clots of hair.

"Hello?"

"Hello?" echoes a voice upstairs, a boy's voice, high-pitched and rich with mockery.

"I came to see Adeline," Julia says—brave or not, she takes a step back and puts her hand on the doorknob, ready to flee.

"I came to see Adeline," says another voice, a girl's this time, but still with that cloying sense of mockery, and then other voices begin taking up the name—*A-de-line, A-de-line*—and all of the doors upstairs are opened and slammed shut, again and again.

A figure in white stops at the top of the stairwell.

It is ghostly in the darkness, this ethereal shape. A child in some sort of nightshirt. Then the child turns on a flashlight and holds the beam beneath its face, every campfire horror story suddenly come to life, and Julia screams, because it *is* a horror: the body remains that of a child but the face, the face is skeletal, sunken and drawn; the flesh of its skull is hairless, and woven threads of black run along its skin like tattoos, like ink taking a jagged path down parchment. She screams again, turns, her hand pawing at the knob of the front door, escape the only thing in her mind, this animal need, but the knob suddenly refuses to turn, that chorus of voices growing louder behind her, *A-de-line, A-de-line,* and foolishly, idiotically, she looks behind her.

A sea of children clamber down the stairs, writhe down them like falling water.

Dozens of them. Some are small, toddler-sized, some her own age, more in between. She notes all of this with a terrible clarity, that dreamlike sense of time grinding to a halt. They are all malformed, the children, all bent and sinuous, and in the weak light she sees that each has that skeletal, emaciated look about them, and *still* the god-damn knob won't turn and she faces the door again and *pulls* and a hand falls upon her shoulder—

She screams, and Frank—it's Frank, Adeline's thrall, the old man—he pulls her deeper into the house and hisses at her to shut the fuck up. He turns her, past the living room, if that's what it is, and into another room with tremendous holes punched into the walls, with drop cloths that lay on the floor like the discarded skins of animals. The children follow them, and he keeps his body between her and them and there is something in Frank's other hand, what is it? A gun? The deeper into the house she goes, the harder it is to see, and then there are these brief kaleidoscopic moments of illumination as the child with the flashlight whipsaws the beam across the walls, and all the while they chant Adeline's name like some nightmarish nursery rhyme.

At the doorway between the dining room and what she notes, even in her frenzied state, is a kitchen, Frank stops and pushes her forward. She sees him turn around and brace the doorway, still holding out his hand. The flashlight beam plays across it for just a moment: the man is holding a fucking *spoon* out at the children, and they hiss and sway but stay clear of him. They could flood the doorway but they don't. Over his shoulder, he says, "She's down there, through that door."

Julia turns, looks, sees a door next to the empty coffin-like hollow where a refrigerator had once stood.

The door has the dull muted look of steel about it, bringing to mind fortresses, dungeons, and she hears Frank say, with a fierceness he never mustered in the park, "Get the fuck back, you idiots," and he tells her once again to hurry up. Adeline's name is a whisper from the mouths of the children now, though a few of them stamp their feet on each syllable.

She tries to turn the knob and it's locked and Frank hisses, "Jesus Christ, you have to *knock*," and Julia knocks, and immediately—as if Adeline had been waiting for her on the other side—comes the sound of chains being thrown, a deadbolt, and then the door opens and she is careening down the half-lit stairwell, past Adeline, her hand tracing the rough, weeping cement wall. She can hear nothing save her own breath and the murmur of the children above, behind the door. The stairs are wood, crazily warped, and she can see the cement landing below, the walls trembling with candlelight. The heavy scent of blood and cigarettes. Adeline chuckles, locks the door and follows her.

Down the stairs, the walls slick with moisture. The basement is fetid and close and she can see mold in dark swaths on the walls, great black runs of it, and candles on their stands with beads and strings of spent wax. The floor is covered in a rug of great arching black and yellow patterns, and there's a massive bed with a canopy of gauze and an oak chest of drawers with a mirror. There is an open armoire and inside it is a line of dresses like the one Adeline wears now, blue and pink and yellow, all of them filthy and ringed in black at the neck.

There are no windows down here, and the candle flames hardly tremble.

Adeline walks past her and sits on the edge of her bed with a cigarette in one hand and an ashtray cupped in the other. She looks very small and somehow this makes Julia more afraid.

"You came," Adeline says.

Julia tries to speak and a croak comes out. She clears her throat and says, "I want you to make me ready for him. Varley."

Adeline looks at her for a long time, smoke twining around her. She is still for so long that Julia wonders if she's fallen into some state, gone someplace else, when she says, "Where's your man?" Puts the cigarette to her lips. *"Uncle Duane,"* she says, drawling it, heavy with contempt. "Does he know you're here?"

"It doesn't matter."

"Girl, you aim for sounding worldly, but you just sound like a fool."

Julia swallows again. "You want a life in trade, right? Do you have to, though?"

"Do I have to what?"

"Make a trade."

Adeline shrugs, seems impatient with her now. "Do I have to? Does the process demand it? Will whatever disgruntled stock boy that passes for God rise up and smite me otherwise? No. But without structure, we're like the animals, dear. We're like your villain, Bad John."

"Does it hurt?"

Adeline closes her eyes, smiles, her eyebrows arching beneath the smart line of her bangs. "Everything hurts. Is that rude of me? Everything hurts, always. Sorrow, vengeance, even joy. Everything's got teeth on it."

Julia, surprising herself with her own impatience. Adeline seeming like she's playacting. Performing a role. "I'll get you a life," Julia says.

"Whose, though?" Adeline looks up at her. There is a flatness in her eyes.

"Mine."

Adeline rolls her eyes. "Oh, please. If I wanted a meal, I'd be swimming in your marrow by now."

And it's in that moment that Julia understands. Understands all of it. "When you say you want a life, you're not asking to, to eat, are you?"

For a moment, Julia thinks she's fucked up, made a mistake. Storm clouds move across Adeline's face. "I don't *ask* to be fed, girl. I want to eat, I eat."

"Okay. I—"

"I don't *ask* anything."

"But you want me to stay here, is what you're saying. Right?"

And then Adeline stands from the bed. Walks over and touches her arm. Her fingers are icy, bloodless, and her eyes crawl across Julia's face. Julia keeps her gaze impassive as a clay mask, hiding any revulsion she might feel. Any sign of disgust or fear and she feels sure that Adeline will fall upon her, sink those teeth in her neck.

"I do," Adeline says, and there's an earnestness in her voice for the first time. Finally, she seems like a child. "I want a companion."

Julia blinks, momentarily stunned by the admission. "What about all the ones out there? What happened to them?"

"They've failed me," she says. "I thought that they would—that *we* would—" She turns away, flicks her cigarette into a corner of the room, and this signals some kind of shift. Whatever momentum she'd had with Adeline is gone now. Decimated. The mask hardens.

"Adeline," she says.

"I've turned every one of them," Adeline says. "Every one. Thinking they might walk the world with me. And every one of them is too softhearted, too weak. Too self-pitying and lamenting of their lot. I keep turning them in the hopes of finding *one* that appreciates this life for the gift it is, and they've all disappointed me."

"What about Frank?"

Adeline makes some dismissive noise and walks over to her bed, gets another cigarette. "A thrall is not a companion."

"Why are they like that? The kids out there?"

Adeline takes a long drag on her cigarette and Julia thinks she'll ignore her. But then she says, "Your curiosity isn't quite the asset you think it is, you know that?"

"I'm sorry."

Adeline smiles, tips her cigarette in acknowledgment. Then she says, "I can't kill them. They're starving to death. But I can't kill them and I can't let them go."

"Why?"

"Do you know how many children there are here? In these houses?"

"No. I mean, I saw a lot."

"Thirty-six. Thirty-six children over Christ knows how many years, and a part of me wants to mother them, and a part of me wants to be their friend, and a part of me wishes they would die. That I had the necessary bravery to kill them and set myself free. But I can't do it."

"Because you turned them."

"Because I turned them," Adeline says.

"So you keep them here."

"Frank and I, yes. And we find people for them to feed on, but for thirty-six mouths? It's never enough. They're blood-stunted, is what they are. Made stick-thin and bent in half against their own needs. I can't just let them go and I can't kill them because of my own small, weak heart. In their own way, they're *of me*. So we live like this, all of us. We live like this and we wait for the time when, eventually, the world falls on our heads. We wait to be discovered."

Julia looks at the stairs, where all's quiet now. The trembling candlelight. "Will I be like that? Like those out there?"

"If you don't eat. Yes."

"Alright."

"But you'll want to eat, believe me."

"And what happens if I—if we don't get along?"

"We will."

"I bet you've said that before, though. Right? I bet you've said that thirty-six times."

Adeline smiles, and Julia sees something strange happen in her mouth, that rippling of teeth, just for a moment. "See, that's why we will. You and your cunningness."

"And because you're lonely."

"Because I'm lonely, yes."

"If you turn me, I'll come back here when I'm done. I'll be with you."

A deep sigh, and then it's Adeline who looks up the basement steps. "Ah, sweet one. You won't come back from Varley. I see the hurt in you, and the fury, and I know you think it's a kind of armor, but it's not. He's of a Maker."

"What does that mean?"

"It means he'll wring your corpse like a wet rag and toss you away. It means he can do things that you and even I can't. It means he's the sort that would pluck the heads from my children out there and stick them on a line of fence posts just for the symmetry of it."

"I don't care."

Adeline sighs again. "I know," she says. "You *should* care, but I know you don't. That arrogance will either damn you or surprise the hell out of him. And if you can surprise him, you might have a bit of a chance. Not much, but some."

"So what do we do next?"

And for the second time, Adeline—the woman-girl, the girl-thing—lays her cold fingers on Julia's wrist. Looks up at her. What does Julia feel? Fear, yes—she thinks she might always feel some nerve-twitch of fear around Adeline, and why not? Shouldn't she?

But beyond that there is a simple willingness.

An understanding, too, of next steps: She should petition this age-less thing with whatever treasure she has, and then fucking go on about it. Wait for her uncle to pass out and then find John Varley.

This thing and then the next. Do what needs to be done. Do the thing in front of you.

"Next," Adeline says, "is you promise me."

"Promise you what?" Julia says, though of course she knows.

"Promise me you'll come back."

And the thing is—she will. Living here with Adeline, inevitably disappointing her—just like all these other children have—and then joining the inhabitants of the Museum, starved and wizened and bent with hunger?

If that's her lot and it gets her moving toward Varley, fine.

She'll do all of that and more still.

Christ, she'll even deserve it, won't she? Failing her mother the way she did. Her brother. Failing Aunt Heidi and her grandparents. She'll come back.

But first?

First, she gets to hunt John Varley the way he hunted.

"I promise," Julia says, and when Adeline takes a step toward her, she closes her eyes and waits.

He almost gets hit running across the intersection of Interstate and Lombard, against the light, a car's tires *whish*ing across the ice, Minor's hands in front of his face, lit up in the headlights. Then there's a long, sustained honk and the car fishtails around him, missing him by inches.

Back to Kenton Park, his chest burning. That headache throbbing behind his eyes, legs gone to jelly.

Down the pathway, and the feeling now like the trees are fencing the place in. He sprints toward the playground, heartbeat loud in his ears.

He sees a figure on the swing set, readies himself for conflict with Adeline, imagining what he'll possibly do against her, against those teeth.

But it's not Adeline.

He slows, his footsteps crunching on the snow.

"Julia," he says. His throat's so dry he sounds like a movie monster.

Her coat's been lost somewhere, and she swings with her arms hooked around the chains and crossed in front of her chest. She pushes slowly with one foot, up and back, up and back. If she heard him, she doesn't react.

He walks closer, peels his own jacket off, lays it across her shoulders. Her hair hangs over her face and when she looks up at him, Julia's eyes are like blown pieces of glass—beautiful and glittering and cold.

"Julia. What did you do?"

"Hi, Uncle Duane." She blinks. Licks her lips, looks ahead. "I went inside."

"Where?"

She hooks a thumb over her shoulder and says, "It's a house back there, through those trees. Across the street. It's a lot of houses, all hooked together like a nest. It's kind of hard to look at, like your eyes want to move past it. All the windows are black."

His head won't let him think. She sounds crazed. "You went inside? The Children's Museum?"

"I knocked," she says. She sounds surprised by the fact. "I knocked, and they let me in."

"Did they—did they hurt you?"

"No. Not really."

"Not really?"

"They didn't."

It's the best he can hope for right now. He puts a guiding hand on her back. "Hon, let's go home."

"There's no home, Uncle Duane. We don't have a home."

"Julia—"

"I did it. I made a deal. With Adeline."

In the distance, he hears sounds like gunshots—but no, it's fireworks. Bottle rockets, the pneumatic *whoomph* of bigger explosions, reminding him distractedly of mortar fire, the pause between launch and impact.

He's confused for a moment and then realizes: it's midnight on New Year's Eve.

A new year.

For a moment, Minor's afraid to speak. "You made a deal? What does that mean? That 'life for a life' bullshit?"

"I still want him," she says. "I want to kill him."

And it's then—God, the drunkenness, the fog inside him, the pain in his head—that he notes the shadow beneath her jaw.

"Julia," he says, the terror pooling in him slow and languorous, "what do you mean? What have you done?"

Gently, a surgeon peeling away an old bandage, he lifts the collar of the coat he's put across her shoulders.

Sees the half-moon of puncture wounds at her throat, wounds that are still seeping blood.

June 1977

Eighteen months later

3

BLOOD ON THE GROUND

1

He's finished digging the grave by three A.M.

It's behind the cabin, a messy hole gouged out of the earth. The loam had quickly given way to a hard, reluctant clay studded with stones, and Minor's hands are raw and blistered as he drags the corpse out the back door. The body—what's left of it—is wrapped in a floral comforter, flowers in white and blue and pale pink, that had been resting across the back of the couch. The bloodied sheets and towels have already been thrown in the grave along with sponges and rags, the gloves Minor had worn to clean the fucking horror show as best he could.

Julia stands off to the side, watching as the wind whips her hair like a dark flag. Her face is still caked in blood, and Minor asks her to leave him alone for a bit.

"I can help, though. I can do this faster than you."

"Just go in the house."

The body lies at the lip of the grave, a mounded shape in the dark. Minor stands before it, bent over with his hands on his knees. He's so tired. His hair has grown long, and the clay has turned his arms red up to the elbows.

"I'm sorry, I—"

He closes his eyes. "Julia, just please, go in the house. Alright?"

She walks inside, and Minor's left with himself, the dark, a chorus of frogs doing their business at the edge of the lake beyond. The cabin had had the air of abandonment about it and they had lucked into two nights here unbothered, but an old man came to the door with a key earlier this evening and surprised them. So, yippee, here we are, Minor up to his ass in an ad hoc grave for the past five hours.

His hands are wrecked, and it smells like a chemical factory inside after all the cleaning he's done, with Julia the picture of sudden piety and remorse. *I can help, my ass. You've helped enough, haven't you?*

He wishes he had a light out here, something to see by. The genny, unsurprisingly, was empty of gas. He imagines that's what the old man was doing, coming out here to get the place ready for the season. Maybe he was the owner, planning on fishing the lake a bit before-hand. Minor slaps at a mosquito and pushes the body into the hole atop the rags and sheets and all the rest. The grave is cloaked in shadow and, with Heidi's face in his mind, he stands upright and goes to work filling it.

An hour later, Julia comes out again. Dawn's approaching. She's got that cagey, penned-in look she gets as morning nears, but still she walks to the grave and crouches down. She's cleaned her face, changed her clothes. The hole is half filled and he stands inside it. She rises, puts her hands on her hips. "Duane. Let me help. Please."

"I got it."

"Duane."

He turns his back to her. He rests his chin on the shovel. He thinks distractedly of a drink but doubts he could even lift a whiskey bottle right now, the way his arms ache, how his hands have frozen around the handle of the shovel. "You should go to bed," he says. "It's getting light out."

"I got scared, is all. He just came in."

"I know. It's alright."

She stands there and he gets back to work and sometime later he hears the back door close.

Soon dawn thumbs the horizon, the barest pinks and oranges across the tops of the trees. He finishes around six A.M., and in the morning light the ground looks like exactly what it is: an ugly, churned-up patch of earth that most likely houses a dead body. Obvious to any cop with half a brain that might have cause to wander back there. Scoggins, he's sure, could walk around here blindfolded and recognize it for what it is.

Minor sits cross-legged next to the tamped dirt and looks at his ripped-up, bleeding palms. Watches the sunrise. He dreads going inside that house, but he does, finally, making sure all the doors are locked. The rooms are ticking and still and heavy with death. Everything smells of bleach. He looks at the floor where the old man was killed and that, at least, looks serviceably clean. Lying on the couch, his back nattering at him, he takes the silver-plated Smith & Wesson .38 from his jacket and holds the revolver in his hand for a moment, staring at its form, its blunt utility.

He sets the revolver between the couch cushions and makes sure the Ithaca 12-gauge shotgun rests on the floor beside him, the safety off.

His eyes close and he leans toward sleep.

Eighteen months have passed since Julia went into that strange, many-roomed house beside the park, and the things he's done since in service to finding John Varley, in service to taking care of Julia, well. Safe to say Ed wouldn't be giving him any stern, disappointed looks, were he alive today.

No. Ed and Joanne and his wife, they'd all run screaming. Screaming from both of them. They'd bar the doors and beg for their lives.

And yet, the metronomic nightmares from his time above the Last Call—Vietnam, Lyle and Ferris and the two lumbering specters with glass in their faces—they're gone now. He doesn't understand why.

Maybe now his waking hours are nightmare enough.

He wakes with the taste of ash in his mouth, shards of afternoon sunlight falling through the blinds and bisecting his body. The room is hot and quiet save for the drone of an airplane somewhere high above. He rubs his face, sits up, fishes the revolver from between the cushions. Starts with his daily ablutions, three good things he remembers:

Ed and the way he would gently pat a regular's shoulder as he passed on his way to the office or the back room. Just this gentle touch, this acknowledgment of another person.

Joanne's smoker's cough, rusty and joyous, her hands silently clapping in front of her whenever someone told a particularly dirty joke.

Heidi at the kitchen table, hair pulled up as she sat cross-legged on a chair, making notes in the margins of The Hollow *with a blue Bic pen.*

When he's done with this, his briefest prayer, mooring these people to his heart once again, reminding him why he's here, he unzips the gig bag that rests on the coffee table, takes out the syringe and rubber tubing, lays a trio of glass vials on the tabletop. Carefully gets to work.

Upstairs, in the dark and dust-plumed attic, Julia sleeps.

2

The clear delineations of her life, how it's now divided into thirds. One, there's the world before she came to hunt John Varley, the world before she was turned.

Then the world where she'd lived for a short while with her aunt and uncle in Portland, the months there a pastiche of heartache and sorrow and calmness and, occasionally, a wild and riotous joy.

And before that, the world she'd shared with her mother, her little brother, and her stepdaddy. Upstate New York, this was. Farm country, a small town called Transom.

Ray Ray's real name was Raymond Sikes, and Julia had not minded a single whit when her mother had taken Ray Ray's own pistol and put a .45 round right through his front teeth one night at dinnertime. This happened approximately ten seconds after he'd sent a still-hot cast-iron frying pan sailing toward her mother's head, and Julia had surprised herself with her own readiness, like a part of her had been expecting such a thing from her mother. Julia'd gone so far as to grab the dead man's wrist where he'd fallen on the kitchen floor, blood and brains still dripping in clots off the cabinet doors, ready to drag him out to the backyard, where they might bury his body. After all, Ray Ray Sikes—he insisted everyone call him "Ray Ray," even his boss at the foundry—was prone to catting around, known for being gone days at a time until he came home either broke or drunk or both, and almost always full of the rage a man carried when he deemed there were too many walls in his own poor life, too many people willfully holding him back. They could say he'd gone off, was Julia's thinking, given such a statement could be backed with historical fact. This she'd known even at eleven years old. Hell, the foundry boss had fired him a half dozen times over the years, only to reluctantly hire him again, as it was also true that Ray Ray had a deftness with the foundry molds that few of his co-workers could manage. Point being, it would come as no surprise to anyone, at least for a bit, if the man were to go missing. They could bury him in the soft ground out back, out there at the dog run by the fence, where Ray Ray's two pitties had already run the earth to mud. She and her mom could take turns digging the grave. Just put Little Kev in front of the TV and bury the body, say the shithead had run off somewhere. Easy as that.

Ray Ray had come home the night before drunk, a number of hours after his shift had ended. The family was already asleep. Hammered, talking to himself in the dark, Ray Ray had, it would be discovered in the trial, whacked his shins on the coffee table, hard, and then pitched a fit, throwing the whole table over by the sound of it, glasses and ashtrays and Little Kev's army men all landing on the buckled hardwood floor of their living room. Everything just shattering. Whole house awake by then, the silence pulled into a single, drawn-out moment before Little Kev, the whites of his eyes gleaming in the bed next to hers, had opened his mouth and started wailing.

"Shut that baby up before I shut him up myself," Ray Ray had barked from the living room, his voice guttural, kicking a shard of something across the floor, and Julia had slipped like water from her bed and picked up Little Kev and held him until he hiccuped his little sobs, until those quieted to nothing. Eventually she was able to lay him back down, but Julia herself had a hard time falling asleep afterward. She could hear Ray Ray's snores cutting through the house not even two minutes after he'd stepped inside.

If her momma and him talked at all about it that next day, Julia didn't know. She doubted it—his rages were simply part of their landscape. Like the way the living room floor sagged in the middle, how the pitties barked at all hours on their chains, and how there was a filthy stack of concrete blocks leaning against the side of the house that Ray Ray insisted would eventually be the framework of an outdoor patio. His rage was water and air and sun, just the way of things.

He yelled and threw shit and hit Julia's momma, grabbed the loose skin at the back of her arms and pinched till they bruised. That was the world running its course.

Julia, the next morning after he'd come in, had got herself ready for school, got Little Kev his breakfast so that Momma could take him to Mrs. Martinson's for daycare, and then ran out to the end of their county road to catch the school bus. It was raining and she almost fell in the mud more than once—none of the roads around Transom were paved. The cuffs of her jeans were filthy by the time the bus doors wheezed open. As ever, Melissa McClaren had openly laughed at the state of her clothes and hair, asking how the poor trash was today, as if Melissa herself wasn't wearing her sister's own hand-me-down dungarees with a patch over one knee. Julia bore it all. She sat down and looked out the window. Like sharing a room with her brother, like Ray Ray's rages, what else was there to do? The house was only a certain size, and the school was only a certain size. The town itself. At some point, the way day followed night, she understood she'd need to stomp Melissa McClaren's teeth in, just as a matter of simple survival. But it wouldn't happen that day.

The house when she came home from school sat heavy with silence. The loaded kind, the kind that meant Ray Ray was home, that there were land mines everywhere. The house with Ray Ray hungover and Ray Ray sober, Ray Ray broke and Ray Ray with money, they all had different *feelings* to them, different rules and parameters. Her mom had finished her shift cleaning rooms at the Breeze Inn in town, and Ray Ray was sitting in front of the television in his work coveralls, his socked feet up on the splintery beer barrel that served as his footrest. The TV was on, that black-and-white show where the Nazis were supposed to be goofy and inept. Ray Ray ignored her when she came in, but he was already angry, she could see it in the way his jaw worked, the way he held his bottle of Michelob in a fist tight enough to whiten his knuckles. This was Ray Ray hungover, the most dangerous of his moods. A man just waiting for someone to do or say the wrong thing so that he might luxuriate in that wrongness, and reward it with fury. She could hear the dogs going wild in the backyard. The frenzied barks and the raucous laugh track of the Nazi show were the only sounds in the house.

It happened at dinnertime. Her mother had made tacos, had seasoned the meat in their cast-iron pan, the sound of the knife blade thwacking against the cutting board as she diced tomatoes and lettuce, the shredded cheese in a plastic bowl at her elbow. The four of them had sat at their scarred kitchen table, the clatter of the dogs' chains like background static. Ray Ray was seated at the head of the table, looking over her mother's shoulder so that he might see the television in the other room. The news had been on, Julia remembers that much, and the man on the TV had been talking about the war, his face impassive as a mannequin with a silver bouffant and brown tie. Listing how many American men had died that day, how a bomb had gone off in some city in Vietnam and killed some people, a man on a scooter throwing the bomb into a Saigon bar that American soldiers went to when they were not fighting.

Ray Ray had left his cigarettes on the arm of his recliner.

That was the thing. Going to get his cigarettes in the living room.

He'd risen after he was done eating—he'd been first served and first finished, before everyone, wiping his mouth with a napkin spotted with orange grease. Little Kev was still eating his tacos one ingredient at a time, taking everything apart, and Julia and her mother were quiet, the two of them weighted by the unpredictability in the room. Ray Ray had shambled past them into the living room for his smokes, his footsteps heavy. A moment later they froze, all three of them, Julia with a taco halfway to her mouth, when they heard Ray Ray bark "Fuck!" Shredded cheese and strings of iceberg lettuce tumbled back down onto Julia's plate, she and her mother both half rising in their chairs.

He came limping into the kitchen, eyes glittering, and held up his socked foot for Julia's mother to examine. A small red spot of blood showing through the dark filth of his heel.

"Linda," he said softly, "what the fuck is this?" He seemed genuinely confused, as if he'd never seen blood before, or a sock. The way he said it made it seem as if Julia's mother had attacked him.

"I'm sorry," her mother said, rising fully from her chair now. "I had to sweep fast before my shift this morning, baby, I'll—"

"No," he'd said, a staying hand held out. "Don't bother getting up. Don't fucking worry about it at this point." He left the room.

Julia and her mother had slowly sat down at the table again. Julia was spearing her fallen lettuce with her fork when Ray Ray walked back into the kitchen, put on the oven mitt that hung from a hook above the stove and scooped up the cast-iron pan on the burner—the *care* inherent in that was one of the defense's key points, the consideration and self-preservation involved in not burning his own hand—and hurled it across the room at her mother's head. Everyone screamed, her mother falling to the floor as the pan sailed past her, through the front window and out into the yard. Little Kev sat in his high chair screaming with glass in his hair. The dogs out back barking like mad, Julia on the floor next to her mother, her shoulders covered in little greasy bits of the pan's ground beef. She saw her mother's eyes settle on her own, some unknowable message transmitted there, a message Julia would spend the rest of her life trying to decipher. Then her mother had stood up and stuck a hand into the purse she had hanging off the back of her chair. The hand came out of the purse holding Ray Ray's own Colt .45, the one that he told Julia, drunkenly and often, that he'd killed a dozen NVA with. He had time to say her mother's name exactly once, the word coming out as if he were exasperated with her. He had time to raise his hands, and to back his ass up against the kitchen counter. He had time to have a kind of terrible understanding light up the flat, cruel features of his face, and then Julia's mother shot Ray Ray through the palm of one hand, and through his mouth, and out the back of his head. The kitchen was not large, and the shot was loud. Ray Ray's skull smacked against the cupboard, spilling a considerable amount of brains and blood through the exit wound, and then he fell to the floor, his face colliding against the linoleum, a fall that would have surely knocked his teeth out had they not been shot out already. Little Kev screamed and screamed. The dogs were in an absolute frenzy out back.

Julia had stood up, wiped at the grease spotting her arms and grabbed one of Ray Ray's wrists. She could feel the bristly hairs there as she started pulling on him, the warmth of him as blood seeped out from that ruined head onto the floor. Her mother had said in a surprisingly even voice, "Leave him be, Jules."

"We can take him out back, Momma. Bury him in the dog run."

Her mother squinted at the gun in her hand, took a careful moment to put the safety on before she turned and placed it on top of the refrigerator, among the jars of dill and oregano, next to Little Kev's dented metal lunchbox with the shooting star on the front. Her hands crept to her face, pulled her cheeks down in a rictus as she let out a slow and quaking breath. After a moment she said, in another clear voice, a voice lent with a strength Julia had rarely heard: "Get your coats. You and your brother's." And then: "Kevin Aaron Sikes, you *stop* that crying right now."

"Momma, we got to get rid of him," Julia had said, panic starting to feather her voice.

"We'll do no such thing. Get your coats. I'm calling Mrs. Martinson to have her come pick you up. And then the sheriff."

"You'll go away, though."

Her mother's eyes had settled on her, and here was *another* thing Julia would spend so much of her life trying to figure out: What was it she'd seen in her mother's eyes in that moment? Sorrow? Triumph? *Relief?* Some embittered, whirling mixture of all of them? Whatever it was, her mother had looked at her and then walked over and picked up the phone hanging on the wall.

"Do what I say, Jules. Time is short."

The State of New York awarded Heidi Minor and her husband, Duane, guardianship even before the trial, provided the two of them met HHS guidelines and agreed to regular scheduled visits with a caseworker in Oregon. Little Kev's grandma—Ray Ray's mother—

agreed to take him in, but only him, steadfastly refusing to be involved with Julia at all, in spite of the state's claim of how painful it would be for the children to be separated like that. Particularly for the boy, who at three years old had already had his entire family ripped apart and had seen his mother murder his father. But Ray Ray's momma would not be swayed. "She's no child of mine, that one, and her momma a killer? God would not permit that girl in my home." Julia could understand it—Little Kev was Ray Ray's boy, blood of his blood; Julia's own father was long dead, a car accident when she herself was two years old. So Ray Ray's momma had taken Little Kev down to Gainesville, Florida, which might as well have been Paris for its distance, and that was that. Julia's whole life uprooted. No mother, no father, no brother. Just an aunt she remembered only vaguely from a few childhood Christmases before Ray Ray got his clampdown on things and her momma stopped being allowed friends or family or much else at all.

Paperwork, then, piles of it, and phone calls galore. A week after the murder, she and Heidi had met with a social worker in Buffalo and shared a room in a Best Western off the highway. HHS fast-tracked everything, given the situation, and signed off on her relocation to Portland. The two of them got into Duane Minor's pickup and headed west, Heidi chain-smoking and listening to rock music the whole way. She was trying to put on a brave face for Julia, she could tell, trying to act like they had not mostly been strangers to each other for Julia's entire life. Heidi talked about her Grandpa Ed and her Grandma Joanne, how they couldn't wait to see her again, and her husband, Duane, who was back home working at the bar. Heidi seemed so young compared to Julia's mother, and she felt another flaring burst of anger at Ray Ray, how he had wrung all the joy out of her, made her old when she really wasn't at all. She sat in the passenger seat and watched the highway markers tick past and listened to Heidi talk about college—God, she was in *college;* Julia tried to imagine her mother getting the chance to go to college and simply couldn't. It felt like the world had been pulled from beneath her.

They drove to Portland, and she stayed above the Last Call for five months. Then there was the trial and she and Heidi drove back to New York State in Duane's truck again.

The trial was quick, and at the end of it, Julia's momma was given a life sentence plus one year in Bayonne Women's Correctional.

Julia sat with her aunt in the second row of the courtroom when the sentence came down. It was two women on the jury, the rest of them men. Momma had been given a haircut in the prison that made her look severe and brutal, and with the bags under her eyes and the jumpsuit and the shackles at ankle and wrist, she'd had any softness, any motherliness, carved from her. Maybe she *was* brutal, Julia thought. Her momma was not asked to testify and would not look her daughter in the eye as she was led away, though the judge would have allowed for a goodbye in the hallway if she'd been willing. But her mother had refused. Another thing to consider, to turn over on long nights. This thing like a knife in the chest.

By then, things had changed for her. She had grown comfortable with Ed and Joanne and Heidi and even Duane, which she didn't think would happen. Even when she fucked up, when she let her anger get the best of her, like at school. They talked to her about it. When she fought—and now that she was away from Ray Ray, she found that she was angry all the time, like the anger was allowed, finally, to take root—they still made room for her. There was a part of her that felt guilty for feeling good in Portland. Guilty for even letting the *idea* of *I love you* escape her lips to anyone but her mother or Kevin. But she said it to herself in the bedroom above the bar, imagined, in the dark, saying it to Heidi, to Joanne. To her grandfather, with his cough and his kind eyes and his gray muttonchops. Portland had felt like home. She made some friends at school, in spite of everything. Duane helped her with her math, Heidi with her writing and history. Joanne and Ed took her to see *Jaws* in the theater, gave her popcorn and a giant soda, her first time ever in a movie theater, Heidi looking at them like they were crazy for taking her to it. She'd loved every second.

But after the trial, yeah, after her momma walked away without saying goodbye, she and Heidi had driven back across the country one more time, the last time, and all the songs on the radio had sounded like sad songs.

Two nights after the mistake in the cabin, she and Uncle Duane are parked at the end of a rutted, unpaved county road. A fallow field on one side and a pasture with a trio of black cows on the other. Leaning barbed-wire fences on both sides. Moon like a fist up in the sky, bright and loud. In front of them sits a small farmstead, which time and disrepair have given a wayward lean. There are KEEP OUT signs posted everywhere, and a rusted yellow gate. Not a window in the place that hasn't been boarded up.

"You sure this is it?"

"Yeah," she says. "This is the directions we got."

"But it's not Varley in there."

"Not yet," Julia says. "But we're close."

"How do you know?"

"I just believe it."

Minor looks at the house, rubs his chin with a knuckle. "I don't know, Jules. There's a reason we haven't tried this."

It's true. Two of them after Varley for this many months, with at least one close call where they missed him by minutes, and there are still roads of inquiry they haven't walked down. Ideas they haven't tried. Some ideas have felt too risky—dangerous for Julia, mostly—while others just sang out as batshit desperate, bordering on the nonsensical. This idea falls in the latter category, Minor thinks, but after all this damn weariness, it's too tempting not to at least look into it.

"It's alright," she says. "Wait for me." She opens the glovebox and reaches under the pages of *The Hollow* to remove the gift. She gets out, shuts the door without waiting for Minor's response. Since the Children's Museum, their roles have changed. She feels bad about the old man in the cabin—he truly had surprised her—but she also knows that Uncle Duane has lost his way. He says he still wants re-

venge, but mostly he wants to keep her safe. And her feedings have
bent him crooked, she sees it; busted his heart in a way that neither of
them have been willing to talk about yet. A part of her feels bad for
him, but to her, everything they do is a means to an end. Everything
starts and stops with Varley's death. Every feeding, every night she
prowls in search of him, every question they ask someone, every dol-
lar they put in people's hands—it's all in answer to that.

She puts a hand on the gate and vaults over it, landing neatly on
her feet. Moonlight paints the grass white. The porch is festooned
in junk, tires and waterlogged cardboard boxes and weatherworn
wooden signs with the text faded to ghostliness. She gets one foot
on the porch step when a craggy voice above her says, "That'll do."

Julia steps back and looks up to see a man crouched on the roof,
arms resting on his knees. Sitting up there like a spider. She hears
Uncle Duane's door open, and without turning, still gazing up at the
man, she says, "It's okay." Then: "Hi, I'm looking for a Jim? Cobweb
Jim's the name I was told."

"Fucking stupid name," the man rattles.

"But that's you?"

A moment, and then: "It's me. Didn't pick it as my own, tell you
that much. You get saddled with something like that, nothing you can
do about it. Still gotta live your life."

"Well, I'm Julia."

"Hello," he says, amiably enough, then he rolls his shoulders up
there, resettles. "Who's your man out there in the truck?"

"He's my uncle," she says.

"I can smell him. Smells good."

"I brought you a present," Julia said. "I was hoping you might be
able to give me some information."

"A present?" the man says, and the greedy eagerness there makes
her go cold. She wonders if she sounds like that in her own hunger.
There is the briefest sense of movement, the shingled roof groaning
in protest a bit, and then Cobweb Jim jumps down into the grass be-

hind her, lands with hardly a sound. She turns. "What sort of present, girl?"

The moonlight does him no favors. Sinewy and small, in tan chinos and a white tank top gone gray with age and dirt, Cobweb Jim looks a hard-earned fifty, though how old he actually is she has no clue. A widow's peak of gray hair and knobby elbows. Teeth that met a dentist both infrequently and long ago.

Worst of all, his left arm is a seeping ruin, dripping ichor, and Julia can smell the pus and rot of it from where she's standing. Moonlight plays across the wetness at his shoulder, and threads of black blood run and drip off his elbow; he holds that arm curled against his chest. Beneath the skin, dark threads radiate from the wound, traceries that run the length of his arm up to his neck, beneath the straps of the shirt. Cobweb Jim stares at her half crouched, a mix of shame and defiance on his face.

"I see you looking at me."

"Sorry. It looks bad."

"Fucking silver, is what done it," he says.

"I know," she says, and hands him his gift: a glass vial of Duane Minor's blood.

Cobweb Jim's eyes go wide, and he comes to her quickly, pops the plastic stopper with his thumb and tilts the beaker back to pour the blood into his mouth. His second set of teeth begin to surface and then retract back into the gums.

"Christ, that's good," Jim says. Dips a finger in the tube and puts the finger in his mouth, slurps at it. "Gotta eat twice as much as anyone else and I still feel like shit all the time."

"Who shot you?"

"Oh, some bastard. Said I killed his wife, which, fine, was true. Shot me with a silver bullet, he did, and it went right through the shoulder. Little .22, but it's doing its work anyway, as you can see. I made him pay for it, though." He peers down at the tube, then back up to her. He sighs. "Still, I'm fucked, honey pie. Got the blood-rot."

"When was this?"

"Oh, pretty near a year back. Slow way to go, and it hurts like a pisser. I ain't got long now." He dips his finger into the beaker again, licks it. "Wouldn't mind another one of these."

"It's all we have."

"I don't know if I believe that."

"You know where he got the bullets from?"

"If you know where you might find another one of these," he says, waggling the tube.

"We might have another one. One more."

"Look," Jim says, "there's maybe four, five people in the whole country making silver bullets, and what I hear is we're unlucky enough to have one of the fuckers working out of Fargo, not seventy miles from here."

"I was thinking I ought to put a stop to it," Julia says, the lie easy on her tongue. "So they can't hurt people like us."

"I would be amenable to an idea like that."

"Got any idea where I could find him?"

Cobweb Jim looks at her, plaintive and hungry. Rot's crawling up into his jaw, she notes. The bad-meat stink of him, meat left out in the sun. "Got an *idea*. But you know the saying: Bullshit walks. Pass it over."

The past eighteen months and Adeline's words have come to carry the weight of truth: trying to find John Varley has been like trying to catch the wind with her teeth. He is always ahead of them, or just behind, or around some corner she hadn't known was there. They track him by the bodies he leaves behind. By doorways festooned in crime scene tape and the red-and-blue lights roving across the fronts of buildings, the anguished faces of loved ones held back by policemen, Minor slipping money into folded hands, or Julia holding council with those few like her that she's come across, offering vials of her uncle's blood to get them talking. Two months ago outside of Cheyenne, they saw what turned out later to be his taillights, and once she thinks she saw him—

actually saw him—in the parking lot of a roadhouse twenty miles out-side of Denver. But Adeline was right: they just cannot fucking catch up with him. He winnows past, around, over, beyond. When he's not in a blood-maddened rage, he's damnably crafty and smart. But they're close, they are, and Duane's convinced her that they'll need something if—*when,* she tells herself, *when*—they do find him: bullets. She remembers Frank in the Museum, holding that spoon out in front of him like some kind of talisman. Some totem. How it had kept three dozen blood-starved children at bay. Finally told her uncle about it and his eyes had widened with understanding. *Silver's what we need,* he said. *A silver bullet.*

Ninety minutes after leaving Cobweb Jim, they're parked outside a Fargo bar. Lester's, it's called, the name done up in red neon in the window. Uncle Duane, she knows, is still upset with her about the old man in the cabin. He's smoking a cigarette, watching the street with eyes that never rest. He's tired. She doesn't think he's gotten a good night's sleep in a long time. Certainly not since they started all this. She can smell his sweat, the pus and watery blood from the blisters on his hands. He's showered since filling the grave, but she can still smell traces of clay beneath his nails.

Duane is angry at himself too, she knows, because he tried to drive the old man's truck into the lake this afternoon and it didn't work. Just sat there, half submerged. It will draw far more attention now than if he'd just left it alone in the driveway. A fucking idiot, he calls himself. Fargo, he says, is too close to all that. They should be run-ning, hiding out. But the promise of bullets is too tempting.

He stubs out his cigarette in the ashtray. Ties his long hair back with a rubber band. Julia flexes her own hands, closes them. The moon up above feels like a song in her blood. This kick drum that strides up her backbone, knocks deliciously against every vertebra.

"Travis is his name?"

"That's what he said. Jim said he likes those shirts, I guess, with the big collars. Gray hair."

"Jim," he says bitterly. "Jesus."

"I believe him."

"Just stay here," Duane says. A few people are standing outside the bar, smoking. She watches them, hears the throb and snarl of music through the bar's windows. A woman tilts her head to the sky and laughs. Playfully slaps a man on the shoulder, who smiles and slinks his arm around her waist. The place makes her think of the Last Call, her grandma working in her office downstairs, and Julia looks away.

"I'll be back in a minute," Duane says. "Don't talk to anybody. Don't get out of the truck."

"Okay."

"I'm serious."

Moon on her skin like a song. Like a hand gripping her.

Cobweb Jim saying, *I ain't got long.*

And the look on the old man's face in that cabin, the last drawn-out moment *before.* Before she had bent her mouth to his throat, before that second set of teeth had pushed from her gums. The wonder of it. The fear. She thinks of Ray Ray holding up his foot with its little dot of blood. *Linda, what the fuck is this?*

How some secret part of her—a part that Julia herself hardly dares rifle through, a part she will never ever tell her uncle about, never ever, nor anyone else—thrills at it every time. What she saw in that old man's eyes, what she always sees. In that second before.

It's terror.

Because of *her.*

She thinks of Ray Ray every time she eats.

Her uncle steps out, crosses the street.

3

ester's is like every bar he's ever been in. Smoke and noise, the press of bodies. The slight give in the floor, the luxuriating stink of cigarettes and spilled beer. There's been a handful of times that he's allowed himself to drink since Julia's turning; most days he's sober and misses it like hell, misses places like this.

He walks up to the bar, catches the eye of the bartender, a tough old boy with muscles and a widow's peak, dark curls touching his shoulders. The flattened nose of a brawler. Minor orders a soda, drops cash on the bar. He thinks of that man on the roof, the wet black ruin of his arm. Minor with his little bandage in the crook of his elbow now, his blood a currency among the circles they run in. Christ in heaven.

How Julia most times can't even be in the room when he does it. The temptation too great for her.

"I'm looking for a Travis," Minor says when the bartender returns with his drink.

"Okay," the man says. "You got an appointment?"

"No. Just dropping by."

"What do you want to see him for?"

"Silver," Minor says.

The bartender nods for a moment, as if Minor has said something particularly interesting, then reaches under the rail and takes out a .45, rests it on the bar, the barrel pointed at him, his finger inside the trigger guard. Minor's hands drift up toward his ears.

"Hey, now—"

The bartender pushes a handheld mirror across the bar. "Why don't you take a look, friend."

Minor does it. Sees only his own terrified, exhausted face looking back at him. Pushes the mirror across the wood.

"Alright," the bartender says, "you mind if I frisk you?"

"Suppose not."

The bartender comes around, makes a show of giving him a pat-down, the other patrons not blinking an eye. Minor wondering, not for the first time, how such a thing becomes commonplace in some circles. How folks like Varley and Julia striding the earth becomes a thing you just accept. Minor's left the revolver in the truck, figuring this exact thing would happen, and when the bartender comes up empty, he slaps Minor on the back and tells him it'll cost fifty bucks to see Travis. Minor digs out his wallet again.

"Wait here," the bartender says, making his way to a back room, past a pair of guys playing eight ball. The ghost of the Last Call stands up all around him, clattering its chains. Every bar he's been in—and he's curried information in a lot of them the past year and a half—feels comfortable and well-worn and also reminds him how damnably far he is from any sort of home. How badly he's failed his people.

The bartender comes out after a few minutes, hooks a thumb over his shoulder. "He's in the back, just go on in."

Minor makes his way to the back office, a room so similar to Joanne's that he once again feels that throb of homesickness. There's a guy sitting behind a felted desk, thumbing through a stack of papers. Tan, gray helmet of hair, big walrus mustache. Maybe fifty, maybe sixty. Indeed wearing a plum-colored button-up shirt with one of those giant collars. Glass ashtray at his elbow.

"You Travis?"

"I am."

"I heard you might be able to help me out with something."

"I bet I can, yeah. Why don't you tell me what it is you're looking for."

"Silver bullets that fit a .38."

He frowns a bit, nods once. "Well, alright, then. I got you covered. It's a cash operation, though."

"I figured so. How many can you get me?"

"For a .38? Let's see. Half a dozen."

Minor wishes for ten times that, a hundred, but also knows he's lucky to find any at all. He sends a silent prayer of gratitude to dying, unwitting Cobweb Jim. "That'll work. How much?"

Travis then states a sum so outrageous that Minor's jaw nearly drops open. Any goodwill that might have been blossoming between the two men is snipped as cleanly as someone cutting a det cord.

"Brother, that's fucking highway robbery."

Travis shrugs. "Try finding another silver bullet anywhere in a thousand miles."

"I could buy my own forge, cast my own shit for that much."

"Well, you're welcome to do it."

And that's that. Even when it comes to things like death, like vengeance, it's money does the heavy lifting.

Minor opens up his wallet and passes a sheaf of bills across the desk. Leaving him and Julia with jack shit financially, but there's the hope in the back of his mind that they're almost done with all this anyway. Always this idea, vague as smoke, that there'll be some sort of life available to him after all this.

Travis compounds the insult by counting the money right in front of him. Then he opens a drawer in his desk and reaches in. Sets a handful of bullets clattering on the desktop. Minor picks them up. Each one's heavy as hell.

"These are hand-cast?"

"They are," Travis says. "Do it myself."

"What happens if they don't fire?"

"First of all, that's rude. Second of all, they will."

"Well, what if they don't, is what I'm asking you."

"What do you mean, what if they don't? If you're using them for their intended purpose and they don't fire? You're probably shit out of luck. Probably be dead shortly thereafter. Part of why the price is so high is that guarantee of professionalism."

Minor puts the bullets in his jacket pocket. "Alright. You got a pay phone here?"

Travis lifts his chin toward the door of his office. "Around the corner, by the bathrooms."

In the hall, Minor finds a cigarette machine by the pay phone and drops his quarters in. Smacks the new pack of Winstons against the back of his hand, peels off the cellophane and lights up. Then he dumps money in the pay phone and dials Bobby's number by heart.

It's early in Portland still, and Minor figures that Bobby's at one bar or another. Usually it's just the act of making these calls that soothes him, and he hangs up before anyone answers. Just an anchor to his old life. But this time, Bobby's old man, Ian, picks up right away, surprises him.

"Hello?"

"Hey, Ian," he says.

A pause. "Yeah?"

"It's Duane. Uh, I was hoping Bobby was home."

Another beat, and then: "*Duane?* Holy shit, hold on."

A rustling, murmured voices, and then, Bobby: "Duane Minor? For real?"

"Hey, bud."

"Jesus, Duane. I can't believe it. What's going on? You okay?"

Minor smiles, looks out at the bar. "Sure."

"I mean, for real?"

"Yeah, man. I'm just calling to see how things are."

Bobby lets out a laugh, sounding a little like his old self. "How things *are?*"

"Yeah."

"Well, if I had to say, things are royally fucked, brother. Let's see. Last Call's now named, what is it? *Lucky's.* Building got sold a while back. It's like a, a cowboy bar now. You believe it?"

"Still a bar, though?"

"Still a bar, yeah, but it's fucking corny, you know? Everything Joanne and Ed worked for, pissed away. Me and Ian don't go there, that's for sure."

"That's alright," Minor says, but of course it isn't. The bar is gone, the apartment's gone, everything upended. He sees in his mind Cobweb Jim lifting a vial of his blood to his lips like a ghoul.

How is there any way this ends right?

"Yeah, well," Bobby says, "tell that to that detective."

"Who? Scoggins?"

"Yeah, Scoggins. Been up *all* of our asses since you took off. Coming into my work, bugging the guys at their new spots. You know he's got a warrant out for you?"

Minor doesn't know anything, but he says, "I imagine so, yeah."

"Kidnapping, for one. You believe that shit?" A pause, where he can hear Bobby inhale his smoke. Softer, he says, "I think they might want you for the murders, Duane."

Maybe so, but he can't imagine making it this long in the world, running around for the past year and a half, if they'd pinned a triple homicide on him. Every highway patrolman and bartender and convenience store clerk would be looking at his wanted poster, wouldn't they? And it seems a stretch, given how buddy-buddy Scoggins had been with him. But who could say. Minor doesn't know anything.

"Maybe he just wants to talk," he says.

"I don't think you're hearing me," Bobby says. "He's roughing guys up. Putting some weight on them."

"Alright. I'll give him a call."

"Well, I didn't say *that*, brother. Just be aware. Keep your head on."

"No, it's alright." Thinks of Scoggins's card in his wallet.

"Just saying, Duane, year and a half's a long time for a cop to keep sweating people. I think you're his white whale."

"One that got away, huh?"

"Something like that."

"Well, thanks, Bobby. I appreciate it."

"Of course," he says, and then, "Listen, Duane. You ever think about coming back? Straightening all this out?" He coughs, embarrassed. "They buried—they buried Heidi and her folks in Lone Fir. Turned out Joanne had the plots already paid up and everything. Me and Ian go there, say hi."

"That's good," he says, a wave of weakness moving through him. Everything just too much. *Name three things,* he thinks. *Name three things you remember about her, and keep her alive that way.*

"So you coming back, brother?"

"Not yet," he says. "I still got to do some stuff."

Another pause, and then Bobby says, almost plaintively, "Jesus, Duane. I mean, at this point, what's left? What's out there that still needs doing?"

4

"You know we'll have to take care of that man at some point. The one you told me about."

"I know it."

"Things are complicated enough, John. If we're really doing Alaska—"

"One thing at a time," Varley says. "We do the thing in front of us. Duane Minor's not here right now. I'm not even sure he's after us, truth be told."

"He is," Johan says. "*Someone* is. I can feel it. Can't you feel it?"

After a moment, Varley says, "I can."

The two of them in the van, waiting. The windows are open, and the smell of grass is in the air, a scent so synonymous with his boyhood, his life before being turned, that Varley is held fast in one of those diamond-rare surges of nostalgia. Crickets chirp in the dusty fields beyond the barn, the moon up in the sky like a curved blade. It's late evening but still explosively hot, yet Johan lies in the back of the van beneath a blanket, insistent on wearing that leopard-spotted greatcoat. Ninety degrees out, sweating his ass off, one hand curled around a cut-down Mossberg 10-gauge, and still wearing the thing. Varley smiles in the dark, moved as ever by his love's peculiarities.

The van, a bright orange VW with a white canopy, is parked snug up beside the splintering wall of an abandoned barn some five miles north of Sioux Falls, South Dakota. Rusted tractor parts rise like revenants from the fields of knee-high grass all around them. A star-salted night, the flitter of bats overhead. Johan's eyeball-deep in a cocaine high and practically vibrating back there. He cut his hair last month in a gas station bathroom, convinced the Colombians were about to turn on them, and now looks like a dangerous and emaciated child. Varley finds it thrilling, the way he and the boy have let loose their respective madnesses; ever since that night at the rest stop, Johan has matched him in ferocity, in passion. Varley, before Johan, had never truly considered letting love take root inside him. There has been no shortage of men and women throughout his life, short-lived as such trysts might have been, but what has happened between them has been different from the beginning. If he does not love Johan, it is something parked near enough to love that he may as well use the word. They've shared beds—so much so that Varley has let Johan lay curled next to him during his day-sleep, at his most vulnerable, his closest to a true death—and he has listened to the boy's every horror, every atrocity he's ever committed. Varley, if anything, has held tighter to him. Bound at the heart, the two of them, and by their shared and simple joy at the matter of killing.

A whole world he never imagined possible, and it's opened up in front of him.

Now Johan giggles, drums his bootheels against the floor of the van; both the stock and barrel of the shotgun have been sawed down so close that Varley's warned him the kickback might break his finger when he pulls the trigger. The thing's loaded with buckshot, and Johan's placed a wager—a wager so carnal that Varley grows heated just thinking about it—that he'll actually cut a man in half when he fires the thing.

Five minutes later, headlights spear the long driveway off the county road, make their way toward the barn and its nearby house, dark and hulking and in a similar state of disrepair. There's no short-age of unused, forgotten places out here, and for people like Varley and Johan, these dead spaces are their nesting grounds.

"Alright," Varley says, "he's coming. Get your head on, boy. Get ready."

Johan drums on the stock of the Mossberg. "Shit, I was born ready."

The car comes to a slow stop some twenty feet away, dust clouding the headlights and then settling. The headlights flash twice and then turn off. It's a dark blue sedan that anyone with half a brain could pin as an unmarked UC ride, and Varley says, "If you do have to fire that thing, remember to aim to the left."

"My left or your left?" says Johan.

"Goddamnit, Johan—"

"John, I'm kidding," he says, drawing out the last word, and Varley steps out, shuts the door behind him.

Doug McCoy steps out of the sedan. A man they are almost sure is an undercover officer, likely with the South Dakota State Police; he's been buying cocaine from Varley and Johan for nearly four months now, since Varley had done what he's always done—found a market and ingratiated himself into it by force. He'd come across a fellow by the name of Moonbeam in a Sioux Falls bar, a nineteen-year-old hippie whose entrepreneurial visions had led him to making the leap from dealing hash to cocaine. Moonbeam was low-tier, an ambitious street-runner, but over one torturous, blood-spattered night in the basement of an abandoned farmhouse outside town—not far from where they were right now, actually—Moonbeam had spilled his guts. Literally and otherwise. Told them everything about the Colombians he bought his cocaine from, who to reach out to, who might balk at Varley's intrusion. Boy didn't know everything but he knew enough to get them started. The Colombians had been reluctant at first, but they also admired Varley's fearlessness; one of the cartel members had stuck a revolver in his mouth at their first meeting and Varley had pretended to chew on the barrel, laughing while he did it. (He hadn't brought Johan along to that meeting—too fearful of the boy catching an errant bullet if things went to shit.) Six months ago, this had been, and Varley started buying street-weight first, picking up Moonbeam's runs while continually pressing the Colombians to sell him more. He needn't have worried: Johan, turned out, knew how to sell dope. He was affable and fast and paid attention.

The Colombians started selling Varley more weight—word got out that he had killed Moonbeam to take his spot in the roster, and this, too, earned him points with the cartel—and he rented an apartment near the university, where he and Johan did brisk business. It was at that apartment on Western Avenue that McCoy and another cop came to do a buy. Johan had picked the two of them out right away as undercover, and Varley wondered if they were on to him about Moonbeam's death. The woman wore a strawberry-blond wig and go-go boots. The man did most of the talking.

You got a light? Oh, never mind, I got one had been Johan's signal to Varley, and when he heard Johan say it, he stepped out of the bedroom, within a hair's-breadth of letting his teeth rise, ready to do grievous harm to whoever was there.

But he found everything in order. Johan was sitting on the couch. There was a man in his mid-forties in bell-bottoms and a corduroy vest with his legs splayed on their loveseat, the redhead in her big white boots sitting on the armrest, playing with her hair. Varley understood: Johan wanted him to see whatever this was.

They bought a bag; the man—Doug, he said his name was—paid in small bills. At the doorway, he turned, asked if they could come back and buy again.

"You bring cash," Varley said, "you can come back anytime."

They left and Johan lit a cigarette and rubbed at a spot on his coat. "Those two were cops, I think, John."

"How do you know?"

"They felt like play-actors. At least the man did. And he was too old."

Varley had smelled the fear on the man and the woman both, but that didn't mean much; most people were afraid when they came into the apartment. "It doesn't matter," he said. "We own the world."

A little snort of derision. "Oh, do we?"

Varley sat down next to him, put his hand on Johan's thigh. "What's the matter?"

Johan looked at the television sitting on an apple crate across the room. It was turned off, and he looked stiff as a statue in its gray curvature, Varley's head and hands in its reflection a wavering nothingness. Johan said, "Tell me, what happens if you get shot?"

He knew where this was going and cursed himself for walking into it like a fucking dunce. Johan waited for him to answer until Varley said, "It goes through me, or it lodges in there and then gets pushed out after a minute."

"Right," Johan said, blowing a trio of smoke rings before exhaling. "Then what?"

"What do you mean?"

"What happens after that?"

"I heal."

"Right. You heal." He ashed his cigarette and then turned to him, but not before gingerly removing Varley's hand from his lap. "Do you know what happens if a bullet hits *me*, John? If those cops had shot me, or if the Colombians do, or if someone breaks in, tries to rip us off?"

"Johan—"

"A bullet doesn't get fucking pushed out of me, John, that's for sure."

"No, I know."

"Tell me the truth. Can you fly? Climb up walls? Turn into a bat?"

"No," Varley said, laughing a little until he saw Johan's face. "It's not like that. I can do some things, because I was turned by a Maker. But I can't lift my cloak and disappear in a puff of smoke. Nothing like that."

"I'm just saying, there's a world of difference between what you can do to protect yourself and what I can do."

"I know."

Johan made a strangled sound, a bewildered, frustrated kind of laugh. "You're going to make me fucking sing it out for you, aren't you?"

"Spell it out," Varley said, knowing he was being a fool.

"What?"

"You mean spell it out, not sing it out."

"Oh, fuck off," Johan said wearily. He opened the drawer in their coffee table and lifted the panel where they hid their baggies. It was empty and he stood up, walked to the bathroom, where they had hidden the rest of the cocaine in a hollowed-out space beneath the sink.

"You want me to turn you," Varley said from the couch. "That's it, isn't it?"

Johan peered out from the bathroom, his face a complicated mask of fury and helplessness. "I want you to *protect* me."

"I do. I will."

"I'm the one in the front room, making the deals. Looking cops in the face, nodding and smiling along to every fuckup imaginable."

"You're the one that told me to stay in the back room, Johan."

"Yes," he said, throwing his arms out. "Because you scare the shit out of people."

"Then what are we arguing about?"

"I'll come out and say it, then, John. Since I have to, apparently. *When* will you turn me?"

The same wall they always came to.

The same door Varley was unwilling to open.

What's mine is mine, he thought. Unable to help himself. This knot of selfishness inside him.

Johan saw the look on his face and turned away in disgust. Slammed the bathroom door.

"Alaska," he called out. "I'll turn you in Alaska." But if Johan heard him, he didn't respond.

Doug had come back three days later, alone. He doubled his first purchase. Varley knew that Johan was right; the guy was playing dress-up. He wondered, if he ripped Doug's shirt open, if he might find a microphone taped to his chest. But they sold to him anyway; Varley, still wounded a bit by what Johan had said, was tossing away any idea of caution. Always at the mercy of his own desire to test the edge of whatever thing the world put in front of him. Within the month, Doug was a regular. Buying from them two, three times a week. Staying for a bit here and there, occasionally throwing out feelers as to who their dealers were, the months moving along, and all the while Varley was buying more coke from the Colombians, putting together a nice nest egg for Alaska. Finally, Doug sat on their couch and did his pitch, the pitch that both Johan and Varley knew was inevitable. It was either the pitch, they knew, or they'd have a dozen Sioux Fall cops raiding the apartment. But Varley knew the cops wouldn't necessarily want him and Johan—no, they'd want the big fish. They'd want the Colombians. *Fellas, I want to buy some big weight* was what Doug had said, and Varley's plan had fallen into place.

Varley had agreed, and agreed further to meet Doug the following week; he had used the cred he'd built up with the Colombians to call a meeting with them at the apartment. He was cashing in his chips, wanting to make a big buy. The Colombians agreed to give him fifteen kilos. Six men came to deliver, to make sure nothing was off, all of them and Varley crowding into that one-bedroom place off Western Ave.

He ran through them quick.

Limbs bouncing off the walls, bodies leaving mad splashes of blood like an artist signing a painting with a flourish, gunfire loud in the small living room, Varley feeding so much—emptying out three bodies after everything had stopped—that he'd regurgitated hot blood all over the carpet, a first in all his long life. Johan had been at a bar down the street and Varley had washed his face at the kitchen sink, knowing he only had a minute before the police arrived, if that. He stuffed the cocaine into a suitcase, put the money he'd saved in a grocery bag that he shoved in next to the coke, and pounded down the stairs and out onto the street, trembling with the power of it all, the joy of it.

Varley imagines the news of the dead Colombians has gotten back to Doug McCoy and the State Police by now, but he hadn't batted an eye when Varley had called him to change the meeting place from the apartment to this run-down, desolate farmstead outside of town. Varley knows that he's pressing things—the Colombians will want retribution, the Staties will be looking for the two of them, almost assuredly the feds will get involved, and there are the pressing rumors he's heard that *someone else* is looking for them as well, a man and a dark-haired girl—and he's got a damn good idea who *that* might be, doesn't he?

And yet.

And yet up until now, he and Johan have experienced an astonishing stretch of good luck out here on the plains. With the money they've saved, and the cocaine in the back of the van, Alaska's become a very real possibility. Depending on the season, there can be twenty hours of night there or more. He's come to realize, come to loathe, how that bone-simple act of nature—the fucking sunrise—serves as the flashpoint for so much terror in his life. What a relief it would be, a near-permanent night.

So, that's the tentative plan—sell this coke to this cop and take the highway up to northern Alaska, where their money will walk far and he doesn't need to live in nightly fear of the coming dawn.

McCoy's overweight, balding, with a thin red mustache. Tonight he's wearing dungarees and flip-flops and a loose, diamond-patterned button-up. No weapon that Varley can see, but he might have a holster at his back. He ambles over and they shake hands; the man's palm is lathered in sweat.

"How's things going, my man?" McCoy says, his eyes bouncing around. Everything about him vibing nervous, on edge.

"Alright," Varley says. "Thanks for the switch-up. The apartment just got too hot. Felt like cops were right around the corner." If McCoy reacts to that, Varley will take his head from his shoulders and they'll run.

But he doesn't. "No problem," he says, not a blink, not an eye-twitch, and for a moment Varley doubts everything. And then the smell hits him.

Fear-sweat, hot and oily, a fug that springs up at McCoy's hairline and armpits, intoxicating in its intensity.

"Where's your buddy?"

"Oh, he had to stay back. Is that the cash?" says Varley, pointing at the leather bag that McCoy's holding.

"It is. Do you have the cocaine?"

The formality snags at him. *Do you have the cocaine.* Like McCoy's reading from a script.

"Yeah, it's in the back of the van. Can you help me carry it to the car?"

"Yeah, what the hell," McCoy says, and they walk over to the back of the VW. He hears the sound of crickets, the dry grass against their legs. Varley pulls the rear door up. The coke is right there, fifteen packages of plastic and brown tape.

McCoy's eyes go wide. He sets the leather bag down next to the pyramid of dope and scratches the back of his head. "Damn," he says. "There it is, right in front of me. Fifteen kilos of coke."

Everything falls in line then: McCoy *naming* everything. Scratching the back of his head—a signal. The fear-stink on him so bright this time compared to others.

It's a setup.

Of course they fucking know about the apartment.

He spins around, sees a dozen flashlights roving toward them from the tree line in the distance, a string of headlights coming in fast from the county road.

"Johan," Varley says, and the boy rises from his blanket behind the stack of cocaine and a point-blank load of buckshot chews Doug McCoy's head and shoulders into a churned cloud of red meat; he flies backward, losing a flip-flop, dead before he hits the ground. Varley's face is peppered with shot and a decent backspray of McCoy's blood. The men with flashlights begin screaming at them across the distance, calling out. The first gunshot zings past. Varley bends, rips open McCoy's sopping shirt. Sees the microphone taped to his chest.

He runs to the driver's seat at a crouch, lead pellets from the buck-shot round pinging as they fall out of his face onto the floorboards, the wounds healing, more gunshots zipping through the dark. Red and blue lights begin trundling toward them on the road. He keys the ignition, jams on the gas, the van fishtailing in the dust.

Past the barn, away from the lights, Johan crying out and laughing as he bounces around in the back, scrabbling to keep the packages of cocaine from falling out the open hatch. Varley hits a gravel road and sees a State Police cruiser blocking his way. He veers into the ditch, clips the cruiser's bumper and keeps going. Johan fires another round from the Mossberg and howls with joy.

Varley grins and runs a hand down his face, clears McCoy's blood from his eyes. There's a fork in the road and he spins the wheel, turns left; they'll go to Sioux Falls, get a new ride, get the fuck out of the state; they're right at the edge of Minnesota, Iowa. Johan's just evapo-rated McCoy's skull into paste. Whatever branch of law enforcement he was with, every cop in the state will be looking for them. But if they can get out of *this spot,* escape this phalanx of cops after them, they'll be alright. They own the world.

"You got that money back there? The cop's money?"

"Bet your ass."

"Open it."

"It's full, John. We're fucking rich."

"Alright," Varley says over the sound of the wind, the scream of the van's engine. "Dump the cocaine."

"What?"

"Do it."

"John—"

"Dump it. We've got the money, we're traveling light."

He peers in the sideview mirror. There's no way they'll make it to Sioux Falls in this van; those trouble lights are getting closer. He counts three, four patrol cars gaining on them.

The world narrows, and then it narrows some more.

Johan dumps the coke, package after package tumbling and bouncing onto the road.

In spite of it all, some part of Varley remains light, buoyant. He turns the headlights off, spins the van down a long dirt side road, aiming for the cutout shapes of the low-rising hillsides in his windshield, and, closer, the smattering of lightless houses, those dead spaces, those forgotten, cast-off buildings where he and his might find some measure of safety, if only momentarily.

5

The Last Call had been dim and quiet, just a few regulars, the overhead fans pushing warm air through the room. It was August of 1972, and Minor had come downstairs to the bar to grab a cup of coffee to try and wake himself up. He and Heidi had just come back from an afternoon at Morrow Lake, and Minor was suffused with that gentle, lovely weariness that comes after spending a day in the sun. He was drowsy, a little horny, a little stoned, and beyond that felt young and at least mildly invincible. He was twenty-one years old and recently married; Heidi's parents had given the two of them run of the upstairs apartment earlier that year, and he had little in the way of obligation. Life felt abundant, simple, chock-full of countless riches.

"Duane," Ed said, sipping his cup of coffee and looking down at the crossword in *The Oregonian*. "You got some mail in the office."

"Okay, thanks." Minor filled a mug of coffee behind the bar, nodded at a couple of the old boys in their usual spots at the rail. He was thinking about what he'd do when he went upstairs—there was another six-pack of Miller in the fridge; he imagined he and Heidi would drink a few beers and listen to records. Maybe he could sweet-talk her into bed.

He found his draft letter sitting on top of Joanne's desk.

The office was warm, painted with deep shadows, and Minor dropped the letter like it was on fire. He knew what it was without opening it.

"I thought of pitching it," Ed said, standing in the doorway of the office with his cup, looking unhappy. "But, you know, that wouldn't do you any good."

"Yeah, no," Minor said, the words sounding like they were coming from far away. "I hear you."

"I'm sorry, Duane. It's a hell of a thing."

"Thank you," he said, looking down at the letter, not knowing what other words fit something like this. It was what it was, and standing there with sand still dusting the tops of his feet and the smell of the lake on him, he felt stupid for not expecting it sooner. For thinking he might be impervious to it. That blinding ability of youth, figuring shit will happen to everyone but you.

The night before he was scheduled to report to the recruitment center, from which he and other local draftees would be bussed to Fort Lewis for basic training, he and Heidi sat cross-legged on the couch, smoking grass and listening to blues albums. It was late. They'd waited until the bar was closed and everyone had gone home—Joanne had been known to clomp up the stairwell and give them a scorching look if she smelled weed while they had customers. It was September now, and moths hung resolutely on the window screens, hoping against hope for entrance. The only light in the room came from the standing lamp in the corner that Heidi had covered with a thin orange scarf. She alternated between little pulls of the joint pinched between her fingers and wiping tears away from her reddened eyes. Minor could feel the pilled fabric of the couch cushions against his back. He tried to focus on the music. Summer was still pounding on the door of this part of the world, and neither of them were wearing shirts.

"I just don't even know, man," Heidi said, and Minor smiled wanly, nodding. To him, the whole thing had taken on an air of inevitability. The draft was the draft. America had flung itself into a war and they needed people to shoot the guns. What the hell could you do about it? He hadn't petitioned the draft board for exemption, hadn't gobbled a bunch of crosstops and stayed up for three days and carved swastikas into his forearms in an attempt to be labeled unfit. Nixon had signed legislation the year before to supposedly end the draft, but that machine just kept churning along. Like Minor was in a car and oncoming headlights were filling the windshield. Heidi said it again, "I just don't even know," and Minor put a hand on her warm knee. It had been her refrain for weeks now, coupled with the same few desperate questions:

What if you don't go?

Then I get a warrant for my arrest. Go up before a judge, who probably calls me a hippie and a draft dodger, and I either get a jail sentence or get sent anyway.

What if you go to Canada?

Are you ready to go to Canada, Heidi? Because we can't come back if I go. We can't come back here.

She was getting ready to start writing *The Hollow,* her novel. She was studying up on it, going to the historical museum on her time off, coming back with stacks of mimeographs, books from the library. She was so excited. She had her friends here, her parents. A life. The whole goddamn world was spreading its arms wide before her.

Can you stay on a base where it's safe? Do you get to pick where you go?

No, baby. I go where they say.

It was possible he'd be placed in an infantry unit, but if he was lucky, he'd get a motor pool job, clerking, something on an FOB somewhere. And there would be time Stateside before and after his tour. Still: those headlights were coming. You could try to scream it away, but the road between you and that other car would shrink down to nothing no matter what you did.

The record ended and Heidi got up to flip it. He looked at the shadows of her back, the ridges of muscle there. Incense and dope clouded the room, seemed substantial enough to swim in. Minor did not want the night to have the quality of a funeral. He didn't feel solemn about it, not really. He felt sorry for Heidi, for her anguish, her fear. But she had her parents and school and her friends. Her writing. She put the needle on the record and sat down next to him, putting the last little bit of roach between his lips. Minor puffed dutifully as the record popped before settling into its groove.

"It'll be cool," he said, the hiss of the joint as he scrubbed it out in the tin lid of the ashtray. Moths still banging against the screen. "It'll be okay." Heidi leaned her head on his shoulder.

"I don't know, Duane," she said. "It's not fair. Those people didn't even do anything to us."

"We're fighting Communists, I guess. Way you hear guys talk about it, you either keep them out of South Vietnam or they'll be, I don't know, planting rice paddies along the Willamette."

"Yeah, right."

"I guess we just wait and see," he said.

Months later he would be stunned at the grand luxury of such a thought. That he'd had enough breathing room in his life to say something so fucking dumb.

He lost fifteen pounds in basic, and he wasn't a heavy cat to begin with. Hardly slept. Learned how to run with a forty-pound rucksack on his back. His fear grew in larger and larger increments as his drill instructors ratcheted up the terror, filling the recruits' heads with all the great and varied ways in which they would likely die. Drills and drills and drills, days of them, and then sometimes the DIs would wake them at one, two, three A.M., screaming and kicking their bunks, ordering them to fall out lest they wind up in some muddy forgotten grave with their buddy's blood in their eyes. Mortars were coming, they screamed. VC had gotten under the wire, come to slit their cocks off and dry them for necklaces. On and on it went. Eight weeks.

When Minor finally stepped up the ramp of that big Boeing transport plane, heading to Saigon to be assigned to his division, he was grateful to be done with this part, to at least be done with men screaming at him.

Again, just the grand stupidity of an assumption like that.

He was indeed placed in an infantry unit, and did his thirteen months in-country. Long stretches of boredom and discomfort punctuated with ball-puckering terror. The *zip* of tracers, snipers taking endless shots at them over fence lines, wiping mud out of your rations while on patrol. That idea that danger was always right there, arched across the span of the next second, the next curve in the path. Life narrowing down to the sweating neck of the grunt in front of you, to the warm beer you got in your bunk before crashing. Dripping trees, snakes, foot-rot, insects of every imaginable variety, the *foomph* of a mortar and that pregnant stretch of silence before it landed. Lyle getting his jaw shot off. Another guy, McFarland, this guy from Tennessee they had carrying The Pig, the M60, he was on guard duty the night after Lyle got shot. McFarland caught a sniper round, this time in the guts, and died two days later, and everyone went apeshit.

The brass mortared the living shit out of the perimeter in response, called in F-100s to crisscross the trees beyond the base with lines of napalm. Some of the boys took to writing Lyle's name on their helmets, or McFarland's, and they were sent out in search-and-destroy squads past the wire in the middle of the night to find the sniper, find any VC at all. Napalm smoke still rising into the sky, little stinking pockets of fire still on the ground; it made your throat close up tight if you smelled the smoke. They didn't find anyone, of course. Only thing that happened was one grunt stepped in a hole and got a heel full of punji spikes smeared with shit and they had to haul him back behind the wire bucking and cursing. Command put a halt to the S&D teams but kept up the mortaring, the napalm. It went on and on like that. Fear and outrage at war with each other and blooming into big flaming trees inside his body.

Everybody was afraid. Guys had different ways of dealing with it. Minor was not creative in his quelling of the fear; he savored the small normalcies that Vietnam offered—beer, cigarettes, music in the bunks, fellowship of other young men who had seen and done insane, terrible shit. And of course he held ferociously tight to Heidi. To her as a person, to her as a body, to what she represented when he came home. To the idea that he would not be too altered, physically or otherwise. Minor wrote her letters, and she wrote back dutifully, even when she attended the occasional antiwar protest with friends from class. She was open about it, and while Minor was initially pissed—everyone in the world seemed to think what he was doing here was shameful, even after he'd been fucking drafted—he eventually realized that if he'd had the opportunity, he probably would've done the same. These two things—this understanding that he was here, there was no way out of it, that he just needed to finish the days to make it the fuck home, and that Heidi was there waiting for him—these were the buoys that lifted him across the unknown waters of that endless year.

When he finally went home, from the FOB to the Tan Son Nhut Air Base down south, then to Germany, then JFK, then Dallas and finally PDX, almost fifty hours of travel, it felt like he was stepping back in time, attempting to reclaim some vestige of his old self, only to find that that old self had been chipped away, sanded and scrubbed and crafted into something new. Maybe into something worse, certainly not better, but irrevocably something different.

He came home and worked at the Last Call, grateful for the opportunity, Joanne's idea, and things felt okay apart from the dreams. The dreams were bad mostly because of their regularity. Drink started to be a salve in a way it hadn't been before he'd left, becoming a new anchor point in each day, how he gauged time and meaning from how many beers he'd had, how many glasses of whiskey. Heidi rarely mentioned it, but it bothered her, and he knew it. He'd look in the mirror and see that same haunted, windblown look that he saw in other men at the bar, men like Bobby Liprinski, men who bought him drinks and told him war stories and grew so intoxicated and weepy some nights they were reduced to leaning over the bar, blubbering and gripping Minor's arm like he was the only thing tethering them to earth.

And with the drink and the dreams came the violence. The anger. The willingness—the strident, ugly *desire*—to fistfight some idiot because he'd looked at him wrong, or Minor imagined he had. Heidi growing cautious around him. Never violent with her, no, but the distance between them expanded. Minor gone quiet, cracking a smile when he used to laugh loud. Scabbed-up knuckles, a split lip that stuck to his pillowcase in the morning. Shit like that.

And then the night he'd surprised two burglars in the midst of robbing the bar, maybe six months before Julia's mother shot Ray Ray Sikes in the face, and what Minor had done to them, and how Joanne had helped him hide it.

You owe me, she'd said, and she'd been right.

And this, Christ, *this* was how he'd repaid her.

It's early afternoon now, the sky blue and cloud-tattered, the sun a white coin in the sky. Minor's standing in front of a motel room a couple miles outside Fargo, North Dakota, and the interstate a half-mile away sounds like an ocean. Inside, Julia sleeps in the windowless dark of the bathroom, a towel stuffed against the bottom seam of the door. Dreaming her strange dreams, the shower curtain covering her as she lies in the bathtub. He keeps imagining there's a way out for both of them, but he can't figure what it might be. They have spent months testing the boundaries of this thing, and the rules are resolute: Sunlight kills. Fresh human blood—a significant portion of it, and regularly—is required to survive. Julia telling him the story of the Children's Museum, Adeline's thrall keeping the blood-starved children away with the silver spoon. There's some joke there, but he can't figure out what it might be.

Meeting Adeline, was that the point that proved too far to come back from? Or the night Julia was turned? Was it when Varley did what he did? Earlier still, when Minor brought that bat down against the table, told those men in the Crooked Wheel vests to leave? You could run it back in your mind to the exact moment Varley was born, or Minor was. It still wouldn't make any sense.

He takes a card from his wallet and dials a number, drops in the requisite coins after the recorded voice tells him to. A long-distance call.

It rings three times and his father answers.

"Hi, Dad," Minor says, shutting his eyes.

He can sense the surprise on the other end: Minor hasn't called the old man in months. Halting, infrequent, minute-long conversations are all he can manage since they started this whole thing. The fuck is there to say? And yet he feels a rankling obligation. Blood is blood.

"Well, hey there, son," his old man says. "How's things?"

"I'm hanging in," he says, looking out at the highway. "Just wanted to see how you and mom were doing."

"Oh, we're fine, we're fine. Your mom's with her garden group, you know, otherwise I'd put her on the phone for you."

"Oh, that's okay, I can't stay on long."

"Got business to take care of, I imagine."

"That's right, Dad, yeah."

"Okey doke, well, how's the family? How's Heidi's book coming along?"

Minor shuts his eyes again, presses a thumb against a lid. "Oh, she's still working on it. I don't know if she'll ever be done with the thing."

"A perfectionist," says his father. "Your mother's the same way."

"Yeah."

"How's that girl? Julia? She still with you two?"

"Yeah, Dad, she's still with us," Minor says, weary now, exhausted, wanting to run away, run through the fields to the highway, where he might either hitch a ride or throw himself in front of a passing big rig. It's all too much. Being a son, a parent. All of this.

"Listen, Dad, I gotta run. Please tell Mom I said hi, will you?"

"Well, okay, Duane," his father says, as surprised that he's hanging up as he is that he called. "We'll be seeing you, thanks for reaching out."

"Thanks, Dad. Love you."

"You too, son. Bye now."

He hangs up, lights a cigarette. Obligations stacked on obligations. This idea of indebtedness. He takes out the business card, its edges age-softened now. More coins dumped in the slot.

"Detective Scoggins, Portland Police Bureau."

Minor's throat clicks—he hadn't expected Scoggins to pick up. "It's, uh, it's Duane Minor, Detective. Hi."

A pause. And then, "I'm talking to Duane Minor right now."

"Yes, sir."

Scoggins clears his throat. "You gotta help me out a bit here, son."

"How's that?"

"Well, no disrespect, but prove it, for starters."

Minor almost hangs up. It just reinforces the idea he doesn't even know why he's calling this cop in the first place. What could he possibly be seeking from this man? Absolution? A sounding board for his sins?

But apart from Julia, from Bobby, Scoggins is the only person with an inkling of what's going on.

The detective seems to sense his reluctance. "Duane, you had some photographs that I thought were pretty interesting, first time we saw each other. You remember? What was in those pictures?"

"You wanted to see a man's face, but you couldn't." He drags on his cigarette, watches trucks drift along the highway, white against the yellow fields, the cornflower sky. "It was filled with smoke."

The slightest exhalation. "Where the hell you been, Duane? I been trying to get in touch with you for a while now. *Long* time now, actually."

"Yeah, someone said you put a warrant on me."

"Well, hell yeah, brother. Yes, I did. You're involved, tangentially or not, in at least seven or eight murders here. As you are well aware. And then you go and run rabbit on me? Absconding with a minor on top of that? Hell yes, you're wanted for questioning. I think that's reasonable, don't you?"

"I suppose."

"I mean, Duane, you never even buried your wife."

He shuts his eyes. "I heard she's out there in Lone Fir? With her folks?"

"Yep. I've been to the graves myself. They take care of them nice there."

She and Ed and Joanne at the old cemetery on Morrison. Quiet and beautiful, solemn with its trees and winding pathways and moss-furred stones. Peaceful. So far away from where he is now. A rip of shame moves through him.

"Did you arrange that, Detective? The burials?"

"I mean, I helped with the details a bit. Your in-laws had already done the legwork. Paid for the lots and everything back when they were topside."

"Well, I appreciate it."

"Why don't you thank me by coming back to my office? Answer some questions. Are you in town now?"

Minor puts out his cigarette against the steel box of the pay phone. Watches a hawk wheel through the sky, its eye on something in the field between here and the highway. "How's John Varley doing," Minor asks. "Any luck tracking him down?"

"No luck yet, Duane. Not here in Portland. But you know what?"

"What's that, Detective?"

"He's one of those guys, you look for him, you start to see him everywhere. Read a police report with some eyewitnesses that say a fellow gave that exact name before breaking a man's neck in a bar in Greenpoint, Idaho. Back in 1969. Description matches too."

"No photographs, though."

"No photographs, no fingerprints, no arrests. Only his name and the stories that follow him. Actually, there was a massacre in Sioux Falls that a buddy of mine just heard about. Six cartel members dead in an apartment. Done same as your people, same as Karen Malone, the Crooked Wheel boys."

"It's him."

"Maybe? Man's taken on the air of a fucking boogeyman, though."

"Except he's real."

"I still don't know how he got in with the Wheel in the first place,

Duane, but yeah. Fits the pattern with this Colombian thing, I guess. Him just horning in on established crews, taking over, making some money, then running. Know what else?"

"What?"

"I been reading all these eyewitness reports. All over, going back to the '30s, like we talked about, and I'm seeing transcripts of grown-ass men—witnesses, some of them looking at serious federal time on other charges, men with everything to lose—and they're *insisting* to these arresting officers, to detectives and district attorneys, that John Varley can rip a man in half. That he has two sets of teeth. That he sleeps in a goddamn coffin. One fellow said he can find you by the smell of your blood in the dark. Crazy shit like that."

Julia, asleep in the bathroom right now, that shower curtain wrapped around her like a burial cloth. "What if it's true, though?"

"Yeah," Scoggins says, and sighs. "I don't know, Duane. I was hoping you could tell me."

"I don't know either."

"How's your niece doing these days?"

"She's fine."

"She in school?"

"We don't have time for school."

Scoggins laughs and he hears someone murmur on the other line, the rustle of the handset being moved. Imagines he's probably got other detectives listening in. Tracing the call, maybe.

"Listen, Duane, why don't you just let her go? You can drop her off at any police station in the country, and she'll get where she needs to be."

Minor can't help himself. Feels that anger unspool in him a little. "You're making it sound like she's a fucking hostage. Like there's people lining up to take care of her."

"No, no," Scoggins says soothingly, "just, maybe you took on something that's become a bit bigger than you thought. Trying to take care of a kid on top of everything else, that's a lot of work. I know."

"Don't give me that shit," Minor says. A slow thread of fury unzippering inside him, mostly because he's thought the same thing a hundred times before, how he's failed Julia again and again. "Acting like you're looking out for us."

"All I'm saying is that it's tough to raise a child in the best of circumstances, and you got it tougher than a lot of folks."

"Just blowing smoke now," Minor says.

"See, I'm not, Duane. I'm trying to throw you a lifeline here. Whoever this Varley is, whatever kernel of truth these stories have, you don't want her involved in that. You don't. Drop her off in front of a cop shop and drive away. Go on with your life. Can you do that for me?"

"I don't think I can." And then: "I want to."

"Oh, Duane, I promise you, you can."

"We're too involved in the thing now."

A pause, and then Scoggins says, "Is she really still alive, Duane? Truly."

Minor thinks of the men he's procured for her to feed on, drunk men from dim bars brought to motel rooms with tarps already laid on the floor. Or how he sometimes simply bids her good night as she walks out into the darkness to seek her own sustenance. Minor in turn hauling himself to the nearest tavern, those rare times he's allowed to drink himself stupid. Both hating himself for it and terrified she'll never come back.

Is she still *alive*? How does he answer that?

"Of course she is," he manages. "I'll be seeing you, Detective."

Minor hangs up, walks across the parking lot back to their room.

6

She wakes with the shower curtain over her face.

The smell of plastic, disinfectant, mold. The slick surface of the tub beneath her spine. Julia's grown accustomed to this status, her body paused in mid-flight. She vaguely remembers feeling refreshed after a particularly good sleep back before she'd gone into the Museum. What happens now is nothing like that. It's a falling, a seizing. She has slept in motel rooms with blankets over the blinds and in the canopy of the truck beneath a stack of sleeping bags. In the attics and crawl spaces of innumerable buildings. Once, they got stuck on the highway with dawn looming and she had to lie in a drainage pipe with Duane wrapping her in a sheet of plastic from a nearby construction site, all he could find, and still she'd fallen into the same loveless, static sort of sleep.

Every night she awakens and expects to find him gone.

Every night she awakens in her darkness and listens for her uncle's breathing, for a cough, the flick of a lighter. Some indication that he is still with her, that he hasn't left. Sometimes she doesn't hear anything, and the fear grows so big in her heart that she can't help herself—she calls out his name. He is the last rock visible in the churning sea of her life.

It's only when they're hunting Varley, actively looking for him, that Uncle Duane seems to know any peace. It's the *movement* that he likes, that sense of heading toward some conclusion. He hasn't said as much, but she knows he harbors some idea that things will change after Varley's dead. And in the meantime, they are, in their ways, detectives. Parsing clues and gathering information. She knows—she *believes,* at least—that he blames himself for what happened, even if she's told him a hundred times she *meant* to go in the Children's Museum. That she would do it again in a heartbeat.

Tonight, she smells his cigarettes in the other room. She rises and folds the plastic sheet into a careful square, puts it in the tub. Washes her face. Trades her clothes for clean ones in her backpack.

She comes out to see him watching television, and he offers her a sad smile.

"Three good things," she says, sitting in the chair by the window.

He turns to her. "Alright. Three good things."

Julia scratches her nose and says, "I told Aunt Heidi once that I'd never baked cookies with my mom and she was just floored, man. She was like, 'Well, *that's* gotta change right now.' So we made this giant batch of chocolate chip cookies. They were amazing."

"I don't remember that," Duane says.

Julia grins. "Yeah, we ate them all before you came home. Every single one."

He looks at the window over her shoulder, the blinds cinched tight. "Okay. One from me. Ed, when I came back from Vietnam, he let me celebrate, you know. We had parties, everyone got wasted, but after a couple days, Ed made sure to sit me down, and he told me that I'd be haunted. By things I'd seen, things I'd done. Hadn't done. He wasn't arrogant about it, wasn't trying to be a hardcase. He just said it real matter-of-fact. It was a comfort to me."

"Alright," she says, looking up at the ceiling. "Grandma. A good thing about Grandma I remember is how she would look at my face and say she saw my mom in me. How I looked like her, sat like her. Walked like her. I missed her so much, and when Grandma said that, it made me feel like she was close. I felt close to both of them." She scratched her nose again, her voice suddenly thick. "To all of you, I guess."

Duane rubs a hand across his mouth. "She protected me once. Joanne did. When I needed it."

"Grandma?"

He nods. "I killed these guys once," he says, and the words sit there like some new person has entered the room. Like someone has walked in and broken something.

"In the war?" Julia says, after waiting for him to say something else.

"No." He's still looking at the window, the blinds closed, his hands in his lap. "No, this was, hell, this was three summers ago. Maybe six months before you came to live with us. I'd been drinking a lot since I came back, you know, another thing Ed warned me on, and my temper, I just—anything set me off. My nights off, me and Bobby Liprinski would go out drinking at other bars, raising hell, and most times it'd end with me starting shit with some guy, making up a reason for it. 'Bobby, he disrespected vets.' 'Bobby, he's a fucking hippie, come on.' 'Bobby, he looked at me wrong.' Didn't take much. Didn't take anything. Then Bobby'd have to pull me off some guy in an alleyway somewhere. Sucker-punching some poor bastard after I followed him into the bathroom. I was having these dreams, couldn't sleep, sick in the mornings. Drinking during the day. Coming home with my knuckles all chewed up. Teeth loose in my mouth, black eyes. Broke my pinkie finger at one point, dumbest shit ever." Julia sits silently in the chair by the window. There is a sense of spillage, of a dam breaking, and she realizes that her uncle has been holding this inside, holding it tight to himself. That in this moment—maybe even in spite of his best intentions—he's decided to let it come pouring out.

"Heidi, she was this close to kicking my ass to the curb. Divorce. I never hit her, you know—Christ, Ed, Joanne *and* Heidi would've taken turns with a bat to my head, I'd ever touched her—but that rage, man, it wears on the people around you. Grinds everyone down. Heidi, she was trying to get me to go to support groups with other vets. Stuff that Bobby and I made fun of. This idea of a bunch of shell-shocked grunts scared of hearing a car backfire. Not for me, I said, like I was above it. Ed tried to have another man-to-man with me, but I couldn't see it this time. There was just this pit in me." Her uncle's words are taking on the momentum of a freight train now. This inevitability.

"That fury, man, it's got hooks. You come to depend on it. Hungover or not, just walking through your life like you were hell on earth? Like you're such a dangerous man that you felt like you owned the street you walked down?" He scratches his chin with the back of his hand. "And then I caught these two guys robbing the bar."

"Grandma's bar? Downstairs?"

"I heard them after hours. Heidi was out with her writer friends that night, trying to keep her distance from me, and I was insecure about *that* shit too, and I come down, and I see these guys in masks trying to break into the till with a crowbar. Trying to pry it open. And I just, I went to town. Beat the shit out of them, stomped one guy's head in. A glass got broken during all of it and I smashed the other guy's face into it on the floor. I felt so *good* doing it, Julia. Because I had *every right*. You know? They were in *my* space, a space I was protecting. This place I lived in, worked at. *Mine.*" He lets out a shaky laugh. "I was *right,* finally. For once."

Julia opens her mouth, no idea what she's going to say, and then closes it.

"And then," he says, "the guilt came. The fear. These two guys on the floor. I panicked and called Joanne. Didn't call my wife, called Joanne. She picked up right away and I told her I needed her to come to the bar, that it was an emergency. And she came, and she saw what happened, and she understood—I could see it in her eyes—that this, this was murder, attempted murder, this was prison time." He looks at Julia then and his face is haunted, bomb-blasted. No relief in it, in telling the story to someone.

"Joanne told me to pull my truck up behind the bar, and we put those two guys in the truck bed, and I put a tarp over them and I drove them out to this stretch of industrial shit up in the north part of the city, near Kenton Park, actually, not far from where we saw fucking Adeline. There was nothing there but train tracks and cement blocks and weeds. And I pushed them out on the gravel bar near the river. And then I drove home." He fishes a cigarette out of his pack and lights it. His hands are shaking. He blows smoke at the ceiling.

"Then I spent—*have* spent—the past couple years waiting for the world to fall on me. Next day there was nothing in the papers about it, nobody ever came to the bar to get, you know, revenge. No cops came by. I never took their masks off. I don't know if they were with a crew, or if they were just a couple of random guys. Sometimes it almost seems like I dreamt it. I don't even know if they were dead, honestly. But, Julia, they were like *dolls* when I pushed them out of the truck. And when I came back to the bar, Joanne had cleaned everything up, the blood and the broken glass. It was like it never happened. But she put a finger in my face, you know how Grandma could get real intense"—and here his voice catches, thickens—"and she said, 'You ever drink again, you touch a drop, I'm telling Heidi, and I'm telling the cops. Get your head on straight.' 'But, Joanne,' I said, 'I think I killed those guys.' 'You didn't kill 'em,' she said. 'I think I did.' 'You did *not*,' she said, 'and you'll sleep better when you understand that. They learned a lesson but they did not die. Now go take a shower and get to bed.' And I said, 'Yes, ma'am,' and I white-knuckled it for almost two years, not a drop to drink, terrified every minute, dreaming bloody, horrible dreams, pushing that sickness in me down. Heidi slowly coming back to me. And now? Every once in a while, you need to eat someone and I go get drunk and I visit those two guys in my mind and tell them how sorry I am. You understand any of this?"

He looks at her, but he can't keep his gaze steady for long. He stares down at his hands.

"You keep asking me to *fight*, Julia. To bring that violence up front, where I live. And I *want* to do it, I do. Because it'd be easier than this. Than *feeling* all this shit all the time. Living like this. Remembering everything." He shoves the palms of his hands against his eyes and lets out a groan, then takes them away. "But I can't. I have to take care of us. I have to keep things— I have to make sure things move forward. One thing and then the next. Or we'll drown." He looks at her and there is unmistakable pleading there. "You want that man to come forward, that killer I was, but I'll drown if I do it. I'll die."

"He murdered her," Julia says softly. "Just to do it."

He looks at her helplessly. "You think I don't fucking know that? Jesus Christ, I *saw* that room, you think I don't understand that?"

You think you love her. She knows enough not to say it to him. *You think you love her, but I love her different. I always have, Uncle Duane. I love them all differently than you do.*

I love them with blood.

7

1903, Seattle, John Varley doing Templeton's dirty work for him, his bootheels clomping down the planked sidewalk to Davis Starling's tavern, three doors down from the Bloody Bucket. Starling's new spot was close enough to spit, and Varley heard the *thunk* of hammers putting a nail home, heard men laughing even before he pushed open the saloon's doors. There had been a moment the night before, fleeting, but still there, when Varley had held in his hands the pistol Templeton had given him and considered if human lives were worth all this. Two men warring over property, over status. Over money. Two men who'd probably never been told no in their entire existence. It was as deep a consideration as a man like Varley was capable of, and an easy enough thought to push away. He buoyed himself instead with the memory of Templeton's fatherly hand on his shoulder. *Makes a man a friend for life.* That, and Templeton's knowledge of what had transpired in Redding; it was all the motivation Varley needed. Templeton wanted a bloodbath, and a bloodbath he would get.

So Varley walked into Starling's still-unnamed tavern, with gas lanterns burning all about, and Templeton's big Browning pistol tucked in the back of his waistband. Men turned at the sound of his boots. Four of them, he saw right away. Two tough old boys laying lengths of pine on what would be the bar top, another seated on a stool at the skeletal frame of the bar itself, a bottle of beer in his lap. Still another one farther toward the back, heavyset and working at a joist with a hammer. All four turned to assess him.

"Ain't open yet," the one at the bar said. "Just about, though. Couple more days."

"I'm looking for Davis Starling, and whichever of you was dogshit-stupid enough to stick Wendell Leblanc last night."

The one at the bar smirked. Leaned back against the bar's frame, which was still just raw two-by-fours at that point. He fixed Varley with a mouthful of brown teeth and said, "I can guarantee your loved ones would be grateful if you turn backwards and walk right on out that door, friend."

"I'd have to have loved ones for that to matter much," Varley said, smiling back at him, and pulled the Browning pistol from behind him, shooting the man at a walk. A small red hole appearing above the man's right eyebrow, a fistful of pulp *splatting* onto the two-by-fours behind him. The man tumbled off his stool, and one of the fellows at the half-built bar began scrambling at something near a stack of pine boards, Varley imagining a scattergun back there, and he turned and fired twice, catching the man in the shoulder and spinning him. He toppled, fell to the floor, and Varley stepped over and put a round in his throat.

The other man behind the bar's skeleton was quailing on his knees, his hands held up. There was a beat where Varley didn't shoot him outright, then another, so he stood up and took flight alongside his friend, the big one with the hammer, both of them running out the front door at a good clip. The room hung heavy with silence then—just the one man gagging and spurting out the last of his life's breath through that ruined throat. Varley's blood felt hot inside him, and he could hear it thudding in his ears, could smell the exacting stink of gunpowder and spilled beer. He'd just killed two men and found it as straightforward as anything else in life.

"Starling," he called out, walking toward the room's rear door, which he assumed led to the man's office. "Put your boots on, friend, let's do this decent."

He pushed open the office door. There was no subterfuge about it. Varley at his wisest was not a creative man and was decidedly less so in 1903. There was little deceit or fool-craft in him.

He opened the door onto a charnel house.

It was indeed Davis Starling's office, or had been. This room, indicating the man's priorities, was more complete than the bar itself. An imposing oaken desk stood at the back, so similar to Jim Templeton's that they may as well have come from the same catalog. Fine gas sconces hung like glowing fishbowls from the walls. Walls done up in exquisite, gold-threaded wallpaper, and a bookcase to the side stacked neatly with leather tomes. A great steel safe in the corner that came up to Varley's waist. Starling had planned on doing business long-term here, it seemed. At the far wall, behind the desk, was a rear door with a deadbolt installed.

The room was absolutely slathered in blood. Gouts of it on the wainscoting, all over that fancy wallpaper. Fanned drops on the ceiling. Varley stood in the doorway, his mouth suddenly dry as paper, the pistol a useless weight at the end of his fist.

A severed foot, still clad in its leather shoe, lay on the floor near him. The anklebone was a small yellow nub amid a blue-red circle of flesh. He smelled cooking blood on the glass of the sconces. Heard blood dripping off the lip of the desk, the measured *pap pap pap* as it fell to the floor, a cadence that marched in tandem with Varley's heartbeat.

Davis Starling's severed head lay in the center of the desk, facing him. Its eyes rolled to the whites, the mouth in a sneer, as if he'd already visited the afterlife and found the accommodations lacking.

A man—the one who had plowed through Templeton's gang the night before, presumably, and Starling's hired hand—stood behind the desk. Behind the head.

Nearly seven feet tall, Varley would guess. Flesh gray as a cadaver, a veil of hair on a ridged skull, white and fine as spider-silk, long enough that it brushed his shoulders. An explosion of minute red veins in the hollowed cheeks. Eyes black—black, truly—and shot through with a cold humor, as if the slaughter was all great fun. His trousers and coat might have been handmade or something sewn fifty years before; where they weren't black with blood, they were a colorless menagerie of grays and browns. Leaning over the desk, fingers tented on each side of Starling's severed head.

"Hello, little one," it said, a fey smile on its lips, a voice sounding as if it was clotted with dirt. "Your timing's a wonder."

Varley began to lift the pistol, and the thing raised a gray hand dismissively. It was—Varley would come to understand this years later—a man only in the barest sense. So vaguely human by that time that Varley would soon stop using the term at all in relation to the creature that stood before him. His Maker was not a man, but instead couched in the land between that and something else. Otherworldly. Undead. Who could say.

"Don't bother," it said of the pistol he aimed. That voice, so filled with rot, the grinding of stones, and still Varley could hear the disdain in it. As if it were watching a child throwing a tantrum, waiting for him to tire himself out. "Your man here tried the same, and look where it got him." With the tip of its finger, it poked the back of Starling's head. The head leaned forward, resting for a second on its nose, and then rolling onto a cheek. Blood on the desk there because there was blood everywhere. How had those men out there not heard it? He had no idea this much blood could *be* in one man.

"Why'd you kill him?" Varley said. The pistol hung at his side.

"Who, this one?" And then the thing lifted Starling's head up, held it aloft by its thinning black hair and spun it so that Varley saw the back of the man's head and then the gray, sneering face and back again. "It was in the natural order of things. And also, it's true, I'm one prone to rashness." The thing sniffed, let out a low chuckle. "The fellow welched on me, in short."

Varley said nothing.

"And why is it you killed those out there? I heard the shots." Those cracked lips purled into something that could almost be considered a smile. "Look at us, doing our work in tandem."

"I killed them because I was sent to," Varley said. "Same reason I'll be killing you shortly."

"Ah. Paid for it, were you?"

"Of a sort," Varley said.

"This is about last night, I imagine. Well, I admire your confidence. And yet"—and here the thing carefully set Starling's head back on the desk—"how is it you'll kill what's already dead, little one? Got some bright idea you might bury me twice?"

Varley sneered. "Who gives a shit about burying you?"

And then, ever moving bullheaded against the currents of the world, and young for only a moment more, he raised Jim Templeton's Browning.

There wasn't a shot fired, though.

Wasn't time for it.

The thing *moved*.

And all this over *money*. He'd spend a lot of time thinking about that.

Over who had more sway on this particular street, this particular neighborhood.

All of it for that strident, buried, nattering little-boy desire to have someone, even a murderous shitbag like Jim Templeton, tell him, *Oh, John Varley, you done good. I was looking for the right man and it was you. I'm proud.*

All this, and all that followed, for such a sad, simple thing as that.

Now, with the howl of a siren near them, bright and ululating across the plains, he and Johan hide in yet another dilapidated barn, with its flutter of bats overhead, its cobwebs and suggested shapes of old farm equipment stacked and tiered in one corner. Smell of dust and old straw and mouse shit. They have tossed the cocaine and driven down a bevy of farm roads with the headlights off, and finally parked the VW in the dark mouth of this barn, the trouble lights of various police vehicles only slightly distanced from them. They are coming, and Johan thinks it's a grand thing, wearing his ridiculous coat and a madman's grin, holding the shotgun in his fists. His troubadour from hell, this one, the whites of his eyes gleaming wildly in the dark. They have driven the VW deep into the barn and closed its door best they could and now they stand inside it, waiting to be discovered.

Johan puts his fist in his pocket, comes up with a handful of waxy green shotgun shells. "If this is it, John, I want you to know something."

"You don't need to say it."

"No?"

Varley looks over at him and smiles. "I feel the same. Never in my life expected it."

Johan smiles back at him. "Well, there we are, then."

"I wish you would stay in the van. I can do this myself."

"No fun in that."

"Johan—"

The siren stops and they hear a car approaching and then stopping on the gravel outside. Beneath the seams of the barn door they see undulating spills of red and blue.

Johan puts a finger to his lips—*my God,* Varley thinks, *he's smiling even now*—as a pair of car doors close, and a moment later the barn door opens with a haunted-house creak of tortured hinges. A single flashlight beam of light moves along the concrete floor, the walls. Limned shapes behind the cruiser lights in the dooryard—the outlines of two men in Staties campaign hats. A single flashlight beam roves along the length of the van and Varley hears the troopers inhale at the sight of it, sees them both pull their revolvers.

He finds peace then, and love.

As ever, the moment guides him.

He steps out from the side of the van. Johan, still hidden, giggles.

"Don't fucking move," one of the troopers barks. Johan creeps around the other side of the van and fires, a gout of flame leaping from the sawed-off barrel of the Mossberg, one of the troopers screaming and falling to the dirt. The other trooper drops the flashlight, a spear of illumination wheeling around the room.

He starts shooting at Varley, backing up, trying to make it outside. One of his bullets takes off the ring finger of Varley's left hand and lodges in his shoulder. A distant starburst of pain and then a flared, maddening itch as the bone and tissue knit themselves together, drawn from nothing, the flattened slug pushing itself out of his body, pattering onto the dirt floor. Another round punches through his collarbone and Varley staggers forward, his teeth rising as he laughs. Johan, somewhere in the dark, yips and howls like a wolf.

Varley catches the trooper around the collar—one more round exploding through his guts and out his back. He lays a hand across the trooper's face and pushes the head back, turning him and pushing him against the side of the van. He hears the oceanic thud of the trooper's blood at his throat. Smells it. Somewhere nearby, Johan fires the shotgun again. "Feel that?" he hears Johan say, and then again and again, "Feel that, do you feel it? Did you feel it?" Varley's jaw distends fully, that second row of teeth pushing forth from the gray gums, inky blackness falling over his eyes. He bends and rips the man's throat open, a jet of hot, glorious blood splashing across his face, into his hair. He burrows in, snarling, nearly convulsing with the sudden rich *life* at his mouth.

Varley's body leans into the pulse of it, his fingers gripping the wound at the man's neck and pulling, sinew and muscle giving way with a febrile tearing. The trooper gurgles, tries to scream, but his vocal cords are shredded, his voice box a dangling knob of yellow-white gristle in the jetting aperture made at his throat. His legs kick. Johan says something beside him, but it's lost beneath the volcanic rush of blood at Varley's mouth. The trooper bucks weakly against him.

Invigorated, deathless, he snarls and hooks his fingers in the wound at the trooper's neck, *pulls harder,* rends the head off, the flesh giving way along with a wet crack of the vertebrae. Varley steps back and the head rolls somewhere. He takes hold of the body, those last vestiges of heated life still throbbing from the ragged stump of neck, and buries his face there. His body now impelled, furious. Then he lets the body go and it leans against him for a moment before sagging against the van and tumbling to the floor. His face and chest slicked with blood, his clothes sopping with it. He turns and staggers and Johan grips him by the hair and kisses him, his mouth against Varley's, the trooper's blood lacquering their faces.

This is love, then.

8

They get confirmation outside a bar in a little town called Brandon. Midnight, so hot Minor imagines the tarmac pulling against his hand like taffy if he laid it down. Minor sidling up to a man who's watching horse races on the television mounted above the bar. He has that look about him—hungry and afraid, the desiccation they got from being blood-starved just starting to take hold on his face, a kind of papery tightening of the skin. Julia had pointed it out to him the few times they'd come across others in the throes of it. He's got a handlebar mustache and a cowboy hat, sitting in front of a glass of untouched beer. Minor's left the revolver in the truck; anyone turned would likely attack him or run away if he even walked by, given the silver bullets inside.

They don't need that. They need answers.

He sits down next to the guy, orders a Bud. Bartender brings it over, Minor pays. Sips. Wants to lift that piss-amber up to the light, wants to drink the whole thing, order another. Order ten more. He hopes this is the right thing to do.

"You feeling alright?" he asks the man without turning his head.

The man's eyes narrow; he turns to him. "Say again?"

"Looking a bit like a dog on a leash, friend. Got something that might help you." Minor reaches into his pocket, and under the bar holds out a pair of glass vials, the blood looking black as oil in the gloom.

The man with the mustache blinks, turns his face back up to the television. He puts a hand on his glass of beer like he's going to drink it, but he doesn't, and that's when Minor knows for sure. He's never gonna drink a beer again, this guy, but he would if he could. The beer's part of the costume.

"How about," the man says, "I just open your neck up and drink that? Lift you up like a fucking soda pop, son, and toss you away when I'm done."

"I'm not looking to start trouble."

The man chuckles, scratches a thumbnail on the bar top. "You come in here and talk to me like that. Say that to me. Might as well have 'trouble' tattooed on your ass."

"Here," Minor says, holding out one vial next to the man's thigh. A muscle in his cheek jumps, and he lifts his lips up in a sneer for just a second, but then he takes it, puts it in his jacket. There's a mixture of noises around the bar—groans and a few yelps of joy—as one horse wins and the others lose. "I want to find John Varley."

"I don't know him."

"He's like you, but real vicious. As in the boy likes to clear whole rooms, sticking ripped-off arms up assholes, things like that. Just did it to a bunch of guys in Sioux Falls, is what I heard."

"Jesus Christ," the man says, and Minor smiles into his beer, hearing the scared little boy in his voice. In their way, all of these things are so close to death. So terrified of it. Sunrise or silver or not enough blood. Almost more fragile than people are.

"Why don't you help me out? You're so blood-hungry your pecker's about to fall off. I see you. You're no hard-ass. Least not right now."

The man looks at him with true hurt on his face, pushes the brim of his cowboy hat up. "You do this a lot? Come up to fellas in bars and bust their balls?"

Minor thinks of how many goddamn bars he's been in since this whole thing started. Where else do they have to congregate at night? What other space offers them the opportunity to find something to *eat*?

"You'd be surprised," he says.

"Yeah, well, kiss my ass, is what I'm saying."

Minor sighs, exhausted with it all, as exhausted as when he'd talked to his father on the phone. "Here." He hands the man the other vial. Finishes his beer, gets off the stool. "Fuck it. Have a good one."

The vial disappears and the man says, "I don't know no one by that name. But I heard about the Sioux Falls thing. Bunch of dope dealers, supposedly."

"Alright," Minor says. "I appreciate it."

"You can still go to hell, though."

"Yeah, okay. I'll save you a seat."

Before they take off, Minor has Julia wait outside the truck while he pulls more vials of blood. She's been quiet since he told her about the bar, about killing those men. He'd thought it might be a relief, to finally tell someone, as if his guilt might lessen somehow in the telling, but he realized almost immediately after that he'd spared his own feelings at the expense of Julia's. Changed the girl's understanding of both him and her grandmother.

They hit the bars in Sioux Falls, Minor taking the revolver with him this time. Using it as a kind of Geiger counter, watching for anyone to buckle or pull back when he walks by. They've chased rumors for so long, and have found that two people saying the same thing is usually worth following. Both Scoggins and the guy in the bar telling him about Sioux Falls? Thinking there's a one-in-a-thousand chance he just comes across Varley, maybe less. Again, there are only so many places to go at night.

But he finds nothing. Just a Tuesday summer night, folks hot and trying to while away the hours.

After the bars close, he puts the gun away and they find an all-night diner where Minor leans over an omelette and Julia slowly shreds a napkin, rolls the pieces into little balls.

"I don't want to stay in town," she says.

"Why?"

"He's not here."

Minor stops chewing, his fork hovering over his plate. "What're you talking about?" He pushes the newspaper across the table with its SIX DEAD IN WESTERN AVENUE APARTMENT MASSACRE headline. "That's Varley. Look, Julia, just like in Portland: he gets into the dope trade and then he flames out and slaughters everyone. This is him. It happened three nights ago."

"Right, but then what does he do?"

He looks at her, chews.

"He runs," Minor admits.

"Exactly," Julia says. "So now he's running." He thinks of the girl who had looked at him on the way to a sleepover at her friend's house and said, *What if I get too scared?* A lifetime ago. Ten lifetimes.

"You're getting a little freaked, aren't you? Now that we're maybe getting close?"

"No," she says. "But I'm tired."

"Alright," he says, softening. "We'll go somewhere out of town, try to find where he's going next."

"Alright."

They head south. Beneath an overpass, Minor pulls over onto the shoulder and Julia gets out and climbs into the truck bed. The windows of the canopy have long been blacked out with cardboard and electrical tape and she buries herself beneath a cocoon of blankets. "It'll be over soon," she says, but if she's saying it to him or herself, Minor isn't sure.

He drives out of the city and before long sees strings of police lights chewing up the night. Then sirens behind him too and he slows the truck, pulls it onto the shoulder again as a volley of emergency vehicles blaze past.

Not even a mile later, he passes a roadside tavern, a small boxy thing with a flat roof and an OPEN sign. Maybe a hint of dawn in the sky now. Across the weed-choked parking lot from the bar is an L-shaped, two-story motel. He can get some sleep of his own, be well-rested for tomorrow, for whatever happens next.

He parks in front of the motel and turns the truck off. Listens to the ticking engine and then turns around and knocks three times on the rear window.

Three knocks come back through the steel of the canopy.

Minor gets out, heads toward the motel to get a room.

9

Varley had not known it at the time—hadn't known shit, frankly—but he'd been turned by a Maker. A Father. That monstrous, white-haired thing that stood in the back office of Davis Starling's saloon, that had bandied Starling's head around like a child's balloon, it had been one of the old ones, maybe three or four of them still walking the earth, and as such, Varley's turning has afforded him things others don't have access to. He knows that he can petition his Maker to come offer guidance—one time only, and the Maker may refuse it, but yes, he may ask for guidance and succor. So far, in all his years, he's never been desperate enough.

Another thing? A little gift born of the nature of his turning?

Varley can perform a blood-calling.

He and Johan are three, four miles north of Sioux Falls, in the third leaning barn of the evening. No shortage of them around here. The changing face of the world, with homesteads, passed on from generation to generation, now succumbing to the death-spasm of industry. Family-run affairs replaced now by factory farms and un-bridled mass production, and in the wake of this new world these broken-down places are left. Dawn's coming, and Varley makes his roost in the barn with its cavalcade of bats and a hole in the rear section of roof like a meteor has struck it. A fallen chorus of timbers back there, and he'll burrow beneath them and dig as much of a hole as he can, and as such will consider himself as safe as one like him can be. He could always sleep in the house across the dooryard, of course, but large houses, with their maze of exits and entrances, their windows, make him nervous. The barn is less secure, but the ways out are more easily navigated.

Because he and Johan have savagely murdered three policemen, every cop across the plains will be looking for them. And Alaska beckons. The two of them in a field of white, a small house, an unbroken horizon.

Duane Minor's the problem. He remains the last damnable logjam in Varley's plan. He's heard mutterings here and there over the past year, year and a half, from a half dozen sources: *Someone's looking for you. Two people—young guy and a dark-haired girl. Guy's got that thousand-yard stare on him. The thralls get that look sometimes, but this one's different.*

And *They paid me with a vial of blood. They already knew your name.*

And *The little girl had the teeth on her, like us, but the man still walked in the sun. The girl called him* Duane, *I remember that.*

And *They're looking for you, sure as hell.*

And he's felt—the both of them have—this sense of being followed. It is not exactly like feeling hunted, but it is close enough to make him uneasy. He's made no shortage of widows in his life, but there is something about that man in particular that's caught like a bone in Varley's throat ever since Portland. He knew the bastard would be trouble. Should have killed him and the old woman that first night in the bar, been done with it. And now it seems this *Duane* has aligned himself with some child vampire, paying her in blood most likely. A man on the hunt, seeking revenge.

He can picture holing up in Fairbanks, or farther north. Barrow, maybe. He and Johan, together, unbothered. Feeling for the first time what it would be like to live without the constant terror of dawn, the killing sun always promising to rise.

And then, imagine it, in that narrow span of daylight hours, this heartsick fool with his little vamp mercenary comes into Varley's house, drags him out the front door, the Alaskan sun doing its work, quick and ugly.

No.

Hell no.

With Duane Minor out there, he'll never feel truly safe. Better to tie up loose ends now, in spite of the cost. The ensuing weakness. A blood-calling will put a stop to him. Meanwhile, they still have McCoy's money, their savings, a van that works. The rest they can deal with as it comes.

Johan roots through the van, tossing things out, convinced that even ten, fifteen pounds of abandoned material will make the piece of shit move faster. Varley has his doubts, but as ever, he appreciates the boy's intentions. They stand in the barn and the sky begins to noticeably lighten, and as it does, steel rods insert themselves slowly in his spine, a spiked fist twisting in his guts. He calls Johan over.

The boy looks at him, sweating. The barn's hot and closed in, and there are blued circles under his eyes. He looks cross and tired.

"You're mad we threw out the cocaine, aren't you?"

"We could have kept *one* package, John. I feel like shit right now."

Varley holds a blade in his hand, a switchblade with a black handle that Johan's picked up somewhere, some novelty under a glass case in this roadside gas station or that one, spied alongside the throwing stars and brass knuckles. A ripple of unease walks across Johan's face when he sees Varley holding it.

"What are you doing, John?"

Varley crouches to one knee. "Putting out a calling."

"A what?"

"Hush now." He runs the switchblade across his palm. A mouth opens on the skin, and blood begins dripping out, black and viscous. Normally a wound like this would close in seconds, but this one doesn't. There are no words to a calling, no spoken incantations. Certainly nothing as lofty as prayer. But it's a thing he's known himself capable of since his own turning; trying to explain it to Johan would be like trying to explain the intricacies of the solar system.

Blood spatters on the dusty cement. A bird twitters somewhere, and as if in response, a ripple of pain marches through Varley's body, bends him. Dawn's coming. He has minutes, if not less.

There's true panic on Johan's face. "John, what're you *doing*?"

"Just wait. If I fall, don't worry. Cover me with blankets. Timber. This'll be my bed for the day." He winks, trying to belie his own fear and unease.

Duane, it comes to him again, the name clunky, silly, *Duane Minor.* An image rises in the murk of his mind, of the young man who'd stuck a gun in Bradley's ear in the bar that night. A fellow trying his best to run a card table and say how things were going to be, without understanding that Varley won, always. That John Varley ran the show. Though he imagines Minor has learned that lesson well enough by now, given the dead Varley's left behind for him. He pictures Minor's face, focuses on it.

Blood begins to pour freely from the wound at his hand, pattering to the earth. Dawn creeps closer, a sledgehammer at his back.

He raises his face to that hole in the roof of the barn, the sky above now a bruise-deep violet, the veins in his neck growing taut. It is a sense of *pushing,* the blood-calling is, an expanding ring of intention that moves out from his offered blood into the world.

He feels Johan's hand at his back. Varley hisses like a cat and shrugs him off.

Squeezing his hand, flaring it open and squeezing again, precious drops continue to fall to the dirt. He imagines a stone in a pond, the concentric circles rippling outward. Pictures the message—*this man, all of you, kill this man the moment you see him, look for him, find him, he's got a little girl with him, dark-haired, a vamp, do it,* kill them, *you will be rewarded by the child of a Maker, you are called to do this, you must*—bouncing between the chinks of buildings, beneath the seams of doorways, sliding along hilltops and amid trees and fields and rivers. The billion unseen pathways and tributaries of the world.

He squeezes his fist once more and then stands on weakened legs. Seconds later, the wound knits itself together.

"What the hell was that?" Johan asks, and now, when the boy puts an arm around his waist, Varley leans against him. He's led, like an old man, to the mad jumble of broken timber at the far end of the barn, a folded stack of blankets nearby.

"Are you sure you don't want to sleep in the van, John? It's safer than this—this garbage pile."

Varley shakes his head. A wave of dizziness overcomes him, and he retches, spits. "You need the van."

"I do?"

"I got to eat, boy. The calling's made me weak, and I'll get sicker still. I need you to bring me someone."

"Alright. Yes, okay. What *is* it, though? You looked—you looked like you were dying."

Varley smiles, though the pain of the sunrise has become significant. He thinks he smells smoke—his own skin perhaps, or just distant synaptic fireworks as dawn approaches—and gingerly crawls beneath a slat of fallen roof. Johan passes him blanket after blanket so that he might better cover himself. The itch of wool against his face, and, at last, sweet relief as he's hidden from the growing light. The glorious pull of sleep in his diminished blood.

From his makeshift crypt, he says, "You know about gangsters, Johan?"

"What?"

"Gangsters, boy. Al Capone, Bugsy Siegel. You know, guys who—"

Above him, frightened, Johan says, "I know what a gangster is, John."

"Well, I put out a hit on him," he says, the blanket's fabric against his mouth, flattening his words. He's smiling.

"What?" Johan says. "I don't know what you mean. How—"

But Varley's gone, flung into merciful sleep.

10

Minor opens his eyes. Julia is standing over his bed, and he rockets up, gasping. Some sleep-addled part of him is convinced, he'll only admit to himself later, that she's come to kill him. The room's cemetery-quiet; electric light falls in razor-thin bands on the floor, cast from the parking lot and the neon of the bar across the way.

"Duane," she says in a whisper. "Something's wrong."

He runs a hand over his face. He's grown used to sleeping in his clothes, and with the .38 under his pillow. He's left the Ithaca under the seat in the truck, not wanting to give the hotel manager anything to eyeball.

"What's going on, hon? How'd you get out of the canopy?"

"I kicked out the glass."

"What?" He locks her in the canopy on the days that she sleeps out there. Too many doomsday scenarios have played out in his mind over the past year and a half: the truck gets stolen, the thief opens up the canopy to see what he's made away with, and if it's during the daytime he ends everything when he roots around and finds a sleeping girl back there. "Jesus. What's the matter?"

"I had a—a dream, kind of? This voice in my head, *loud,* Uncle Duane, saying I had to kill someone, *find him and kill him,* and the image, the face I saw, it was you—"

"Julia," he says.

"—I'm not *going* to, but I *saw* you, is the thing, and the voice kept saying *kill him, kill him,* and *he has a dark-haired girl with him* and I just, I don't know what to *do,* Uncle Duane, it was so loud and I don't know what it *means*—"

Someone knocks on the door to their room, and Julia's eyes go wide in the dark.

On the other side of the door, a man says, "Duane? You in there, buddy?"

Julia shakes her head wildly, that dark hair flying, and Minor puts a finger to his lips and reaches under his pillow.

Softly, quietly, he stands up and walks over to the door. Peers through the peephole, the .38 near his chin.

There's a man with a black beard and a green-and-black button-up standing in front of the doorway. He sniffs, his nose curling, and then a boyish smile rises beneath the beard.

"There you are," he says, and kicks the door in.

Minor's quick enough to put an arm up, but still the door strikes him, cracks off a hinge, and the man steps in and grabs Minor by the collar of his shirt and runs him backward into the wall. A deep *pong* of his skull denting the drywall, a whiff of bad meat, and he hears Julia scream once as his vision grays. His brain bellows at him to move. There are snarls rippling around him—animal sounds straight from a nature documentary—and he leans against the wall and sees Julia and the man doing a mad pirouette. Minor touches the back of his head and looks at his fingers; no blood. Pushing himself off the wall, he sees the man turn at the hip and toss Julia across the room. Her body horizontal with the floor, she slams against the back wall so hard that something in the bathroom falls and shatters. A buckle in the wall two feet wide, and she falls out of sight behind the bed.

The man pivots, stands there in a half crouch. He opens his mouth and hisses, shows Minor his teeth. Since the murders, he's seen Julia converse with perhaps a dozen others like her in their attempts to find Varley, and their palavers have always been conversations stiff with formality and a veiled curiosity.

Never had one come right fucking at him, though.

Where's his gun? He can't think. He sees it on the carpet near the chair, and he's leaning over, reaching for it, his brain slow and muddied, when a cold hand grasps the back of his shirt and yanks him up. Sees the black eyes and the gleaming teeth inches from his face and then Julia's small hands wrap around the man's throat from the back and he lets go of Minor and twists again, the two of them staggering around the room in another embrace, their jaws snapping at each other. Minor crawls over and grasps the revolver and stands up. The man runs Julia into the wall next to the television, plaster and lath dusting her hair. She lets go and he turns, hooking a hand around her throat, pushing her up the wall as her feet kick, pawing weakly at his wrist.

Minor walks up to him and puts the barrel of the .38 behind his ear.

"You feel that?" he says, his own voice sounding far away. "You do, huh? How it makes you feel all fucked-up straightaway? Silver bullets, brother. Let her go, or I park one in your brain."

They tie him to a chair in a ridiculous mishmash of duct tape and cut-up strips from the room's shower curtain. It's something he could easily shrug off; it's only the bullets that are giving him pause. Minor's dumped one out of the revolver and stands behind him while Julia sits in front of him, cross-legged on the bed. The room's door rests crooked on its hinges, and it's frankly amazing that the manager, as old and deaf as he was, hasn't come in to toss them out.

"Who are you?" Julia asks the man. Her hands are folded in her lap. She looks small and diminutive and her voice doesn't waver, even though he knows her well enough to know she's scared as hell.

"Nobody."

She rolls her eyes. "For real, though."

"I don't know, man. Ronald McDonald, I guess."

"Alright. Hi, Ronald," she says tonelessly and looks at Minor, and Minor presses the bullet against the flesh at the base of the man's neck, above his collar, and he sputters in his wrappings and lets out a strangled shriek, the chair jumping. Dark smoke spurts from the wound and Minor takes the bullet away, nauseous. The man looses a string of curses and the smell of cooking meat fills Minor's nose. Looks like putty at his neck, weeping and ringed in black.

Julia says, "What is it?"

"What's what?"

"I woke up and I felt this thing in my head, this loud voice, and I saw a picture of him"—and here Julia lifts her chin toward Minor— "and the voice was just like, *Kill this man the moment you see him, look for him, find him, kill him.* It was so loud. It still is."

Even standing behind him, Minor can hear the smirk in the guy's voice when he says, "Yeah, kid, you must be new."

Julia blinks. "What do you mean?"

"This chickenshit behind me? Guy got a blood-calling put out on him. You did too, far as I can tell."

"What does that mean?" Minor says.

"It means you both fit the description."

Minor looks up at Julia and says, "That's what you were talking about?" She nods. It's been a while, since that day in the drainage ditch, maybe, that she has looked this panicked, and Minor's working hard at pushing down his own fear.

"The hell is a blood-calling," he says to the back of Ronald's head.

Ronald turns and sneers. "It's like a hit. A contract. Except just the old ones and the children of old ones can do it."

"My friend, I don't know what in the blue fuck you're talking about."

"Yeah, I can tell."

"So who did it?"

Nothing.

"Who put out a hit on me, Ronald?"

"Listen. I don't even want to say his name."

"Why not?"

"Because he's bad news, is why."

Minor holds the bullet between two fingers and a thumb and begins pushing it into the soft spot behind Ronald's ear, there where he'd put the barrel of the .38 minutes before. It sinks into the flesh like warmed butter, black threads of rot spilling from it, threads that fan out along the back of Ronald's skull and beneath his hair. Ronald bucks in his chair and shrieks again.

"*I'll fucking* kill you *stop stop—*"

All this for vengeance, Minor thinks. *Christ. Like Heidi's gonna walk through this broken door, whole and alive, if I hurt this guy enough.*

And yet he wants this man to name his adversary, to say his name so that they might make him real, not just some errant ghost they've been chasing for a year and a half, so he pushes the bullet in deeper. More smoke, more rot, more screaming and bucking. "Who put out the hit, Ronald?"

"*Varley*," Ronald roars, his ear blackening like stop-motion now, shrinking like a flame-curled rose on the side of his head. "John Varley, alright? Stop fucking *doing* that, God."

Minor walks around, crouches down so he's facing him. "What's he offering you?"

"What?"

"What's he paying you?"

Ronald's face is a complicated rictus of agony, eyes wild as a horse in a burning barn. "It's not like that." Drool falls to his lap and his head falls to his chest.

"What's it like?"

"It's a blood-calling. It's like a command. We have to do it. We're *compelled* to do it. Like she said, I seen your face in my mind."

"How'd you know where to find me?"

Ronald lifts his head. Minor watches as black threads crawl from his glistening, smoking ear, across his temple, into the white of his eye. "Man, *everybody's* looking for you. Kidding me? Every vamped-out asshole in four hundred miles has got your number, motherfuck. I sleep nearby. I decided to start hitting the motels and bars and bookie joints the second I woke up. I just got lucky, is all. Talked to the old man at the front desk, he said you fit the description."

"That simple, huh?"

"Guy sold you out for five bucks. I said you were my cousin."

"Where's John Varley?"

"What, he tells me his whereabouts?" Ronald licks his lips, his eyes moving from Minor to Julia and back. His eye's blackening, seems to be caving in on itself. "You got shit confused. *We* answer to *him,* you know?"

Minor stands up, his knees popping, and walks back behind him again.

"You ever seen him in person?"

"Fuck you," Ronald says, and Minor hears the weariness in his voice. Thinking one more time that Heidi, her memory, who she was, lives on another planet entirely from where he is in this moment. He holds the bullet an inch above Ronald's skull, as if probing with a metal detector, and a moment later, Ronald sputters, starts coughing. Minor takes the bullet away and walks in front of him again.

"That's *really* messing with your brain, isn't it? When I do that?"

Ronald nods, grimacing. A drop of blood falls from his right nostril and then it's like someone's inched open a spigot, it just starts pattering from his nose, this steady drip.

"It hurts?"

"Bad."

"So can we just finish this? I don't want to do this anymore, Ronald. Have you seen the guy before or not?"

"Yeah, once. Alright? One time. He started moving dope all through here. Mostly in Sioux Falls. He muscled in on a crew of Colombians, is what I heard."

"Colombians in South Dakota?"

"Money's money."

"And we're talking heroin?"

"Coke."

"Where's he move it out of?"

"I don't know, man. Town, like I said. I steer clear. I don't want nothing to do with him or his thrall. Both of them scare the shit out of me, be honest."

"Who's that?"

"What?"

"The thrall."

"I don't know. Some fruity guy."

"That's not nice," Julia says from the bed.

Ronald laughs. He's drooling blood now too. "*European,* then. How's that? Wears a long leopard-print coat, comes to his knees. Blond hippie, hair practically down to his asshole. I don't think he's been turned. But they're a pair, man. He's as mean as Varley is."

"What's his name?"

Ronald looks up at him, sneering; the one eye not laced with black-rot is clouded red with burst blood vessels. The silver near his brain has done more damage than Minor imagined. "Brother," Ronald says, "you get a calling, you do what you're told. I've heard three of them since I been turned, and I tracked every one of those people best I could. You see a face, you find the face and kill the guy it belongs to. That's all. You're *obligated.* I don't know names or nothing about Varley's man, if he's a Pisces or a fucking Communist or nothing like that. You try to murder the face you see in your mind, that's how a blood-calling works."

Minor has a vision of Heidi, how one arm had come to rest in a V on the floor, bent the wrong way at the elbow, a puzzle his mind hadn't been able to understand at first. The cold blowing through the room from the broken window. The roughly sphere-like shape of her severed head in the corner by their rattan chair. Other pieces of her, other parts.

Minor smiles. "Three blood-callings, huh? When were you turned, Ronald?"

"I got bit in St. Louis in 1910."

"Oh yeah?"

"Lady who did it, I thought I was in love with her, actually, and she—"

"How many people you murdered in sixty-seven years, Ronald?"

"Duane," Julia says softly.

"I don't know," Ronald says, his eyes skirting away. A plaintive edge creeping into his voice. "A bunch, I guess. It's not like I *like* it, man. I don't *like* any of this. I miss summertime, I miss being warm. Catching fish at the creek and then taking a nap. Walking down the street, looking at girls, the outfits the girls wear now, I tell you, it's a whole other world," he adds, his voice gone singsongy with fear, and Minor thinks of Heidi flipping a record that night before he went off to basic, the smoothly defined muscles of her back in the dim living room, thinks of Ed's body shot through with cancer, Joanne desperately trying to keep all their lives afloat. Varley promising her to turn Ed, and then Joanne saying he didn't want it anyway. All those missing people in Portland, those dismembered girls. How Heidi's never going to be laying out in the sun again, ah, never get to lay at the river with a transistor radio near her towel, laughing low and throaty with her face against the fabric when he says some terrible joke, her face implacable and beautiful as a statue with those big dark sunglasses she liked to wear, how that whole world is dead to him now, that life dead and gone, none of it coming back.

He takes the bullet and sets it in Ronald's ear and pushes it with one finger through his ear into his brain. The bullet sinks in like a penny into warm wax. Ronald judders and lets out a kind of rusty sigh, someone clearing their throat, and blood spills out of the ear like oil, sumptuous and thick. Blood pours from his mouth too, and his eyes liquefy into jelly and fall in clots down the wrapped, taped-up mass of his chest. Ronald's feet thump madly against the floor. That side of his head blackens and smokes and caves in on itself, even as he continues gurgling and sputtering blood. Minor stands over him, hoping to feel something. Hoping rage or redemption or horror might march through him. Hopes even to feel the sickening twine of regret tighten his throat.

But there's nothing.

Julia feels something, though: she sits on the bed, weeping, a fist pressed to her mouth.

"We need to leave," Minor says, his voice cracking at the sight of her. He thinks for a moment of retrieving the bullet from the ruin of Ronald's head and instead walks to the broken door and carefully opens it on its one fragile hinge. Steps out on fawn legs over to the truck, into a night that smells of cut grass and gasoline. Next to a scatter of glass from the canopy's broken window, he heaves once, spits, lights a cigarette with shaking hands. Smoke burns his lungs, and he's grateful that it replaces the chemical reek of Ronald's liquefying body.

Across the parking lot, a pair of headlights wheel in from the road, the vehicle rattling to a stop on the motel side. It's a rattling VW van, a white top, the body orange as a safety cone.

A man gets out, starts walking toward the bar. Doesn't give Minor a glance, his footsteps hurried. He's almost running toward the small, boxy tavern with its Christmas lights around the windows.

A tall man, his blond hair cut short.

But what's he wearing? What *is* that?

The middle of summer, and this fool's wearing a long leopard-print coat, its hem coming to his knees.

t's early evening, but the bar's already chock-full of good old boys in cowboy hats or workman's coveralls, women with bouffants and tight jeans. American flags from last year's bicentennial festooned all over the walls. Minor exhales and threads his way among people, looking for the blond man in the ridiculous coat. If he's here, it's likely that Varley is too. Still, he's told Julia to wait in the truck. *If he's here, I'll bring him out,* he's told her. He feels the reassuring weight of the .38 in his coat pocket. He thinks of the easy give of the bullet in Ronald's head. Thinks of Ronald saying, *They're a pair, man.* Saying, *He's as mean as Varley is.*

In the back of the bar, there's a small stage in the corner. No band, just a dance floor with a few people milling around, cans of beer held to their chests. Minor finds the blond man at a small circular table.

He looks to be about Minor's age. Drawn cheeks and cunning, sullen eyes. Minor tosses his cigarettes and lighter on the table and sits across from him, smiles. "All the bars in South Dakota," he says, "and you pull into this parking lot. I finally caught a break."

The man takes him in, smiling blankly at first, and then Minor says, "Where's John Varley?" and the man's eyes go glassy with panic.

"I don't know who that is."

Minor leans back in his chair, pulls out the handle of the Smith & Wesson from his jacket pocket. "You don't have any idea how long I been looking for you, do you?"

He doesn't answer.

"It's pointed right at you," Minor says. "Right at your guts. Keep your hands on the table. Don't bullshit me."

"Alright."

"Is he here?"

The man's eyes pinball around the room. "No."

"Do you know who I am?"

"No." He has an accent. European, hard to place. Swedish? Norwegian?

"You're lying."

The clatter of pool balls, the jukebox howl, wood paneling and hanging lights, the whole room a haze of cigarette smoke.

The blond man nods, seems to settle a bit. "Alright," he says again.

"If you run," Minor says, "I'll shoot you."

"You already showed me the gun."

"What's your name?"

The man tongues a molar, seems to think about it, then says, "Johan. What's yours?"

"You don't know it? It seems like you'd know it. Considering what you did."

"I didn't do anything."

"No?"

"He put out some kind of calling on you. A hit, he said."

"That's right. Do you know why I'm after him?"

"He says because of Portland. He did something in Portland."

"That's right," Minor says acidly. "He did something in Portland. What do you think he did?"

"I wasn't with him then." Johan seems calm, but even in the poor light he can see a tic jumping near the man's left eye.

Minor laughs. This ugly, bitter sound. "That's convenient, Johan. You must not know anything about him. You must not know anything about what he does." He fishes a cigarette from his pack. Lights it. His hands are still shaking from the motel room, the bullet. He drops the lighter on the table. "You're his thrall?"

"What?"

"I said, you're his thrall?"

"I'm not," Johan says.

"No?"

"I love him." Johan swallows, his eyes flashing bright and defiant. He lifts his chin. "We love each other."

A blade turns in Minor's heart at the words. "You do? After all he's done? All he *does,* you still love him?"

"I love him *because* of what he does."

Minor grins, his heart cut out from him entirely now. Eager to move forward. "Alright. So what's the plan here?"

Johan gives him a pained smile, tilts his head. "The plan?"

"Don't fuck with me."

"I'm just having this drink."

Minor gestures at Johan's face with his cigarette. "I'll put a bullet right there. Right at the bridge of the nose. And then I'll walk out the door, and get in my car, and no one will ever think about you again, because Varley will die next. You're *alone.* Lie to me one more time and me and you will try our luck."

Johan's eyes cut to the table. He takes a drink of his beer.

"So what's the plan?"

"I convince someone to come with me."

"And?"

He smiles, shrugs, while still staring at the table. "And sometimes it's easy. And then there are other times, like this. Where no one will talk to me."

Minor does not examine the similarities between their lives, pushes down the realization that he does the same for Julia. Think like that and you'll freeze and Varley will get away. He offers Johan a cruel smile and says, "He's hungry, is that it? Man's got to eat, right?"

Johan shrugs. "Something like that."

The bedroom he shared with his wife. That smirking, benevolent way Varley had left the bar that night at gunpoint, like he was doing Minor a favor.

I love him because *of what he does.*

That rage inside him comes uncoiled again. He leans forward, wearing the smile that feels in its madness like he's cutting his own face apart. "Hell, I'll go with you, Johan. You can take me."

Johan shuts his eyes, murmurs something, splays those thin, pale hands on the table.

"Get the fuck up," Minor hisses.

They stand up and walk through the bar, Minor's hand latched around Johan's biceps lest he try to run. A few hoots follow them, a few kissing noises. Someone calls out, "Bye-bye, sweethearts," followed by scattered caws of laughter. They step out the front door into the parking lot.

The night air is a glorious thing after the heat and smoke of the bar. The noise. Crickets chirring in the grass behind the motel. The highway sounds.

They start walking toward the far end of the lot, toward the orange VW.

Behind them, seconds later, Minor hears footfalls, giggling. He turns, already knowing what to expect.

It's a trio of men, red-faced and laughing. Bearded and beer-bellied, wearing grimy ball caps and mean, mirthful eyes, the three of them so similar as to be interchangeable.

Minor hears one say the word *faggot* and already knows how things will go if he pauses. Sees it like he's divining the future. He'll be jammed up with these three and Johan will run, will get away, and they'll never find him again, never find Varley, will piss away this astronomical stroke of luck, and someone else will jump them when they aren't ready, heeding the blood-calling. That'll be the end of it. He'll die. Julia will die. All the sorrow for nothing. So he turns and strides toward the three men and pulls the silver revolver from his pocket. He thinks, *Don't you run, Johan. Don't you do it.* The men, seeing the gun, all buckle and bend, hands covering their heads, their faces. One of them says, "Jesus Christ, man. We wasn't gonna do anything."

"Get your ass back inside." Minor spits, and they turn and scuttle right back through the door they just came out of.

He turns around and Johan's already gone. Hauling ass toward his orange van at the end of the lot. Minor curses, runs after him. He shouts Julia's name.

At the far side of the parking lot, Johan's furiously trying to jam his key into the door of the VW when she bolts from the passenger side of the truck, silent as smoke. She kicks at the back of Johan's leg and he buckles to one knee, the key scraping a white line in the van door. Julia shoves him onto his back and then crouches over him, laying one hand on his chest and one on his jaw, pushing his skull to the asphalt. The pale arch of his throat exposed. Minor watches her teeth rise. She looks very small above him, and strong, this single arrow of intention. Johan takes a juddering inhalation, his eyes wide, looking right at Minor. "Please," he gasps.

"Was he there?" she says, her words misshapen from the teeth in her mouth. "With Grandma and Grandpa? Aunt Heidi?"

"No," Minor says. "We need him, Julia."

"Please," Johan says, his coat fanned out on the asphalt like dark wings.

"We need him."

Julia waits a moment and then stands up.

She gets in the back of the van. Minor sits in the passenger seat, holds the gun on Johan. In the rearview mirror, the squat box of the tavern looks quaint now, pretty. He hears the faintest drift of sirens.

"Go," he says, and Johan reverses out of the lot, heads toward the highway.

"I don't know where he is," Johan says.

Julia lays a hand on his neck, and the man flinches, draws his shoulders up. "Then you're useless to us," she says.

"I might be able to find him," he says, and Minor smiles.

The sirens grow louder, and as they nose onto the highway, they pass a pair of police cruisers going the opposite way, the noise splitting the night apart.

"You still might make it through this, Johan," Minor lies. "You understand? Get me to him and we'll see how things go."

•

Bugs in the funnels of the headlights. Spatters on the windshield. Barns and fields and fences alongside the windows in the dark. The weight of the gun in his hand is a comfort.

Johan squints through the gloom beyond the windshield. They are off the highway and on some county road. Parallel to them he can see the rotating red-and-blue lights of a police cruiser. "Lot of cops out," he says.

Johan grunts noncommittally.

Minor wonders what would happen if they broke down right here. Would they make it through the night, he and Johan and Julia? What truths might be revealed between the three of them? What stories? *All the bodies we've made,* he thinks. *The heartache that trails behind us all, like a string of tin cans.*

Finally, Johan hits his blinker and they turn onto a gravel road. Rocks ping the undercarriage. The air becomes charged with the threat of the future, with what the next few moments might bring. A farmhouse slowly takes shape in the darkness. It looks decrepit and shuttered, paint flaking and chipped down to the raw gray wood in spots. The barn next to it is in similar disrepair, with a crater-sized hole in the roof like a great dark eye.

"He inside the house?"

Johan shakes his head, casts a sidelong glance at the gun in Minor's lap. "The barn." He licks his lips and, for the first time, Minor sees that veneer of bravado entirely dismantled. Johan's true face is one of fear and uncertainty.

Welcome to the club, Minor thinks.

He tells Johan to leave the keys in the van and they step out onto the driveway. Hears the insects in the grass, the thud of his heart. Julia gets out behind him, her head swiveling back and forth.

He walks around the van and seizes Johan's arm, digs the revolver into his back. Walks him to the middle of a dooryard of beaten dirt, everything around them fringed in shin-high wild grass. Julia stands on the other side of Johan; she doesn't want to be near the gun.

A form stands in the doorway of the barn, black on black.

Ice pricks Minor's scalp. His legs go watery. He squeezes Johan's arm.

John Varley steps forward. He wears clothes so aged and matted as to be indistinguishable from the dust at his feet, the weather-worn planks of the barn. He's as large as Minor remembers, but skeletal now. His hair is blond like Johan's but hangs in his face in clotted strings. A pale and bloodless face, the cheekbones jutting. He looks at Johan, notes Minor's hand around his biceps. The girl.

"You brought dinner," he says to Johan, and smiles. He looks like he's dying.

Minor licks his lips. "You remember me?"

"Course I do." Varley lifts his chin at the two of them, scratches his chin. "Been a royal pain in my ass for a while now, Duane. Nice of you to jump right in the fire."

In his periphery, Minor sees Julia dip her chin down, open her mouth. Watches those second teeth slowly slide out.

Varley smiles at her. "Brought yourself an ankle-biter."

"You look like shit," Minor says.

"Bit under the weather, won't lie." He can't seem to take his eyes off Julia, says to her, "How'd you come to run with this one, girl? What's he promised you? Whatever it is, I can offer you more."

Her teeth slowly slide back up. "You killed everybody I love," she says. She's tensed like a coiled spring. "My aunt, my grandparents."

"Oh," Varley says, drawing the word out. He looks at Minor. "Is *this* Julia? I remember now. You were so damn *concerned* about her, Duane. You let her get turned? Really? What kind of caretaking is that?" And to Julia: "You went to that house, I bet? The Children's Museum. Adeline and her cute little names for everything. Loitering in the same park she played in as a girl. Always trying to turn someone. Always trying to make a *friend*. Never understanding the less of us, the better off we are. What a sacrifice you've made, girl, just to die here in the dirt."

Heat pushing through Minor now. All those nights of death, all those harrowing dreams of vengeance, and it comes down to this half-assed showdown in an overgrown dooryard, Varley treating their hollowed-out hearts with the most casual, offhanded contempt.

"Are you sorry at all," Minor says, "for what you've done?"

Varley frowns, then smiles. "*Sorry*'s not a word I bandy about much. Hell, are *you* sorry?"

"Because I wouldn't let you sell dope in some bar? You fucking—"

"Because you had the *gall* to think you could tell me no, boy. That's why they died. That's why you should be—"

Minor squeezes the trigger, shoots Johan in the back. The crack of the round, a spray of blood from his chest. He utters a single guttural cry and falls to the dust, Varley's eyes widening in shock and surprise.

Julia sprints at him.

Varley crouches. His face ripples, teeth rising. Julia leaps at him and he plucks her from the air and turns, tossing her against the side of the barn. Its wall gives way with the snap of rotten wood and she tumbles into the dark.

He turns, his eyes moving from Minor to Johan's body and back.

"You killed him," he says, his voice glottal with shock. "My Johan."

"How's it feel?" Minor says. Fifteen, twenty feet away, and he sights down on Varley and pulls the trigger again.

Through luck or grace, the bullet gets him in the gut somewhere, Varley buckling, and Minor walks toward him, the .38 like a rock at the end of his fist. He lays the barrel against the part in Varley's hair. Pulls the trigger again.

A dry click.

The revolver's striking pin hung up on the hand-hewn bullet.

Exactly what Travis had told him wouldn't happen.

Varley's *fast*. Looks up with those black eyes and grabs Minor's wrist. He squeezes, pulping his ulna and radius bones into paste.

Minor screams and backpedals, almost falls, but Varley won't let him go. He drives a fist into Minor's guts, a white-hot burst of agony. Minor drops the gun, feels ribs explode. He gags, staggers, finally falls into the dirt. The revolver's lost—he has no feeling in his hands;

they've become these strange, useless appendages, comets drifting miles away from his own body. Dimly he feels Varley drive another fist into his spine. Another starburst of pain, but farther away this time. Pain mailed to him from another location.

He can taste the dirt. Pebbles in his mouth. He spits. He's on his stomach. He feels Varley's cold fingers atop his skull, feels him start pulling back on his head. Hears him screaming, or maybe it's Minor that's screaming. Maybe both? *He's going to pull back until he breaks my neck. Until he cracks my spine like a stick and takes my head right off.*

Blood in his mouth, spilling warm over his lips. His lungs arrowed with bone fragments.

Heidi, I tried.

I love you.

Julia, I'm so sorry.

At some point, he doesn't hear the screaming anymore.

At some point, he doesn't hear anything.

4

SUCH GRIM FINALITY

varley finds a ride • *julia makes a decision* • *the trunk* •
the barest outline of a plan is made • *an insistence to go west* •
the maker is petitioned • *all the old haunts* • *the cemetery* •
running • *vengeance is mine* • *last call*

1

Varley's on his hands and knees in the dooryard as the van's tail-lights careen madly through the dark. Minor's shot him, hurt him badly somehow, and just as Varley had been about to relieve the fucker's head from his shoulders, the girl had come out of the barn and they'd fought again. Wounded the way he was, they were too even a match for his liking, until she'd knocked him down and taken Minor's broken, dead body with her.

Varley's certain he's shattered the man's ribs into his internal organs, cracked his spine like green wood, but still they've gotten away. Christ, she'd even managed to grab that wretched gun, and all he'd gotten was a bloody scrap of her shirt.

He coughs. Spits red. Closes his eyes. The pain is significant, and that alone holds some kind of wonder. When was the last time he was truly hurt? Been years.

Sounds envelop him: Insects in the grass. A weathervane somewhere creaking in the breeze. And Johan gurgling, the hissing-snake perforation of his punctured, flattened lung. He lets out a pinched mewling sound of fear and pain. The galvanizing iron-stink of his blood not ten yards away, and it's this scent that finally stirs Varley to movement.

The bullet's inside him good, hung up somewhere in the dark meat of his guts. Something's wrong. By now he should have expelled it, the muscle and bone knitting themselves back together.

Might be in some trouble here, he thinks.

Righting himself, he stands with his hand at his stomach, and calls out Johan's name. A pair of syllables that fall from his mouth like stones, spill more blood from his lips. He's become, suddenly, a weak and diminished ghost of himself. Even before he was shot, he'd been starving. The blood-calling, he'd had no idea how frail it would make him. His first mistake.

He walks to where the boy is splayed out. Falls to his knees. Johan is on his face, his coat all twisted around him. Varley turns him over, cups the boy's head in his lap.

The eyes are like candles with their wicks pinched. Dead now, his love, dead as anything, blood all over his mouth.

Varley looks up at the sky. He lets go a single guttural expulsion of sorrow, close as one like him can manage to weeping. He dips his head then, his mouth fanged, and he settles upon Johan's throat and sups on what he can. What's left. Gossamer teeth breaking off in the cartilage and sinew. His mouth to the river of his lover's throat, the blood cooling so fast, and oh, a drumbeat of vengeance already beginning its metronome in his heart.

After, he sits there next to Johan's body. Putting his forehead to his knees and closing his eyes, he grips the scrap of the girl's shirt between his bloody fingers like something totemic.

I should have turned you when I had the chance, boy. I'm sorry.

Me and you in the dark and the cold up there? Our own kingdom up there in the ice? What a world we'd have made. What a life.

He stands, wiping his blood-splashed hands on his pants, and while the bullet is still lodged inside him, still stridently *wrong*, his back is now straight. Johan's blood doing its slow revitalizing work inside him. He pulls the boy's body from the ground gone mud-like with spilled gore and brings him over to the pile of rubble at the rear end of the barn. Had he more time, he would dig a hole and bury him. There is, yes, laughably or not, some dim part of him that still believes in the holiness of it. But mostly because a buried corpse takes longer to find by creatures, both two-legged and four.

Suddenly, he turns and spits on the floor of the barn. Something's *wrong* with Johan's blood. The taste is off, bitter.

He drops the body next to the jumble of fallen roofbeams. Johan's eyes are wide, a face gazing past the veneer of the world now. Varley lifts a fallen roofbeam, the wound in his guts muttering distantly, and then, still holding it aloft with one hand, crouches down and grabs the boy, tossing him beneath the beam. Dropping it, the latticework of timber obscures most of the corpse. Varley, having not seen daylight beyond films and photographs in the past seventy years, still remembers that what is obscured now will be visible then, so he spends some time lifting more debris and tossing it onto the pile. Eventually—tomorrow, or the day after—animals will enter the barn and perhaps wonder at the body, though only the hungriest and most desperate will attempt to eat: the strangeness of Varley's scent will keep the majority of them away. Another minute of moving planks and debris and he considers the work finished, as finished as such a thing can be. He finds the leather bag of money he's stored behind a stack of loose lumber and walks out of the barn, begins trotting down the gravel drive toward the road until it hurts too much, then keeps walking. A big-boned man with blood in his hair, heavier now than he was minutes ago.

Soon enough he makes it to the road and chances on a pair of headlights closing the distance. A pickup crests the rise and passes him, then stops and slowly reverses. Varley stands on the shoulder and the man leans over and rolls down the passenger window.

"You okay, bud?" the man says, his eyes skating up and down Varley's body, the blood all over him, the red still painting his mouth. "Christ, you get in an accident?"

Varley stands there, looks at his features warp in the pickup's sideview mirror. The mirror, the back of it silvery, coming to a point that's shaped like a bullet. Shaped like—

"Silver," Varley says.

"What's that?"

"He shot me with a fucking silver bullet." Varley reaches out and puts his hand on the sill of the truck's door and the man panics, fishtails off, engine roaring.

He walks on. If Minor had managed to land that round in his

heart, or if that one he'd nearly put into his skull had actually fired, Varley wouldn't be here right now. Once, in Manitoba, maybe sixty years before, he'd been nearly beheaded by a woodsman who'd hunted him with dogs and a silver-headed hand ax for the better part of a week, getting him once badly in the neck, and Varley afterward had spent perhaps a dozen nights in a snowed-in warren three feet underground, weeping in pain and gagging on his own blood, nearly drowning in it until his flesh stubbornly knit itself together. And a wooden stake had once been driven through his mouth, a near miss, driven through both cheeks and the bone of the lower jaw. That one had truly made him wish for death, for true death, though the poor clergyman who'd done it obviously suffered afterward. It is impossible for his kind to live a life like this—a tremendously fragile life, in its way—and not be hurt. But Christ, pain like this, it's been decades.

He feels another savage rip of sorrow move through him. Johan and his silly coat, how he mended every tear, how he brushed his hair each night and counted the strokes, even when the two of them slept among the dirt and the bugs.

Another pair of headlights, and this time Varley sticks out his thumb like a hitchhiker. He needs wheels. Needs to find the girl.

It's a police car, Varley's only marginally surprised to see, and it slows. The headlights pin him in the glare and the officer inside turns on the trouble lights as well, the night colored red and blue, red and blue, a brief blip of siren as accompaniment. Varley raises his hands.

The door opens—with the headlights upon him, there is only the barest suggestion of a body behind it. "Put your hands up," the shape says, and Varley smiles. Man sounds scared.

"Yes, sir."

Varley begins walking forward, hands aloft, the bag of money still in one fist, and the voice screeches, "Don't you *move,* son, I got a gun right on you," and it's as easy as that. Varley passes the headlights and the trooper's revealed. Quailing jowls and beautiful blue eyes, something from a painting. A black revolver that Varley bats away like a toy. He drops the bag of cash and sinks his thumbs into the trooper's eyes and the man howls and tries to skirt away, but Varley is too strong. Too savvy and too sad and too furious. The man gibbers like a child, slaps at Varley, sinks to his knees, and Varley slams the back of the trooper's head against the side of the cruiser. Again, again, the back of the skull growing soft, jellied, the white side panel of the cruiser reddening with spatters and drips. The body now like a vessel Varley might move about, a doll's body, but he keeps slamming the head against the side of the car until brain and hair lie in clots and smears, again and again until the head is a loose red bag of pulped bone and skin. Varley finally removes his hands and the body falls heavily to the road.

Son of a bitch put silver *in me,* he thinks.

In me.

Killed my Johan. Shot him in the back like a coward.

And shot me with silver.

What I'd give to kill that fucker twice. But the girl will have to do.

Someone screams, and Varley jumps a little, then realizes someone's been screaming through all of it, that in his blood-fog he was only dimly aware. He peers into the cruiser and there in the back, behind a mesh screen, a man's pushed himself into the corner of the seat. Far away as he can get. The man sees Varley—gore-slathered, exultant, black-eyed and grinning with rows of glimmering teeth that are only now starting to sink back into their gums—and screams again. He's in handcuffs, and his face is green and pallorous from the dashboard glow. There's a brief burp of static on the radio and he screams once more, as if it were his sole and singular purpose on earth. A regular scream-machine, this one.

Varley smiles, his heartache forgotten for the moment. He tucks a hank of hair behind one ear with a dripping, blood-wet hand and says, "Hey, bud. How we doing tonight?"

S he fishtails the van along the gravel road, tree branches scraping across its top. Her uncle is a silent, bent shape in the seat beside her. Everything in him broken, blood falling in strings from his mouth, drizzling into his lap. Her momma had taught her to drive during Ray Ray's benders, there in the parking lot of the motel she cleaned at. It was a thing they did more and more often as Ray Ray got meaner, as if her momma was laying the groundwork for her to run someday. She sobs, dips one side of the van into a culvert, the engine suddenly screaming until she turns the steering wheel and rights it.

Uncle Duane is dying. Clearly. There are fields on each side of them, a line of white buildings, some sort of manufacturing plant, then more fields. She chances a look over at him and cannot tell if there's any life left in him at all.

"No no no," she whispers. "Oh no no no. Please. I'm so sorry, please—"

She turns onto another road, fenced in on both sides with bracken, blackberry bushes nearly as high as the roof of the van. Almost a tunnel. She steps out and runs around to his door, bugs beating themselves against the headlights, a dog barking somewhere, and pulls him onto the hardpacked road. *Sorry I'm so sorry Uncle Duane I'm sorry for all of this* a mantra in her head as he bleeds and stares slackly at the darkened sky. Momma and Little Kev and Heidi and Grandpa and Grandma and now Uncle Duane. Death stacked on death, everyone lost to her, everyone taken. Death insisting on devouring every last fucking thing. She crouches there, puts her fingers to Duane's neck, a thing he taught her; she feels the weak, fluttering cadence of his pulse.

Alive! Oh God sorry I'm so sorry for everything, please don't die—

But he will. He will die. He's hurt too bad.

And then, inside her, some dim knowledge. A spark, a flit of light caught in amber.

He's all that she has left. She's sacrificed everything to do this, to honor the dead in her life, to even things out.

Duane, her uncle, flawed and broken as he is, has sacrificed everything too. They've gone through this hell together. He doesn't deserve to die.

He doesn't *have* to.

And she can't do this without him.

Julia moves forward, pushes the side of his face to the road so that his throat is exposed.

Her teeth slowly rise, catch the moonlight.

She bends to him.

3

Darkness. A sense of being—what is it? Untethered, somehow. Adrift in the murk.

Pain too, though. Christ, yes.

Pain at his throat—a starburst of it, some dimmed part of his mind insists, a pulse and pull and draw—and also a floating, free-formed agony all throughout his body. He smells blood. Tastes it in his mouth.

Heidi is looking at him over her shoulder and laughing, rolling her eyes at something he said, sunlight shining in her hair. Lyle is hooting in surprise, staggering around with his jaw gone, and the sound of the sniper shot comes drifting across the valley seconds later, a distant pop like a firework. Minor's bones feel liquid, like they're melting and reknitting themselves. READYMADE MEAT. Joanne looking at him from behind her desk in the Last Call, saying *I know you're just looking out.* A hundred pay phones he's spoken into, searching for Varley and finding nothing. Pulling his own blood into a syringe, filling vial after vial, the way the glass tubes go red. The greedy way they tilt them to their mouths.

Watching across the parking lot as Julia steps out of a gas station bathroom, wiping blood from her lips. Seeing his niece like that, how it feels like he's tied a chain around himself, leapt in the sea.

Heidi in pieces on the bed, in pieces on the floor. The walls. Her head like that, her hair clotted with blood.

Those two men in the Last Call that night. The happy red ruin of it, falling into madness.

The past year and a half has been a slow, measured descent into hell.

He blinks. Feels hard pills of fabric against the back of his skull. A rug? A blanket? He smells piss and the pong of gasoline. The coppery tang of old blood. His arm drifts down and he feels the pilled surface beneath him with his fingertips. He looks up, blinking, surrounded by windows covered black. Feels, somehow, a moon above him—*coffin moon,* he thinks distantly, *I'm dead and that's a coffin moon up there for sure*—and then drifts back to sleep, that moment seeming no more or less real than all the others.

Heidi leaning over, flipping a record.

Heidi in pieces.

Ferris. READYMADE MEAT.

The old man in the cabin, split apart, Julia bent to him, greedy with it.

Lyle, Lyle with the red jaw.

I love him *because* of what he does.

He's moved at some point. Dragged somewhere. Feels himself being pulled—shit *hurts,* God—feels his heels making divots in the ground.

Awakens in a space all dark and musty and closed-in. Smell of motor oil fills his nose. Gasoline and rubber. He reaches out and right near his face his hands stop. He feels the confines of a box. An entrapment. Hard like steel. His bones are on fire. And then he sleeps again.

He blinks—keeps blinking, this is his life now, these odd valleys of sleep and not-sleep—and this time he's in the backseat of a car, not the van with the darkened windows but a car, and the world is in clearly delineated planes of nearly iridescent moonlight. Lunar in its whiteness. He's in a car on a dirt road and there's a leaning wooden fence to one side with trees beyond it. Wild grass and small white flowers here and there. Pretty. He can hear the bending of those flowers in the breeze. And then something slams against the side of the car and Minor flinches and that hurts. He has been sat upright and he looks out the window toward the noise. Moving his head feels like an act of profound will. The world is so bright. The flowers ripple in the breeze. Outside the car, Julia is locked in mortal combat with a man in a black T-shirt and an ugly snarl of a mustache; his hands are wrapped around Julia's throat, and when he opens his mouth, his wicked teeth gleam. Minor croaks and paws at the door handle. The man slams Julia against the side of the car again and her skull smashes a webbed star into the driver's side window. *Not a dream,* he thinks. *Not a dream. The blood-calling. People are still after us.*

He pulls the door handle. Tries to push himself out and falls to the road, dust on his hands. The man lets out a grunt of surprise at seeing him and Julia twists one of his wrists and bites off the man's thumb. He screams and falls back, blood jetting from his hand. Julia leaps onto his chest and begins savaging his face, the grunts and gurgling screams and footfalls clouding the road with dust as the man staggers backward into the weeds, Julia still atop him. Minor slides into darkness again, the dirt cool and soft beneath his cheek.

Back in the coffin with its steel walls. He is more aware now. Recognizes it for what it is. He's in a car. He feels the pebbled mat of a trunk, the rough steel walls. The car doesn't seem to be moving. He presses against its top, tries to bring his knees up to push against the trunk, push through it. Can't manage it.

Why the fuck would Julia put him in—

No.

Minor runs his hands to his throat, his breath suddenly pinched with panic. He finds the wound there, that arcing ridge of punctures. A small half-moon of teeth marks.

No.

Oh, Christ, no no no, *please no—*

Minor begins screaming, his body bucking in the dark. He screams and hits his fists bloody. Doesn't stop screaming for a long time.

4

Varley drops the dead trooper's body in the trunk. The bag of money follows. The boy in the backseat screams again and Varley, jubilance gone, cross and hurting now as the silver does its work, sighs and considers killing him just to get him to shut up. He opens the back door and peers in.

"Close your yowling gob if you want to keep breathing, for fuck's sake."

Backed against the window, the boy takes a breath, nods feverishly, handcuffed hands at his chest. Varley closes the door, then goes back to the trunk. The trooper has a five-gallon jug of water in there, and Varley takes it and spends a few minutes cleaning the blood and hair and brains from the side of the cruiser's panel, hoping he might lessen the inevitable scrutiny. Considers putting on the trooper's uniform, but it's ruined. Still, his mind is working, attacking the angles of the thing, the big picture.

The bullet inside him is silver, and he's feasted on Johan's silver-tainted blood. He's sick and will only grow sicker. He knows it.

He sets the jug in the footwell of the passenger seat and then spends a moment figuring out how to release the 12-gauge shotgun that's locked in the rest between the two front seats. He manages it, remembering there were cartons of shells in the trunk, and spends another stretch of precious time loading the shotgun. Back in the driver's seat, a voice comes over the CB radio, a burp of static. Varley spends more time examining the thing, then finds the knob that turns it off. All the while the boy in the back is quiet.

For perhaps the first time in his life, Varley wants—*truly* wants—revenge.

In the front seat, he turns and lays an arm across the headrest. Looks at the boy through the wire mesh. Asks what his name is.

He's young—young as Johan, Varley thinks, and that throb of sadness flares inside him again—with a cap of auburn hair like someone put a bowl over his head and went blindly at the rest with scissors. His face, Varley thinks, is untrustworthy, ugly, a boy who was probably picked last for games and grew up clandestine and sneaky. Grown into his own cruelty like a vine curling along a branch. Johan had been mad in his way, gloriously so, but the meanness in this boy's eyes feels small and blackhearted.

Still, he recognizes it: *Here's one I can use.*

"Cat got your tongue, youngblood? Well, let's get a move on, then."

It takes Varley another moment to find the switch that shuts off the trouble lights on the roof, and then they're on the road. John Varley, driving a damn cop car. What a life this has been! Even shot through with heartache the way it is. He hears the young man whimpering like a whipped dog in the backseat. His sweat, Varley smells it: that sharp, cloying tang of terror. Perfume to him. He breathes deep, starts looking for another building where he might perform the business at hand. No way in hell he's going to find that girl just driving around, and certainly not in a stolen cruiser with a dead cop in the trunk. Unless . . .

Maybe there's a way through this after all.

Often, dirt-bound in a shallow grave, or in a windowless room with the door boarded shut, John Varley would sometimes allow himself the grand luxury of remembering what had happened in Starling's office after he'd lifted the Browning pistol up to the ancient, unnameable thing behind the desk. How he had raised the gun and the thing had smiled at him. How it had been the smile of a parent humoring a child's foolishness.

With, Varley believes to this day, something of love in it.

It had smiled and then leapt over Starling's dripping desk, the teeth springing from the gums, the eyes with a sudden black film falling over them. It had wrested the gun from his hand so easily, and then pushed Varley's jaw up and latched those teeth at the side of his neck. But had it ripped the bone from the flesh? No. Taken his head off? No again. Could have but did not.

It had bitten, supped a bit, even gently, and that was all.

It had turned John Varley, *made* John Varley, there in that red-spattered room with the light of the gas lamps trembling against the walls and the stink of Davis Starling's shit and spent blood a fragrance that Varley would forever equate with rebirth. He'd stood there, his skull cradled in the palm of the thing's hand, and he had been held in a kind of ecstasy.

That room, where Varley met his true father.

How old had he been then, Varley's often wondered. Had his Maker slept his sleep in the darkened crypts of Galilee? Skulked the narrow, labyrinthine alleys of Athens? Strode the killing fields of the Civil War like some revenant, there and gone with the sunrise? He was not a wondering man, Varley, but he has wondered about this. After, it had walked him over to Starling's chair like one would help an elderly grandparent, a guiding hand at his back.

"Your life has ended," the Maker said with a smile. The words strange and misshapen behind those doubled teeth.

"Has it?" Varley touched his fingers to his neck, and they came away bloody. He felt a dizzying thrill shoot through him.

"Ended and begun, yes."

Varley peered down at his boots, strangeness coursing through him. He looked for the revolver on the floor, couldn't locate it. Not that it mattered—some pact had been forged between them.

"Did you poison me?"

"Ha! I like that. Poisoned you." His Maker knelt before him on the rug, its chin still glistening, its eyes black and catching the curve of gaslight in them. Skin cadaverous and drawn, like flesh cinched tight over a skull. How old? Varley watched as the bloody second teeth crept into its gums once again. "A great number have raised guns against me, boy, but you did it without pause. Fearlessly."

"If it's fearlessness," Varley remembers having said, "then why are my drawers wet?" His Maker had lifted its broken face to the lamps and laughed. A sound like bones cracking. Varley looked into those black eyes, swam in that gaze. It put a white hand on Varley's knee and it was cold, cold, a thing of the grave. Its grin without the second teeth was somehow more terrible.

It said, "I offer you your life, little one. Better than before. A gift, for your fierceness of spirit."

"Why, though?"

"Why let you live?" It lifted its chin toward Starling's head. "Why not do you like I did him there, who tried to double-cross me?"

"Right."

His Maker had stood, walked to a lamp, traced a sconce with one bloody finger. The light nearly warmed its features but couldn't quite manage it. The hair that hung from the skull lit up like tendrils of fire. "A lark, I suppose." It shrugged, turning to him. "Or perhaps I see my viciousness in you. This truly is a dark and wondrous life, boy."

"I don't understand you." Varley's voice like someone speaking in another room.

"You will. With cautiousness, you'll have time to understand everything. And if you're careful, time will cease to matter at all."

It turned then, and Varley swore he could hear the creaking of sinew, though perhaps it was only the thing's garments, tightened now with drying blood.

Voices, then, beyond the door. Muttering, a holler. Feet on the floorboards.

"They're coming for you," the Maker said, touching a gray finger to the wound at Varley's neck, then licking its finger with a tongue white as a grub.

"Me?"

"You." It walked to the rear door and threw the deadbolt, opened the door onto a muddied, narrow alleyway carved in moonlight. "You're the only one here, after all." The Maker stepped out, then crouched suddenly, as if shot, this arching movement, so fast that Varley expected the sound of a pistol. Instead came the sudden, terrible elongation of bones, the cracking, wet rearrangement of flesh. A tuft of fur here, the splintering of a femur, a body in profound alteration. The thing's clothes fell from it in a bloodied heap, became as dark and indistinguishable as the ground itself.

A wolf stood in the alley now, panting, its fur mottled black and gray and white.

Varley did not see its eyes, for the thing turned, loped away out of the mouth of the alley. Better apparently to be a wolf trotting through Pioneer Square than a seven-foot-tall cadaver wanted for murder.

Varley, standing there with Davis Starling's head still resting on the desk, and a number of murdered men in the front room, did the exact thing that went against his nature. He stepped out the same door and ran away. Two pairs of bloody footprints on the floor of the office, and then only one in the alleyway.

It's the witching hour now, and the highway is sparsely populated, mostly ghostly big rigs running their freight along the black ribbon of road. The flare of sodium lights, the ticking of billboards as they pass: Marlboros, a Chevrolet lot some miles ahead, a local radio station. Varley's euphoria over escaping the police cordon has faded, and an assemblage of pain begins to pronounce itself in his guts again. He thinks of Johan, shot in the back on a plot of abandoned land. All good things eventually lean toward murk and shadow, and his sorrow bangs an iron cup against the cage of his heart. The boy in the rear-view mirror will not stop peering at him with those wet, watchful eyes.

Varley asks again what his name is.

"Emmett," he says this time, his voice a husky croak.

"How old are you, Emmett?"

"Twenty."

Varley nods. "Emmett, twenty years old. What brings you to be seated in the back of this police car, Emmett?"

He says nothing for a moment, and then, "My truck broke down." The truculence unmistakable.

Varley smiles; a born liar. The way life handed you these people. "And you just come to find yourself handcuffed back there because your truck broke down? Doesn't sound fair to me."

"Well, also I stoled some shit," Emmett says after a while.

"There you go," Varley says. "What'd you steal?"

Emmett sniffs, disdainful. "A six-pack. And some cigarettes."

"What kind?"

"Camels. I only smoke Camels, unless somebody buys something else for me."

"Pack of smokes and some beer, and they act like you're the prince of the Graybar Hotel? Doesn't seem like something to get cuffed over."

"That's how I feel about it too."

"Beer and cigarettes," Varley muses, shaking his head. "Fuel for any reasonable man, I figure."

Silence then, the mileposts ticking along. Varley waiting.

"Sir, you mind if I ask you a question?"

"What's that?"

"Well, I'm wondering if you got plans to kill me. Like you did to Trooper Meachum back there. I mean, not that I mind. I'm grateful, honestly."

"Meachum, his name was?"

"Yes, sir," Emmett says. "Biggest pain-in-the-ass trooper in the county. Corliss Meachum. Man broke my ribs last time he took me in."

"What were you in for that time?"

"Well, robbery, same as this one."

"You got a pattern to your work, it seems."

Emmett takes on the wistful tone of a man reliving his glory days. "It's true. There was this old lady on Joe Bean Road one time, that county road gets all curvy by the lake? Couple of real nice houses out there, supposed to be empty around autumn-time. I went in through the kitchen window, wiggled in over the sink. She got the drop on me, sat there with a scattergun put on me till the cops come."

"The old lady did?"

"Yuh. So there's me, sitting in a chair, my hands up in the air for an hour, waiting for Corliss Meachum to walk in and bust my ribs up while he's arresting me. Saying I 'fell down on the way to the patrol car.' Lady gave me a glass of water at least, that was nice." Emmett leans forward again, deciding, Varley supposed, that his life has been spared, and at this revelation grows suddenly animated. "Sir, you mind turning the heater up a bit? Pretty cold back here, and Corliss caught me without a jacket."

Varley spends another minute finding the heater. Turns it on, the roar of it filling the car.

"Appreciate it."

More silence. Varley realizes he can actually feel the bullet in his guts now, this glowering little kernel of poison.

They move beyond a big rig, the truck's headlights filling the interior as they pass. Varley locks eyes with the boy in the rearview, and he sees Emmett's face tighten with sudden horror—noting in the cast of the rig's lights, for the first time, Varley's fog-shape reflecting back at him in the mirror.

"Emmett," Varley says, "I'll tell you what. I am a sorrowful man. The love of my life was shot in the back tonight, shot in the back by a coward, and vengeance is on my mind. And you, son? Well, I think you might be able to help me."

Emmett swallows so loud Varley hears his throat click. "I—I'm not sure if I can, sir."

"Oh, you can."

"Sir, I—"

Varley holds up a hand, moored once again in that image of Johan beneath the rubble of the barn. His empty eyes. "No more," he says, and Emmett wisely shuts his mouth.

The backbone of night, brief islands of illumination here and there as they move down the road. He is looking for just the right place. Heartache moves through him, yes, and the pain in his guts has truly begun to sing. But this boy in the backseat, he's a gift. Varley thinks of his Maker standing on the other side of that bloody desk, saying, *How is it you'll kill what's already dead, little one? Got some bright idea you might bury me twice?*

A plan forms. Loosely made, but sure enough to gamble on.

He turns the cruiser down one more dirt road, fence posts ticking past. He touches the scrap of the girl's shirt in his pocket, looking for one last tucked-away building where he might do his work.

5

Minor's sitting in the backseat of the car Julia's procured. A 1973 Chrysler Newport, olive green, big as a schooner. Plains and scalloped hills outside, the dark sutures of power lines running longways in the distance.

"Why?" is all he asks. He wipes sweat from his forehead and looks at his palm. It comes away red with blood. He's *sweating* blood. Jesus Christ. He remembers the same thing happening with Julia, those first terrible weeks after she'd been turned. Vomiting blood, sweating blood, pissing it out. Her own blood expelled so she'd become reliant on devouring others'.

"Why?" he asks again.

Julia's made herself a small shape in the front seat. Her chin's tucked to her chest and he sees the pale stalk of her neck. The black wings of her hair on each side. "He broke all of your bones, is why. He broke your back. You'd have died if I didn't."

He will not allow himself to touch the bite, that half-moon of delicate scabs at his throat.

"You should have let me."

"What? Die?"

"Yes," he says. "Hell yes."

Two nights now since she bit him, and it's bright now in a way he's never seen before. Julia has talked about the moon sometimes, since turning, and he had listened, but he hadn't *understood.* It is like something alive on his skin. A kind of caress. It is a good feeling, the moon up there, a pure feeling, and Minor loathes himself for it. Almost hates Julia for it, but can't.

"I couldn't do that," Julia says, her voice suddenly thick. "Uncle Duane, I *couldn't*. You're all I got left."

"I'm not me, though."

"Duane—"

"No," he says, "listen to me," and ah, shit, he's crying now, his vision blurring, "I stayed with you after Adeline, after you went into that house. After I told you not to. Told you that you wouldn't be able to see how big it was, Julia, a decision like that. I protected you. I followed you through all this. And then you turned me? Julia, goddamn. You *turned* me?"

An edge to her words when she says, "What, was I supposed to *ask* you? He smashed your bones into your lungs. I could *feel* your bones, Uncle Duane, they were *soft*."

"I didn't want this," he says, his voice cracking. He runs his hands down his face, looses a hitching sob. His palms come away wet and red again. "Look at me." She doesn't move.

"Julia, look at me."

She turns and looks at him, her eyes crawling across his face.

"I'm sorry," she says.

"Where's the gun?"

She looks away. "I hid it."

"Give it to me."

"No."

"Julia—"

"*No.*"

"I don't *want* this," he says, looking at himself in the Newport's rearview mirror. Sees his face blood-pocked, red oozing from his pores. The whites of his eyes bright in the gloom. Sees, though maybe it's just his imagination, the first blurring of his features peering back at him.

"Too bad," Julia says, her voice steel now. "This is where we are."

Ten minutes later they're on the road. Minor's driving.

He insists on going west. "The gun's in the trunk, isn't it?"

She's in the backseat. Knows he wants space, time to think.

"Yes," she says.

"Does it hurt you back there? Being that close to the bullets?"

"I'm fine."

"If I was in the trunk during the day, where were you?"

"I ran the car over a tarp so the wheels were on it. Then I kind of burrowed in underneath."

"Jesus."

After a while, she says, "How far do you think it goes?"

"The blood-calling? I don't know."

"But you want to outrun it?"

"Look, we tried with him," Minor says, peering at her smoke-shape in the rearview. "We tried to do it how you wanted, tried to kill him, and look where it got us. We can't beat him, Julia."

"But you hurt him," she says.

"Not enough. Clearly."

"Duane—"

"I want to go *home*." He wipes at his bloody face with a rag. "I want to be with Heidi."

"What do you mean?"

"I want to see her."

He turns on the radio, gets static, turns it off.

"It's just," Julia says, "he's not dead, Duane. We didn't get him. That was the plan, wasn't it?"

"We *lost*," he says, almost spitting it. And then, softer, "We lost, Jules."

She opens her mouth to say something and Minor shakes his head. "I am *tired*. Alright? Tired of all of it. I love you, Julia, but I'm going home."

service station on a country road, the pumps off, doors locked. Gas stations and bars and abandoned buildings, his palaces in the dark. He and Emmett go in the back, where Varley kicks the door in, waits poised at the threshold for an alarm to sound. When he doesn't hear anything, they step into a back office, and Varley turns on the lights there. Then he walks into the front part of the station, bag of money in his hand, the boy following at a cower.

He's careful not to turn on any lights up here. There's a cash register, a few shelves packed with goods and a humming glass case in the back, which Emmett zeroes in on. Opening one of the doors of the case, he finds himself a six-pack of Stroh's and cracks a can, his hands still cuffed. Varley roams the aisles, smiling at his luck: he finds a small section of one of the shelves dedicated to tools.

Emmett drops a can and belches, loud and airy. Varley looks around the front room of the station, notes the wooden column in front of one of the aisles. It rises up to the ceiling. Good enough.

"Ah, damn," he says, careful to make his voice sound wondrous, shocked. Emmett's drawn from the case like a moth, another can of Stroh's held between his cuffed hands.

"What you got, boss?"

Varley holds up a hammer, the price tag still on the steel head, and before the boy can register shock, register anything, really, he swings the blunt end into the boy's throat. Emmett's eyes go pinwheel-big and he drops his beer, bent over, his hands clawing at his neck. Varley hoists him up by his handcuff chain, the can exploding foam all over the floor. He raises Emmett's arms up and drives a clean tenpenny

nail—box of fifty of them for sale right next to the hammer—into one
of the eyelets of the handcuff chain, pinning him to that wooden column, arms above his head like a flamenco dancer. Emmett gags, kicks
out at him. Varley grunts and takes it, then drives a nail through the
palm of one of Emmett's hands for the trouble. The boy screams and
bucks as blood runs down his arm and Varley, tongue peeking out
between his teeth, gets a few more nails through his hands into the
column, just for safety's sake. Just for the hurt of it.

Varley stands before the boy, who continues to howl, eyes bulging,
veins like worms on each side of his neck.

There's a significant concern about the noise—yes, the front
door's locked, and yes, surely most of the screaming's blocked out,
and yes, they're on a somewhat rural thoroughfare. But Varley's also
seen a pair of cars pass by on the road out front just in the few minutes they've been here, and his luck, clearly, seems to be on the down-
swing.

And for this next piece of the plan, he'll need silence and attention; this fool, screaming his head off, offers neither.

Varley drops the hammer to the floor, looks at Emmett with his
hands on his hips. "You need to quiet down, son. Or I'll have to quiet
you."

Emmett, to his credit, has more string than Varley had first
thought: he shrieks and spits at Varley and then shrieks again. His
voice cracking with the effort. Kicks at him, though pulling on the
nails in his hands like that must hurt terribly.

Varley sighs, his own guts banked with that slow fire, and he's losing an alarming amount of blood too. He walks back over to the meager home improvement section. Sandpaper, scissors, a dusty tube of
caulking and—there it is.

He takes the hacksaw off its peg on the shelf and walks back over
to Emmett, whose hair lies plastered to his forehead in sweaty whorls.
If it's possible, the boy's eyes widen even more. He kicks desperately
at Varley and Varley slaps his leg away and places the hacksaw's teeth

against Emmett's neck, the flesh dimpling, the boy *truly* screaming now as Varley begins sawing at the hard knob of Emmett's voice box. It's a delicate matter, given the closeness to the carotid; Varley doesn't want him to bleed to death. He'll be useless then. Emmett gibbers and tries to turn away but his nailed hands keep him in place. Blood spatters warm on Varley's face as he grinds the saw through the knob of cartilage and the boy gags and sputters, his voice strangely insectile now as his feet *shish shish* against the cement floor. Blood darkening his shirt like a bib. But at least it's *quiet* now, relatively so, and Varley drops the hacksaw to the floor.

Much like the blood-calling, a summoning is a knowledge inherited with his turning. Intuitive. Simply known.

He stalks the aisles one more time and finds a container of salt. Anything would be fine, but salt runs no risk of evaporating. He doesn't know how long this will take, or if it will even work. But he pours a circle of salt around the column, around the writhing boy nailed there, and begins his ablutions. Dropping the container, he walks across the circle and presses a hand to Emmett's throat, wetting his palm with blood, the boy absolutely slicked in the stuff now, Varley a little incredulous he hasn't passed out yet. He crouches, sets his bloody palm inside the circle at Emmett's feet. Thinks of Johan's coat, his effete brutality, his joy in the thousand small moments they shared together.

I should have turned you when I had the chance.

You should be here with me.

You would have loved this.

A short incantation is performed. A petitioning. The words are guttural, bone-simple, and his voice cracks with loss throughout. Above him, the aperture in Emmett's throat makes a hissing sound. Varley goes to stand again and the bullet in him twists in his guts and he cries out. Walking at a crouch, afraid to look at the wound, to see the blood-rot that will inevitably be there, he gets the bag of money from the back room and then staggers behind the counter, where he finds a folding chair and sinks into it like an old man, groaning in pain. Though it's still night out, he falls into the uneasy slumber of the ill, images of Johan at play behind his lids.

Varley awakens sometime later to the sound of *chewing*, intimate in its closeness. He lifts his head, confused. He'd been dreaming of Johan's golden hair in braids, what he'd have looked like with the teeth on him, turned at last.

He blinks in the dark.

There's something crouched before Emmett.

It's on its knees, dining upon the hanging strings of the boy's intestines. The form is smoke-black, skeletal, limbs like a gathering of charred sticks. Varley rises from his chair, groaning again as he does—the bullet still working its slow brutalities through him. He imagines Emmett must be dead, but no. A foot twitches, the silent head shivering upon the neck.

The thing sees Varley move from behind the counter and stands as well. A gray rope of Emmett's guts is speared on its teeth and it's pulled taut before falling, slapping against the boy's leg. The thing crouches, clawed fingers splayed wide. It hisses at Varley like a cat.

"Father," Varley says.

His shock and disappointment are unmistakable: he'd hoped for a reckoning. Christ, he realizes now he'd dared hope for some sort of *welcoming* from his Maker. But this? Whatever it's become, it's a far cry from the malevolent, cocksure thing that had toyed with him in Davis Starling's office all those decades back.

"It's a gift," Varley says, gesturing at Emmett's body. "For you."

The thing lifts its misshapen head inquisitively, takes a cautious step forward, black eyes on him, and then goes back to dining upon Emmett's insides. The boy, finally, appears to have died, chin dipped to his breastbone.

Is this, Varley wonders, what the future holds for him? This amalgam of skeleton and char, looking like some trash the devil might piece together?

Varley walks around the counter, approaches the thing. Talking softly, the way you might approach something wild, he says, "I called you. A summoning."

The thing's skull is nearly buried inside Emmett's rib cage, rooting in the chest cavity. Animal sounds in there. One of the boy's hands comes undone from the nails, ripped free through the bones of the palm, and that arm falls, slapping the creature's back. It grunts in surprise, still rooting.

Varley reaches into his pocket, holds out the scrap of the girl's shirt like an offering.

"I was hoping you might find her for me, Father. I gave you this boy, after all. A gift. I was hoping it might curry your favor? Revenge is my business, see, and I was hoping you might bind me to her, so that I might hunt her down." He's babbling—he hadn't expected his Maker to be so *changed*. Everything has veered off course.

Finally, it rises, takes a step toward him. Teeth crowding that distended jaw, wisps here and there of filthy charred hair that hangs lank on its shoulders. "A gift," it says, surprising him with speech. Sounding as if the aperture of its throat were cast in ground glass, and yet the mockery in its voice is impossible to miss. The jelly of Emmett's insides sheens its face.

Varley takes an involuntary step backward, hardly aware that he's done it.

"And yet," the Maker continues, "this gift comes with a request." The teeth slowly slide back into its jaws. "Which sounds less like fealty to me, and more like you seeking favors."

"Father, what—what happened to you?"

"Me?" the thing says, mock-coquettish, laying a hand across its chest. "Whatever do you mean?"

"You've changed."

The Maker nods. "One thing you can be certain of, boy. Things change. Even for those such as us." It casts a sideways glance at Emmett's corpse, as if there might still be meat worth dining upon.

"But what happened?"

"Caught a sunrise, is what happened, boy. Got caught wanting and had the dawn fall on me."

"All this from the sun? Jesus."

"Hell, one such as you would have been nothing but ash in the breeze." It distractedly slips its fingers in the hole at Emmett's throat, the divide Varley made with the hacksaw. Hooks its fingers in there and pulls. Emmett's blood is cooling now—Varley can smell it—but it still spills, and his Maker puts its mouth to the rip. After a moment, it rears its head back and says, "Revenge, you said?"

"Yes."

"Why is it you want revenge on this child?"

Varley looks away. "My thrall was murdered." Even as he says it, he feels shame—Johan from that first night had been more than a thrall. The shame comes from using language his Maker will understand. Varley, made weak like that. Small like that, and dishonest.

His Maker turns, looks at him. The black eyes rove his face, his body. The bloody lips split into a grin. In that grin he sees some minute vestige of the being he'd met in Davis Starling's back room. The glee. The boundless, sweeping arrogance. "And you want vengeance?"

"That's right."

He gestures at the scrap of Julia's shirt Varley holds in his hand. "You want me to bind you to the killer of your thrall."

"Yes, Father."

"Who was murdered."

"Yes."

The grin splits wider. This sun-blackened death's head. The spindled arms. The xylophone rib cage, the shriveled little cock hanging there. "A thrall can't be *murdered*, boy. They're in service to you. They're an object to be used."

The words acid in his throat, Varley says, "Yes, Father."

His Maker steps toward him, again with this inquisitive, doglike tilt of its head. The eyes close languidly, and then open, and a tremor moves through Varley. There comes from the thing a hissing sound, like sand sifting to the floor, and it takes Varley a moment to realize that his Maker is *laughing*. Laughing at him.

"You fell in *love*," it croons. "Didn't you? With a *thrall*. Oh my. All that and with the stink of silver on you too."

"I was shot," Varley says, his voice small.

"You're a disappointment for certain."

Varley sneers, steps forward, resentment and rage suddenly pulsing through him. "Oh, please. I've left a *sea* of bodies in my wake. And you? Calling *me* a disappointment? You look like you got a bit too close to the smoker, old one. I'd watch my tongue."

"I remember you now," his Maker says. They have begun a dance, slowly revolving around Emmett's body, around the column. The tight space between the counter and the aisles of the station. Varley puts the scrap of Julia's shirt in his pocket once more, flexes his hands. "The back room of that tavern. Seattle. That fellow's head on the desk."

"That's right."

"You screamed like a child when I turned you."

"That's not true."

"And look at you now. To think I traveled here at your calling. You think I'd *help* you, little one? For a *thrall*? You've squandered this life I've given you."

"And for me," Varley says, the bitterness unmistakable, "to have held you in regard for this long. I was a goddamn fool, wasn't I?"

His Maker crouches, splays his burnt-kindling arms. The two of them have tracked a loose circle of gore around Emmett's body, darkening the cement with his blood. Smeared the salt into bloody paste. Varley can still feel the silver in him, and he thinks of Johan, laughing, that blond hair trailing behind him as the wind whipped through the car. Thinks of them in bed, Johan tracing a pattern on Varley's chest, nestled there in the crook of his arm. The heat of him.

His teeth rise.

They rise, and he runs headlong toward the one who made him.

•

He leaves the cruiser behind the service station.

He walks toward the highway, leather bag in hand, blood-soaked and exultant, and finds after some miles walking the dark road a motor court, the neon VACANCY sign pulsing in the night. The parking lot is half full. There's a pay phone outside. Through the lobby window, he sees the proprietor, a man wearing glasses and a pink collared shirt. He's watching a small TV on the counter and eating a sandwich. The TV is reflected in his lenses as he chews.

Beneath his shirt, Varley touches the tender flesh where his bullet wound had been; the skin is still divoted and pink but the bullet's gone, expelled and left there amid the broken matchstick ruins of his Maker, in the shadow of Emmett's body still hanging from the service station column by one hand.

In the dented metal of the pay phone box, Varley grins, watches his features warp.

Who made these rules? he wonders. Who was the first old one? Who, when it came down to it, had made his Maker? The one who Varley has just bested? Whose throat he's just supped from? Ill or not, weak or not, dining on his Maker's blood has affected him profoundly, wondrously—the silver has been pushed from his body, and he feels new and furious life moving through him. Had he known that fratricide would have offered him all this, he'd have summoned his Father to him decades ago.

He *feels* the girl now, has somehow bound himself to her. A kind of archaic, ancient homing radar.

She's going west. She's not far.

I'll find you wherever you go, girl.

But he already *knows* where she's going, doesn't he?

Where does an animal go when it's injured? When it's frightened and alone?

It goes somewhere familiar and hides.

She's going home. Going back to Portland.

He dials Information, makes a request. The operator asks him to wait.

There is a sense, just riffling the outskirts of his consciousness, that the Maker's blood holds possibilities for him that Varley's only dreamt of. Sick or not, the judgmental old fuck was a treasure trove of abilities and power. And without its body sun-weakened as it was, Varley would have never stood a chance against it.

He's told to deposit money for the call. The coins *thunk* home. He hears a voice on the other end of the line. Varley's already grinning against the mouthpiece.

"Portland Police Bureau," the voice says. "How can I direct your call?"

"I'd like to speak to the officer in charge of the murder of those folks from the Last Call Tavern, back in '75? I got some information."

Twenty or thirty seconds of silence and then a voice, keen with attention: "Yeah, this is Detective Scoggins. Who is it I'm speaking to?"

"Well, hey there, Detective Scoggins." Varley looks at the red neon VACANCY sign out there by the road. Sees the name of the place above it, done up in cursive script: *The Hi-Brite Motor Court.* "My name's Hugh Bright. You the one working the murders that happened to the owners of that bar couple years back? And the lady that lived upstairs? If so, I got some information you might want to hear." He peers up at the moon. "It's pretty late, glad I caught you."

"I am," he says slowly. "And how is it you came by your information, Mr. Bright?"

Varley can't stop smiling. "Oh, gosh, truth be told, I'm privy to all kinds of things, sir."

Something clatters to the floor on the other end of the line, and he imagines this Detective Scoggins in a mad scrabble to get a fellow cop to pick up another handset, jump on the line and listen in. Man's eager, just what Varley wants.

"Alright, Mr. Bright. What kind of information is it you have for me?"

"Well," he says coyly, "it's not so much about the murders, as it is Duane Minor."

Silence on the other end, a feeling like the air is electrified. And then Scoggins says, "It's been a while since I looked at the case. Can you remind me who exactly Duane Minor is? Where he fits into all this?"

"Look, can we avoid the dance, Detective? I was a regular there in the Last Call. He was a bartender there, related to the owners. Before his old lady was killed, he had a, a niece, I believe." Here's the tricky part, where he must glean information without giving too much of his own away.

"Okay, Mr. Bright. Have you and I talked before? I did some extensive interviews with regulars at the bar after the events that happened, and your name's not ringing a bell."

"Well, I did my drinking elsewhere after all that."

"Huh. Fair enough. What exactly is it I can do for you tonight? Like you said, it's a bit late, and I'd like to head on home."

"Of course, Detective. It's just— I was thinking of the girl, you know. His relative, his niece."

"Yeah, unfortunately, I'm not at liberty to discuss an active investigation, Mr. Bright."

"Well, the word among us regulars was that she was either kidnapped by Duane, or went off with him by choice, after all that terrible business went down with the murders."

Another pause, and then a stiffness in Scoggins's voice—thinking, most likely, that he's landed some ghoul on the line. "Yeah, I can't be discussing any of the particulars of this case with you, sir. Have a good night."

A catalog of abilities held tight inside his Maker's blood, and Varley, having imbibed of that blood, weakened or not, sun-diluted or not, has now taken ownership of them.

"Detective Scoggins," he says, and he *pushes*, this *flex* in his mind, "what is the girl's name? Duane Minor's niece, what is her name? It's Julia, isn't it?"

Scoggins clears his throat, sounding uncomfortable as he says, "Julia Shaw, that's right."

"Where is she from?"

Woodenly: "I shouldn't be telling you."

"You will, though. Where is she from, Detective?"

A sharp intake of breath, like the detective's cut his finger or stubbed his toe. "What are you doing to me?"

Another *push*. "Where is she from?"

"She lived with the Minors above the Last Call. Until the murders. And then Duane took her."

"But she's his niece, correct? Not his daughter. His niece."

"That's right. God. Her mom's in prison."

"Where?"

"New York. Ah, Christ. Upstate New York. What're you doing to me?"

"If the girl—Julia Shaw—if she was to come back to Portland, where would she go?"

"I don't know."

"If you had to guess."

"I'm really not sure."

"Any other family in town? Anyone that's not in prison?"

"I—I'm not—"

He *pushes* again, imagining the push traveling through the phone lines, skittering along the scaffolding of power lines and deep underground, this *command* that bursts forth at the other end of the phone and arcs this faceless cop's will into his own.

Scoggins sounds like he's choking. "The bar's been remodeled, sold. Someone lives in the apartment upstairs. Minor never arranged burial services"—he starts coughing, a smoker's hack that trails off into heavy breathing—"but the family, the wife and grandparents, have plots in Lone Fir Cemetery." He clears his throat again and says, as if waking from a deep sleep, "This is John Varley, isn't it? You killed all those bikers in the garage. And Ed and Joanne Shaw too, right? Heidi Minor? Karen Malone? You did all of them, didn't you? All the things they say about you are true. Even back in '31—"

Varley hangs up and walks into the lobby of the motor court. The proprietor's finishing the last bite of his sandwich. Varley approaches and the man wipes the crumbs from his hands, holds up a finger as he chews. "'Scuse me," he manages. "One sec." Still watching television.

"Do you have a car?"

The proprietor frowns, swallows. "Pardon me?"

Sweet Christ, his Maker's blood moves through him like a baptism. He reaches over, palms the man's head into the counter. Once, twice. The proprietor squawks, glasses breaking across the bridge of his nose, blood bursting from the split.

"Car," Varley says, his hand around the collar of the man's pastel pink shirt, the proprietor slapping at his pocket, pulling out a key chain bristling with keys. He holds it up and Varley takes it.

"Which key?" He smells the blood on the counter and can't help it—his teeth rise. He swipes at the spatters with his free hand, puts the smear of it to his tongue.

The man blubbers. "What?"

Varley has to focus to push his teeth down. Concentrate. "Which key?"

Weeping now, the man points at a large gold key on the ring.

"And the car?"

"N-n-*Nova!*"

Varley turns back and sees a tomato-red Chevy Nova parked right there in front. "Christ," he mutters. He lets go of the man's collar, turns around.

At the front door stands some outraged, puffed-up South Dakotan—baseball hat, beard, cowboy boots. He's spied the shakedown through the window, and has the temerity to be holding a tire iron in his fist. Varley grins and moves to him and the two of them collide in the doorway of the lobby. The man tries to bring the iron down and it smacks ineffectively against Varley's raised forearm. Varley laughs and drives his hand into the man's guts as the iron clangs to the ground. Blood spills slow from the man's mouth, his eyes roving Varley's face with shock and wonder, like there's some great mystery he must suddenly decipher. He squeezes Varley's shoulder like a friend saying goodbye.

Varley takes his hand away; it's gloved in blood up to the wrist. He marvels at the four-inch-long claws now tapering the end of his fingers, sheened in light from the parking lot. The man drifts softly, almost gingerly, to his knees, his baseball hat sliding off before he falls in the open doorway. Varley wipes his bloody hand on the man's shirt as best he can, and there's another odd sense of *pulling* as the claws slowly retract, his own fingernails made visible again. These new possibilities leaping around inside his body.

Hearing the proprietor making panicked half words behind him, Varley walks out to the Nova. Whistles as he does it, jingling the man's keys. His good fortune has returned. Christ, he thinks, making himself wolfish might not be too far off from here. A bat? Maybe so. Might find himself able to walk up walls soon enough.

The Nova starts easily. Three-quarters of a tank.

He turns on the radio, finds himself a country song. Smiles in the mirror, grins big at the serpentine smoke-shape he sees there.

Child, here I come. Ready yourself for the whirlwind.

7

They're outside of Billings, Montana, when Minor asks her how she compartmentalizes it. They're driving west and he's been quiet most of the ride. Radio tower lights pulse like eyes out in the distance.

"What's that?" Julia says.

"How do you do what's needed? How do you live with it?"

Looking out the window, she says in a small voice, "You're asking me?"

"I am."

"Eat people, you mean? Drink their blood?"

"Yeah." He drives for a while longer and then says, "Every person I ever hurt, killed—even VC, and they never wanted us to see them as people—I think about. I dream about them. They fucking, they *roost* in here, you know?" Taps his temple and looks over at her. His window's down, warm air ripping through the truck's interior, and her hair whips around. "How do you live with yourself? I don't mean it like an asshole, I just—"

"I get you," she says. And then, after that: "I think my mom saved my life. Me and Kev's. I think that Ray Ray would have killed us. Killed her. Maybe not that day, but that shit just gets bigger and bigger. He was so angry at all of us and I never could figure out why. I think he was angry with everything, really, and we were just the people in front of him."

"I hear you."

"Well, no, I'm explaining what I mean. I think my mom killed him to set us free. Because she knew that sooner or later, he'd get one of us. He didn't let her make phone calls, did you know that? He'd check the phone bill every month and mark calls with a red pen that he didn't know what they were. She had to explain each one. 'Oh, that's the doctor's office, hon, remember when Little Kev got that cough wouldn't go away?' 'That's the gas company, I called to make sure they got the check before they shut everything off,' all that. Pinching her arm when she walked by, leaving bruises, for no reason at all. Slapping her on the butt when she was cooking, but so hard that she was a little scared, and then doing it harder, to the point that it hurt, daring her to say something. I felt so relieved those Fridays when he would get paid, because he would almost always go get drunk for a few days. And then by Sunday you'd start to get nervous again, because maybe he's coming home today, maybe tomorrow, maybe Tuesday."

"I'm sorry."

"There's no way he would have let her leave. So she did what she had to do. And that's what I'm doing."

"What do you mean, Julia?"

"I'm doing what I have to do. To get him. Varley. Me and you tried all kinds of things, remember? So I wouldn't have to eat? We tried saving up your blood, tried giving it to me a vial at a time. The blood got too old, or there wasn't enough of it. I have to eat. That's the way it is."

"I can't do it," he says. "I won't."

Wait till you get hungry, she thinks, but doesn't say it.

He finds another motel, parks the car around the side of the building, pays the sour-faced clerk in dimes; their treasure after Julia punched through a vending machine some miles back.

"You can have the room," she says, "just be sure to let me out."

"Are you sure? The blood-calling?"

"No one's going to find me in here. And we're all asleep during the day, remember?"

Then she clambers into the trunk. A dim, shameful part of him tells him to run, run, that he still might escape all this. But he can't do anything close to it, not with Varley out there.

And after all that's happened, he can't leave Julia.

He puts their gun in the glovebox, surprised to find that he's already growing somewhat nauseous with the proximity to the bullets, and takes out Heidi's manuscript. Walks into the motel room.

Shutting the blinds and locking the door, he pushes the dresser in front of it, then undresses and gets under the covers, holding the pages of *The Hollow* to his chest. He has never read it, and never plans to. As long as he has it, it's like there's a part of her that he has yet to discover. There is more of *her* left in the world, more of Heidi continuing to unfold past that red room, past that one terrible night.

He sleeps.

His sleep is different now; he's like a man frozen in ice.

If he's bedeviled by any dreams, they're ones he doesn't remember.

He wakes to a red outline of his body on the bed, like every pore has stippled the sheets with blood. Blood flowered now on the title page of the manuscript.

They continue west, up through Spokane, then dip down and cross the border into eastern Oregon. Toward dawn, there's the goddamn sun again. The implication of it puts molten iron into his spine. The pain of it has already become both maddening and familiar.

"Why don't you get sick anymore, Julia? With the sunlight, I mean?" His voice shakes when he asks her this. They've found a maintenance shed at the edge of a farm. Cobwebs fur the room's corners. The place has no windows and is explosively hot, though this hardly bothers him now. There are no blankets to cover themselves with, just cardboard boxes, a wall of maintenance tools. The fact that they're well-kept and organized worries him; seems like a place that's visited frequently. But what else is there to do? He stacks boxes in front of the door to keep out any shards of daylight that might spear through the cracks. The darkness then is like a kiss, like his mother's cool hand on his brow when he was home with a fever.

"I do," she says. "Just not as bad as I did at first."

He looks around the room. "We could dig a hole," he says. The floor is hardpacked dirt. Even now, the insistence of sleep is pulling him down.

"We'll be alright," Julia says. "I'll protect you."

Minor smiles. It's a sad smile. The world's been turned on its head.

They hit Portland's downtown around three A.M. The revolver in the trunk, as far away from them as they can manage it. Even at this hour there are signs the city is awake; the rumble of a glasspack engine tearing up and down the street, people walking in clusters, catcalling each other. Summer raucousness, and it pulls at Minor's heart. Every corner seems inhabited by a haunting of his old life.

They cross the Hawthorne Bridge, the night-ink of the Willamette beneath the Newport's wheels all scattershot with lights from the high-rises across the river, and he asks himself if he wants a drink, but that's not it. A drink would be nice, yeah, would smooth the edges of this panic he's feeling, but that's not it entirely. He probably can't even drink anymore; such a thing would likely be poison to him.

No, he's *hungry,* is what it is, and with that comes a starburst of terror so profound he inhales like someone's burned him with a cigarette. Julia looks at him like she knows what he's thinking, but doesn't say anything.

They drive by all the old haunts. He can't get that phrase out of his mind. *The old haunts.* Because that's what he's doing, right? He is haunting these places, saying hello to them again. Feeling even more a ghost now than when they'd left back in the winter of '75. Neither of them talk.

The Last Call is now called Lucky's, and as he slows the Newport, he sees a bartender going about his business of closing up, a friend perched on a stool near the rack, the two of them smoking cigarettes and bullshitting. It's otherwise empty. It might have been him and Bobby. Mopping the floor, setting the chairs up, his buddy with the puck of an ashtray at his elbow. The two of them only occasionally saying something to the other. Then the friend turns and looks out the window, sees the idling sedan, and his face darkens with suspicion. Minor moves on. Wonders what's happened to the upstairs apartment, what the police and the city and the movers did to all of his stuff, to all of Heidi's stuff, Julia's, the flotsam of their lives jettisoned, tossed away, and for a moment he feels a sorrow so violent he's not sure it can be contained in his body. He lets out a single choked sob and Julia looks at him, alarmed. Asks him what's wrong. Tears blur his vision and when he wipes them away, his fingers come away red. He tells her he's fine.

He goes past Ed and Joanne's house, the lights dark, the driveway empty. It clangs like a bell inside him. Did someone move in there too? Do the new owners know what happened to the two of them as they'd slept in their beds? Do their ghosts march loud in the hallways, carom off the doorways some nights, demanding exit? Justice? Minor's never been sentimental, but now, here, he can't help himself.

He goes to Bobby's apartment. There's a light burning in his third-floor window and Minor entertains the idea of ringing his buzzer. But what is there to say? How would the telling of his sins, of Julia's sins, help anything?

And there's the matter, too, of his own hunger. This widening impulse.

This fear of what he might *do* to Bobby, to Ian, the two of them sitting across from him. So concerned, so worried. Maybe his only friends left in all of this.

So they rove the city instead, they *haunt,* and then he drives a block down from Lone Fir, the acres of cemetery ringed in iron bars, the trees a dark canopy above. The mausoleums scattered throughout like ghostly miniature witch houses. The gentle slope of the hillside. He shuts off the sedan and for a moment it's just the sound of the engine ticking.

"This is where they're buried?" Julia says.

He nods. "I'd like to be alone for a bit. I just— I want to see her by myself first, Julia."

"Alright," she says, even though he can tell he's wounded her.

"I'll come get you when I'm done," he says. "And then we can go up there together, or you can say goodbye to them by yourself. I just— I want to talk to her for a little bit."

8

He vaults the spiked iron fence and spends some time walking among the gravestones. It's a warm night and the trees overhead offer him a cowl of trembling shadows. The cemetery seems to have no discernible pattern to its plots—folks who have been interred a century ago are buried next to those who died at the beginning of the decade. Some headstones are so aged and moss-furred and weatherworn as to be illegible, and through it all are the scents of summer—lilac, cut grass—that make Minor ache for the past, wish he could wind the clock back.

He wanders the cemetery for half an hour before he finds their graves.

Ed and Joanne and Heidi. Three rectangular stones rising only a few inches from the ground. Angled and polished marble. The dates of their births and deaths.

The graves are festooned in flowers. Fresh, still wrapped in paper. Lilies and brightly colored Gerbera daisies and white roses. Bobby, maybe?

Beyond her name and her dates of life and death, Heidi's headstone is adorned with three words. When he reads them, fresh heartache nearly bends him in half:

Daughter • Aunt • Wife

He is about to say something—perhaps to her, or to whatever God that would consider making a thing like Varley walk the earth—when he hears an unmistakable metallic *click* behind him.

"Duane, put your hands up right now. Put 'em behind your head. That's it."

Minor can't help smiling. The cosmic joke of it. "Scoggins?" he says. "That you?"

Scoggins puts Duane's hands behind his back, cuffs him, the steel biting into his wrists. He turns Minor around, and even in the moonlight it's impossible to miss the shock on the detective's face. *I'm going through some changes, aren't I,* he thinks.

"How'd you find me? I just got back into town."

"Little bird told me."

"A little bird?"

"I got a phone call."

Minor is mystified. "From who? Someone said I'd be here?"

Scoggins tilts his chin toward the street, keeps his revolver on him. "My car's over there, Duane. Let's take a walk."

He imagines all the rigmarole, the bullshit, the hours of questioning in the station. Scoggins sitting there with his yellow pad. He remembers the window in the interrogation room they put him in the first time, imagines all too well the shards of morning sunlight coming through the slats. Depending on how far he's turned, everything might end right there.

Would that be a bad thing, really?

If I'm going, I want to pick my own way.

"I can't do that," he says.

Scoggins nods as if he understands. "Yeah, see, you will, though. I don't know what horseshit you and Varley pulled on me the other night, Duane, but it's not happening again."

"Wait, what? Varley? What're you talking about?"

Scoggins gestures with his free hand toward the cemetery entrance.

"Backup's on their way, Duane. Don't start fucking with me now." He's a good liar, Minor thinks. Scoggins asks him where Julia is.

"She's on her own trip now," he says.

"The hell does that mean?"

"I promise you, she doesn't need your help."

Scoggins looks like he's about to press the point, but he shakes his head. "Car's that way. Just down that path there." After a moment, when Minor doesn't move: "You got three seconds before you are forcibly moved, brother, and I won't mind it a bit if that's how you decide to do things."

"There's no backup. Is there? Why'd you really come out here, man?"

Scoggins laughs, looks up at the sky for a moment, but his revolver doesn't move. "I tried being straight with you a year and a half ago, and you went rabbit on me. I'm not telling you—" And then the detective frowns, squinting at him. "You're bleeding," he says, gesturing toward his own nose. And then, for the first time since he put the cuffs on him, there's a softness to his voice. "What is going on with you, Duane?"

"I'm sick."

"Yeah? What kind of sick?"

Minor smiles, looks down at Heidi's gravestone. *Daughter, aunt, wife.* "The kind there's no coming back from."

"Alright," Scoggins says wearily, as if some decision's been made, and he walks around him and puts a guiding hand on Minor's elbow, starts moving him toward the cemetery entrance, the street. "I'm gonna Mirandize you now. Duane Minor, I'm placing you under arrest for the suspicion of murder of Heidi Minor and Edward and Joanne Shaw, as well as the kidnapping of Julia Shaw. You have the right to remain silent. You have the right to—"

A sense of movement behind them, the slightest draft, and Minor thinks, *Julia.* Scoggins coughs, just once, quietly. His hand falls away. Minor feels warmth on the back of his neck.

He turns and there's John Varley, his hand a blade of black-clawed fingers. Scoggins, wide-eyed, presses his hands to his throat with the red all spilling down, his revolver dropping to the grass.

Varley grins and grips the detective by the back of the neck, shakes him, Scoggins's neck going this way and that, blood pouring, the mouth agog, eyes already glassy with death. Varley laughs, drops him to the ground, Minor backpedaling. Feels the tense of the cuffs behind him, trying to break them.

Varley walks toward him, grinning big.

"Howdy, Duane," he says, blood-spatter dotting one side of his face. "Figured you were dead. Gonna have to make extra sure I rip your fucking head off this time."

Minor takes another step backward, his heart in his throat, and then trips over his dead wife's headstone.

9

I n all his vast and expansive life, Varley's never quite gotten the handle on the act of *living*, not really. He knows it about himself. All this room, supposedly, to *live* in deathlessness. But it's all built on sand. He's never been afforded space to breathe.

After all, how could he? How, he's wondered so many times before, is one supposed to accrue wealth when a beam of sunlight might smite you to dust? How to gain power when the touch of a man's ring during a handshake might leave a scabrous burn that sends you howling to some shadowed corner of the room?

And the big one: How is one supposed to ever truly *rest* when your daily bed is, in essence, a motherfucking grave?

Alaska, he'd wanted that. Wanted that badly. Chasing the night with Johan across those plains of winter. The two of them together, untethered from the constant, belittling terror of the sun.

Almost a century striding the earth now. Countless bodies, hundreds of them. Thousands, perhaps. Bodies torn and scattered on roadsides, in stands of forests. Beheaded in barrooms and barren fields. Left alone in clots of weeds. And Varley in all those years never turning another soul, no matter what they might have done for him. This notion constantly present in his heart: *What's mine is mine. If you become like me, of me, I am less myself than I was.* And then Johan had stood there against the brick wall of that gas station in that silly coat and stuck a hand fierce through Varley's rib cage and squeezed his heart, made him come alive for the first time.

To have *hoped* and *loved* in that one and only instance—in nearly a century?

And to have it all taken away.

By *this* man.

He sees Duane Minor fall to the grass, hears the snap of the cuffs that held his hands behind his back. It'd been a surprise, seeing Minor talking to that other fellow, someone Varley had clocked as a cop straightaway. Had it been Scoggins? The one he'd talked to on the phone?

Minor crabwalks backward and Varley follows, slow and patient. He steps on a bouquet of flowers, white and orange and pink, still in their paper cone.

"I thought I killed your ass, Duane." Minor's head comes up against another gravestone—the back of his skull knocking against a cherub's feet.

Minor rolls over, gets to one knee.

"She turned you, huh? Your niece? I can smell it on you. How's it feel, playing for the other team?"

He stalks over and palms Minor's skull into the cherub's granite body. An explosion of stone, a chalk-like puff of dust, and Minor sags to his knees and then falls to the yellowed grass again.

Varley picks him up by the collar and runs him through the remains of the statue. Minor groans, his face whitened with dust like a mime, granite chips in his hair. He tries to push himself up from the grass, and Varley, even as he laughs, feels a grudging sense of admiration. Any unturned man would have died by now, the insides of his skull turned into paste.

Varley picks him up by the collar of his coat and his belt and hurls him; the man drifts through the air like something from a cartoon until he lands on his back on another headstone, shattering it into rubble. He lies there, unmoving, looking like he was dropped from the sky.

"I tell you what, Duane. I get why you two had it out for me. I didn't understand at the time, but then I *met* someone, you see, and well, I fell prey to the nature of things. Had no plans for it, but it happened. So I understand now." He crouches before Minor, who blinks up at the stars. "I did a few of yours and you did one of mine, and that's how it goes, right? Tit for tat, eye for an eye, all that happy horseshit." He looks down at his hand, watches the claws rise from the nailbeds, watches them grow black and gnarled and knife-sharp at their five points. Clacks them together, an almost celebratory sound. "Except here's the thing. My boy *mattered*. My love *mattered*. More than yours, and that's the simple truth of it."

He splays his other hand over Minor's face, covering him in death, and then raises his claws, prepares to drive them into his heart.

"Hey." A girl's voice, and he looks up and there she is, stepping from behind a mausoleum. That dark-haired child.

Varley smells smoke, sees that her hand is on fire as she raises it toward him, flames licking the palm, the wrist, the smell of char on the air, and what's that she's holding? Is that—

A sharp *crack,* and a sizeable section of John Varley's face disappears.

An explosion of pain, white-hot and full of an exacting agony, one previously undiscovered, unknown, and Varley screeches, slaps at his shattered jaw, falling back onto the grass. His nails retract, and he lurches up, reduced to an animal now, an animal's fear, an animal's insistence that he *run,* and the girl, closer now, shoots him again. This time right above the elbow. Most of that arm shears off in a black cloud of gore, the lower half becoming a shriveled, smoke-curled remnant before it even hits the grass.

Varley *runs.*

He runs breathless and slaloming among the graves, his face blackened on one side, jaw mostly gone, yellow bone shining beneath freshets of blood. One arm's a chopped-up gathering of meat that drips ichor like spilled ink. The rot's already climbing, rippling up to his collarbone.

The Nova's parked on a side street, just right there, but he drops the keys and hears footfalls behind him and so he pivots and just keeps running. Abandons the car, thinks of his Maker behind Davis Starling's bar, his cracked-bone transformation into a wolf, but oh,

Varley's heart pounds, fear making him blood-blind and stupid and reactive as any terrified thing. He'd thought he was *strong*?

He runs. Down the middle of the street, a car slowing and then veering around him in a wash of illumination and speeding away. Varley sobbing like a child. His body lighter and lighter, his body filled with air, his body a balloon that pain is filling. He staggers, turns, sees no one following him, and pushes down a narrow slot between two brick buildings. The stink of garbage in his nose, the skittering of rats. He kicks a wooden door he finds in the alley and kicks again until it breaks and then he's inside. A place he might hide in. This sense of safety lasts all of three seconds before he realizes a lantern burns inside and there near the doorway is a man sleeping on a bed of cardboard, cocooned in a sleeping bag, eyes wide in fear, and Varley bends to the man and lodges his teeth—fuck, his *top* row of teeth still work at least—there in the man's face, and then his neck. *Eat, make me strong again.* But God, the piss-blood taste, shit-blood floods his mouth; the silver ruining everything, and he strikes at the man's face, his chest, digs a thumb in an eye, batters him, howling, this petulant outburst of horror and rage. The man squeals and hits a glancing blow against Varley's ruined jaw and Varley shrieks in the man's face, shrieks in agony, in fury, his blood falling into the man's eyes, and then Varley pushes away and staggers farther into the darkened room, his breath like a bellows in his own ears, panic seizing him by the scruff and shaking him like a dog.

10

M inor walks down the narrow mouth of the alley, sees the door hanging on its hinge, the dim glow of a lantern inside. He steps in and sees a man gurgling on his bed of cardboard, frothing blood, his hands held to his neck, his face a wet ruin.

Minor steps farther inside. His footfalls rasp on broken glass. The windows are boarded, and in the lantern's meager light he sees a warring scatter of spray-painted tags across the walls. Stacks of lumber, rusty half gallons of paint stacked in tiers in the gloom. A large, paint-spattered tarp divides half of the space, and a dozen dented folding chairs lean in a stack against the far wall.

Minor tries to imagine his life a year from now, ten years. Fifty, a hundred. These half-lit places that would be his empire. His future reliant on a door that might hold back the morning sun.

He stands in the dark, listens. The wounded man on the cardboard moans.

Varley's blood, black as paint, trails behind the hanging tarp.

"Come on out," Minor says, weary. Tired of everything.

Varley coughs, steps out. That one arm all hanging gristle beneath the shredded sleeve, still dripping black. His face gaunt, something carved from hell.

"You got me," he says; even with the silver gone through him, his jaw is healing enough to speak. The power in him is something Minor can't fathom. The yellowed bone is already knitting itself together, worms of tendon and muscle, the pinked beginnings of new flesh. Varley grins, and his eyes shine black in the light. "Never imagined I'd be shot with silver from one of my own kind. Girl's worth ten of you, Duane. You ought to thank her. She's saved your ass twice now."

Minor says nothing. Heidi never farther away than she is in that moment. His old self—the kid who'd smoked grass with his young wife while listening to records, moths banging themselves against the windows, both of them assuming the machine of war, of violence, would not chew him up, that it would be just, or perhaps even forgiving in its brutalities—that kid seemed very far away. The man who had tried and failed to be a guardian, a parent to his niece, felt farther still. All these past selves laid to waste, cut down by time and circumstance and choices made. He didn't know who he was in this moment, what was left.

"I ain't got much of a showdown in me," Varley says, laughing wetly, limping toward the folding chairs leaning stacked against the far wall. "You mind if I sit?"

"Go ahead."

He takes a chair, opens it, sits down. Gasping as he does, bloody hair obscuring his face. He tucks a hank of it behind his ear with a hand that shakes. "Hell of a life I've had." He pulls up a wad from deep in his throat, spits its blackness onto the floor. Already his words are returning to their former clarity. "I have loved exactly one time in my life, and I fell into that like a dream. Fell into it against my own understanding of how life worked. And you up and shot him."

"I pictured this moment about a thousand times," Minor says, the words leaden in his mouth. "Ten thousand. It felt like killing you would mean something. But I'm just— I don't know."

"You don't know what?"

"You're a small man. I thought you'd be the devil, but it turns out you're just small."

A leer, a lift of the face up to that wan lantern light. "Your redhead didn't feel that way. *She* thought I was the devil. She begged for mercy, Duane, begged for a moment more to live, was *talkative* there at the end, while I tore her apart. Blood in her eyes. Wept for her mother like a baby would. And the *joy* in that, boy, knowing that I already had the mother's blood running through me. The father, the old man, he had a sickness in him—that's why she wanted me there in the first place, you know that? If I got to move dope through the bar, make some money, I told her I'd turn the old man."

"I know it."

"You know what else?"

"What?"

"I never turned anyone in my whole life. Not even Johan. Because *I* run the fucking show, boy. *Me.* And then you pissed me off, and I cut through your world like a goddamn hog knife. Painted whole rooms with the blood of the people you loved. I want you to know that. They died because of you, each one."

"I know," Minor says softly.

"You do?" Varley seems surprised, almost happy. "Good. And I want you to know that she *screamed,* that she *begged* me to take you instead, take the girl, to give her just one more minute. Cords on her neck like *this,* man, like fucking *wire* as she screamed for me to kill you instead."

Lies or not, none of it mattered. "You're just talking to hear yourself now."

"But, Duane, listen, *listen,* she asked me why I was doing it, *why,* and I told her because of you, because you were stupid enough to tell me no. To get in my way. And she died *blaming* you. Died *hating* you. I need you to know that."

"It doesn't matter."

"It *matters.*" He spits again. "I remember it all. I'm a fucking *repository* of memories, Duane. Tip me over, watch the memories fall out. My father, my Maker, Johan. I lay down to sleep and the fucking movie starts. You understand me? It *all* matters." He sniffs, looks around the room. "You'll be the same, I promise."

"Alright."

"You eaten yet?"

"No."

Varley grins with that terrible, glistening, re-forming jaw. "Oh, you're in for it. You know I tried to eat a goddamn *cow* when I first started out? A *dog?* Just made me sicker. Hungrier. It comes on slow, first couple of days, then it gets hold of you. And when I knew I *had* to do it? That I *had* to? I told myself, 'I'll only kill bad men.' And there were bad sons-of-bitches around me in plentiful supply, Duane. But there will come a time when circumstances demand that you eat or you die. No breathing room, sun coming up in fifteen minutes, you're starving, made skinny as a fucking branch, bent over from the ache of it, *and you will choose to eat.* Every damn time. Just like I done and that girl of yours done. Why do you think there's so few of us?"

"Because it's hell."

"Because it's hell, that's right. Because we go mad as shithouse rats. It's why half of us decide to walk into the goddamn sunrise. Those are your choices: you eat the people you used to be like, or you go mad and take a walk outside come morning time. But *not eating* isn't in the cards. Disabuse yourself of that fucking notion right now."

"You done?"

Sighing, Varley says, "I don't suppose we could work some sort of barter."

"Looking at you, I'd say your bartering days are over."

"Give me half an hour and I'll rip your fucking throat out."

"You don't have half an hour, John."

"I can make you more than you already are, boy. I got the blood in me now. Blood of the old ones. Got the keys to the kingdom."

"I don't want anything you got."

A sound then—footfalls in the alley. Minor turns, sees a shape in the doorway.

Varley sees it too, grins big.

"There she is," he crows, like a proud parent.

Julia comes in. She stops, looks around the room. She holds her jacket in a bundle at her chest and blood runs in dark rills from her eyes, her nose.

"Julia—"

Minor settles a hand on her shoulder as she passes and she shrugs it off and keeps walking. She sets the coat on the floor and picks up the revolver nestled in its center. The hand that holds the gun is already a blackened gathering of bones and sinew, ruined up to the elbow. Minor watches as small pockets of flame light up here and there—one on her wrist, her forearm. Char-smoke curls.

Varley manages to stand, gasping. Even with his jaw's re-formation, the brachial climb of silver-rot has moved up onto his face, whitening one eye into a dead orb.

And then he falls back down into the chair, says nothing. Makes no proclamation. Begs not, says not a word. Julia walks to him and he opens that bloody jaw and his teeth rise half extended, all he can manage. She puts the barrel to his forehead and it sinks an inch into the curve of his forehead.

"You and me could run the whole goddamn world, girl," he says in a croak as small blue flames rise from Julia's hand and smoke purls from where his flesh and the barrel meet. Julia is silent, her lips pulled back, and he hisses, that black film slowly sliding over his remaining eye—

She pulls the trigger. Red and black paste erupts from the back of Varley's head, the blond bloody hair flicking, and he falls off the chair to the cement.

Julia's hand is a charred club, the revolver clattering to the floor, and she turns away from the body with a woodenness, walks past Minor like something pulled on a string. On the way out she says, in a voice soft with either shock or contentedness, "One more bullet left, Uncle Duane. If you want it. I hope you don't."

At the doorway, she holds her ruined hand to her chest and bends down. Crouches. She bites the wounded, dying man who lies there bleeding on his bed of cardboard. Bites him carefully, with consideration, just once.

Enough to ensure that he lives. In a sense.

Enough to ensure his transformation.

11

He drives the latticework of streets in the industrial section, warehouses and loading docks trundling with life and commerce even at this dark hour, the taillights of vans and trailers flaring red as they back up to loading docks, freighted with goods. This secret life while the rest of the world sleeps.

He drives past the men unloading the trucks and finds himself leaning toward their lives, leaning toward their thudding blood like a flower bending toward the sun. At a stoplight, he flexes his hand and he can hear the sinew creak, the bones pop. This need inside him is like some animal taking up residence. Growing larger.

Down Grand Avenue, he passes an all-night diner done up in jeweled neon, and through the windows he sees the line of heads at their booths, shoveling food into their mouths, sees them speaking as bitter saliva crowds his tongue. The revolver in the trunk with its one bullet throbs at his back. He'd picked up the gun with his jacket, the way he'd seen Julia do it.

The pain of the silver's nearness has already become familiar.

He rolls down his window, spits. Wishes for a cigarette. Wishes for a drink. Wishes that those echoes of his old life might hold some lasting meaning.

There's a choice to be made, he'd said to Julia just before they'd parted ways. Before she'd walked out of that killing room and down the mouth of that alleyway, her silver-burned hand cradled to her chest.

Minor still can't say if he was talking to her, or himself.

Julia had walked out, and Minor had gone after her.

"Wait," he'd said, and she'd turned, her arm shriveled and useless. "Will she even take you in? Like that?"

"I don't know."

"Julia, we could run."

She'd shook her head. "I was always running *to* something, Uncle Duane. This whole time."

"How will I find you?"

A smile. "Come to the Museum. I'll be there."

"Julia—"

"I have to go. You're supposed to keep your promises, remember?"

"To who? Adeline?"

"I told her I would."

"But I'm supposed to keep you safe," he said, the words ridiculous in his own ears.

That smile hadn't left her face, though. "You did. I love you for it."

She'd walked on then, into the dark, and he'd stood in the doorway and looked down at the injured man there, blinking in shock and fear.

Would Lyle, he wondered, have wanted to live after that sniper round came drifting low across the valley? What would he have done if he'd been given another chance?

Would Lyle have wanted to be turned? Ferris?

Those two men in the bar that night? What about them?

He'd walked over to the man on his cardboard bed and smelled the blood, luxuriated in it.

It would be so easy to crouch down and just *eat.*

But he'd walked outside. Walked away.

I will only eat bad men, Varley claimed to have once believed of himself.

Bad by whose standards? Minor thought. *Who gets to decide?*

He spies a pay phone, parks the car. Crosses the street and dials 911. Tells the operator about a man dead in Lone Fir Cemetery. Wishes there was more he could have done for Scoggins, who had basically walked across broken glass to give Minor a second chance, and a third. Another whittled mark on the yardstick notched with his failings.

He drives to the Last Call. No, it's Lucky's now. Once again he parks the Newport. Takes out Heidi's manuscript, puts it under his arm. Fishes the .38 from the trunk, wraps it in his coat, holds it to his chest. *Hot potato,* he thinks grimly, feeling the first purling of blood from his nostril. The building's dark now, hours past closing time, the bartender and his buddy long gone. No lights burn in the apartment upstairs. Cradling his jacket and the revolver inside it, he punches through the glass door with his free hand. Reaches in and unlocks the handle.

It's like walking inside the rib cage of a ghost, being in here.

He knows the route by heart. Walks behind the bar, sets his coat on the bar top. Smooths out *The Hollow* with its bloody title page, then shakes out his aching hand, the cuts from the glass already knitted closed. He pours himself a beer. Stands there watching the foam rise and then dissipate, trying to ignore the hunger walking through him, strident and demanding.

All his past jumped up and howling. All his dead. He takes out the Polaroids—soft-edged, a sharp crease across the one of Bradley where it was folded at some point—and lays them next to Heidi's book. These artifacts, making it all this way with him. He turns and looks in the mirror behind the bar, and is strangely relieved to see his warped, vaporous face looking back at him.

You can dump that bullet in yourself, or you can eat.

You can walk into the sun.

You can find Adeline in Kenton Park, see if you might be made an addendum to the Children's Museum. Be with Julia again.

Even now, after all this, there are choices.

He thinks he hears the floorboards creak upstairs.

Putting his hand around the cool pint he can't drink from, the glass sweating beneath his fingers, he whispers again, "There's a choice to be made." The silence swallows each word.

He looks down at the stack of typewritten pages before him. The rust-red spatters on the title. Heidi's name beneath it.

So, what'll it be?

He flips over the first page.

Starts reading her final story.

5

EPILOGUE

• a knock at the door •

They'd been sitting at the kitchen table once, above the Last Call. She and Heidi had been counting out Duane's tips, she remembers that, dividing them up into neat stacks by denomination, coins and dollars both. Julia's job was quarters, there were a lot of them, and she was supposed to count ten dollars' worth at a time and then roll them into their paper tubes. Plan was her mother was going to call her that day from Bayonne Correctional and she hadn't. Heidi, her hair in a ponytail and a cigarette burning at her elbow, had sensed Julia's distractedness, the way she kept counting the same stack of coins over and over again. She'd taken a drag of her Parliament and said, "She got held up, hon. She didn't forget about you."

"I know," Julia had mumbled, a little surprised that her thoughts had been so obvious.

"I promise you, she wants to talk to you. She'll call next week. She loves you."

"I know," Julia had said again.

Duane had been sleeping on the couch in the other room, ankles crossed, hands tucked into his armpits, a football game playing low, and Julia watched Heidi occasionally look through the doorway at him, her husband; her smile had been a small and tucked-away thing, equal parts love and concern. She probably didn't even know she was doing it. A part of Julia was secretly relieved that her mother had not called collect that night, that they had not had to haltingly grind out the retelling of their lives, all of it punctuated with long beats of silence and the telephone hum of the great distance between them. Both of them trying so hard to find each other's hearts in the dark like that, Julia struggling, too, with the guilt inherent in the fact that she was happy here. Happier, anyway.

The kitchen had smelled of the soup cooking on the stovetop, the breadsticks in the oven that Heidi had braised with garlic and butter. Condensation filmed the kitchen windows, and she could hear the occasional thump and rattle of the bar beneath her feet. Julia sat for a moment, wrapped in that weird, confusing collusion that she had so often felt living in that apartment—a heavy sorrow coupled with relief at having *gotten away,* and the shame that she should be relieved at all, given the tremendous price people had paid for her to wind up here. That feeling of shame strung through everything like wire scaffolding. She ached for her mother and missed her mother and blamed her mother for what had happened. And there was Little Kev there in Florida with Ray Ray's mom. Kev getting bigger every day, and how he always managed to be sleeping, or on a playdate, or just out whenever Julia called to talk to him.

"Alright, listen up," Heidi said, standing up and putting all the tips into a coffee can they kept above the fridge. "You have been through the wringer. Alright? Gone through shit that no kid—no person, but sure as hell no child—should have to go through. We tell you this all the time, Julia, because it's true. And then you have things like this, these little hurts that get sprung on you." Julia's face had suddenly burned with embarrassment, and she'd turned away, blinking away tears. "So I'm just gonna tell you one more time," Heidi said, "that it's not your fault. None of it. You're doing everything you're supposed to. The way you feel is exactly how you're supposed to feel."

Julia had looked at the fogged kitchen window, worried a thumbnail between her teeth. "Whose fault is it, then?"

"Well, which part?"

"What do you mean?"

Heidi sat back down at the table and took another drag from her cigarette, blew smoke at the ceiling. "I mean which part, hon? Because your mom shot that man and killed him. She owns that. She pulled that trigger. That's why she's in Bayonne and not calling you on the damn telephone when she's supposed to." In the other room, Duane had whimpered in his sleep, rolled over onto his side. "And Raymond, the shitbag"—Julia had smiled at that, looking down at the table—"he brought a lifetime of misery down on all of you your whole life. So he's to blame too. And there's enough for me to take some on too, I figure."

"You?"

Heidi gave her an *Of course* look. "Hell yes, me. My sister disappears? Takes up with a man who moves her across the goddamn country? Won't let her talk to me on the *phone*?" She laid the flat blade of her hand on the kitchen table, drew it across in a sweeping motion. "I mean, Linda was my big sister. I should have flown out there and knocked down the damn door, is what I should have done. But I just nursed my hurt, right? Felt distant from her, felt like it was something being done *to me,* right? Didn't see it as a thing *she* was living through. Not until it was too late. So, no, Julia. I'm not innocent either."

"I like it here," Julia had said quietly, rubbing the edge of the table-cloth between her fingers.

"Good," Heidi had said, leaning forward, putting a warm hand on hers. "We like you here too. We're glad you found your way to us."

She doesn't remember much more than that. Doesn't remember the soup, or Uncle Duane waking up. What followed was likely predictable: dinner, then homework and TV, the three of them in the living room together. In that apartment, Julia's heart, her entire body, had felt like a raw wound that was slowly scabbing over. The predictability, the calmness, had been its own treasure. She'd thought, *There's room to breathe here. The quiet isn't dangerous.*

That's what she wants to remember. Her and Heidi and Duane in the old creaking apartment, the sound of all that quiet life around and below them.

The windows misted and obscured by their breath, their warmth.

How the night was a thing that happened outside, beyond the walls of the house.

•

She walks the length of the city, miles of it, back toward that dark and crumbling block of homes across the street from the park. Those houses with their peeling skins, their shuttered windows and strange walkways between the upper floors like the ventricles of some malformed heart. Near the park a car slows at one point, the driver with either malevolence or concern in mind, but the look she gives him, the blackened curl of her arm held to her chest, the blood, makes him drive off without a word spoken.

Finally, she walks past the chain-link fence into the yard, stands before the Museum, remembering all that had happened inside. Adeline and her wish to be with someone. To have some sense that all was not lost, that even as *changed* as she was, she was not alone. *I keep turning them in the hopes of finding one that appreciates this life for the gift it is, and they've all disappointed me.* The oath she'd made to Adeline, who also would never age.

The house stands before her. Some dark monolith. She hears the distant cat-wail of a siren somewhere, then two.

Up the cement steps, onto the creaking porch. A debt is a debt.

But, also, a debt is not forever.

She owes Adeline, yes, for this half-life she's given her. For the gift of vengeance.

But she doesn't owe her *everything*.

Eventually—maybe in five years, maybe ten, twenty—Julia will consider her debt paid. Perhaps she won't live that long. Perhaps she'll be caught by a silver bullet herself, or a sunrise, or have her head taken from her shoulders. Perhaps the char blackening her arm will continue to creep up to her heart, like Cobweb Jim. Perhaps Adeline will contest the debt's fulfillment when the time comes. They'll cross that bridge then.

She hopes she'll see Uncle Duane again. Maybe he'll decide to sleep, and wake, and sleep again. Decide to *eat*. Make those infinite choices that need to be made on any given day in order to live. At one time she might have been consumed by the guilt of what it took to survive—might have been frozen by it, rooted to the ground—but not anymore. Julia's got no use for guilt anymore. When has it done her any bit of good?

So one day, if she survives her time with Adeline, her debt will be paid, and she'll travel.

Take a trip to New York.

To Bayonne. Over the wire and inside and among the cells.

And she'll give her mother a choice.

And then she'll go to Florida. By then, Kevin will be big and strong.

And she'll offer him a choice too.

And she'll have some vestige of family again, maybe.

God help anyone that tries to stop her.

She's small, and eternally young, with one ruined arm held to her chest, but oh, the heart inside her. Fierce as a gunshot. Fierce as wicked teeth.

She knocks, and her fist is heavy against the door.

She says, "It's Julia."

She says, "I came back. Like I said I would."

After a moment, the door opens.

Darkness within, and then a face.

ACKNOWLEDGMENTS

Thanks to:

Caitlin McKenna, Chad Luibl, Robin Corbo, Jesse Stowell, Joe Hill, Gordon White, Wendy Wagner, Luciano Murano, Steve and Tabitha King, Michael Kortya, Craig Grossi, Jeremy John Parker and the University of Maine, Roma Panganiban, Kristina Moore, Jamie-Lee Nardone and undoubtedly many others I've forgotten.

All of the folks at Random House, Janklow & Nesbit, UTA and Black Crow. Dream-makers, every one of you.

Most of all, my god, thanks to all the readers, reviewers, blurbers, booksellers and librarians out there. What a gift you've given me, that I get to do this, get to continuously share these stories with the world. As ever, thank you.

Alright. Let's move on to the next one, shall we?

Eyes forward, hearts full.

ABOUT THE AUTHOR

KEITH ROSSON is the author of the novels *Fever House, The Devil by Name, Smoke City, Road Seven,* and *The Mercy of the Tide,* as well as the Shirley Jackson Award–winning story collection *Folk Songs for Trauma Surgeons.* He lives in Portland, Oregon. More can be found at keithrosson.com.

ABOUT THE TYPE

This book was set in Bulmer, a typeface designed in the late eighteenth century by the London type cutter William Martin (1757–1830). The typeface was created especially for the Shakespeare Press, directed by William Bulmer (1757–1830)—hence the font's name. Bulmer is considered to be a transitional typeface, containing characteristics of old-style and modern designs. It is recognized for its elegantly proportioned letters, with their long ascenders and descenders.